I0675830

A Duty to Family

A Duty to Family

Douglas Falls: Book Three

By J L Dawson

Butterfly Books
PUBLISHING

Cover photograph used with permission from: Darlene Munro Photography.
Cover silhouette from Shutterstock
Cover design by: Kyle Keogh
Edited by: Amber Smith

ISBN (Paperback) 978-1-7385962-0-1
ISBN (E-book) 978-1-7385962-1-8

A CiP catalogue record for this title is available from the National Library of New Zealand.

First edition, 2022 Butterfly Books Publishing

Contact the author or subscribe to newsletter:
jldawsonauthor@yahoo.com
www.jodawsonauthor.com

This book is dedicated to:

Karen Waters

You've always supported me in my writing journey. I value your encouragement and friendship more than you'll ever know.

Contents:

Some of the Characters in Douglas Falls.

Sergeant Adam and Katherine Morgan
    RNWMP officer and his wife 'Katie' – a former teacher at Douglas Falls.
        Their children: Rose, Callie, Anna, Lizzie, Sarah & Hope

Pastor Daniel and Louisa Coleman
    Pastor at Douglas Falls – Adam's best friend and Katie's older brother. Married widow Louisa Maxwell.
        Their children: Andy (Louisa's boy from her first marriage, adopted by Daniel), Timothy, Emma, Jack & Samuel

Doctor Owen and Becky Randall
    Doctor at Douglas Falls – Married Katie's best friend Becky.
        Their children: Louie & Vinnie (twins) & Kate.

Sergeant Samuel and Jo Ferguson
    RNWMP officer at Pine Crest – The closest town to Douglas Falls.
        Their children: Jamie, Esther, Michael & Henry

Theodore Morgan 'The Commander'
    Sergeant Adam Morgan's father and RNWMP Assistant Commissioner

One
Sweet Sixteen

Becky Randall put her knitting aside and stretched her back. A smile curled her lips when her eyes fell upon the lovely girl sitting under the nearby oak tree, with her nose buried in a book. "Rose is a beautiful young woman, Katie; you must be really proud of her?"

Katie Morgan looked up at her daughter and smiled. "Yes, I can't believe she's sixteen. Where did those years go? I don't feel nearly old enough to have a sixteen-year-old daughter." She shook her head.

"You aren't old, Katie; it's just the by-product of us all having children when we were young, I guess." Joanna Ferguson smiled.

Their conversation was briefly interrupted by loud shrieks. The four women sitting on the wide porch looked up in alarm. Two young girls ran across the meadow towards the house, with the Reynolds twins following them, holding grasshoppers in their hands. Alarmed frowns turned to wide smiles, and the women shook their heads and turned back to their handcrafts.

Across the meadow, a cry of, "Yoooooou're out!" travelled through the crisp March air. Lizzie Morgan triumphantly held the ball above her head, thrilled to have caught out her cousin. Andy Coleman groaned, shook his head in defeat, dropped his bat and stormed back to his waiting team. Baseball was so common an occurrence up on The Rise, that the bases and outfield were worn permanently into the ground by their feet.

It had been an unseasonably mild winter for Alberta, much to the people's relief. The previous few had been long and hard, but that year the snow had been shallow, and by March, almost none remained. Spring bloomed early, and The Rise was alive with beautiful wildflowers in every colour they could imagine, their aroma wafting across the eight acres. It was a rare occurrence for Rose's birthday.

Katie lay down her knitting and looked around. The boys and Lizzie were involved in their game, the doctor and pastor in the midst of it all. Her eyes travelled across their land. A group of smaller girls picked flowers off to the side, and their old husky Jack darted back and forth on the trail of something; butterflies were his favourite to chase, although he was seldom successful in his hunt. Two pretty teenage girls sat on a blanket under one of the large trees, deep in animated conversation. As always, Rose sat on the chair her father had built under the large oak. Her head and shoulder leaned against the tree and her stockinged feet up on the seat. She almost always had her nose in a book.

Louisa Coleman looked up at Katie noticing her wide smile and misty green eyes. "A penny for your thoughts, Katie?"

Katie's cheeks coloured a little, and she turned to smile at her friend. "I was just looking at all these young people. It makes my heart proud."

Lou surveyed the scene and nodded. She reached across to squeeze her friend's arm. "It's quite a legacy we've all built."

"I was thinking the other day we've all been friends for nearly seventeen years." Jo lifted her tea cup to her mouth.

"Has it been that long?" Louisa lay down her crochet hook and rubbed her sore neck.

"Yes, that sounds about right." Katie nodded. "So much has happened in that time."

"Remember when you first moved in here, Katie, right after you and Adam were married, and we all dreamed about raising our children together." Becky smiled nostalgically.

"Yes, and we have certainly made that dream come true." Jo scanned the scene before her. "Even the distance between our two towns hasn't stopped us from coming here regularly. Of course, it's so much easier now that we have a car."

The women nodded and grinned. "This place sure has changed, Katie. You and Adam have built a real little farm for yourselves up here." Becky lifted her tea cup to her lips.

"Two cows and some chickens hardly constitutes a farm." Katie laughed. "But yes, Adam has extended our house, built stables, fenced the place, built a chicken coop, built swings and a cubby house for the girls. He's built a wonderful life for us up here." Katie sighed contentedly. "I can't imagine living anywhere else." She stood to refill their tea cups and peered through the kitchen window towards the clock. "Oh, I'd better get the meal started." She placed her knitting in its basket and headed inside.

"I'll help." Becky leapt up to follow her.

Jo and Louisa looked at each other and grinned. "Us to," Jo said on their behalf, and they followed. The four women were soon working side by side in Katie's large kitchen, chatting and laughing as they always did. Becky stopped stirring the biscuit dough and grinned.

Katie, looked up from the potatoes she was washing. "What is it?"

"I was just trying to work out how many times we've done this over the years, how many meals we've all shared together, how many times we've all worked together in this kitchen."

"Way too many to count," Jo smiled. "We've shared some times over the years, haven't we? I really wouldn't have wanted to do any of it without you all. I'm so blessed to have you three amazing women to share the good and bad of life with."

"Yes, we sure have been together in all the joyous and all the hard moments," agreed Louisa. "I'm glad we've not had to go through any of it alone. I can't imagine three more amazing friends."

"Friends that are really family." Katie put her arms around Becky and Jo. Jo reached her arm out to Louisa, and they stood holding each other for a brief moment.

"Most people aren't this blessed." Becky squeezed Katie. With a nod and a smile, they returned to their cooking.

Becky removed the pie from the oven, placed it on the counter and wiped her brow. "Shall I call Owen and the boys to come and set up the tables?"

"Yes, call that old pastor, too," Katie said of her brother, Pastor Daniel Coleman.

His wife Louisa grinned. "Hey, he's not so old."

Becky headed for the door, untying her apron as she walked and flicking it over the nearest chair. She hurried from the house and called out to her doctor husband and teenaged sons. The baseball game was quickly dissolved, and its members came running across the meadow. In a true display of 'many hands make light work', they had the tables set up in no time, and Becky and Lou laid crisp gingham table clothes over them. Just as they were heading indoors, the two Mounties rode up, leading a rather unusual horse behind them.

Adam halted Ebony, and Sam pulled his borrowed horse to a stop. Children came running over to investigate.

Twelve-year-old Anna tipped her head to one side. "Who's that new horse, Pa?"

"You'll see, Darling." Adam Morgan winked at his daughter as he dismounted. "Where's your ma?"

Katie and Jo walked out of the house with plates of food and laid them on a table. Both women walked across to their Mountie husbands to receive loving embraces and kisses as always.

"Good timing, Sergeant. The food is nearly ready."

Adam grinned at his wife as she stepped out of his embrace. "Excellent. May I give Rose her gift now?"

"Yes, of course." Katie smiled at him.

Adam whistled loudly, and children came scampering across the meadow; Jack, the old husky, followed along, his pink tongue hanging out and ears pinned up, always ready for the next excitement.

Rose and Callie walked behind the others much more gracefully than the stampede of little girls and boys. Adam waited for them to gather around, and he beckoned Rose to him with his finger and a wide smile.

"Oh, Pa." Rose screwed up her face and rolled her eyes. "You promised you wouldn't make a fuss."

"Too bad, my oldest daughter is turning sixteen. I want to make a fuss."

"Oh, Pa." Her cheeks grew red as he placed his arm around her shoulder and kissed her hair.

"I love you so much, Rosie Girl. You are my firstborn daughter, and watching you grow up has been the greatest joy of my life. Your ma, sisters, and I are so proud of you and the woman you are becoming. And I have a really special gift for you." Adam nodded to his friend.

Sergeant Samuel Ferguson led the striking palomino towards them. The creamy-coloured horse, with an almost white tail and mane, was adorned with a brand-new saddle and bridle.

Rose gasped. "Pa!" She ran her hand over the intricately carved leather saddle. It had a rose engraved in the leather and 'Rosie' carved below in decorative letters. The bridle was leather with blue rope woven into it. All lovingly hand-made by her father.

"Rosie, I know most fathers give their girls jewellery for their sixteenth birthdays or take them on trips or out to supper. Some lavish them with beautiful dresses, but I wanted to give you something very meaningful to me. You know how much I love horses, and I believe every girl should have a horse of her own. I brought your ma Copper all those years ago, and now I want to carry on that tradition. This is Buttercup, she's three years old, and I've been training her for the last six months for you."

"Oh, Pa! She's so beautiful." Rose reached her hand out to stroke the neck of the horse. "Hello, Buttercup." The horse sniffed at Rose and nudged her with her head. "I love her, Pa, thank you. Thank you so much. This is a much better gift than jewellery." She threw her arms around her father's neck, and he held her tightly. He closed his eyes and kissed her hair again; his heart nearly burst in joy as he held his grown-up daughter in his arms. It was a privilege he'd never taken lightly.

"You're most welcome, Darling." She stepped back from him. "I chose her especially for you." Adam's six daughters had grown up in the saddle. They'd all grown to love horses as much as he did.

For eight years, Adam had kept his compensation money from the Police Force to be used for his girls. It was his intention to buy each their own horse for their sixteenth birthday.

5

Standing near the back of the group, Pastor Daniel Coleman cupped both hands around his mouth. "Speeeeechhh."

Rose blushed. "Oh, Uncle Danny, I'm not one for making speeches." She giggled; she and her mother were the only ones who ever got away with calling the pastor 'Danny.' Not even his own wife called him that.

"Well then, just say whatever's on your mind, Darling." Katie slipped a supportive arm around her look-alike daughter's waist.

"Alright." Rose patted the neck of the horse again. Her eyes sparkled in joy. "Family." She looked around at all the faces before her. Twenty-four sets of eyes swung to her.

The four families had been close friends for so long that Rose felt at ease with them all, they had long since stopped being friends and were thought of instead as family. "Turning sixteen is no great achievement, and it isn't because of anything I've done. I feel like I'm being rewarded for something not of my doing. I'm no hero like Pa or Sergeant Ferguson, or a doctor or pastor." Her eyes moved from face to face. "I'm not a mother, or a nurse, or even a teacher yet." She shrugged. "I'm just plain old Rose Morgan, but I am the most blessed girl in the world today."

She stopped and reached for both of her parents, linking arms with each of them. She kissed her mother on the cheek and then stood up on her toes to kiss her father too. "I have the best parents any girl could ever ask for. You've made me who I am today, and I'm grateful for you both. We've been through so many hard times but so many wonderful blessed times too. I have five beautiful sisters." Rose curled up her face into a sideways smile. "Despite all the arguments we've had over the years, I love you all very much." She dropped her parents' arms and hugged each of her sisters who stood before her. Even Lizzie was happy to embrace her sister, just this once.

Rose stepped back up and continued addressing the crowd. "I have all these wonderful friends who are much more like family, and now, I have this beautiful horse. Thank you so much, Pa. She's wonderful. I've always wanted a horse of my own."

She hugged her father again.

"I know, Darling, and I agree with your words. Except that you're wrong about one thing. You are a hero. You're my hero, Rosie. It's you, your ma and your sisters, these good friends; you're all heroes in my mind. It's all of you that have saved me on so many occasions. This horse is the least we can do to celebrate the very beautiful and lovely young woman you are. We can't wait to see what the future holds for you. I'm really gonna miss you when you head to teacher's college in the fall." Adam curled his face up and pursed his lips out comically, but his eyes betrayed the wistfulness and fear of her leaving his home. "Thank you, Rosie Girl, for the joy and beauty you have brought to this old Mountie's heart."

"Oh, Pa, you aren't old!"

Adam winked at her and turned to his wife. "Katie, have we got time for a quick ride before lunch?"

"Of course." She smiled at her husband.

Adam turned and grinned at his daughter, his eyes sparkling in excitement. He raised his brows. "Want to, Rose?"

"Oh, Yes."

Adam helped her up on Buttercup and adjusted the stirrups to fit her.

Rose wriggled in the saddle and found herself the most comfortable position, suddenly wishing she wasn't wearing her new boots. She leaned forward, wrapped her arms around the horse's neck, and whispered, "We are going to be great friends, Buttercup." The horse gave a short whinny in agreement.

"You two look great together." Adam smiled as Rose sat back up. He stroked the horse's soft neck. "Like you were meant for each other."

"I can feel that, Pa." She grinned and winked at him. "Race ya." She clucked to the horse, flicked the reins and sped away, managing to knock over one of the tables as she ran. Her long hair flowed out behind her, her eyes sparkled, and she laughed as she galloped off.

Adam hesitated and grinned. "Hey, that's not fair." He leapt up on Ebony in one bound, and with a wink at his wife, he took off after her. He was an expert horseman, and he quickly caught up with her. They galloped across The Rise for a time, and then Rose pulled her horse to a stop overlooking the valley below. Adam pulled up next to her.

Rose's face shone, and her eyes were alight with joy. "Thank you, Pa; thank you for Buttercup. She's wonderful."

"You're most welcome, Darling. You're wonderful too." The rather sentimental Mountie smiled broadly at his lovely daughter.

"I love you, Pa."

"I love you too, Rosie Girl." He grinned and reached over to squeeze her arm. "Now we better get back for lunch, or your ma will tan our hides."

Her eyes twinkled. "Alright." She nudged the horse and sped off, flying like the wind on the swift horse. Adam chuckled and rode after her.

* * * *

Katie sat before the mirror in their room and brushed her hair in long strokes. She looked up at her husband's reflection and caught his eye and wide smile. "That was a wonderful day, Adam. Your gift to her was very generous."

"I really wanted to give her something meaningful to me. Anyone can give jewellery, and I have many times in the past, but other than my girls, horses are my love." Adam unbuttoned his red-serge jacket and hung it on the hook by the door.

"I know, Husband; I remember when you lost Midnight, it was almost like you'd lost your best friend."

He nodded slowly and walked over to touch the faded sepia photograph on the wall. It was of him on his graduation from the academy, mounted on Midnight with his old husky, Bear, at his side. "He was a good friend. We served together for a long time. He was very loyal to me, like a faithful Mountie." He paused as his memories travelled back in time. He ran his fingers through his hair and turned back to Katie. "I hope that Buttercup will be the same for Rose."

"That saddle you made was very beautiful, like the one you made for me."

"It was a joy to make it for her, like it was for you."

Katie placed her hairbrush back on her cabinet. "You're a thoughtful man, Adam." She stood, walked to him and slipped her arms up around his neck.

He grinned at her and wrapped his arms around her waist. They shared a sweet kiss.

"Me and the girls, we're so blessed to have you in our lives. You really are our hero."

Adam slid his arms up to rest against her back. He looked into her mesmerising green eyes and grinned at her. "Nah, Katie, I'm not a hero. And it's me that is blessed. All that I've achieved, and all that I've done, has been because of you and those six little girls. I don't know how I got to be so favoured by God that he'd give me so many wonderful blessings."

He raised his eyebrows, and his dark eyes softened and misted over. "It's my highest calling, my greatest duty, the duty to my family. I feel it very deeply, especially since I was away from you all for so long when I was jailed." He closed his eyes and swallowed. His false-imprisonment eight years ago was still hard for him to think about. It had been an extremely difficult portion of their lives, Katie believing he was dead, he in the most horrific conditions for more than half a year. All the compensation money in the world couldn't make up for that. "Sitting there in the dark, I vowed if I ever got out of there, I would never ever, for one moment, take any of it for granted, and I never will." He raised his brows and flashed her the sideways grin she loved so much. "When I was finally home, I felt I'd been given a second chance. I mean, life was wonderful before then, but getting to watch my girls grow up and being here with you in this place has been the greatest blessing of my life."

"Mine too, Adam." Katie laid her head against his chest. Adam leaned his head against hers, his bride of nearly seventeen years. He was even more deeply in love with her than he had been when they first married. He took a deep breath, breathing in the scent of her lilac soap and, with it, the strength he drew from her.

"I love those girls, Katie. You sure did me proud giving them all to me."

"They're a testament to you. Such a wonderful caring man who loves, honours and values women the way you do is rare and special. Rose is the lovely young woman she is because of the example of the father she has. I know that someday when the young men come calling, she'll only want to choose one of the highest character because that's the example she's had. Even her Uncle Daniel, Owen and Samuel are men of great character. She'd never settle for anything less."

Adam closed his eyes and sighed. "I hope not. I couldn't give my daughter away to just anyone. I can't even imagine giving her away at all."

"You're a good man, Adam." Katie stood up on her toes to kiss him on the cheek.

"Because I have a good woman behind me. I truly believe men are only strong because of the women supporting them. How can I not love and honour them? They are remarkable young ladies. I'm the proudest Mountie alive."

She laid her head against his chest again. "I'm sorry you never got to have a son." Her voice trembled with emotion.

Adam lifted her chin to look her in the eye. "You mustn't be sorry. I'm not." He grinned. "I'm proud to be a father to girls. They are so precious and such a joy to me."

"I did always want to give you a son, though." Katie gulped and stepped back from him. "I often imagine the baby I miscarried was a boy. I think of him often." Her lips trembled. "I wonder who he might have become. Would he have been a Mountie like his daddy?"

Adam reached for her and wiped away the tear that sat on her cheek. He pulled her close to him again, cradling her head in his hand. Katie could feel a slight tremble in him as he spoke.

"I don't know who he or she would've been, just that they would've been loved like the others. Whoever they were, they would be five or six years old now, I guess." He closed his eyes and laid his forehead against hers again. "When you haemorrhaged like that, and I thought I was gonna lose you, I've never been so scared in all my life. I pleaded with God to save you. When Owen told us we couldn't have any more children after that, in some ways, it was a relief."

Katie leaned back and looked at him. "A relief?"

"I don't mean that as in I didn't want more children. I would've happily had twelve if the Lord allowed." He closed his eyes. "But I didn't want to risk you going through that again. Losing the baby was awful. But we hadn't been anticipating him or her; we didn't know they even existed until then. But the thought of losing you was worse than the pain I went through in that jail." He swiped at the tears forming in his eyes and then smiled at her. "So, I'd much rather enjoy the family we have knowing you didn't have to go through that again, than risk losing you."

He grinned and raised his hand to cup her face, stroking her soft cheek with his thumb. He kissed her, looked deeply into her eyes, and smiled with his whole face. "I'm not upset we didn't have any more children. I'm delighted, over the moon, thrilled and content with the family we have. Those six beautiful girls are everything to me. You are the greatest joy of my life." He paused as Katie brushed away a rogue tear that slipped down his cheek. He ginned at her and continued. "I have absolutely no regrets; no yearning for more children I can't have; no longing or pining for a son, and no resentment whatsoever."

Katie nodded and smiled at him. "Thank you, Adam. You make me so happy; I couldn't have asked for a more wonderful life." She kissed him deeply, her arms around his neck. "I love you. Now come on, let's go to bed. It's been a long day."

Adam scooped her up in his arms and carried her to their bed. She chuckled as he placed her down, brushed her nose and winked at her.

They spent time praying as they usually did, each thanking God for their love, their life and the family they had been blessed with. Adam prayed for Rose, their beautiful daughter who was becoming a woman. At last Adam pulled his wife into his arms. "I can't believe my Rosie is sixteen!" His voice sounded wistful.

Katie nodded and snuggled up to her husband.

Two
Rose

Adam returned from his run, and Jack wandered over to his rug and curled up in front of the fire. The old dog looked relieved to be back indoors again. He still managed to plod along behind his master a few times a week, but Adam knew his faithful companion didn't have many years left; he'd already exceeded the expected lifespan of a husky by several years. He squatted down and petted the dog's head. "Just rest, Boy. The girls'll be up soon."

He grinned as he headed for the bathroom to clean himself up. That dog sure did love his girls. He'd been with them since before Rose was born. Jack had romped the bushes on adventures with the sisters on countless occasions. He'd followed Adam on assignments and even saved the Mountie's life a few times with his acute hearing and sense of smell. Adam was grateful for that dog. Knowing he was there with his ladies when he couldn't be, was a great sense of comfort to the Mountie. He believed it was because of his love for the girls that Jack had lived so long.

As he bathed, Adam thought back to when Rose was born. He and Katie had been married less than a year when she'd made her appearance rather abruptly out in the woods on their land. Adam chuckled. "It was because of Jack," he said aloud. Katie had gone out after the adventurous puppy, and while there, she'd gone into labour. Rose had been born there in the woods under a large Douglas Fir tree.

He shook his head as he dried himself and dressed. Katie would be awake any moment, and he wanted to get the fires lit and the house warm for her and the girls. He buttoned up his shirt and lifted his suspenders over his shoulders as he walked out to the living room. He lit the fire in the kitchen stove and added more wood to the main fire in the living room. He squatted and petted the head of the old dog. "Just think, Jack, that little baby girl you guarded all those years ago is graduating today. She's sixteen and finished school. She'll be off into the world soon, Boy, and I'm just not sure I'm quite ready for it all." The dog lifted his head, tipped it to the side and whimpered. Adam chuckled. "You either, huh?"

Katie entered the room dressed simply in a white blouse with a lace collar and her long pale green skirt. Adam stood, crossed his arms over his broad chest, and grinned. He looked her up and down slowly and deliberately. "Katherine Morgan, you take my breath away. You are a truly beautiful woman."

"Oh, Adam, your eyes are deceiving you. I'm getting old, and these are just work clothes. My hair is a fright, and I probably have bags under...."

He stopped her by pulling her close and kissing her passionately. "Nope, you are still the most beautiful woman I've ever seen, bar none. I mean it. You still make my heart skip a beat. Your smile still makes me weak at the knees, and your kisses and embraces, they thrill me! I love you so much, Mrs Morgan. I can't believe how blessed I am. I still can't believe you ever married me!"

"Adam." Katie blushed. "Of course, I married you. You're the most wonderful man I've ever met and the most handsome. You still make me blush, and when you kiss me, I go all giddy like it's my first kiss."

They held each other for a moment. They relished these small quiet moments when they could declare their love to each other. Theirs was a home of love and laughter. It hadn't always been easy, but they'd all held together as a family and supported one another, and that is what had got them through; family and faith.

Adam sighed as he held her. She pulled back from him so she could look her husband in the eye. "What is it, Adam?"

"I was just thinking about how Rose was born out there in the woods, and then when at last you were settled and sleeping, I held you both in my arms. I remember thinking I was the richest man in the world, and now that sweet little girl; my Rosie, is graduating. Where have all those years gone, Wife?"

"I don't know. I just know how proud I am of her. She's a really lovely young lady."

"She's just like her beautiful ma."

"There is a lot of her daddy in her too. You two have always been very close."

Adam couldn't help but grin. "She's the apple of my eye. I love that little girl so much. One of the most treasured things in my life is having her arms around my neck and holding her tight. Of course, I used to have to kneel, but now she can almost look me in the eye. I still love it when she throws herself in my arms, kisses me, and says, 'I love you, Pa.'" He shrugged. "I guess that's one benefit of having girls; I think boys would have grown out of hugs and kisses long ago. I hope my girls never grow out of that. There's just nothing like it. The privilege of being that girl's father overwhelms me sometimes."

"Oh, Pa." Rose walked to him. He released Katie and stood looking at the beautiful dark-haired girl. She had dressed carefully that morning in a lovely lemon-yellow dress that she had made with her mother's help especially for graduation, and this was the first time that Adam had seen it. He grinned at her.

"Oh, Rosie. You look so beautiful. You've done a wonderful job on that dress. You're so talented, my darling." A tear ran down his cheek. "I love you, Darling. I'm so proud to be your father."

"Oh, Pa." She threw her arms around his neck.

He squeezed her and cradled her head in his hand; his eyes tightly closed. "Holding you is such a privilege, Rose. I'm not looking forward to you going away, away from my arms and into some young man's," he spoke into her hair.

She stood back and kissed him on the cheek. "Even when that does happen, I'll always want your hugs. I told Ma years ago that your arms are about the safest place I know, and that hasn't changed, and it never will. I'll never be too old for your hugs, not ever." She hugged him again, and he kissed her hair.

He gulped and sniffed back the bubbling emotions. "I'm glad, Darling, my arms will always be here to hold you; my shoulders are always here for you to cry on, whenever you need them, no matter how grown up you get."

One by one, the girls entered the room, all in various stages of 'waked-upness', as Hope often said. Lizzie was always full of energy no matter what time of the day it was, but Hope slithered out and immediately slumped down on the couch. It was obvious she wished she was still sleeping. The other girls were usually somewhere in between the two extremes.

Adam sat at the breakfast table with his family. He was feeling nostalgic that day as he observed them all. Occasions such as these often made him reflective. He couldn't help but think how absolutely beautiful they all were. Each one so very different and unique in her own right. Two with their Uncle Daniel's dark auburn hair, the rest dark like their mother.

He observed each of them while he ate and grinned.

"What's so amusing, Pa?" Callie raised a spoonful of oatmeal to her mouth.

"I was just thinking how beautiful all my girls are. I feel like the most blessed man alive to have such wonderful ladies in my life."

"Pa." Lizzie rolled her eyes. "You can be so sentimental sometimes."

"Can't help it." He reached across and placed his hand on her cheek. Lizzie smirked, but it quickly changed to a wide smile. "With beautiful girls like you in my life, it turns even the toughest of men into great big saps, and I'm not even ashamed to admit that."

His eyes travelled from face to face. Rose, his strong and tenacious firstborn. Callie, their domestic queen; Anna, the studious and quiet scholar. Lizzie, his red-haired firecracker who was always moving and oozed gumption and spunk from every pore. Sarah had the same red hair as Lizzie but a much gentler disposition. Lastly, his precious Hope. The girl couldn't be more aptly named. She truly had been his hope and his strength at the darkest time in his life.

Adam finished his review of his lovely little ladies and grinned. He'd always wanted to have lots of daughters, it had been his dream to have six little girls, and he'd really never thought it would happen.

Men often commiserated with him for only having daughters as though he was somehow cursed, and they felt sorry for him. His reply was always the same "Have you seen how beautiful they all are? Why on earth would I want any of them to be boys?"

*   *   *   *

Rose's graduation ceremony was bittersweet. Adam sniffed back his emotions as his beautiful daughter got up to give a speech on behalf of her classmates. He looked around and saw several young men with shining eyes watching the lovely girl in the lemon dress. He frowned slightly and scowled, but then a wide smile crossed his face as he heard the teacher announce, "Rose Katherine Morgan."

He stood and applauded rapturously with the rest of the parents as she received her diploma. Rose waved enthusiastically to her whole family, then gracefully made her way off the stage. Samuel leaned forward to whisper to his friend in the row in front of him. "She's a striking young lady, Adam." He patted his friend on his shoulder. "I've seen at least three young men admiring her," Samuel continued with a frown; all four men were very protective of each other's children, especially Adam's girls.

"I know." Adam's face curled up into a mock scowl, he patted his holster. "It's okay. I've got a gun!"

Sam patted his back again and chuckled. "You might be needing it soon, my friend!"

Rose made a bee-line for her father. She threw herself into his arms, and he held her proudly. Her cheek rested on his red serge jacket, and Adam whispered to her. "I'm so proud of you, Rosie; your speech was wonderful." He kissed her hair.

"Thanks, Pa." When he released her, he could see her eyes shining, and she handed him the rolled-up piece of paper. He held it while she hugged her mother, her sisters, and the entire extended family. They were never ones to shy away from hugs, even in public.

Daniel sidled over to Adam and Katie and put his hand on both of their shoulders. "That's a pretty special young lady you two, a real testament to you both as parents."

"Thank you, Danny. We think she's pretty great." Katie smiled at her brother.

"I noticed some young men eyeballing her." Daniel raised his bushy auburn eyebrows and stroked his short beard.

"I did too." Adam curled up his brow. "I'm gonna have to keep my wits about me."

"You can't keep her at home forever." Owen approached the group. "Some young man is going to sweep her off her feet one of these days, and there's nothing you can do about it."

"Why must you torture me so, Doctor? I thought we were friends," Adam groaned. "I'm not quite ready to give her up yet. It's bad enough she's leaving in a few months to go to Edmonton to study."

"We're all going to miss her, Adam." Becky approached the group.

* * * *

Adam sat at his desk, finishing up records. He sighed, ran his fingers through his hair, dipped his pen again, and leaned his chin against his left fist on the elbow propped up on his desk. Paperwork was so tedious, it was the least favourite part of his job, but it had to be done.

Finishing up the report, he stood to file it in the cabinet in the corner. He glanced up at the clock and grinned; it would soon be time to take his girls out for ice cream. He chuckled as he reached for the pile of correspondence. He knew how it was going to go, the squabbling over who got to choose first. Who would give the money to the clerk, what flavours they would get and the unreasonably long time they all took waiting for Anna to decide. Adam laughed out loud at the memory, and Jack lifted his head and whimpered. The Mountie nodded to the husky sleeping in front of the fire and chuckled. The dog lay his head back on his paws and promptly fell asleep again.

Adam shook his head. *That dog sure does sleep a lot.* Slicing open an envelope with his pocket knife, he slipped out the latest updates from headquarters and perused it. Startled by a knock at the door, he dropped the letter and looked up. A young man poked his head in the door.

"Sergeant Morgan, do you have a moment?" This was nothing unusual; he was used to people popping in at all hours to ask for help or report a problem, or even just to chat. He always had his door open and welcomed his people at any time.

"Certainly, Mr Murray, take a seat and tell me what I can do for you." Adam gestured to the chair opposite his desk.

The young man took the offered seat and then noticed Adam's paperwork in front of him. "I'm sorry, Sergeant, if you're busy, I can come back later?"

"No, it's fine. I welcome the interruption." Adam knew the young man well. Marcus Murray attended their church with his family. He was seventeen, and had recently started an apprenticeship under master craftsman, Arthur Campbell. It was a running joke in the church that the Murrays had six boys and the Morgans, six girls. "You seem a little nervous, Marcus, is something wrong?"

"Um... well, no... well, you see... that is...." He swallowed rapidly, tapping his fingers on his knees.

"Take a deep breath, Son, and tell me what's on your mind?" Adam smiled at the tongue-tied boy, he sat back in his chair and folded his arms.

Marcus inhaled deeply, held his breath for a few moments, then released it slowly. "Sergeant Morgan, Sir." His lips trembled as he tried to get the words out. "I was wondering, well, Sir, I'm here to..." He paused and swallowed, took a deep breath and began again, he looked Adam in the eye and squared his shoulders, attempting to look more confident than he felt. "Sergeant, I'm here to ask your permission to take Rose to the dance." He swallowed again twice in quick succession and clasped his hands together, leaning forward on the desk.

Adam's grin suddenly vanished, and he exhaled loudly, like he'd been kicked in the stomach. He'd always known this day would come, but he hadn't been prepared for it. He grimaced. *And so it begins.* He shook his head, and a wry smile crossed his face.

Marcus was visibly shaking, his request still hanging awkwardly before them.

Adam took a deep breath, and his lips quivered ever so slightly. He stood up, came around the desk, and sat on the front of it near the boy's chair. "Marc." He reached his hand out to touch the boy's shoulder, trying to put him at ease. "My answer is yes." He smiled.

Marcus released the breath he was holding and grinned; his face lit up. "Thank you, Sir." He exhaled deeply and started to stand up.

"Marcus." Adam's stern voice stopped him before he could even get to his feet.

"Yes, Sergeant?"

Adam crossed his arms over his chest and raised his eyebrows, holding Marcus in his steely gaze. "Rose is very special to me."

Marcus nodded. "Understood, Sir. You have my word that I will be the perfect gentleman. My folks raised me to value women; my intentions are honourable."

"I know that, Marcus, or my answer would've been no." Adam's lips held a slight smile, but his piercing brown eyes and creased brow assured Marcus that he was serious.

The young man swallowed. "Understood." He confidently looked the Mountie in the eye. Marcus rose to leave, and Adam stood up. He was very foreboding in his red jacket with his broad shoulders and square jaw. He put out his hand to shake Marcus's hand, gripped his shoulder and nodded. The young man returned his nod, thanked Adam and then left.

Adam sat back down in his seat and tried to concentrate on his paperwork. It was no good. He put his pen down, leaned back in his chair, thrust his arms across his chest, and sighed deeply. He shook his head and ran his fingers through his unruly hair. He heard a chuckle, and Daniel walked in. "Got something on your mind, Sergeant?"

Adam gestured for Daniel to reach for the coffeepot. The pastor smiled, poured two cups of the strong coffee and sat down in the still-warm chair. This was a common scene. The two had been best friends for more than twenty years and were close confidants as well as brothers-in-law.

The pastor slid a cup across the desk. "What is it, Adam?"

"Dan, I'm afraid it's begun." Adam raised his eyebrows and shook his head nostalgically. He took a long draft of the hot coffee and let it soothe him.

"What has?"

"Not ten minutes ago, a young man sat in that very chair and asked to take my Rosie to the dance."

Daniel put down his coffee, and his smile vanished. "Oh. What did you say?"

Adam sighed. "I gave my permission. Caught me by surprise though." He chuckled at his own sentimentality.

"And who is this young man that's got his claws into my niece?" Daniel grimaced.

Adam grinned; he knew anyone who finally did marry his girls was going to have more than just her father to contend with. "Marcus Murray."

Daniel raised his eyebrows, then smiled and nodded slowly. "He's a good lad. Theirs is a good family, Adam."

"I know. I wouldn't have said yes to just anyone."

"I should rather hope not; I might have to talk sense into you otherwise."

The two men drank their coffee in silence for a few moments.

Adam cocked up an eyebrow. "Do you suppose this will ever get easier?"

Daniel sipped his coffee and placed the cup down. He reached up to stroke his short beard. "I don't suppose so. And this is just a dance; wait till he wants to come courting."

"Ohhhhhhhh," Adam groaned and covered his face with his hand.

Daniel chuckled. "You wanted six daughters, Adam!"

"I know, it's just, I kinda wanted to keep them to myself forever."

"Well, you always knew that wasn't going to happen, my friend." He drained his coffee cup, stood and slapped Adam on the back. "It's the duty of a man, to bring his children up to leave his home."

Adam nodded slowly and toyed with his coffee cup, a look of nostalgic sadness on his face.

"I have to get going, my commiserations." Daniel grinned and left, chuckling. "Poor man." He put his hat on as he stepped out into the sunshine. "It's not easy giving up your girls."

*   *   *   *

Rose arrived home carrying a large bouquet of flowers, her cheeks rosy and her eyes sparkling.

Katie looked up from her cooking. "You look happy, Daughter."

"Yes, Ma." Rose blushed and smiled. "A boy asked me to the dance."

"He did?" Katie grinned. Adam had whispered to her over their ice cream cones about the meeting with Marcus.

"Marcus Murray, he's a nice boy, Ma."

"I know. Your pa and I know his family well."

Rose nodded.

"So, what did you say to him?" Katie raised her eyebrows.

Rose lifted her eyes to look at her mother; her cheeks reddened further as she smiled. "I said yes."

Katie squinted at her daughter and tipped her head to the side. "Do you have feelings for this boy?"

Rose shrugged. "I've never really spoken to him much, except at youth group events. He was a grade ahead of me, and they've only been in town a few years. But I know his brother, Archie, and he's nice too."

"I'm happy for you, Daughter." Katie squeezed her arm.

Rose reached up into the top cupboard for the vase and filled it with water from the pump. She placed it on the countertop, lifted the flowers to her nose, and breathed in their scent. Smiling, she lowered them into the vase. "I'm awfully nervous. I've never even given much thought to courting."

"It's just a dance, Rose. Don't get ahead of yourself. Don't even mention courting around your father. He's likely to have a heart attack." Katie laughed.

Rose screwed her face up. "Oh, Ma, do you think Pa will be mad?"

Katie furrowed her brows. "Mad about what, Darling?"

"About a boy asking me to the dance? I know how he is about his girls." She placed the vase of flowers on the mantle and turned to look at her mother.

"Your pa already knows. Marcus asked his permission."

"He did?" Rose frowned and then grinned, "And Pa said yes?" She walked back to her mother in the kitchen

Katie gripped her arm and smiled. "Of course he did."

Rose's eyes grew wide, and she shook her head. "I thought he'd be chasing all the boys away with his gun."

"He would if he didn't think they were good enough for his daughter."

Both women turned their heads as the door opened. "Well, that's a sight to walk in on, two beautiful ladies." Adam strode into the house.

Rose ran to throw her arms around his neck. "Thank you, Pa." She kissed his cheek and ran to her room.

"You're welcome, Darling." He laughed and turned to embrace and kiss his wife. "What am I being thanked for?"

"For saying yes to Marcus."

"Oh." He grinned. "Got any coffee, Wife?" He winked at her.

"Of course, my darling." Katie kissed him, and he unbuttoned his red serge jacket and sat down to remove his boots.

Katie placed the coffee and cookies on the table next to him.

Adam patted his knees for Katie to sit on his lap. She climbed up and put her arms around his neck, and they enjoyed a rare moment of peace together. He kissed her deeply, and she leaned her forehead against his for a moment.

She sat up with a grin. "So, how was your day?"

Adam groaned and rolled his eyes. "I wasn't expecting that."

"I know, Husband."

"The poor lad was so nervous he was visibly trembling." Adam laughed.

"Well, you're pretty intimidating, Adam."

"It made me glad I only had to get past your brother."

"I wasn't sixteen."

"No, you were nineteen!" Adam nodded. "I think that's the hard part. I was kinda hoping this wouldn't happen for a few more years."

"It's not a courtship. They're just going to a dance."

Adam nodded slowly. "I know, but I can't shake this foreboding feeling that I'm going to lose her soon."

"Don't get ahead of yourself. Just enjoy this time. It's beautiful watching your daughter grow up and become a woman."

"I wish they could just all stay as they are, where they still need their daddy." He sighed and raised his brows. His dark eyes grew nostalgic.

"I'll always need you, Pa." Rose entered the room. "That's not going to change." She had changed out of her work dress and into house clothes; still, she was lovely. Her shining eyes and blushing cheeks were very becoming.

Katie climbed off Adam's knee, and he stood up. "That's good, Darling. I'll always need you, too." He embraced her. "You look very happy."

"I am. I'm looking forward to the dance." Her cheeks reddened.

Adam raised his brows. "And I suppose those flowers are yours?" He nodded towards the mantle.

"Yes, Marcus gave them to me." Her cheeks coloured.

Adam sighed.

"It's just a dance, Pa."

"I know, Darling. It's just hard for a father to watch his precious daughters grow up. I'm happy for you, but it's tough on me."

"I know, but I don't even really know Marcus. I'm just going to a dance with him, not marrying him." She pursed her lips.

Adam flashed her his sideways grin and shook his head.

Three
The Dance

Adam was busy tying ribbons and combing hair when there was a knock on the door. He stood to open it, welcoming in the young man. "Marcus." He nodded and gave the young man a slight smile. He put a hand out to Marcus and welcomed him in.

The young man held a small posey of flowers and wore a crisply laundered black suit with a pale yellow waistcoat his mother had made him to match Rose's dress.

Marcus refused the offered chair and leaned nervously against the wall. The girls twirled around in their party dresses and waited for their parents to be ready. Callie and her mother walked into the room, and behind them came Rose wearing her pale yellow gown and long white gloves. She wore a simple silver necklace and her mother's yellow earrings, and her long brown hair tumbled down over her shoulders. Adam's eyes misted up, and Marcus swallowed nervously several times, his lips trembling and his knees threatening to buckle.

"Oh, Rosie, you're truly beautiful." Adam embraced his daughter. "Your dress is lovely, and your face is glowing so."

"Paaaaaa." Rose blushed deeply as she stepped back from him and then shyly looked up at Marcus. "Hello."

"Hello." Marcus' heart skipped a beat. He took a deep breath and walked towards her, holding out the posey to her. "These are for you." He swallowed again. "Ma told me they are peonies."

"Yes." Rose smiled. "They're lovely, thank you." She smiled, her usual confidence returning.

"You're lovely too, Miss. Morgan." Marcus shining eyes confirmed his words. "Are you ready to go?"

"I just need my shawl." She pointed to the white shawl hanging on the hook behind him.

"Allow me." Marcus took a deep breath to swallow down his nerves and remembered his manners. Reaching for the delicate crocheted shawl, he wrapped it around her shoulders. Time slowed down and her heart raced as she lifted her long hair over the top and thanked him with a nod.

He put his arm out to her. Rose gripped it shyly.

"I'll see you at the dance, Sir." Marcus shook the Mountie's hand and looked him in the eye. Adam was pleased about that. The young man seemed confident and polite after his initial nervousness.

"Drive carefully, Marcus." Adam clenched his jaw and raised his eyebrows.

"You have my word, Sergeant." He nodded, turned, escorted Rose out of the door, and helped her up into his father's small gig.

Adam closed the door on them. He shook his head and sighed. He reached out to embrace Katie and smiled sadly. "That was more difficult than I thought." He closed his eyes for a moment and took a deep breath.

Adam looked wistfully at his five other daughters and grinned. "Look at you all, so beautiful. I'm going to be the most envied man on the dance floor tonight with all these beautiful girls surrounding me. Are you all ready?"

Four of them nodded enthusiastically. Lizzie rolled her eyes and groaned dramatically; she tugged at the bodice of her dress, looking very uncomfortable in ruffles and lace.

Adam entered the saloon with his wife and Callie on his arms. The four younger girls walked along behind. Lizzie immediately made her way over to the punch station to purchase a cup with the dime her father had given her.

Adam looked around and noticed Rose and Marcus already on the dancefloor; they looked at each other shyly as they waltzed together. Marcus turned out to be a very good dancer. His mother had taught all her sons how to dance. Adam caught Mr Murray's eye and nodded to him. The man was also watching his oldest son dancing with the beautiful girl. His mother had misty eyes, and her hands clasped together before her as she watched them.

Daniel came over and put his hand on the shoulder lapel of Adam's red serge coat. "How you holding up, Pa?"

Adam shook his head and chuckled. "It's not easy, Dan, but I'm learning to accept it. They do dance nicely together."

Daniel looked in their direction and grinned. "They sure do."

Adam sighed. "I have to admit, they seem well suited. They'd be good together."

"You're getting ahead of yourself, Sergeant. It's just a dance."

Adam ran his fingers through his hair. "I'm just preparing myself for the inevitable." He gave the pastor a sideways smile.

Adam was on duty that evening, as always; but he would take the time to dance with each of his girls and his wife. He hoped Marcus would spare Rose for one dance with him. As it turned out, after he'd danced with Katie, the next was ladies' choice. Louisa was busy behind the lemonade stand, so Katie winked at her husband and headed over to ask her brother to dance.

Rose whispered something to Marcus. He nodded kindly to her and took a seat.

Walking across to her father, she put her hand out to him. "Sergeant, might I have this dance?"

Adam grinned and took her offered hand. "I'd be honoured, Miss. Morgan."

They took up the waltz together as they had so many times in the past, and he noticed her shining eyes. "You look happy, Daughter."

"I am. Marcus is a perfect gentleman. He even brought me some coffee and a muffin from the cake table."

"I'm glad, Rose." He raised his eyebrows and patted his holster. "If he's anything other than a gentleman, he'll have me to answer to."

"I know, Pa. And Uncle Daniel and Dr Randall and cousin Andy and...." She laughed. "You're all so protective of me."

"Because you are so precious, Rose." His eyes betrayed his seriousness.

"Thanks, Pa. I love you."

"Oh, I love you too, Darling." The music stopped, and he escorted her back to Marcus, kissed her on the forehead and walked away, back to his wife.

"How are you doing, Pa?"

"Fine. Marcus is a perfect gentleman, and she is happy. What more can I ask?" He sounded wistful.

"Did you notice, Callie? The young men are lining up to dance with her." Katie gestured across to Callie, who was being whisked around by a young man from her class.

Adam followed her gaze, and observed three young men standing nearby watching her. He sighed. "I'm gonna lose them all before too long." His frown turned to a grin. He eyed his wife up and down, winked and put a hand out to her. "Please, Mrs Morgan, will you dance with me? I must have the most beautiful woman in the room dance with me. I'll be the envy of all the other chaps."

"I'm not so sure, Sergeant," she teased. "I don't know what my husband would say."

"Well, I've heard he's a reasonable and very handsome man. I think he would wholeheartedly agree." Adam's eyes sparkled.

Katie raised her brows. "Is that an order, Sergeant Morgan?"

"No. It's a request, but if you refuse, it will become an order."

"Then I shan't refuse." She took his offered arm.

"I love to dance with you, Katie. I always have." He grinned as they took up the waltz.

"I love to dance with you too. You're a wonderful dancer."

"Because I'm dancing with you. It's always made me so proud to have you in my arms and watch your eyes shine while we dance. Do you remember the first time we ever danced together?"

Katie grinned. "It was here. I was trying to get away from that man that eventually kidnapped me." She shuddered and curled up her mouth. "You were courting Delia."

"Don't remind me." Adam rolled his eyes and then flashed her a wide grin. "I may have been trapped in a courtship with Delia, but I was already in love with you, and seeing that man roughly handling you, made my blood boil. Then when I danced with you and got to hold you for the briefest time. It was such a delight to me. It still is. I love you even more now than I did then." He leaned in and whispered in her ear, "Only difference is now I don't have to try to hide it, and I can kiss you whenever I want." He winked at her.

Katie blushed and grinned back at him. "You didn't do a very good job of hiding it back then. I knew you had feelings for me, even way back then."

Adam tilted his head to the side. "Really?"

"You aren't quite as mysterious as you think, Sergeant."

He shook his head and laughed. "You've always been able to see right through me, Katie, and I don't mind at all."

Hope fell asleep on Owen's knee. He'd asked her to dance with him since Louie was dancing with his mother and Vinnie with his sister. Afterwards, Owen had sat down, and Hope climbed up on his knee. They watched her parents dancing, and Hope lay her head against the doctor's chest and fell asleep.

Adam walked over, he grinned. It was wonderful how much his friends adored his girls. He knew they'd always be protected even when he wasn't around, and he was grateful for it. "Little sleepyhead. I never could work out how she could sleep in such a noisy room. I better get her home." He smiled and scooped her up in his arms. He nodded his thanks to Owen. "At least I'll get to keep you for a few years yet, little one." He chuckled.

He walked across to his family, waiting at the door. Marcus led Rose over to farewell them.

"Have her home by ten thirty, Marcus." Adam fixed the young man with his steely brown eyes, just a hint of a furrow to his brow.

"I will, Sir."

Adam nodded, kissed Rose's cheek and turned to lead his family out.

* * * *

28

"Where is she, Katie? She should be home by now." Adam paced the living room, his jaw set firmly, and fists clenched. He squinted and scowled. "It's eleven o'clock. I'm going to find her, and I swear if he's laid so much as a finger on my daughter, he better not come within a mile of me." Adam threw on his boots, reached for his jacket and hat and headed for the door.

"Adam, don't do anything rash. Perhaps they just lost track of time."

Adam swallowed and clenched his teeth. "I don't care. I trusted him with my daughter. I'm going to get some answers."

He reached for the door handle and heard frantic footsteps on the stairs and a voice calling for help. Adam yanked open the door, and a very dishevelled Marcus stood before him, with his clothing ripped, bruises and cuts on his face, and a haunted look in his eyes.

"They took her, Sir. You've gotta help me; they took her." His lips trembled.

"What, who took her?" Adam's blood began to boil.

"Michael James and Terrance Parker, Sir. I tried to fight them off. I told her to take the horse and get away, but they were beating me. I passed out, and when I came to a few moments later, I could hear her calling my name as they dragged her away." Marcus trembled as he spoke.

Adam took a deep breath. "Take me to where you last saw her." He turned to his wife. "I will find her, Katie." He clenched his square jaw tightly.

The anger in his eyes frightened her. "Adam, don't do anything you'll regret."

"I'll regret nothing," he hissed through his teeth.

"Adam!" Katie called to him as he disappeared out the door with Marcus. "Oh no." She immediately sat down to pray.

Adam took the reins of the small gig, and pushed the horse as fast as he could. He swallowed over and over, struggling to keep his cool. He took a deep breath. "Who are these men, Marc, and what do they want with Rose?" He clenched his jaw.

"Michael James and Terrance Parker. They both work at the mill. They kept asking Rose to dance. They seemed sinister to me, Sir, and I refused to let them near her, but they kept pestering me. After you left, they only stepped up their game. Rose became very agitated at how they looked at her. She told me they've come into the store a few times and made her feel uncomfortable."

"I wonder why she didn't tell me." Adam frowned.

"Because she knows you and didn't want you risking your job as a result of them. They hadn't done more than just leer at her. She thought it wouldn't go any further than that. I suggested we leave early, it was just before ten, but they followed us. I tried to drive away, but Parker galloped up beside me and leapt on the gig. He wrestled me to the ground and started beating me." Marcus touched one of the wounds on his head and winced. "James yanked Rose off the gig and told her if she fought him, he'd kill me first, then her family, starting with Hope and working his way up all the sisters. He picked her up in his arms and carried her away. I could hear her calling my name." Marcus was almost in tears by the time he finished his lengthy explanation.

Adam breathed deeply and deliberately. "They threatened my girls." His eyes blazed and he set his jaw. "If they've hurt her in any way...."

"They went up here, Sir. That was the last I saw of them."

"There's an old abandoned barn up there. Homestead burnt to the ground a few years back, but the barn still stands. I'll wager they've taken her there." He flicked the rein over the horse's back, hoping to get more speed out of him. Before he reached the barn, he could hear Rose screaming.

"Help me! Pa! Marcus! Help me... Stop, get your hands off me..."

A man had Rose pinned up against the wall; his body pressed firmly against hers. "Come on, Love. all I want is one dance...." She wriggled and punched out at him with all her might, crying out and trying to push him away. The other man was standing nearby, taunting him. "Kiss her, Michael. Then I wanna kiss too."

Adam didn't wait until the horse came to a complete stop. He leapt off, reached for his pistol and ran to the barn. He kicked the door open and fired a shot into the ceiling. The men spun their heads to look at him and froze on the spot.

"Paaa." Rose turned frightened eyes to him and tried to push the man off her.

Adam marched up to the man, still holding Rose tightly. "Take your hands off my daughter, Mr James and back away, or I'll put a bullet in you." He dug the barrel of his pistol roughly into Parker's ribs. The man groaned but didn't let go of Rose.

Terrance moved his hand towards his pistol. "I wouldn't do that if I were you, Parker," Adam growled through his teeth. "I strongly suggest you both put your hands in the air." It took every ounce of self-control he could muster to resist putting a bullet in the heart of both men.

They sneered and backed away. "Okay, red coat, we meant no harm," Parker scoffed.

Rose collapsed to the ground in tears, and Marcus ran to her. "It's okay, Rose; I've got you." He put his arms around her, and she clung to him. He held her gently and rocked her in his arms while she cried into his chest. Adam disarmed Parker and kicked the gun away. He pulled the handcuffs from his pocket and cuffed the men's hands together. He took the second pair of cuffs out of his jacket pocket and hooked one end to Terrance Parker's free arm and the other to a steel bar on the top rail of the corral.

With a scowl at both men, he strode over to his daughter, and squatted down. Marcus released her and Adam took her in his arms. He cradled her head, and she buried her face in his chest. "Oh, Rosie. I've got you, Darling. I've got you. You're safe now." His voice was gentle and full of relief as he spoke into her hair, despite the burning anger growing in him.

"I knew you'd come for me, Pa. I just knew it." She sobbed into his chest.

Adam kissed her hair and looked up at Marcus. "Go into town and fetch Dr Randall and Pastor Coleman. I could use their help with this. I'll stay and keep an eye on these two. Rose will be fine." He stroked her back.

"Yes, Sir." The young man fled to do the Mountie's bidding.

Adam continued to hold Rose until she stopped sobbing. "I'm so sorry, Rosie girl, you don't deserve this, and you can rest assured I will see to it these men never come near you again." He glared at them in the low lanternlight. For a brief moment, he wished Rose wasn't there and he could have just five minutes alone with those men. But he knew better; no matter how angry he was, Rose needed him.

"Lighten up, Constable. It was just a bit of fun. We just wanted to dance with the pretty girl since she refused to dance with us." James thrust his free arm out towards Rose.

"Yeah, Officer, we wasn't gonna hurt her." Terrance tugged against the cuff that joined him to the rail.

Rose sat back, and Adam gave her his handkerchief. He stroked her cheek and winked at her. She smiled at him to let him know she was okay.

Adam stood, strode over and gripped Michael James by the chin. He brought his face so close to his that the man could feel the Mountie's breath and see the fire in his eyes. He gritted his teeth. "If you so much as look in the direction of my daughter or any member of my family ever again, I'll see to it that even your mother can't recognise you." Adam's voice was shaky in his effort to remain calm.

"Pa. That's not the way."

Adam let go of him and walked back over to Rose. James lifted his free hand to rub his jaw and spat on the nearby straw.

"Pa, they didn't hurt me. They just frightened me. They aren't worth risking your career over."

"Rose, you're much more important to me than my career. Duty to my family is much more important than my duty as a Mountie."

"Listen to her, Constable; she's a smart girl."

"It's, Sergeant, Mr Parker, and she's the only reason you aren't dead right now." The Mountie marched back towards the men.

Marcus came running in, followed by Daniel and Owen. Marcus ran to Rose and put his arm around her shoulders. "Are you okay, Rose?"

"Yes, they just frightened me. I'm alright now." She laid her head against his shoulder.

Seeing Rose was safe with Marcus, Adam turned to his two friends.

"Adam, what's going on?" Daniel tugged on his short beard. His nightshirt stuck out from under his suit jacket, where he'd hastily tucked it into his trousers as he ran out the door.

"I need your help to escort these men to the cells."

"For what, Sergeant?" James sneered. "Even the girl said we didn't hurt her. You ain't got no case."

Owen marched up to Mr James and grabbed him by the scruff of the neck. "He may not have a case to arrest you, but you should know there are many people in this town that care about that girl, and if any of you comes within a mile of her, we will make an airtight case you can't worm your way out of. Are you hearing me? I suggest you get your sorry selves out of this town and never come back because if you go anywhere near that girl again, I'll...." Owen paused. Adam raised his brows. He'd never seen Owen so stern. He nodded, he knew his friends would do whatever it took to protect any of the family. He was grateful to them.

"You'll what, Doc?" The man spat in Owen's face. Owen stood back and wiped the spit out of his eyes.

"There ain't nofin' any of'em can do to us, James. A Mountie, a doctor and a pastor, they can't do nofin'."

"No, but I can." Rose shook off Marcus's arm, stood up and marched up to Michael James. He sneered at her, but before he even had a chance to say anything, she slapped him as hard as she could and kicked him in the shins. He yelped in pain and hopped on one leg. Marcus grinned, and Adam was working hard not to laugh.

"Atta girl," Daniel muttered under his breath, and Owen nodded.

"You see that, Sergeant? That girl attacked me. I'm innocent, and she came at me unprovoked." Mr James affected an indignant air.

Marcus found his courage before Adam could even speak. He strode up to the men. "Are you gonna press charges against a woman for hitting you? If you do, I'll press charges for the beating you two gave me, for kidnapping Miss Morgan, and threatening an officer of the law."

"I told you we weren't gonna get away with this, Parker."

"You didn't tell me her pa was a Mountie."

"I thought you knew."

"I didn't know her name was Morgan. They just called her Rose at the store."

"I've heard enough. Let's take these two to the cells. I need to get my daughter home." Adam clenched his jaw.

"I'll take her home, Sir," offered Marcus. "I'll see to it she gets there safely."

"Thank you, I appreciate that, Marc." Adam cupped Rose's cheek. "Are you okay, Darling?"

"Yes, Pa, these men don't scare me. I'm not afraid anymore."

"That's my brave girl." He embraced her and kissed her on the hair. "I'll be home as soon as I can. You tell your ma not to worry."

"I will, Pa."

Marcus put his arm around her, and they left the barn.

* * * *

Adam closed the cell door on Parker and James. "I'll have to stay here for the night, keep watch over these two."

"I'll stay, Adam. Rose needs you."

"It's okay, Dan. Her mother and sisters will be with her. It's my job."

"At least let me stay with you. I'll just go tell Lou, and I'll come back." Before Adam could argue, Daniel marched out the door. It wouldn't be wise to leave Adam alone too long with people who tried to hurt one of his girls.

"Do you want me to stay, too?" Owen crossed his arms over his chest.

"No, you go back to Becky and the kids."

"Very well." The doctor walked towards the door.

"Owen."

He paused and turned back to look at Adam.

"Thank you. It means a lot to me to know you've got my back, and my family's."

"You'd do the same for my daughter, Adam." Owen clenched his teeth. "I hope Rose is okay."

"She's a tough girl. She'll be fine. I'll make sure she is."

"She's your daughter, Adam. I know she'll be fine." Owen nodded to Adam and left the office just as Daniel returned.

The pastor and Mountie took shifts staying up to watch the two men. When Daniel was alone with them, he pulled up a chair outside their cell. "What were you men thinking? She's an innocent girl?"

Parker lay on the bed staring at the ceiling while James sat on his bed and answered the pastor. "What's it to you, Pastor?"

"She's my niece."

"We meant no harm. We weren't gonna hurt her."

Daniel crossed his arms over his chest and raised his thick auburn eyebrows. "When the sergeant arrived, you had your hands on her."

"I just wanted to dance with her, I swear it. But that man she was with wouldn't let us. I just wanted to dance with the pretty lady, I seen her in the shop and I wanted to dance with her. I'm a hard-working man, and I deserve to dance with a pretty girl. Is that too much to ask?"

"Yes, if she doesn't want to! You can't force a woman to dance with you if she doesn't want to." Daniel's tone was uncharacteristically stern.

"She danced with other men in there. What they got that we don't have?"

"Manners." Daniel scowled.

"What's that policeman gonna do to us, Rev?"

"I'm a pastor, not a reverend. He's going to wire Mountie HQ and have you charged with assault."

"You have to let us out of here, Rev." Parker sat up on his bed to join the conversation.

"Please, we promise to never come back. Just let us go, and no harm done. We've learned our lesson." James backed up his friend.

"I don't think so." Daniel frowned.

"If you let that Mountie come near us, he'll kill us," Parker protested.

"Do you blame him? That's his sixteen-year-old daughter you assaulted."

Parker's mouth dropped open, and his eyes widened. "That woman is only sixteen?"

"Yes!" Daniel stroked his beard. "She's just finished school."

"Oh, we're dead men." Parker grimaced.

"Shut up, Parker. You fool, I was gonna get us out of this."

"No, you weren't, James. I wasn't going to let you go." Daniel frowned at them.

*   *   *   *

Samuel arrived before noon the next day with orders from headquarters. He gripped Adam's shoulder. "I'm sorry about Rose. How is she?"

Adam nodded and grinned. "She slapped James clear across the face, and I've never been so proud in all my life!"

Sam's smile grew wide, and his eyes sparkled. "That's my girl. She's made of tough stuff."

"Yes! She's her mother's daughter, that's for sure."

Sam nodded. "I have orders from HQ."

"What do they say?"

Sam passed him the telegram. Adam frowned and clenched his teeth as he read it. "They've done this before and been run out of town. They have prior charges for brutalising women, says here James had a wife, and she died under suspicious circumstances."

Sam nodded. "I'm glad you got to Rose when you did."

"Me too, Sam." Adam gritted his teeth.

They stepped into the office together. "I'm here to escort these two to Edmonton. The Mounties there have been looking for these men for some time. How long have they been in Douglas Falls?"

"Less than a month."

Sam nodded. "Atkins is here with me. We have our car. If we leave at first light, we'll make it to Edmonton by nightfall."

"I want to come with you."

"No, Adam, my orders were for you to stay away from it; too many emotions involved. Besides, Rose needs you here."

Adam let out an exasperated sigh. "Sam, I need to see these two get justice."

"Adam." Samuel placed his hand on the older Mountie's shoulder. "I love that girl too. You can count on me, Brother."

Adam sighed loudly and nodded his head twice.

"Now go home. Rose needs you."

"Will you come too? Katie will insist you stay for supper."

"Of course." Sam grinned. "Atkins will stay here overnight, won't you, Constable."

"Yes, Sir." The young Mountie removed his hat and hung it on the hook. He strode over and took a seat behind Adam's desk. He put his boots up on the desktop and put his hands behind his head.

Adam raised his brows at him. The young man hurriedly removed his feet and sat up straight. Adam nodded and turned to Sam. "Well then, let's get home."

"I have my car; we'll drive up."

"Rose!" Adam immediately ran to his daughter without stopping to remove his boots. "Rosie, are you okay, my darling?"

"Yes, of course, Pa. They gave me a fright, but I'm okay."

"You're a brave, strong girl. I'm proud of you." He stroked her cheek. "I was sure proud of you when you slapped him." He grinned.

"Adam," Katie scolded. "Surely you don't condone violence."

"Of course not, my darling." He winked at her. "But my girls have my permission to defend themselves against anyone that tries to hurt them."

Rose nodded. "Marcus was so kind to me, Pa, but he's blaming himself. He thinks it's his fault because he couldn't fight them off."

Adam frowned. "A seventeen-year-old boy is no match for two thirty-year-old men. He did the right thing coming for me."

"I told him that, but he still blames himself. I have to make it up to him. He was so kind to me."

"You will, Darling. He's a fine young man."

Four
Marcus

"Marcus," Rose called to his retreating figure after church two Sundays later.

"No, Rose," he muttered under his breath and walked away.

"Marcus."

He paused, turned, shook his head and smiled sadly at her. He thrust his hands in his pockets, turned back, and continued walking.

Rose sighed and shrugged. She walked back to her family.

Adam raised his eyebrows to ask the question.

"He just left, Pa. He must still be feeling guilty." She frowned.

"Give him time, Rose. He'll come around." Adam put his arm around her and kissed her hair.

Rose shrugged. "It's a shame. I thought we might be friends." She had really enjoyed his company at the dance, found him caring and attentive, and interesting to talk to. She had even dared to dream of the possibilities the friendship could have.

After their family lunch, Rose saddled Buttercup and went for a long ride over her family's property. She loved feeling the wind in her hair as she rode. She and Buttercup were absolutely in sync with one another; somehow, riding her always made Rose feel better. She rode right to the edge of the property to one of her favourite places in the world. There was a little grove of trees that made a sheltered spot which overlooked the valley, and in the distance, she could see the majestic mountains. It was a spot that made her feel close to God.

She sat on a tree stump as she so often did, and enjoyed the warmth of the sun for more than an hour, thinking and praying. By the time she left, she was determined to leave the whole situation in God's hands. If He wanted her and Marcus to become friends, or maybe even more than friends, it would happen in His timing.

*   *   *   *

Adam was much more upset about Marcus's response than Rose. On the night of the dance, he'd seen a great strength of character in Marcus. He hadn't shied away from coming to get help, and he'd been tender and caring to Rose.

When Rose was out riding, Adam headed out to do his rounds. Mountie life didn't stop just because it was Sunday. But he did admit he had a specific purpose in mind that day. He wanted to speak to Marcus. He took his usual route, checking in on his people and making sure his presence was noticed in town. Satisfied his job was done, he pulled Ebony to a halt outside the Murray homestead. Herbert Murray had a large farm, and his six sons helped him to work it. It was Sunday, so they did the minimal amount of work. Still, the farmer was in the barn tending to his animals when Adam rode up. Herbert walked out and swiped his sleeve across his brow and put his hand out to shake Adam's. "Afternoon, Sergeant."

Adam removed his Stetson and returned the man's handshake. "Herbert." He nodded in greeting.

"What brings you out this way this afternoon?" Herbert leaned back against his corral fence.

"I was hoping to speak to Marcus. Is he here?"

"I'm afraid not, he left straight after lunch, and I haven't seen him since."

"Do you have any idea where he might have gone?"

"Fishing, I'd wager. His pole is gone, and it's usually where he goes in his spare time."

"The river or the lake?"

"The river. Usually goes down to the bend at the back of old Roger Edwards homestead. Lots of catfish there."

"Thank you, Herbert."

"I'm sorry I couldn't be of more help, Sergeant. I hope you find him."

Adam placed his Stetson on his head, nodded, unhooked Ebony's rein, leapt on and galloped away. It didn't take him long to reach the spot, and sure enough, Marcus was sitting on a log near the river with his pole in the water. He didn't hear Adam pull up, and he didn't look much like he was interested in the fishing.

Marcus stared into the river blankly with a look of dejection on his face. Adam tethered Ebony to a tree and walked towards the young man, Stetson in his hand. "Marcus."

Marcus didn't look up. "I know why you're here, Sergeant. I've been expecting you to come and find me." His voice was sombre and full of remorse.

"And just why is that?" Adam sat down on the log next to Marcus and placed his Stetson next to him.

"You've come to tell me I let you down. You trusted me with your daughter, and because of me, she almost...." He sighed. He couldn't say the words; it was too horrible to even think about. He was certain the sergeant would never trust him with his daughter ever again. "...Well, you know," he concluded with a loud sigh.

Adam nodded but didn't say anything.

"It's my fault, Sergeant Morgan, and I admit that. I'm sorry it happened, but I can't take it back. I thought it best I just stay away."

Adam folded his arms over his chest and stared intently at the float of Marcus's fishing line. "Best for whom?"

Marcus jerked his head around to look at Adam. He'd been expecting Sergeant Morgan to yell at him, but he didn't appear to be angry at all. In fact, the look on his face was sympathetic and kind. He frowned. "Well, best for Rose, Sir."

Adam turned to Marcus and raised his brows. "Why is you not being around best for Rose?"

"Well... I just figured... you'd rather I not come around her. After all, I let you down... you trusted me, and I let you down. She almost... got hurt, and it's because of me." Marcus hung his head again.

"Did Rose say you'd let me down?" Adam ran his fingers through his hair.

"No, Sir." Marcus studied the scuffed leather of his boots.

"Did I say that?"

"No, Sir."

Adam raised his brows again. "Then why do you think that?"

"Like I said, you trusted me, and she got hurt."

Adam nodded slightly and put his hand briefly on the young man's shoulder. "I didn't come here to tell you off. I didn't come here to tell you to stay away from my daughter. I came here to thank you."

Marcus's eyebrows flew up in surprise, and his mouth dropped open. He stared at Adam. "To thank me?"

"Yes, for saving Rosie that night."

Marcus frowned and gave Adam a sideways smile. "Respectfully, Sir, you saved her. I just stood back and watched."

"On the contrary. You did your utmost to protect her. Even when they were beating you, your thoughts were still for her. When you couldn't stop them, you came for help immediately. When she needed you, you comforted her, ensured she felt safe and got her home safely. I wasn't able to take her home and apprehend those men at the same time, but you never left her until you knew she was safe." Adam looked him in the eye, squeezed his shoulder and smiled kindly. "That makes you a hero in my book, Marc."

Marcus closed his eyes and thrust his arms across his chest. "But I should've fought harder. I should've fought them off."

"Marcus, they were two fully grown men, armed and drunk; a dangerous combination. You did your utmost to protect my daughter; that's all a man can ask. You are not responsible for the choices of evil men. You were my daughter's hope in the midst of that horror. I'm grateful you were with her."

Marcus smiled for the first time, the burden of guilt having lifted off his shoulders. "Thank you, Sergeant. I'm sorry it happened, and I'll not bother her again."

"If that's what you think is best." Adam folded his arms and stared at the river again.

Marcus turned to him again, his brow creased. "Don't you?"

"No. But it's not up to me. It's up to Rose. She's a wise girl, and I trust her judgement. If she wants to see you, then it should be up to her."

A light shone in his eyes, and his mouth twitched slightly in hope. "Do you think she'd want to see me again?"

"Can't speak for her. But she's been miserable the last week or so, thinking you were blaming yourself. She really wanted to talk to you at church today because she hasn't seen you."

"Really? She was looking for me?"

Adam nodded, and a smile crossed his face. "Yes, she told me she had a wonderful time at the dance with you."

Marcus grinned. "Are you saying you give me permission to keep seeing her?"

"I can't tell my daughter who to be friends with, Son." He raised his brows and fixed his eyes on Marcus. "If you plan to court, I'd expect a conversation."

Marcus shook his head. "It's too soon for that. I don't even know how she feels about me, but I'd certainly like to be friends with her." An involuntary smile crossed his face, and his eyes sparkled with hope.

Adam nodded, stood to leave, placed his Stetson on his head, and started to walk towards his horse. He took two steps and turned back. "Marcus?" He raised his brows and flashed him his sideways smile. "How long have you been in love with my daughter?" There was no condemnation in the Mountie's eyes.

Marcus blushed. "Two years, Sir. Since the day after we moved to town, and I saw her at church." He grinned. "Am I that obvious?"

Adam chuckled. "When a man has six beautiful daughters, he notices who has their eyes on them, Marcus. I saw how you looked at her at the dance. My wife tells me men are not as mysterious as we think we are. Your reaction to this confirmed to me you have very strong feelings for her."

Marcus raised one eyebrow. "And you are okay with that, Sergeant?"

Adam closed his eyes and took a deep breath. He gave a sideways grin, and his eyes became wistful. "I don't suppose I have a choice. I know first-hand what it's like to love a woman."

Marcus grinned. That was almost approval.

Adam fixed his steely eyes on Marcus again and raised one eyebrow. "But, Marc, she's very young and has her heart set on going to teacher's college in the fall."

Marcus nodded. "I understand. I'm not in any hurry, Sir. I don't even know how she feels about me. I'm just excited at the chance to spend more time with her."

Adam nodded, leapt on Ebony and galloped away.

* * * *

Adam and the four younger girls were making the most of the long summer evening by playing a game of tag outside. Callie was inside working on her latest sewing project with Katie, and Rose was sitting under the oak tree on the small bench reading 'Little Women', one of her favourite ever books. She was so engrossed in the story she didn't see Marcus ride up, tether his horse, and walk over to greet her pa.

"Good evening, Marcus." Adam left the game to come and shake his hand. The four girls kept right on playing. People came to see their father all the time, and they were used to ignoring it.

"Good evening, Sergeant Morgan."

"What brings you out here?" Adam grinned.

Marcus gulped. "I was wondering if I might speak to Rose. I think I owe her an apology. Sir."

Adam nodded, patted him on the back and gestured with his other hand to Rose under the oak tree.

Marcus grinned. He walked slowly towards her. Adam rounded up the four younger girls and took them inside, with the promise of cocoa and cake. Rose and Marcus deserved their privacy.

Marcus paused for a moment to watch her. She leaned against the tree, her feet up on the seat next to her, and her beautiful dark hair hanging long and tucked behind her ears. He watched her animated face as she laughed at something, and her eyes sparkled. He knew he shouldn't be standing there just watching her, so he spoke. "Good book?"

She gasped and dropped the book, quickly put her feet down and adjusted her skirts, hastily slipping her feet into her shoes. She blushed at having been caught in such a casual position. Rose took a deep breath to regain her composure. She smiled at Marcus. "Yes, it's my favourite actually." She held the cover up so he could see it.

"Little Women." He grinned. "It sounds like it should be about your family, Miss Morgan." His eyes twinkled.

She smiled at him. "There are certainly similarities. Have you read it?"

"No, not completely, but I've had parts of it read to me, at school."

Rose nodded. They were both silent for a time. "Why are you here, Marcus?"

He gulped, looked down and kicked at the ground. "I wanted to talk to you."

He heard a chuckle. "Then it's probably a good idea to talk rather than just standing there."

Marcus looked up at her and smiled. "You're right, Miss Morgan." He gestured to the spot beside her. "May I?"

"Of course, and please just call me Rose." She moved over so he could sit down.

"Rose, I wanted to come here and apologise to you."

She looked at him, waiting for him to continue.

"I've been avoiding you, and I'm sorry."

She nodded. "How come?"

"Well... I... I blamed myself for what happened to you. I thought if I'd just fought harder, I could have stopped them. I thought your father wouldn't want me anywhere near you ever again. I let you both down."

Rose looked him squarely in the eye. "How could you think that?"

Something about the intensity of her brown eyes made his heart flutter. "Because I couldn't stop them! It was my fault, and then that man had his hands on you and...." He exhaled loudly.

Rose closed her eyes and took a deep breath, trying to bury the thoughts from her mind. She put one hand on his arm. "Marcus, you didn't let me down, or my pa." She removed her hand and blushed. She hadn't meant to touch him, it had just been an impulse. She carried on. "You were the perfect gentleman at the dance. I really enjoyed myself and... well... I had hoped...." She stopped. Was she being too forward?

Marcus tipped his head to the side. "Hoped what, Rose?"

She shrugged. "I hoped we could be friends."

He frowned. "But I couldn't even protect you. Why would you want to be friends with me?"

"Marcus Murray, you did everything you could, and you came back for me with my pa. You made sure I was safe. That's all you can do."

"But I should've been able to protect you." He stared at his boots.

"Even my pa can't protect me all the time, Marcus. You can only do the best you can. None of that was your fault." She touched his arm again as if trying to convince him. "I was grateful you were there, and I don't blame you for any of it. I wanted to thank you, actually."

"What for?"

"For being kind to me. For taking me to the dance. For doing everything you could to protect me. For going for my pa. For being there for me. For making me feel safe."

"You're welcome. It was the least I can do, Rose."

"Well then, can we please just get on with being friends?"

Marcus smiled, and his heart backflipped. It had all turned out much better than he'd hoped. "I'd like that."

"Good." She smiled at him. "What made you come here tonight?"

"The Sergeant talked some sense into me." He smiled wryly.

"He did?"

"Yes, he came and thanked me this afternoon for being there for you and told me he wasn't angry and would be happy for us to be friends."

Rose's eyes shone. "That's so like him."

"Really? He always seems so intimidating to me." Marcus grimaced.

"It's just his job, but he's really a very kind man underneath the red serge, provided you don't hurt his girls." She chuckled.

Marcus nodded knowingly. "Well, I hope that we can be friends, Rose."

"I'd like that. And now I must be getting inside."

"Will you let me walk you home?"

"Marcus, it's less than fifty yards."

He grinned. "Nevertheless." He stood up and lifted his elbow to her.

Rose smiled and shook her head. She picked up her book and stood up. Marcus gestured to carry her book.

She giggled. "I can carry my own book. It's not heavy."

He lifted a brow. "This is what a gentleman does, Rose."

She nodded and grinned.

"You don't have to walk me to the door, Marcus."

"Gentleman, remember." He lifted his brows at her.

She chuckled. "I could get used to this."

That's the idea. He grinned. But that was getting way ahead of himself.

Rose opened the door and walked inside. Marcus passed her the book, and she grinned.

"Goodnight, Miss Morgan." He tipped his hat to her.

"Goodnight, Mr Murray." She smiled and closed the door on him.

Rose greeted her pa and kissed him on the cheek. "Goodnight, Pa. Thank you." She walked to her room.

"Goodnight, Darling." He raced out the door. "Marcus?"

The young man was untethering his horse and turned to look at Adam. "Yes, Sergeant?"

"I'm glad you came to clear the air with Rose."

"Thanks for setting me straight. Sir."

Adam nodded. "So I trust you two are friends now?"

"Yes."

Adam nodded again and raised his eyebrows. "No doubt I'll see you at our supper table from time to time then."

"I hope so, Sir." Marcus's eyes shone. "And don't worry, I have no intention of getting in the way of her dreams. I just want to get to know her more. She's...." He stopped himself and shuffled from foot to foot.

"She's?" Adam tipped his head to one side and folded his arms.

The young man smiled. "She's quite remarkable."

Adam grinned. "I couldn't agree more."

"My intentions are honourable, Sergeant Morgan. You have my word on that."

"I know. You wouldn't be welcome here otherwise." His expression gave Marcus no doubt the man was deadly serious despite his jovial tone.

*   *   *   *

Andy walked to his favourite fishing spot. It had been some time since he'd got a free moment to just fish, but his ma had requested catfish for supper, and he was happy to oblige. *I think she just did it to humour me. She knows how much I love fishing.* He thrust his pole over his shoulder and whistled while he walked.

He stepped out of the trees to the small clearing and stopped his jaunty tune. Marcus sat leaning back against the old Douglas fir, with his pole propped up, and his line in the water. His face wore a wide grin and a faraway expression. Andy chuckled to himself and walked up to his friend. "I bet I know what's got you grinning like that."

Marcus snapped his head up in surprise, jolted out of his deep musings. He frowned and looked up at Andy. He smiled slowly and raised his eyebrows. "Really, and what is that?"

Andy placed his bucket down, cast his line in the water and sat down next to Marcus, whose question was still hanging in the air.

"Rose Morgan."

Marcus nodded. He shrugged one shoulder. "She's all I seem to think about these days."

Andy slapped him on the back. "Good for you, Marc. I know you've loved her since you first laid eyes on her. Does she feel the same way about you?"

Marcus squinted and stroked his chin. He sighed deeply and leaned forward to place his forearms on his knees. "I'm not sure."

"What's stopping you from asking her?"

Marcus shrugged. "She's leaving for college in a few weeks."

"So?"

Marcus turned his head and squinted at his friend. "I can't ask her to court just as she's going away."

"I never said anything about courting. You'd have to get past the Sergeant for that one." Andy grimaced.

"What're you saying? You don't think he'd give me permission."

Andy shrugged. "I dunno 'bout him, but it sure would take a lot of courage to ask that man to court one of his girls. Woe be told to anyone who so much as thought of hurting one of them."

Marcus nodded. "I have absolutely no doubt that he'd move heaven and earth to protect them, die trying if he had to."

"That's for sure." Andy nodded. "He's a brave and fearsome man sometimes. I've seen him take down a crook or two."

"And yet I've never met a more fiercely loving and protective man in my life. He's the most tender-hearted and compassionate father." Marcus brushed away a fly that landed on his arm.

Andy grinned. "He sure is. He's like that to all of us, though. Anyone who earns his favour is blessed indeed. If you earn the honour of his daughter's love and you treasure her, he'll love you forever." He took a seat next to his friend.

"Is he sad he never had a son?"

Andy chuckled. "Not even a little bit. My pa told me he always wanted a house full of girls. I think it's just in his nature; he's a natural-born protector of the innocent. You couldn't get a man more suited to his job."

Marcus nodded. "That's for sure. It's like he was born wearing red serge."

"Just about. His father was a Mountie, and he was raised at the training camp for a lot of his growing-up years. He's lived and breathed the Mountie life since his childhood."

"He's very intimidating sometimes." Marcus grimaced.

Andy shrugged. "The only people that should be intimidated by him are those who try to hurt others. If you treat those he loves with respect, he'll be your biggest ally. But if you hurt Rose in any way, it'll be your last chance. He's got zero tolerance for those who hurt others, especially the innocent. He struggles to control his anger at times. I know Pa has stepped in to help him cool his temper on occasion. Still, other than my pa, he's the man I look up to the most in this world."

Marcus nodded. "Thanks, Andy, it helps to get some insight from an 'insider'."

Andy chuckled and slapped his friend on the back. "Happy to help, Friend. Anytime you want to talk, I'll listen. Pa always says men need close friends just as much as women do. He and The Sergeant couldn't be closer if they were blood brothers. From them, I've learned that talking makes all the difference sometimes."

"I appreciate that."

"So, are you gonna talk to Rose?"

Marcus scratched his head, and his eyes glowed. "You know what? I think I will. I can't ask her to court, but maybe I can ask her to wait."

Andy frowned. "Wait?"

"You know, like agree to not court anyone else, and we can write and get to know each other while she's at college."

"How do you feel about her going?"

"I'll miss her, that's for sure. Even not seeing her today makes my heart ache. But I want her to do this; it's her dream. I could no more keep a butterfly from flying, than deprive her of this. She was born to be a teacher." Marcus's face lit up while he was talking about Rose, and he grinned without meaning to. He shook his head, and his eyes grew far away. "She's really something."

Andy slapped his back again. "Then I'll pray it works out for you."

Marcus nodded. "How about you?"

"What about me?"

"Anyone caught your eye?"

Andy's cheeks reddened. "Perhaps."

Marcus raised his brows. "Do tell..." He was interrupted by Andy's rod twitching. Both men leapt up to check their lines, and both found fish on the end. Andy's confession never happened as the two focused their minds on catching supper.

* * * *

Hope skipped into the living room just as Adam arrived home. "Hi, Pa."

"Poppet." He reached his arms out to her, and she leapt into them. He lifted her up and spun her around. He kissed her cheek and leaned back from her. "What have you been up to, Missy?"

"I've been helping Mama prepare for Rose's party tomorrow."

"Good girl. Where is your ma?"

"In the root cellar fetching some preserves." Hope pointed to the open trapdoor in the kitchen floor.

Adam nodded. He sure was glad he'd built that cellar on. He'd equipped it to house all the canning and their extra supplies but also as a shelter should it be needed. It was set up in case his family ever needed to hide, with a disguised escape hatch to the outside. His Mountie instincts meant he was always prepared.

"Pa?"

"Yes, Darling?"

Hope tipped her head to the side and frowned. "Why are we having a farewell party when Rose isn't leaving for three weeks?"

Adam chuckled and put Hope down. He unbuttoned his coat while he spoke. "Because you remember Uncle Samuel and Aunt Jo are very busy the next few weeks, and this is the only time they can make it."

Hope thought for a moment. "And it wouldn't be much of a party without the whooooole family." She grinned.

Adam chuckled and brushed her chin. "You're right, Poppet." He lunged forward as Katie climbed the stairs out of the cellar. He took the jar from her hand, and passed it to Hope, who placed it on the kitchen counter. Adam reached out his other hand to help Katie up the stairs.

"My knight in red serge armour, always ready to rescue a damsel in distress." She chuckled.

He embraced and kissed her. "Are you in distress, my darling?"

"No, only teasing. You sure are my brave knight."

He winked at her and bowed. "Sir Adam at your service, M'lady."

Katie chuckled. "You're home early, brave sir knight."

"I came to see what more needs to be done for tonight."

"Thank you, I could do with some manly strength to move tables."

Adam made an exaggerated display of looking around, he eyed Hope suspiciously, and the little girl laughed. With a shrug and a mock scowl, he turned back to Katie. "I don't see anyone who fits that criteria. Perhaps I'll do?"

Katie put her arms around his neck. "You'll more than 'do', Husband."

Adam brushed her cheek and kissed her. "Thank you, Darling. I'll just wash up and put on some working clothes and join you."

"Certainly." Katie kissed him again and stepped back.

*   *   *   *

Rose and Callie worked in their mother's large kitchen alongside the four older women. Jo looked out the window at the ball game that was taking place. She watched as Marcus stepped up to bat. Looking across at Rose, she noticed the younger woman was watching the same scene, and her cheeks reddened. Jo placed down the potatoes she was peeling, wiped her hands on her apron and sidled up to Rose. She slipped her arm around Rose's waist and squeezed her. Rose looked at her aunt. Jo nodded to the scene out the window. "So, young lady. Who is that wonderful young man?"

Rose blushed deeper. "Marcus is just a friend, Aunt Jo."

Jo nodded knowingly and winked at Katie over Rose's head. Katie grinned and nodded slightly.

"I think he's an excellent young man. I like him very much." Jo squeezed her again.

"Thank you." Rose dropped her eyes and blushed again.

"We all think he's great," Becky added. "We're happy for you, Rose."

"Aunt Becky, we're just friends. You're all getting way ahead of yourselves." But the shy blush to her cheeks and the fluttering of her eyelids gave away her real feelings on the matter.

Becky squeezed her. "We're just hopeful, is all. There's nothing more beautiful than falling in love."

"I'm only sixteen," Rose groaned. "We aren't even courting. Besides, I'll be leaving in three weeks." She hung her head.

"If it's meant to be, he'll wait." Louisa joined the conversation. "He'll be right here when you get home, and so proud of you."

Rose nodded shyly. The four older women gave each other knowing smiles. It was only a matter of time for the young couple.

* * * *

Four men sat on the wide deck sipping at their coffee. They looked out over the gathered family, children running and playing. Women tidying up from the meal, and young people chatting.

Samuel noticed Marcus leaning against the oak, watching Rose while she helped her mother clear away the dishes, a wide grin crossed the young man's face and his eyes fixed on the beautiful girl. "I believe that young man is head over heels in love with your daughter, Sergeant."

Adam nodded and smiled wryly. "He as much as told me so."

Owen slapped him on the back. "How you holding up, Pa?"

Adam ran his fingers through his hair and sighed. He chuckled. "It's not easy. I am thankful he's prepared to take it slowly. She's still very young and headed off to college."

Daniel stroked his ginger beard. "You think he'll wait for her?"

Adam thought about it. "I hope so. They aren't courting just yet, so I guess he's got no obligation to her. But I have a feeling he will. He seems to care about her very deeply, and he seems to be honourable. He's not tried to push her or make any moves on her, and I admire him for that. If he's prepared to wait for her, then he'll have my blessing." He grimaced at the thought.

"You're a good man, Adam. I thought it would be much harder for you than this. You're taking it much better than I expected." Samuel gripped his friend's shoulder and grinned.

Adam groaned. "It's not easy, but I want my daughter to be happy. He's a fine young man, and I appreciate that. He'd make a good son-in-law someday." He sighed and looked wistfully towards his daughter, who was now sitting with Marcus and Andy, sharing some joke. He lifted his brows and his eyes misted over. "Look how happy she is." They watched her grip Marcus's arm and laugh about something. Her beautiful laugh rang out across the meadow. Adam sniffed away the threatening tears and his lips trembled. "How can I get in the way of that? I imagine when she returns from college, they'll be courting."

The three men nodded and watched the young people, Sam patted Adam's shoulder again and they sipped at their coffee.

* * * *

Marcus helped Rose down off the horse overlooking the waterfall. He took the basket from her and spread out the blanket. They sat down and spread out their lunch, enjoying the vista as they ate. Marcus swallowed the roast chicken. "Mmmm. This is great, Rose. You're an excellent cook."

"Thank you, Marcus, it isn't much." She shrugged. "Mostly just leftovers."

He held her gaze and smiled. "No, it's quite delicious."

They ate quietly for a moment, each alone with their thoughts. At last, Marcus put down his plate. "Rose?"

"Mmm?"

"Will you wait for me?"

She frowned. "What do you mean?"

"I mean, at college, there'll be a lot of young men there who'll fall in love with you."

"Don't be silly, Marcus. I'm going there to study, not court."

"Yeah, but they'll fall in love with you for sure, Rose. How could they not? You're so..." He stopped, unsure how much he should say.

"I'm so what?" She squinted at him.

"Beautiful, talented, funny and sweet. How could the young men not fall in love with you."

"Marcus." Rose blushed. "I'm not going to college to find a beau."

"You never know what might happen."

"What are you trying to say? I don't understand." She frowned.

"I was hoping... well...." He sighed and decided to be honest. "Rose, you must know I have feelings for you."

She blushed, dropped her eyes and nodded. He reached out and lifted her chin. "Rose? Do you have feelings for me too?" She bit her lip and nodded just slightly. Tears raced to the corners of her eyes.

He grinned, took her hand and kissed it. His heart was backflipping. "I'll wait for you, Rose, for as long as it takes."

She smiled shyly at him, uncertain of what to say. She began to regret that she even had to go. The situation was so overwhelming. Her heart pounded in her ears, and her cheeks grew warm, and her breathing sped up.

"Will you wait for me?"

"Are you asking me to court?"

"No. I can't do that, not while you're gone. It wouldn't be fair. I'm just telling you how I feel, and when you get back, then we'll talk about courting. I know it's not fair to expect you to wait when I can't make any commitments to you. But we're both young, and we have our whole lives ahead of us." He gently stroked her cheek. "So you go, Rose, follow your dream, and I'll be here when you get back."

She nodded, and her eyes sparkled. Her emotions were beginning to calm. "If I wasn't going, would you ask me to court?"

"Probably. With your pa's permission, of course."

She sighed and looked down.

"Rose. Will you wait?"

"Yes." Her voice was quiet, and she was unable to look him in the eye. His heart soared, it wasn't exactly a declaration of love or a promise, but it was a start. Knowing she wouldn't court anyone else in the meantime meant the world to him. How he wished he could ask her to court before she left, but he knew it wasn't right. The Sergeant certainly wouldn't agree to that. Besides, it would be horrible to be apart from her. At least now they could build their friendship and get to know each other, with hope for the future. While she was gone, he was determined to work hard and make her proud, and when she returned, he'd have something to offer her.

"I won't see you until the day before you leave. Remember I have to go out of town for a few days? I promise to be back to see you off, though." He helped her pack up the picnic.

"I remember. You'll be in Pine Crest helping to build a house. It's fine; I'll be much too busy packing anyhow."

Five
Rose's Choice

Adam lowered himself into the armchair opposite Rose. He winked at Katie as she handed him his coffee cup. The five younger girls were in bed already, and Katie was finishing up the last few dishes and wiping the countertops.

Adam lifted the cup to his lips, took a long sip and placed it on the small table in front of him. "How's your packing going, Darling?"

Rose lowered her book. "I'm not going, Pa. I don't want to go." She crossed her arms determinedly across her chest.

Katie gasped and walked out of the kitchen, wiping her hands on her apron.

Adam frowned and squinted his eyes at Rose. "What do you mean? Of course, you're going. You've been looking forward to this since you were ten years old."

"You're just getting cold feet. It's natural," Katie suggested.

"No, I don't want to go. I want to stay here, not go so far away. I can keep working at the store. I'll be fine." Rose began to weep. Her mother sat down beside her and put her arm around her.

Adam stood up and walked over to her. He knelt before his daughter and took her in his arms until she calmed. He smiled kindly and brushed away a tear from her cheek. "What is this all about, Darling?" Adam's deep brown eyes searched her face, longing to understand. "Why don't you want to go? I thought you wanted to be a teacher?"

"I do, Pa, that is, I did," she quickly corrected herself. "I just... well... I just don't think I'd be any good at it." She scrambled for excuses to avoid the real reason.

"Rosie, that's not true, and you know it. You're already a wonderful teacher, with all the work you do with your Sunday school children and your sisters. You're a natural-born teacher, just like your ma. That's not the reason, and I know it. Tell me, what is this really about?" He flashed Katie a look which said he was fairly sure he knew. She gave him a slight nod in response.

"I just want to stay here with my family and M...." Rose caught herself.

Adam lifted one eyebrow. "With Marcus?"

She looked down, blushed and nodded twice.

"Rosie, look at me." She obliged. Adam lifted a hand to her cheek. "You can't give up your dream for a boy, especially one you've just got to know. You'd never be happy. Teaching is what you're meant to do.".

"Ma did."

Adam frowned. "What do you mean? Your ma taught here for four years."

Rose shrugged. "Then she gave it up to be a wife and mother."

Katie took her hands. "That day may come for you in the future, Rose, but you deserve to have the choice, not to have it chosen for you. Being a teacher has always been your dream, and whether you do it for one year or twenty-five years, the point is you'll be a teacher. One day you'll lay aside your dream to raise a family, and you'll do it willingly with no regrets, as I did. But that doesn't make me less of a teacher.

"I'll always be a teacher. It's in my blood. It just turns out I don't do it in the school anymore. Instead, I teach my children and my nieces and nephews, and Sunday school. Everywhere I go and everything I do, I'm still a teacher, Rose." Katie reached up to brush some hair back from Rose's face. She smiled kindly and squeezed the hand she still held. "If you don't do this now, you'll regret it. Marcus will regret it because he'd not want you to be miserable. If he loves you, and I suspect he might, he'd not want you to give up your dreams for him."

"He told me today he has feelings for me. He asked me to wait for him. He told me that if I was staying, he'd ask me to court. Ma, how can I go knowing he's waiting here for me? What if he finds someone else while I'm away."

"He'd have to have my permission to court in the first place." Adam crossed his arms and sat back on his feet.

"Are you saying you'd say no if I stayed?"

"Probably."

"Why? To punish me?"

"No, because if he allowed you to stay and give up your dream just to court, then he's not the man I think he is. When you truly love a person, you're willing to put aside your own desires and your own needs to see that person happy and living their dreams." He turned to look Katie in the eye, but his words were directed at Rose. "If your mother asked it of me, I'd lay down the serge in a heartbeat and happily be a carpenter for the rest of my days."

Katie reached a hand out to touch his cheek. "I'd never do that, Adam. Being a Mountie is who you are. You'd be miserable without it."

"And I know you'd be miserable if you couldn't teach, my darling and any time you want to go back to the school, you say, and I'll support you." He leaned over to kiss Katie on the cheek.

Rose leapt up from her chair, and hurried to her room in tears, racked in confusion.

"Rose." Katie knocked on her door. "May I come in?"

"Sure." Rose kept her face buried in her pillow. Katie sat on the bed and stroked the girl's long hair.

"I know what it's like to be young, and in love and confused."

Rose sat up. "I never said I was in love, Ma."

"But you do have feelings for him?"

Rose nodded.

"And you'd like to court."

Rose nodded again, sat up and clutched her pillow to her chest.

Katie brushed back some wayward hair from the girl's face and tucked it behind her ear. "Rose, you're sixteen, and you have the whole world before you. Your pa and I love you more than life itself, and we want the very best life for you, but most of all, we want you to be happy. We cannot and will not make this decision for you, Darling, but we don't want to see you throw away your dreams and do something you regret. If you and Marcus are meant to be together, then a year or two years or even ten years is not going to change that. Remember how I always say you can't stop true love?"

Rose nodded.

"Well, I mean it. If what the two of you have is true love, or at least will be in the future, then it's worth every moment of the waiting. Uncle Daniel waited for some time for Aunt Louisa's heart to heal, and he'd have carried right on waiting for just as long as it took. He told me not long ago that even if he'd had to wait ten years, it would've been worth it, and he would've continued right on loving her. I know he meant it because I would've waited a lifetime for your father."

Rose nodded again. "I understand, Ma."

"I guess you have a decision to make, my darling." Katie ran her hand down her daughter's arm.

"Thanks, Ma. Thanks for letting me choose."

"Of course, Darling," came Adam's voice from the doorway. He walked in, sat down on the other side of her, and cupped her chin. He looked into her dark eyes. "Whatever you decide, your mother and I will support you. But promise me you won't make a decision without much thought and prayer. You deserve to be happy and to live your dreams."

"Thanks, Pa." She leaned her head against his chest.

Adam wrapped his arms around her and kissed her hair, cradling her head in his hand. "I love you so much, Rosie. I'm proud of you no matter what." She knew he meant it. There was no safer place in the world than her father's arms. Everything was secure and clear there. Outside of them, the world seemed confusing some days. The closer she got to leaving, the more apprehensive she became. But there were another set of arms ready to reach out and hold her, Gods!

She nodded her head against the flannel of Adam's shirt. "I promise."

* * * *

Rose was in turmoil. She wandered around for a time in a daze. She went through the motions at work, but her mind was far away. She took long rides on Buttercup and spent a lot of time thinking and praying. Several times she made a certain decision. She'd go. But then she'd get to thinking about all the other young women in town, and what if one of them caught Marcus's eye while she was gone? He'd made no promises to her really. He could easily meet someone else. Then she'd decide to stay, and court Marcus. Then she'd think about standing in front of the classroom and all those shining eyes looking to her, and her passion for teaching would bubble up inside her, and she'd decide to go again. She broke down in tears several times in frustration and indecision.

* * * *

Marcus came riding into town and straight into the RNWMP office, with a frantic look in his eyes. "What's wrong, Sergeant? Your telegram said you needed to see me urgently. Is Rose okay?"

"No, she isn't. She's very confused and upset."

Marcus closed his eyes and screwed up his face. Agony stabbed at his heart. "Why?"

Adam stood up and closed the door. "Please sit down."

The young man obliged, swallowing rapidly.

Adam took his seat and folded his arms over his chest. "Did you tell Rose that if she stayed home, you'd want to court?"

Marcus gasped. He had an inkling of what was happening. "Yes, she asked me hypothetically, so I answered. I told her I wouldn't ask her to court until she got back from college because it wasn't fair on her. I did tell her I had feelings for her and asked that she'd wait for me, and agree not to court anyone else in that time. I promised her the same. She's the only one I'd even consider courting." He couldn't help but grin.

Adam nodded. "You're a fine young man, Marcus. I appreciate you being prepared to wait for her. But do you realise she's talking about not going to college now? She's thinking of staying here so the two of you can court. She's afraid if she doesn't, she'll lose you. I don't want to see my daughter throw away her dreams."

"What are you saying, Sergeant?"

He took a deep breath, quite unable to believe what he was about to say. "What if she could have both?"

Marcus frowned. "I don't understand."

Adam grinned. "I've given this a lot of thought. If you are really serious about my daughter..." he exhaled loudly and ran his fingers through his hair, "...then I think you should ask her to court, so that she will be assured you'll be waiting for her."

Marcus raised his brows. "But to still go?"

Adam nodded. "How do you feel about that?"

Marcus stood up, walked to the far wall, and stood for a few moments looking at the photograph of the Morgan family. He walked back. "Sergeant, I want her to go. I want her to have her dreams. I want her to have the whole world, and if I could, I'd give it to her. I know I'm young, and I have nothing to offer her yet, but I plan to, Sir. I'm working hard so that I can offer her those things in the future, but I'd never want her to give up on her dream. She's so excited about teaching, and the way her eyes light up when she talks about it, it's more than just a dream to her. It's her calling. I can't ask her to give that up. I won't let her."

"She does have to make her own choices, Marc, but perhaps if you talk to her, ask her to wait for you as a courting couple with intentions for a future; she might be less reluctant to go."

Marcus shook his head and scratched at his cheek. He raised one eyebrow. "You're giving me permission to court your sixteen-year-old daughter?"

Adam chuckled. "I believe that I am." His face became very serious, and his gaze stern. "But if you aren't one hundred per cent sure, then tell her you have no future together and let her go because I won't have her throw it all away for nothing."

"I understand, Sir. Sergeant Morgan, you have my word. I hope to marry your daughter someday and spend the rest of my life doing whatever it takes to make her happy." His mouth stretched into a broad grin.

"I'm glad to hear it." Adam stood, came around the desk and gripped the young man's shoulder. "On that day, I'll be proud to call you son."

Marcus's face lit up, and his heart began to sing. "I have to go and find her."

"She's got a lunch break at twelve-thirty. I'm sure you can persuade Mr Scott to let her out for the afternoon. I believe you have some talking to do." Adam gave Marcus his sideways smile.

The young man whooped and ran out the door. He'd never for a moment dreamed that Sergeant Morgan would let him court Rose until at least after she'd returned. In all honesty, he thought he'd have to wait until she was eighteen. He very nearly collided with Daniel on his way out the door.

Daniel grinned and walked into the office. "He's got a spring in his step."

Adam shook his head. "How do you do it? Always turn up right at the pivotal moments."

"I told you, I'm just canny like that. God guides me to be in the right places at the right times, I guess."

"I'm glad, Dan. I appreciate your listening ear."

"Now, are you gonna tell me why that young man bounced out of here like the mouse who got the cheese?"

Adam gestured to the coffeepot and slumped into his chair.

Daniel nodded, fetched the coffeepot and two cups. He poured the hot liquid into both cups and leaned back to wait.

Adam gave him a short description of all that had happened. Daniel sat in silence for a few moments stroking his beard, trying to drink it all in. Both took great solace from the hot liquid. Daniel put his cup down and shook his head. "They're courting! I can't believe it."

"Well, not yet, Dan, but I imagine she will be this evening." Adam shook his head, and his eyes were moist with unshed tears.

"Do you think she'll decide to go?"

"I sincerely hope so. I'd hate to see her throw away her dream. If he's worth his salt, he'll not let her."

"What if she decides to stay?"

Adam closed his eyes and sighed. "I gave her my word Katie and I would support her choice. Whatever it is."

Daniel gripped his shoulder. "You're a good man, Adam, and a wonderful father. It's going to work out. I'm sure of it."

"I wish I had your confidence, Daniel." Adam grimaced and ran his fingers through his hair.

*   *   *   *

"Now, will you tell me what all this is about, Marcus?" Rose tethered Buttercup to a tree and turned to look at the waterfall.

"You have to go to Edmonton, Rose. You have to go to college, and become a teacher. It's your dream."

"But, Marcus, what about us?"

"What about us?"

"What if I go and I come back, and you've met someone else? What if you change your mind?"

"That's not going to happen, but just so that you are sure, your pa has given me permission to ask you to court."

She gasped. "Marcus?"

He turned to take both her hands and searched her face with his dark eyes. "So will you, Rose Morgan? Will you let me call on you, make a commitment to you and no other? I promise to be here, to wait for you, just as long as is necessary."

"But, Marcus, I could stay. We could court here. We wouldn't have to wait."

"Rose." He lifted her chin. "I won't let you."

"What do you mean?"

"I want us to court, Rose; and truth is, I'll ache for you when you're gone, but you have to do this." He cupped her soft cheek and brushed it with his thumb. "You have to go and pursue your dreams. I'll not be the one to stand in the way of that."

"But people can have new dreams."

He did something bold and leaned forward and kissed her cheek. "Rose Morgan, I love you. I've been in love with you for a long time, and I want to marry you someday and give you the life you deserve. But more than all that, Rose," he tucked a strand of hair behind her ear and stroked her cheek. "Beautiful Rose. I want you to be happy, and being a teacher is all you've talked about. You have to do this." He rested his hand on her cheek again. "And I'll be here waiting for you, loving you and being your biggest supporter."

"You really love me?"

"I really do." He smiled. "And it's okay if you don't say it back yet. I know it takes time to be sure, but I know one thing for certain, I'll love you for the rest of my days. You don't have to worry. There isn't any other woman I ever want to be with but you, Rose Morgan." He brushed her cheek with his thumb again.

Rose's eyes shone with unshed tears. "Oh, Marcus, you'd really wait for me? For a whole year?"

"I'd wait twenty years for you, an eternity if I had to."

She threw herself against his chest, and his heart leapt as he held her. It felt so wonderful to have Rose in his arms. He'd ached to hold her so many times, and he knew it would be worth it, and he was right. Holding her was a dream. He leaned his head against hers and breathed deeply of her perfume. *Lilacs.* He smiled. He released her, and they stood looking into each other's eyes. "I love you, Rose. I always will."

She smiled at him, and without breaking eye contact, he slowly leaned in to kiss her. She closed her eyes, and her world began to spin. He pulled away from her and sighed. Rose kept her eyes closed and lay her cheek against his chest again, her heart racing and mind swirling. It took some time for her to regain her composure.

Marcus was glad for the brief moment of silence. His own heart was pounding and mind singing, her soft kiss still dancing on his lips.

"A year won't be so long, will it?" she murmured against his chest.

He squeezed her. "No, and you'll be home for Christmas, so it's really only a few months until we'll see each other again."

"And you'll write?" She still didn't let him go, and that was quite fine by him. He'd hold her like this all day quite happily. He loved how perfectly she fitted in his arms, like they'd been made just for her.

"You bet, Rose, and I'll call you on the telephone as often as I can."

She felt so safe and warm and loved in his arms. She wasn't sure yet whether she loved him, but she cared for him deeply.

"Come on. Ma will be expecting me to help with supper. You must join us."

"Does this mean you agree to court?"

"Of course, Marcus, there couldn't be anyone else." She looked up at him again.

He kissed her cheek. "You don't know how happy you've made me, Rose." He reached for her hand, walked her back to her horse, helped her up onto the palomino's back, and then leapt on his own mount.

She grinned and raised her brows at him. "Race ya." She clucked to the horse and galloped in the direction of her home.

"Hey, wait up." Marcus nudged his horse and chased after her.

Rose paused on the top step and reached for the door handle. "Well, are you ready to face my family?"

Marcus flashed her an exaggerated grimace. "Now is as good a time as any." They both took a deep breath. Marcus let go of her arm, opting to hold her hand instead. He lifted it to his lips and kissed it. "For courage." He winked at her.

Rose chuckled and opened the door. "Hi, Ma."

Katie looked up from the kitchen. She saw the shine in both of their eyes, the smiles they couldn't hide, and their joined hands. She shook her head slightly. She and Rose walked towards each other and embraced. "Rose, you look so happy," Katie whispered in her ear.

"I am, Ma, we are." She beamed. "And, Ma... I'm going to college."

"I'm so glad, Rose." Katie squeezed her tightly. "But I sure will miss you."

Katie turned to look at Marcus. "Welcome to the family, Marcus." She smiled and put her arms out to embrace him too. "We are proud of you both."

He blushed deeply and grinned. "Thank you, Mrs Morgan."

"You're most welcome, Marcus, anytime...." She was interrupted by Adam coming through the door. He grinned as he saw the two of them. He turned to hang his Stetson on the hook and took a deep breath. He paused and walked towards the young couple, stopped before them and folded his arms across his chest.

Sitting back against the dining table, he raised his brows. "I take it you two have something to tell me?"

Marcus looked Adam in the eye. "Sergeant Morgan, Rose has agreed to court."

Adam nodded slowly. He stood forward and drew Rose into an embrace. "Oh, my Rosie. I'm so happy for you both. I love you, Darling." He kissed her on the forehead, stepped back and put his hand out to shake Marcus's. "Welcome to the Morgan family, Son."

Marcus merely nodded and swallowed, overwhelmed by the welcome he'd received. He couldn't understand why he'd once trembled in fear of Sergeant Morgan. He was a loving and kind man, provided you didn't hurt the ones he loved.

"I hope you're staying for supper, Marc. You're a part of this family now, Son, and you'll be treated accordingly." Adam raised his eyebrows, and his lips quivered.

"I'd like that, Sir, if Mrs Morgan doesn't mind."

"I don't mind at all, Marcus." Katie touched his arm. "You're family to us now and will always be welcome."

"It's just a shame we only have three days before I go to college." Rose tucked her lips under, raised her brows and looked her father in the eye.

Adam swallowed and sucked in a deep breath. He lunged forward to hug her. "Rose, I'm beyond happy you're following your dreams."

Rose and Marcus had always been so comfortable around each other, but now they were awkward. They made shy glances at one another and blushed at every touch. Adam and Katie gave each other knowing glances and chuckled internally.

"Rose, Darling, will you come and help me dish up the meal?"

"Sure, Mama." Marcus touched her arm lightly, she blushed, and swallowed and stood to walk to the kitchen.

Rose stood up on her toes to fetch a dish from a high cupboard. Katie walked over and slipped her arm around her daughter's waist. "Relax, Darling. You just have to be yourself."

Rose blushed and nodded. "I'm nervous, Ma. I feel all giddy and shy."

Katie chuckled. "That's normal at the start of a courtship, Darling. The two of you will get used to it. He's a wonderful young man, and I'm delighted for you." She squeezed her daughter.

"Thanks, Ma."

"Of course, Rose, your Daddy and I are on your side. Always! If you ever feel confused or need to talk about anything, we're both here for you. You know that. No subject is off limits."

"I know. Thank you." She smiled and carried the dish of roast vegetables to the table.

Adam stood to fetch some firewood and Marcus followed him. Adam opened the barn door. "I'm glad she's decided to go to college, Marc. I know that'll be hard on you both, just as you begin your courtship, but I really think it's the right thing. She'd have regretted it later if she didn't go."

"I agree, Sir. I want her to live her dreams, to get her teacher's certificate and teach for just as long as she wants to. It's in her blood, and it's who she is. I'm proud of her. How could I ever want her to be someone other than who she is?" His grin was so wide his face hurt.

Adam nodded knowingly, and put his hand out to grip Marcus's shoulder. "You're a good lad, Marcus. As much as I hate to lose my daughter, I'm glad you're the one that's here for her."

"I always will be, Sergeant, until my dying day."

Adam patted him on the back. "I'm glad. It's a pleasure to have you join our family."

Marcus gulped. That vote of confidence from the Sergeant meant so much to him. *Lord, help me to live up to his expectations and be worthy of Rose.*

"Thanks for having me this evening, Sergeant and Mrs Morgan, especially at late notice. I really appreciate it." Marcus stood at the door and put on his coat.

"You're most welcome, Marc." Adam shook his hand, placing his other hand on the young man's shoulder. "You'll always be welcome at our supper table, even when Rose is at college. I meant what I said to you. You're one of the family now, and you never need to feel unwelcome or wait for an invitation. We hope that you'll come and see us even while Rose is away. It'll give us a good chance to get to know you."

"I'd like that, Sir. It'll be a welcome change from farm chores."

"I have stables you can muck out if you get to missing it." Adam's eyes twinkled, and both men chuckled. They farewelled Marcus, and Rose slipped out the door to say her own goodbye.

Six
College

Rose squirmed on the rough train seat, trying to find a comfortable position for the long trip ahead. She smiled across at her father on the opposite seat. "Pa, I can't believe it. I'm actually on my way to college."

"I'm proud of you, Rose. You're going to be a wonderful teacher."

"Thanks, Pa. I'm excited but very nervous. I'm glad you're here with me. I'd probably have chickened out before we even made it to Pine Crest."

Adam reached across and squeezed her arm. "I'm glad to be with you too, Rose, but I know you. You wouldn't have chickened out. You're a Morgan, and you're strong and brave."

"Thanks for your faith in me, Pa."

"Of course, Rosie Girl. Hey, you didn't show me what Aunt Jo gave you?"

"Oh, Pa, look." She pulled the gift out of her small bag. "It's the photo of all of us from my farewell party. I can't believe the photographer got us all in."

Adam looked at the photo and grinned. "Look at my beautiful girls in the front. Stunning, all of you."

"Oh, Pa, you're just biased."

"Yes, I am. But I'm not wrong. I see the young men eyeing you all and the fathers of the town are envious of my army of girls."

"Pa." She smiled, and he laughed.

He sighed and ran his fingers through his hair. "Sure am gonna miss you, Rosie."

"I'll write as often as I can, and I'll phone you."

"I know, Daughter, but it won't be the same as having your cheery face at my breakfast table each morning and your hugs and kisses each evening. I'll miss that very much."

"I'll miss you too, Pa."

* * * *

Two weary travellers disembarked from the train in Edmonton, early in the morning. Rose hadn't slept because she was too excited and Adam because he was watching over his daughter.

A Mountie stood stoically on the platform and approached. Adam returned the young man's salute. "At ease, Constable."

"Good morning, Sergeant Morgan, Miss Morgan. I'm Constable Jonathan Scott. I'm at your service today as requested." He was a very young new recruit not long out of the academy, and he'd pulled escort duty for a Sergeant's daughter. He'd grumbled somewhat about the assignment at first, but when he met Rose, his face lit up. *Escorting her won't be so bad.*

"Thank you, Constable. I'm most obliged to you."

Constable Scott stepped up to help Adam with Rose's trunk. "Ohhhh. This sure is heavy, Ma'am. What's in here?" His face curled up with the effort, and he gritted his teeth. He strained so hard his ears turned red.

"Books mostly, Constable, and my clothing and shoes." Rose laughed heartily.

"It sure is heavy." He puffed as they walked along.

Adam chuckled and tried hard not to strain. "I remember when I first lifted this trunk, it was full of her ma's books, and it was twice as heavy as it is now."

"Like mother like daughter, eh?"

"She sure is." Adam winked at Rose.

They loaded all the luggage in the waiting car, and Constable Scott drove them to the boarding house where Rose would be living.

They were greeted at the door by a stout woman, Mrs Hilda Green, a widow in her fifties who'd converted her husband's fine house into a busy boarding house to help her make ends meet. She took in several young people from the university each year but also had rooms available to the general public. In all, there were fifteen bedrooms as well as her small quarters on the ground floor by the kitchen.

Mrs Green greeted them warmly. Constable Scott nodded to the woman as he staggered past with Adam carrying the heavy trunk up the stairs. He hurried down the stairs to bring up her suitcase.

He turned to Rose as he prepared to leave. "Call whenever you need me, and I'll come and get you." The young man's eyes twinkled. "Honestly, Miss Morgan, whatever you need."

Adam frowned slightly and nodded at the man, "Much obliged, Constable. Good day."

Constable Scott nodded to Rose and bounded down the stairs to his waiting car. Adam and Rose followed and waved to him as he drove away.

"I sure am glad I pulled escort duty today. I'd be happy to escort her wherever she needs to go." He grinned as he drove away.

Adam turned to his daughter. "What do you want to do first?"

"I should unpack first. Ma told me to hang my dresses right away to get the wrinkles out."

Adam raised his brows. "Well, if your ma said, then we should do so." He grinned and escorted her up the stairs, and they took a chance to properly inspect the little room.

Rose shrugged her shoulders. "This is my home for the next year, Pa."

Adam frowned. "Not much to it."

The long narrow room had a rather lumpy-looking bed against one wall and a mattress underneath for her father to sleep on. The bed had two quilts laid on it and a feather pillow. Rose had already known she'd have to see to her own sheets, and she'd come prepared.

A narrow window beside the bed had a small side table and lamp below it. In the far corner was a high table with a basin and jug. Against the wall opposite her bed was a desk, with a chair and a shelf above it. In the corner at the foot of her bed sat an old free-standing wardrobe with a full-length mirror on the front next to a small chest of drawers.

Rose grinned. "I like it. I think I'll be very happy here." She smiled. "I sure hope the other girls are nice."

Adam nodded. He was glad she could see the possibilities in the small room. "You'll make it your own in no time." He grinned as she opened the trunk and began lifting out dresses. The men had placed it next to her desk.

Rose paused mid-way to the wardrobe. "Pa, I can put some pillows on top of the trunk and make it a little couch."

"That's a lovely idea." Adam placed her books on the high shelf.

Rose stood a family photograph on the side table and pinned the photograph of Marcus that he had given her on the wall above her desk. Adam smiled as she pinned up the one dried rose she'd kept from the day he asked her to the dance.

At last, she looked around the little room. She turned to her father and shrugged. "Well, I'm all unpacked, Pa."

"Me too." He nodded. "Thank you for giving me some space in your wardrobe." He laughed at his few clothes that hung next to her gowns.

"Of course."

Adam ran his fingers through his hair and looked around. "You've got this place looking great."

A young lady poked her head through the door and smiled.

Rose turned to look at her. "Hello." She smiled kindly.

"Hello." The girl stepped inside and looked from face to face, somewhat confused to see a Mountie in the room. "I'm Alice Harvey. I'm in the room right next door."

Rose welcomed her in. "I'm Rose Morgan, and this is my pa."

Alice's eyes widened. "Your father is a Mountie?"

"Yes."

"I thought he may have just been an escort."

"No." Rose touched her father's arm. He beamed at her. "Pa's a Mountie, a Sergeant even."

"It's an honour to meet you, Sergeant Morgan."

Adam tipped his head to her. "And I you, Miss Harvey. I hope you and Rose will become good friends. Will you be at the teacher's college, too?"

"Yes, Sir, all of us on this floor are. Across from you is Sadie Cook, and next to her is Mandy Brooks. They're out exploring town today, but I wanted to stay back to meet you. I hope we'll all be good friends." She bit her lip and asked sheepishly, "Do you go to church, Rose?"

"Yes." Rose smiled. "I'm a Christian."

"That's great!" Alice's face lit up. "We can all go together."

Adam grinned. He was so pleased she'd have three other Christian girls to spend time with. He knew the boarding house owner was a Christian and ran the place with Christian values, but she would welcome anyone who needed a place to stay. He prayed a silent prayer of thanksgiving to God for orchestrating this.

Alice was a chatty girl. She had a round face and long, almost black hair that she wore long with the sides pinned up in twists.

"Where do you come from?" Rose gestured for her to sit on the bed next to her. Adam took the seat at the desk and enjoyed the girls' happy chatter.

Alice screwed up one side of her face. "I'm not sure you'll have heard of it. It's some ways north of here, Pine Crest."

Rose and Adam looked at each other, their mouths gaped open, and their faces lit up.

Rose touched Alice's arm. "You're from Pine Crest?"

"Yes, you have heard of it then?" Alice grinned.

"I'm from Douglas Falls. I've lived there all my life, and we go to Pine Crest all the time. My parent's best friends live there."

"It's a very large town now, I doubt I'd know them." Alice shrugged.

"My friend is the Staff Sergeant there. Samuel Ferguson." Adam smiled.

Alice's face fell, and her eyes grew wide. She turned to look at Adam. "You know the Fergusons?"

"Very well. Our dear friends."

"Henry is my younger brother's best friend. They're in the eighth grade together. He's told me about a family in Douglas Falls they always go and visit. Wow, isn't it a small world." She shook her head. "We're practically neighbours."

"Yes." Rose grinned and squeezed Alice's arm again. "I won't feel quite so homesick knowing there is someone from so close to home here."

"Is there no one else from your school at college this year?"

"Not at the teacher's college. There is one man who'll be studying law, but I doubt I'll see him."

"You'll like Sadie and Mandy. Sadie is from Moose Creek, and Mandy lives in Stone River."

Rose nodded. "I look forward to meeting them."

"Have you seen any of the city yet?"

"No, we just arrived about an hour ago. I'm awfully hungry. Do you know anywhere good to eat?"

"Mrs Green serves breakfast and dinner, but we have to see to our own lunches. I've been here two days now, and yesterday we went to a café just down the street. Do you want me to show you it?"

Rose turned to her father. "Pa?"

"Sounds great." Adam smiled. "I'm hungry too. Lead the way."

* * * *

"Are you sure you're okay with this?" Rose looked contrite.

Alice smiled kindly and touched her new friend's arm. "Of course, Rose, you go, spend the day with your father. I completely understand. We have all year to spend time together."

Rose smiled and embraced Alice. "I just know we're going to be wonderful friends."

"We will! I know it." Alice squeezed Rose and stood back from her. She nodded to Adam and turned on her heels to walk back to her own room.

Rose turned to her father. "We've got a whole day together, Pa. What do you want to do first?"

Adam winked at his daughter and grinned. "I have business at the office for a short time. Let's get that over and done with. I can't imagine I'll be longer than half an hour. Then I'd like to find the house where your ma grew up."

Rose nodded. "With her Aunt Polly?"

"Yes." He reached for her arm and led her down the stairs. "I'm sure she's downplayed the value of their home. Come on, and we'll get that young constable to be our chauffeur for the day."

Rose nodded and grinned. "Okay, Pa, we can walk to the RNWMP office though, it's not far, and I do like to start the day with a brisk walk."

Adam tipped his Stetson to Mrs Green as they stepped out the door into the sunshine. He flashed his daughter a cheeky smile. "At your service, Ma'am."

Rose swatted at his arm and rolled her eyes. "You're incorrigible, Sergeant."

Adam leaned over and kissed Rose on the hair. "I sure am, Rosie Girl." They headed towards the RNWMP station. Adam walked strong and tall, so proud to have his lovely, grown-up daughter on his arm. As was his way, he nodded and smiled, and tipped his hat to the people they passed as they walked. Rose smiled. She really admired the way her father loved people. He was easy and confident with them all.

Adam noticed a woman struggling to load heavy crates on a wagon, while a baby wailed in its basket on the wagon bed, and a two-year-old boy ran around. The flustered woman tried to keep hold of the little boy. Without hesitation, Adam led Rose over, let go of her arm and approached the woman.

He kindly touched her arm. "Allow me, Ma'am."

The woman looked as though she wanted to protest. A grateful, frustrated smile crossed her face, and tears flooded her eyes. She reached for her wailing baby as Adam made short work of her crates.

Rose squatted down before the small boy. "What is that you have in your hand?"

"Twain." The boy passed her over a small, somewhat sticky tin train engine, with paint flaking off it, his prized possession.

Rose gave the train a thorough examination and grinned at the boy. "It's a beauty." The boy's face lit up at the stranger who was kind enough to appreciate his toy. "What's your name?"

"Archie."

Rose smiled. "I'm Rose. Thank you for showing me your train." She looked up at her father, who had finished his task, and the boy's mother, holding the baby. Both watched her with warm smiles on their faces. Rose's cheeks reddened. She turned back to the boy. "It looks like your ma is ready to go now." She handed the train back to him.

The boy smiled and nodded. "Fanks, Wose."

Rose stood and grinned, meeting her father's adoring gaze. He offered her his arm and turned to tip his hat to the woman. "Good day, Ma'am."

The woman's lip trembled. "Thank you, Sergeant. I'm fairly new to town. I don't know anyone yet."

Adam placed his hand gently on her elbow. "Do you mind me asking, are you on your own, Ma'am?"

The woman's eyes flooded with tears. "We moved here 'bout three months ago. I've not had much time to get out and about to meet anyone. But my husband fell ill, and I've been trying to take care of things on my own. He'll be out of the hospital in a few days and requested I pick up these supplies for his store. I've done my best to keep it running while he's been laid up, but I'm afraid I rather have my hands full." She gestured to the baby and the little boy.

Adam squeezed her arm again, moved with compassion for the woman. "I'm glad he's on the mend. What store does he have?"

She smiled proudly then. "We own the confectionery just over yonder." She waved in that direction. "Now, I must hurry and get these supplies back to the store."

"Do you not have any help?" Rose asked.

"Yes, I have a store boy and a clerk, but I really thought I could manage this simple job on my own. I wasn't aware the crates were so large and heavy." She chuckled and flashed them a sideways smile. "Nate is always telling me I'm much too headstrong for my own good."

Adam grinned and turned to wink at Rose. "I know a thing or two about headstrong women, Ma'am. My wife and my six girls are about as headstrong as you can get." He squeezed Rose's hand. "And, honestly, I wouldn't have my girls any other way. Headstrong, stubborn and tenacious, just the way I like them."

The woman, whose name they never did find out, chuckled. "Thank you, Sergeant. Your girls are blessed to have a fine man in their life. I thank you again for your help. I'm foolish really. I should've let the store boy help me like he offered. I'll be very glad when Nate is up and about again. Now I must be going."

Adam stepped forward to assist her and the children into the wagon and nodded to her. "Good day, Ma'am. All the best to you."

They watched the woman drive away, and Adam looked quizzically at Rose, who had a wide grin on her face and shining eyes. "What is it?"

Rose reached for her father's arm. "I just love the way you really care about people; you're so kind and compassionate, even to a stranger."

Adam removed his Stetson and ran his fingers through his mop of hair. He shrugged. "I can't help it, Rose. Really it's quite selfish of me. When I saw her just now, when I see anyone in need, I imagine your ma, or you girls in need with no one to help you." He closed his eyes and sighed. "I'm simply doing what I'd hope and pray others would do for my girls." He shrugged again. "I can't bear to see innocent people suffer."

Rose stood up on her toes and kissed his cheek. "You're a good man, Sergeant. I'm proud to be one of your girls."

Adam gulped back a wave of overwhelming pride and put his arm around her. "Not nearly as proud as I am." He winked at Rose and nodded towards the RNWMP office. "Now come on, we have adventures to get to."

Rose threw her head back and laughed. "Of course, Pa."

Rose waited in the foyer. Constable Scott brought her a cup of coffee while her father conducted his business with the Staff Sergeant. He was soon back, accompanied by the older Mountie. He nodded to Rose to signal he was done, and she stood to wait for him.

"Much obliged to you for lending me Scott for the day." Adam reached out to shake the officer's hand.

"Least we can do for a fellow officer's family. I'll leave your daughter in his special charge for the duration of her stay here. You know we watch out for our own."

"That gives me great peace of mind." Adam nodded to Constable Scott, who'd returned from taking Rose's coffee cup back.

"My pleasure, Sergeant." The young constable's eyes danced as he spoke, bringing a slight furrow to Adam's eyebrows.

He chuckled and led his daughter out. "We'll wait out front for you, Constable."

"I'll bring the car round, Sir." Constable Scott turned to salute his superior officer, received the man's nod, and hurried from the room.

The younger Mountie acted as escort and driver for the day. They made their way to Katie's former home. Both mouths gaped open as they observed the decadence and expanse of the property.

Rose's eyes grew wide. "Pa." She gripped his arm. "Ma owned all of this?"

Adam nodded and shrugged. He was without words for a time. "She chose to sell it. She said it meant nothing to her without Aunt Polly."

"How much do you think it would have been worth?"

"I can't begin to guess, thousands if I had to...."

"Pa, Ma gave up all this to live on the frontier."

Adam grinned, and his eyes sparkled. "She's quite a woman."

"I agree. It's beautiful here. This house is amazing, all these gardens." Rose sounded wistful. She stood back then and looked her father in the eye. "But you know what, Pa?"

"What, Darling?"

"I'd rather live with Marcus in a tent, than have all this wonderous finery without him."

Adam bit his lower lip, swiped at his eyes and pulled her into an embrace. After holding her for a time, he kissed her hair. "You're quite a woman too," he whispered.

She pulled back from him, and he stroked her cheek.

"That's all a man wants, Rose, to know he is loved for exactly who he is and not for how much he can provide."

"Pa, you've taught me there is so much more to providing than things. If all I got were things and there was no love, it wouldn't be much of a life. I'd far rather be poor and marry for love." Rose shrugged and looked around one more time. "I have no doubt that Ma didn't even give this place a second thought. She'd much rather live life up on The Rise surrounded by love, than have all this."

Adam nodded, kissed her hair again and led her back to the car.

Constable Scott drove them to the university, and they walked around trying to familiarise themselves with all the buildings. Together they worked out which building was which, and Rose found her way to the classroom she would be meeting in on Monday at precisely nine a.m.

Dismissing their Mountie chauffeur, they chose to walk back to the boarding house to measure the distance. To their surprise, it was only a ten-minute walk. Rose was thrilled. She had hoped not to have to walk too far each day.

*　*　*　*

Adam clung to Rose for some time. "I'm going to miss you, my sweet Rosie Girl," he whispered into her hair. "I love you, Darling. You're going to have a wonderful time here. Make the most of this opportunity."

"Thanks, Pa. I'll make you proud, I promise.

"You always have, Rose." He kissed her forehead, climbed up into the train and headed for home.

"Thank you for the ride, Constable. You've been most kind to me."

Constable Scott removed his Stetson and nodded to her. "It's my pleasure, Miss Morgan. You need anything at any time, just call. You know the Force looks after our own."

"That's most appreciated, Constable." Rose smiled and turned to walk into the boarding house.

Jonny watched her go, replaced his Stetson on his head and entered the car.

Rose sat down at her desk to pen Marcus another long letter. She opened the drawer for an envelope and found one with her name on it. *That's odd.* She screwed her face up in a sideways smile as she recognised her father's handwriting. She opened it and found twenty dollars inside. She gasped. "Pa. You didn't need to do that." Her cheeks coloured. But this was just like him. There was a note accompanying the money.

Rosie, my darling daughter.

I know you'd never have taken this money if I offered it to you, but now you have no choice. It's from the pay-out I got from the RNWMP. I vowed the moment I got it that it would be used for my girls, and so I want you to have this. Make the most of this year and every opportunity. Please take some time to enjoy yourself and have dinners with your friends. You can use this money to treat them sometimes, or to make new friends and show them the love of Jesus.

Use it to buy stationery and stamps for writing to your old pa, who's going to miss the apple of his eye. My heart already aches, knowing I'll not be getting my goodnight kisses and hugs from my precious Rosie. I love you, Darling. You're a delight to me, and I'm so very proud of the woman you are becoming.

I'm proud of you for making this your home in just a few days, and I'm glad you've got good girlfriends here to spend your spare time with. Don't forget us though. We'll be waiting to hear from you just as often as we can, and if you need anything, anything at all, call! Don't forget you can also contact the RNWMP station if you need anything.

I'll keep you in my prayers. Enjoy your first day of college tomorrow, and do your best. That's all we can ask of you.

Your loving, Pa."

"Oh, Pa." A tear slipped down Rose's face as she prepared for bed, reluctant to admit that she was homesick already. She lay awake for a time, praying for God's comfort and peace to be with her in all that the next day would bring.

*   *   *   *

"I'm so excited." Sadie slung her satchel over her shoulder as the four girls strode out into the fall sunshine.

"Me too." Rose's eyes sparkled.

Alice was about to agree when a deep voice from behind them broke into their thoughts.

"Say, Miss Rose, will you let me escort you to college?"

Rose shuddered and froze. She turned to frown at the man. "Mr Russell, I assured you over breakfast that I don't require an escort, and I meant it. I am more than able to walk to college with my friends."

"Come on, Rosie. I'm just being friendly."

Rose thrust her hands on her hips. "Don't call me Rosie. We're not familiar enough for that. I insist, if you refer to me, that you do so as Miss Morgan; anything else would be inappropriate."

Leo Russell flashed her his wide false smile. "Very well, Miss Morgan." He exaggerated the nicety in his voice. "Will you allow me to escort you?"

"No, thank you, Sir." Rose turned back and strutted away, her friends fell into step with her.

"Well, I never!" Leo scowled and turned to his friend Joseph Simmons. "Mark my words, Joey. Before this year is out, she'll be mine."

Joseph shrugged. "Why would you want her? A poor little country waif, and her Pa's a Mountie, so they'd have no money."

Leo tipped his head to the side and smirked at his friend. "Because, Joe, she's beautiful, and naïve. I could happily entertain her for a time. A country girl would make a dutiful little wife and would be naïve enough to not know how I spend my time."

Joey shook his head, and they followed someway behind the women. He shrugged. "Still, if she's not interested, what're you gonna do?"

Leo squinted at his friend. "I always get what I want, Joe, Always! She WILL be my girl, and I'll have her eating out of my hands in no time. She'll not be able to resist me."

Joey raised his eyebrows and merely shrugged.

*   *   *   *

Rose hurried up the stairs to her room with her friends on her heels. "What is it with Leo? He makes me feel so uncomfortable."

"I can't believe he was so brazen as to seat you at the table at supper as though you were his girl and then sit next to you." Alice closed the door behind them and slumped down onto Rose's little trunk couch.

"I think he likes you, Rose." Mandy grinned.

"He doesn't even know me." Rose rolled her eyes.

"You're very beautiful. I bet you catch the eye of many young men, like Franky at college today." Sadie shrugged.

"You're so lucky, Rose. I wish the boys would look at me like that." Mandy sounded a little wistful.

"Well, you can have them. I'm not interested in any of them." Rose blushed and smiled. "I'm courting Marcus, and he loves me."

"Still, Rose, you're a long way from him, and besides, things can change."

"Sadie, what are you trying to say?"

"What Marcus doesn't know, won't hurt him, will it?" She raised her eyebrows twice, somewhat suggestively.

"Sadie!" Rose chastised her.

"I'm not saying to court them, but a little harmless flirting never hurt anyone."

Rose stamped her foot and scowled. "Sadie Cook, flirting is never harmless, and people do get hurt from it all the time. I'm not going to behave that way. It would not be honouring to Marcus or to myself."

"Okay." Sadie chuckled. "I didn't mean any harm, but it looks to me like you're going to have to get that message across to more than one young man here."

"I'm perfectly okay with that. I'm only interested in Marcus." Rose smiled and turned her eyes to the photograph on her wall.

"But you aren't engaged, Rose. How do you know he won't court someone else while you're gone?" asked Mandy.

"Because I know him. He promised he wouldn't. I trust him, and he trusts me, and I have no intention of breaking that trust."

The three girls nodded, but they weren't so sure. It was easy to say that now but they'd just wait and see. They were sure Rose would change her mind, with all the handsome men that surrounded them.

Seven
Marcus Visits

"You know you don't have to check up on me all the time." Rose flashed the Mountie a wry smile over their coffee cups.

Constable Scott grinned and tipped his head to her. "Just following orders."

Rose scowled at him and squinted her eyes. "I'm just duty am I, Constable."

Jonathan put down his cup and chuckled. He dared to reach out one hand and place it on her arm. "Not at all, Rose. Yes, your father asked me to look out for you, but it really is my pleasure. You're good company."

Rose smiled. She took a sip of her coffee and looked around the small café. She looked back at the Mountie. "You're good company, too. It's nice to have a male friend that doesn't have ulterior motives." She raised her brows and curled up one side of her mouth.

"You've made it clear that Marcus is the only man for you, and I respect that. I'm just happy to have a good friend, and you know we'd do anything for a Mountie's family."

"Well, I thank you. I enjoy our time together." Rose glanced at the clock and reached for her coin purse. "We'd best be getting back, Constable."

Jonathan jerked his head around to look at the time. He drained his cup and thrust it down on the table. "You're right. Keep your money, Miss Morgan; I'll get it."

Rose scowled and thrust her hands on her hips as they stood up. "Constable Scott, I can pay for myself. Policeman or no Policeman, I don't need your charity."

He threw his head back in laughter, reached for his Stetson and grinned at Rose. "Yes, Ma'am. Forgive me." He gestured towards the counter and followed her, still chuckling.

Rose screwed her face up and swatted at his arm. "You'll keep, Constable."

"Oh, is this assault of a Police officer, Ma'am? Do you need a night in the cells?" Jonathan gave her a mock scowl.

Rose shook her head at him and laughed heartily. They each paid for their coffee and walked out into the crisp air.

Rose smiled as she walked to her room, grateful to the Lord for such a kind friend. It certainly was refreshing to have a man in her life that wasn't trying to pursue her. She felt comfortable and safe with Constable Scott. It was the red serge, of course. She loved it and all that it stood for. But it was more than that; he'd become like a brother to her, and while his protectiveness frustrated her, if she was truly honest, she loved it. He was so much like her father.

* * * *

The second week of November was freezing. A blizzard blew down from the north overnight, and the girls had to make their way through the snow to school. By the time they got to class, their shoes and skirts were drenched, and they were shivering. Leo had offered to hire a carriage to take them all, but they refused. They huddled around the stove in their classroom and tried to get warm. By the time class started, they were beginning to unthaw.

Franky walked in on the girls shivering around the stove. "Good morning, Rose. Need some warming up? I'd be happy to oblige." Rose shuddered.

"No, thank you, Mr Hamilton, I'm just fine. Please leave me be!" Rose said, as kindly as she could manage.

"Don't be like that, Miss Rose. I'm just trying to help." He placed his hand on her shoulder. Rose closed her eyes and shuddered. She was about to cry out.

"Hey, Franky, don't worry about them. Come over here with the chaps." Edmund Patterson gestured to him from across the room.

Rose shrugged off Franky's touch. Franky turned and walked towards Mr Patterson. Rose shot Edmund a grateful look, and he just nodded his understanding.

By the end of that week, Rose was tired of being cold all the time. So Thursday afternoon, she headed to one of the local stores with some of the money her father had left her and bought two pairs of thick stockings and a new heavy winter coat. She really wanted some new mittens too, but she just couldn't afford to spend more money. She'd just use her old mittens and put her hands in her pockets while she walked. She'd budgeted her money carefully, but still had Christmas gifts to purchase; and the prices were much higher in the city.

Rose returned from the store to find two letters waiting for her, one from parents and one from Marcus. She squealed in delight and hurried up the stairs to devour the news from home. Tears trickled down her cheeks as she read about the precious family moments she was missing. There were three November birthdays in her family, and she was homesick for all the fun she was missing out on. She sent gifts home and long letters, but it wasn't the same. Her mother's birthday would be coming up soon, and she was devastated she'd miss it. Their birthday tradition of pancake breakfasts would be one of the things she missed the most.

She wiped away her tears and tore open the letter from Marcus. It was full of all the news from his work and the houses they were building.

Rose put her letter down and sighed. She missed him. She couldn't wait for the Christmas break so she could go home and visit. School was only out for ten days, and two of those days would be spent on a train. Still, it would be worth it. She longed to see Marcus, and her family. She looked up at the clock and gasped. Her family would be at her father's office waiting for her call. She jumped up, put the letter in her pocket and headed for the back stairs where the telephone was.

* * * *

Marcus sighed. The Graham house was taking longer than they thought, and part of the problem was being able to source the goods they needed. Mrs Graham was very specific about what she wanted, but the recent storm had meant the supplies couldn't get through from Edmonton. They'd had no end of trouble trying to get the things they needed. Twice the shipment had come in, and it was incorrect, and now the storm had delayed things further. The only way Mr Campbell could be sure to get the precise pieces Mrs Graham wanted was to go to Edmonton and fetch them himself. But he couldn't. He had four apprentices working for him.

"You'll have to go in my place, Lad." Mr Campbell nodded knowingly. Marcus beamed and listened carefully as his boss gave him specific instructions, to organise exactly what they needed, and make sure it got on the freight train. "Do you suppose you'll be able to find a way to spend the time over the weekend?" His boss gave him as wry smile.

Marcus grinned. "I think I can manage, Sir. Thank you."

Mr Campbell gave Marcus the money for the products, helped him with the company horse and wagon and waved him off. "See you Monday, Lad. Thanks for being prepared to do this."

"You're most welcome, Mr Campbell. I won't let you down."

"Make sure you kiss that girly of yours and take her out for a decent supper."

"I plan to, Mr Campbell. I can assure you of that."

*   *   *   *

Marcus sighed. The train crawled ever so slowly, inch by inch, towards the woman he loved. He'd phoned ahead, and Mrs Green would have a room waiting for him. He chuckled to himself at the woman's delight in being a part of the surprise.

He looked at the seat next to him and grinned. The box of small gifts the family wanted to send to Rose had grown and grown until it became a large crate. Every family member had wanted to include something. He could only barely carry it, but was delighted to be able to take it to her. He knew how happy it would make her.

Finally, the train pulled into the station in Edmonton. Marcus knew from Rose's schedule that she'd be in class, so he hired a wagon and got all his things and the crate taken to the boarding house.

Mrs Green greeted him at the door and wrapped him in a warm hug. "It's so good to meet you, Lad. Miss Rose has been lonesome for you."

"I'm glad to be here. Thanks for accommodating me, Mrs Green."

"It's my pleasure, Mr Murray. I can see why Rose likes you; you're a handsome one."

"Thank you, Mrs Green." Marcus laughed. She showed him to his room and took him upstairs to show him where Rose's room was. As it turned out, it was right above his own room. He grinned. He'd sleep soundly knowing that right above him, the woman he loved was sleeping too.

He unpacked what he could, left the crate near the door, and locked up the room. Slipping the key into his pocket, he headed out to see to his business. In short order, Marcus got all the supplies they needed, including the very ornate door knocker and doorknobs Mrs Graham wanted. The price made him shudder. He was relieved when they were able to find the last of the stained glass windows the woman had requested. It was the last because they'd changed the design and it wasn't very popular anymore. Mrs Graham could be unpleasant when she didn't get her way, even when it was out of their control.

He had it packaged extra carefully. It had to make it home in one piece. All the supplies were crated up and marked with their destination. He followed them all the way to the train station, where they were put in the pile for Monday's train. Satisfied his job was done, he grinned. Rose would be home from class in just over an hour.

He hurried back to the boarding house and bathed, shaved and dressed in his finest suit. He collected the small bouquet of flowers he'd found in a year-round flower store. He'd much rather have given her a posy of the wildflowers that grew behind her pa's office or from their eight acres, but store-bought would have to do.

Mrs Green gave him permission to wait in Rose's room with a stern warning that he wasn't to touch anything. She had a responsibility to her paying customers. He chuckled. "Don't expect us for supper, Ma'am. I've booked a table at the restaurant of a small hotel just down the road."

"You're a fine young lad, Mr Murray. I can see why Miss Morgan thinks so highly of you."

"And I think the world of her, Mrs Green." He kissed the older lady on the cheek, pulled out one long-stemmed flower from the bouquet, and gave it to her. "Thank you for all your help." He squeezed her arm and skipped off up the stairs to Rose's room.

Mrs Green chuckled, sniffed the flower, and shook her head slightly. Slipping the flower in a buttonhole, she chuckled again and walked into the kitchen to get supper on.

There were no locks on the doors, but people respected each other in the house, so Marcus was surprised to see her door was open. He hurried down the hallway and looked in.

"May I ask what you're doing in Miss Morgan's room, Sir?" He eyed the well-dressed young man.

Leo turned around and smirked, seeing another young man with flowers hoping to call on the same young woman. "I'm afraid you're too late. Miss Morgan is already spoken for." He grinned and placed his enormous bouquet of flowers on her desk. He eyed Marcus and scoffed at his cheap home-sewn suit.

Leo's bouquet was very expensive wrapped in ribbons and bows and brightly-coloured tissue paper. It made Marcus's small posy look like a handful of weeds.

"Spoken for?" Marcus raised his brows.

"Yes, Rose is my girl!" Leo smirked. "I've been seeing her for some time." He leaned back against the desk, and crossed his ankles.

"Is that right? How long exactly?" Marcus cocked up one eyebrow. He could see right through Leo's brazen manner and pretentious suit. *This must be the young man that Sergeant Morgan talked about.* But he played along.

"Over a month now. I'm sorry if you came here asking to court. You're out of luck; she's with me." Leo's smarmy smile and dull eyes caused concern to rise in Marcus's mind.

"I see." Marcus eyed the clock. "Perhaps I'll just wait in here too, and we can ask her which of us she wants to see."

Leo grinned. "She knows me well. We've been together for a while and see each other every day. You can't match me for money or looks." Leo flicked his head and swiped at his slicked-back hair. "Anyone can see how cheap your clothing is," he scoffed.

"Do you really think that's what matters to her? You know she was raised on the frontier, right?"

"Yes, I'm well aware, but I know what women want."

"And what's that?" Marcus flashed the man a crooked smile.

Leo stood up straight. "They want a confident, bold man with prospects and money. They certainly don't want some pauper wearing a poorly cut suit bringing a posy of the most pitiful flowers I've ever seen." He gestured spitefully towards him. "My Rosie deserves a big bright bouquet of these expensive flowers, beautifully wrapped. What is that yours is wrapped in?"

"It's a piece of rawhide I tied around them." Marcus's eyes twinkled.

"Rawhide, Pfffft," Leo scoffed, with an exaggerated loud laugh. "Rawhide! You're a country boy, aren't you? You think you're going to win the heart of a beautiful girl like Rosie with wilted flowers and rawhide?"

Marcus smiled. "Yes, I think she'll like them very much."

"Huh! Well, we'll see. You just sit here and wait, and we'll find out who she prefers," Leo spat condescendingly. He stood by the desk, and Marcus stepped back further into the room, and sat on her bed. He glanced at the clock; it was eight minutes past four. He knew Rose would be here any moment, and he couldn't wait to see her.

Marcus looked around her room and smiled. It was such a small, dreary room, but somehow she'd made it cheerful. Her books, and photographs, the small potted plant, the colourful quilts and even her old ragdoll gave it a homely feel. He grinned. It was like her to make even a drab space feel inviting.

At last, they heard footsteps and the girl's laughter. Marcus stood to his feet, anticipation and delight raising in his heart.

"It's so cold." Sadie shivered as they stepped into their hallway. "I can't wait to change into some warmer clothes and out of these wet ski..."

The men heard the conversation stop abruptly as the girls came to a halt suddenly. "Rose, your door is open." Mandy gasped. "Do you think there's someone in your room?"

"I doubt it. Mrs Green likely placed my mail in there and left it open." Rose shrugged. The four girls gingerly crept forward and peered in. They didn't notice Marcus, behind Leo and his giant bouquet. Rose stepped in, and the other three hung back and gasped.

Leo grinned smugly at Rose, and she stopped in her tracks and frowned at him. She paused to say something when a movement caught her eye from behind Leo, and her face lit up. She threw her books on the trunk and grinned. "What are you doing here?"

Leo beamed, put down the flowers and opened his arms out to her. *Finally! Finally, she sees me as a gentleman. The comparison to this poor waif must've made all the difference.*

Rose was temporarily frozen to her spot, her eyes sparkling and her mouth hanging open. Marcus opened his arms and grinned. His whole face lit up with joy. She bolted towards him, completely ignoring Leo and running into Marcus's arms. "Oh, Marcus. I can't believe you're actually here."

Neither of them noticed the three girls still standing in the doorway or the look of sheer disbelief on Leo's face. None of the others thought to leave, and stood watching as the two young lovers clung to each other and Marcus kissed her on the cheek. Alice clasped her hands together and the girls gushed to each other.

"I had business for Mr Campbell in Edmonton, and he suggested I take the whole weekend."

"Oh, Marcus." Rose loved being held by him again. "Where are you staying?"

He thought for a moment. "Mrs Green's boarding house, ground floor."

"Here?" Her eyes lit up. "Oh, this is the best surprise ever."

He held out the flowers to her. "These are for you, Rose. I'm sorry they aren't much, but they were all I could find in the flower store given the time of the year." He hung his head. "And all I could afford."

Leo scoffed, but Rose ignored him, grinned at Marcus and reached for the flowers. "They're beautiful, thank you." She put them to her nose and drank in their scent. "I know they aren't easy to find at this time of the year, and I really wouldn't want you spending all your money on flowers. These are really quite lovely, thank you." She kissed him on the cheek, and her eyes shone.

Leo couldn't stand it anymore. "Rose, you can't possibly prefer this pauper over me."

She turned on her heels. "Mr Russell." Rose scowled, gritted her teeth and thrust her hands on her hips. "I have told you numerous times that I am not in the slightest bit interested in you and your flattery. You can take your expensive bouquet of flowers and pretentious suit and leave my room immediately."

All three girls watching on grinned. "Go, Rose," Alice whispered and turned to grin at Sadie.

Leo thrust his hands out to Rose. "Are you serious? You'd prefer this poorly dressed hick with wilting flowers wrapped in rawhide to me?"

Rose reached for Marcus's hand, and stared Leo in the face. "Yes, I prefer him. I don't want your expensive gifts. I've given every one of them back to you. None of your gifts, endless notes, or flattery has come with any love or concern for me. You haven't taken the time to get to know me or anything about me, or you'd know that I love peonies. They don't grow this time of year unless someone especially tends to them indoors. I know that Marcus must have worked hard to find a flower store that has them. And as for the rawhide, it's special to me too." She grinned and winked at Marcus. "My pa gave my ma flowers wrapped in rawhide a few times, and it reminds me of home. He could have put fancy ribbons around them, and I would've thought it was nice, but this tells me he really knows me. He knows I always carry rawhide in my saddlebags. You never know when your halter might break or if you have to tie something securely. Rawhide is about the strongest thing there is for that job. This was just a little piece of home that he brought me. Not some tacky store-bought gesture.

"I know if we were home and the season was right, Marcus would have brought me the wildflowers that grow in our town. I love them because of their vibrant colours and how their scent wafts in the spring air and makes the whole world smell magical. You just picked the most expensive bouquet in the store, thinking that would impress me. I'm not one bit taken with your fancy suits and city upbringing, Mr Russell. I prefer kind and honest; thoughtful and caring; gentle yet strong." She looked Leo in the eye and continued. "My Marcus is all of those things. I don't care how much money he has. He is everything I want in a man, and well... I love him." She blushed.

Marcus gasped and grinned. The girls at the door squealed and clapped. Leo stamped out dejectedly, taking his expensive flowers with him.

"Rose? You love me?"

"Yes." She beamed. "I love you, Marcus Murray. I realised it just now."

"You have no idea how happy that makes me, Rose. I love you too, with all my heart." Marcus leaned in and kissed her tenderly, and the girls at the doorway swooned. Finally, he released her. "Thank you for your words just now. I knew he was full of hot air. He told me you were his girl, and you'd been seeing each other for over a month."

"Oh, Marcus, that's not true. I despise him actually, and I've told him I wasn't interested and had a man back home waiting for me, but he wouldn't listen. He's so puffed up with his own importance."

"It's true, Marcus." Alice walked in. "She's talked about you constantly and hates all the attention the men are always giving her."

"Oh, Marcus. This is Alice Harvey, my friend, Sadie Cook, and Mandy Brooks. I've written about them." Rose gestured to each one.

"Yes." Marcus smiled and nodded to each girl. "It's nice to finally put faces to the names. I thank you for your friendship and kindness to my Rose." He put his arm around her waist.

"You're welcome, Marcus." Alice grinned. "She's so kind to everyone. Even Leo, who has been nothing but a pain to her."

"That's just like her." He grinned and winked at Rose.

"You have nothing to worry about, Marcus," Mandy confirmed.

"I'm not worried." Marcus looked squarely at Rose. "I trust her completely."

"Thank you, Marcus." Rose gave him a wide smile.

"Well, Ladies." Alice grabbed the other two girls by the hands and led them away. "Let's leave these two to it."

"Stay if you like." Rose smiled.

"No." Alice smiled and shook her head. "I know how much you've missed him. You two deserve some time together."

Rose nodded. "I'll see you later, Girls."

Finally, they were alone, and Rose threw herself back into Marcus's arms, and he kissed her gently. Then she gestured for him to sit down. She sat on the bed and he on the chair at her small desk. He couldn't take his eyes off her, and he grinned broadly.

Her cheeks reddened. "What is it?"

"You're so beautiful. You're a sight for sore eyes, Rose." He stroked her cheek.

"Thank you. I'm sorry about Leo." She creased her brows and dropped her head.

"Hey." Marcus lifted her chin. "Don't be sorry. It isn't your fault he's so brazen. I'm just sorry you have to endure that. Isn't there anything your pa can do about it?"

"No, he hasn't done anything physical. Today was the first time he'd ever been in my room. I'm glad you're here, Marcus." She beamed then. "It's such a wonderful surprise. I just got your letter yesterday."

Marcus remembered something then. "Rose, I'd like to take you out for supper tonight, if you'll let me."

"You'd better, Marcus Murray. I don't think you wore that suit just to sit around with me in my boring life."

He smiled and reached out to touch her arm. "I would sit here for hours on end just watching you read and be happy as a clam. But from what you've told me, your life is anything but boring. Yes, I want to take you out for supper. I have dinner reservations at the hotel around the corner."

"What time?"

"Six o'clock."

"I need to change and take a bath. My skirt is all wet and dirty from the snow."

"How long do you need?"

"Come for me at five o'clock? We could take a walk before we eat?"

Marcus grinned. He stood up, and so did Rose. He kissed her on the cheek and squeezed her arm. "I'll be here promptly at five." She grinned, and he turned and walked out of the room.

Rose headed for the bathroom and hurried to get ready.

Eight
Marcus vs Leo

Marcus grinned as he walked away from her room. He took a deep contented breath and walked down the narrow staircase. He met Leo coming back up.

"Well, well, if it isn't the country boy!"

"Give it a rest, Leo," Marcus responded, turning sideways to let Leo pass him. "And leave Rose alone," he threw back over his shoulder.

Leo turned on his heels and bounded back down the stairs. He grabbed Marcus roughly by the shoulder and yanked him around to look at him. Standing a step above him menacingly, Leo grabbed Marcus by his collar. He squinted his eyes and scowled. "What did you say to me?"

"Let me go, Leo." Marcus, unafraid, rolled his eyes at the man's bravado. He yanked himself out of Leo's grip and continued down the stairs. Leo stood and watched him go, his eyes ablaze and his lips pursed. Marcus reached the landing and stepped out into the dining room. Leo bounded down the rest of the stairs back towards Marcus.

"You think you're better than me, don't you. Marcus?" Leo spat. Several pairs of eyes turned to face them from the dining room. Three of the borders were trying to enjoy coffee and the local newspapers. They turned to watch the scene.

Marcus stopped walking and looked at Leo. "I don't think about you at all." He chuckled and turned to walk to his room.

"Don't walk away from me, country boy," Leo growled. "I'm talking to you."

Marcus took a deep breath and turned to face Leo again. He crossed his arms over his chest. "I really don't have any problem with you, Leo, and I don't want to make one. Rose has made it clear she isn't interested in you. She and I are courting. Why can't you accept that?"

Leo grabbed Marcus by the collar again, bringing his face very close to Marcus's. "Because no one says no to me. She can't choose a country bumpkin like you over a refined gentleman like me."

Marcus raised his eyebrows. "This isn't exactly the behaviour of a refined gentleman." Marcus was not one to be easily baited.

"Perhaps she isn't much of a woman then. Simple frontier girl with no brains...." Leo got no further. Marcus didn't care if Leo insulted him, but to slander Rose, that was not on. Marcus pulled himself forcefully away from Leo, stepped back, and gritted his teeth.

"Take that back, Leo, or I'll make you."

"How are you going to make me, country boy? You two deserve each other, pathetic poor little uneducated country waif like you pretending you're someone in a homespun suit. And a pretty but scatter-brained girl...." Marcus's eyes blazed. He sucked in air through his teeth and swung his fist, collecting Leo right in the jaw, knocking him off his feet and to the floor, where he slumped against the wall.

The three gentlemen who were seated nearby gasped at first but then, in unison, began to applaud. No one in the house approved of the brash and vain Leo.

Mrs Green heard the commotion and hurried from the kitchen, drying her hands on her apron. She arrived in time to see Leo, with his blazing eyes and a loud growl, leap up from the floor, and grab at the retreating Marcus, spin him around forcefully, and punch him right in the eye. Marcus fell to the ground. Leo kicked at him viciously until two of the boarders jumped up to subdue Leo.

They grabbed him and pulled him away forcefully. Mrs Green walked over to him, her hands on her hips and lips curled up in a scowl. "There will be no fighting in my boarding house. Now get out." She gestured to Leo. Somehow she knew it was all Leo's doing. He'd been making life difficult for Rose since she moved in. "Go outside and cool off." She thrust her hand towards the door. Leo slunk off, and the two men helped Marcus to his feet and into a chair. Mrs Green sat down next to him and began to examine his injuries.

"You're gonna have quite a shiner there, young man."

"It's worth it, Mrs Green. He can sling insults at me all he likes, but anyone who speaks that way about my Rose is going to get the same treatment."

"You hit him?" She raised her eyebrows.

"Yes, Ma'am. I'm sorry for making a ruckus in your boarding house. I tried to walk away from him. He just kept on goading me."

"What brought that on?"

"Rose paid him no mind. He's jealous that she would want to be with a 'country boy' like me rather than a 'refined gentleman' such as him. He insulted Rose, and I hit him on the jaw. I didn't strike him hard. I just wanted him to stop saying awful things about the woman I love." Marcus gritted his teeth.

"I understand, Mr Murray. He's been giving her trouble for some time."

"Why don't you do something about him?"

She shrugged. "Nothing I can do if the lady doesn't press charges, and he's not done anything physical to her."

"So we have to wait until he does?"

"No, we'll see to it he doesn't come near her again," one of the boarders commented, looking up from his newspaper. All of the residents in the house loved the four young girls and were very protective of them. Especially the Mountie's daughter. "I'll tell that Mountie that comes around from time to time to check him out."

"Mountie?" Marcus raised his eyebrows.

"A young constable that knows her pa." Mrs Green twisted her hands together.

"The Sergeant has charged the Constable to keep an eye out for his daughter," the man with the newspaper added.

"That's good." Marcus nodded and smiled. "Now I have to get cleaned up. I'm supposed to be taking Rose out for supper."

Rose opened the door to his knock and gasped. "Marcus, whatever happened?" She raised her hand up to gently touch his face. He had a small cut below his eye where bruising was beginning to show.

"Leo." He shrugged and screwed up his mouth.

"Oh no. What did he say to you?"

"He was goading me, but I didn't care. I never would have hit him, but he dared to insult you, and I lost it and hit him on the chin. He stood up and punched me."

"Oh, Marcus, I'm so sorry about all this fuss. It's all because of me." She moved her hand to his cheek.

He reached for her hand and kissed her fingers. "It's not your fault, Rose. You don't deserve any of this. You did nothing to cause it."

"But you got hurt." She knitted her eyebrows together and searched his face worriedly.

"It's okay. I'd take a thousand punches to the face for you every single day of my life if necessary. You're worth it." He grimaced. "I won't abide you being insulted by anyone." He gritted his teeth.

Rose kissed him on the non-injured cheek. "You're a good man, Marcus. Thank you for sticking up for me."

He reached for both of her hands and lifted them to put around his neck. She grinned. He put his arms around her waist. "Rose, I will always stick up for you. You mean more to me than any other human on the planet, and I will always be your biggest fan. I promise to always do everything I can to keep you safe." He squeezed her and closed his eyes briefly. "I'm sorry I can't stop what's happening to you here. I hate that I'm not here to help you bear with it all."

Rose stood up on her toes and kissed him gently. "Marcus. You're the most caring, loving, and protective man I know, and I love you. You're not responsible for what other people do, not after the dance, and not now. You can't be with me all the time. It's enough to know that you're at home loving me from afar."

"I don't deserve you."

"Oh, stop that. Of course, you do. You're a wonderful man, I'm proud of you, Marcus."

"Thank you, Rose. You really are amazing and so very beautiful. I'm the luckiest man alive to have you in my arms."

"And I'm the luckiest woman in the world to be in your arms. It's the safest place I know."

"Good." He grinned at her. "I'll always be here to hold you."

"Well, are we going to supper?"

"Do you still want to go out with me looking like this?"

"Of course. You're still incredibly handsome. You look great in that suit, by the way."

"My cheap suit that my ma made for me?" He grinned.

"Yes, because it was made with love, and I'm much more interested in the man beneath the suit anyway."

He grinned. "Well then, we shall go. But first, I have something for you. Wait here." He released her and disappeared outside the door where he'd left the crate. He picked it up, brought it in, and laid it on her desk.

Rose's eyebrows flew up. She covered her mouth with both hands and gasped. "Marcus, what's this?"

"A gift from your family." He groaned as he finally put it down.

"A gift? It looks like they sent me the entire town." She laughed.

"Just about heavy enough." He chuckled and lifted off the lid.

Rose reached in and pulled out several packages. She clasped her hands together. "Have we got time?" Her shining eyes pleaded with him.

He grinned and touched her arm. "Of course." Marcus sat on the trunk and watched her beaming face as she pulled out each gift, wept, gasped and clapped over them all.

"My family is so thoughtful." Her eyes misted over as she pulled on the new mittens, crocheted in a soft turquoise wool. "I love these. I couldn't afford to buy new ones. Please thank my ma and tell her it means so much to me. And Callie and Anna made the hat and scarf according to the note."

Marcus took delight in her joy. He loved it when her whole face shone and her eyes sparkled. He vowed he would do whatever he could to keep that look on her face for the rest of her days!

She laid the last gift on her desk and glanced at her clock. "We should get going if we're going to make our reservation."

She reached for her coat, but Marcus stopped her, took it from her, and helped her into it. "I have a gift for you too, Rose."

"What is it?" She looked up at him, the question shining in her eyes.

He leaned in and kissed her deeply. It hurt his bruised lip, but he didn't care. It was worth it.

"Thank you. I like it very much," she whispered, with her eyes firmly closed. She opened them and her cheeks coloured under his adoring gaze.

"Will you allow me, Miss Morgan?" His eyes twinkled as he offered her his arm. With a nod, she accepted. He placed his other hand on her hand that was tucked under his arm. "I can't get enough of having you on my arm, Rose. It makes me strong and proud. And might I say you look beautiful. That pale green really makes your eyes sparkle."

Rose blushed as she pulled the door closed. "Thank you, Marcus. I love being on your arm too."

"Good." He gave her a wink.

They passed Leo sitting at the table in the dining room holding Mrs Green's poultice on his chin. He scowled at Marcus and Rose as they walked past arm in arm. "Don't get lost in the big city, you two. It's no place for country folk," he shouted to their backs.

Marcus cringed.

"Ignore him. He's not worth it," Rose said as they walked out the door.

Mrs Green clipped Leo across the ear. "That's enough from you, young man. Accept that she's chosen another man and move on."

He muttered under his breath and scowled at her.

* * * *

"Now, when I read your letters, I'll be able to picture where you are." Marcus grinned as they wandered around the college and peered in the window at each of her classrooms. She told him about each professor and the classes, but she didn't mention Franky. She didn't want a repeat of Leo.

On Monday morning, he walked her to class carrying her satchel over his shoulder. He enjoyed walking with the girls and hearing their laughter. The girls walked into class, and Marcus pulled Rose around the corner into the shadows. "I have to go, Rose. I have a train to catch shortly."

"I know, Marcus. I'll miss you so very much."

"I miss you every day, Rose. But I'm so glad we got this time together."

"Me too. It was the best surprise."

"I'm glad. I just love to see you happy." He kissed her and gripped her tightly. "I love you."

"I love you too."

He closed his eyes and grinned. "You have no idea how much it thrills me to hear you say that. It makes my heart sing."

"Well, you better go. You don't want to miss your train."

"I do want to. I'd much rather stay here with you." He chuckled.

"Marcus, you have to go. I'll see you in a month when I come home for Christmas."

"I'll be waiting, my sweet Rose." He held her tightly and kissed her again. He stroked her cheek and winked at her. "See ya."

"See you." She grinned, and taking her satchel from him, she walked into class.

Nine
Crazy Lizzie

"How come you never play with us girls, Lizzie?" Eliza Clarke threw at her.

Lizzie hoisted her bat over her shoulder and followed her classmates out of the room. "'Cause I wanna play baseball."

"But that's for boys? Wouldn't you rather come with us?" Amelia Adams walked down the stairs next to Lizzie.

Lizzie shrugged. "That depends. What're you gonna do?"

"We're going to sit in the shady area under the trees and take turns on the swing, and jump rope." Eliza pointed to the rope that Stella Edwards was carrying across her shoulders.

Lizzie paused and swung her eyes to the boys who were setting up bases. "Nah, I'd rather play ball."

Amelia screwed up her nose. "You sure are weird, Lizzie Morgan. Sometimes I wonder if you're even a girl."

Lizzie scowled. "You take that back, Amelia."

"No! I won't. You sure don't behave like a girl."

"What are girls supposed to behave like?"

Eliza smiled as Sarah and Hope joined them from the junior class. "Like your sisters, at least they behave like girls."

Sarah and Hope scowled at Eliza. "Don't pick on Lizzie. She doesn't have to play your games if she doesn't want to." Sarah flicked a braid over her shoulder.

Lizzie grimaced. "I can speak for myself, Sarah. I don't want to play your games. I don't care what you think about me..."

"Come on Lizzie, we're waiting for you," her cousin Jack Coleman called her over.

"Coming," she yelled, poked her tongue out at Eliza and ran to join the ball game.

"You go then, Crazy Lizzie, see if we care," Amelia yelled and turned with the other girls to walk to the meadow where they jumped rope.

"Don't call her that." Hope stamped her foot.

"What're you gonna do about it? I can't help it that your sister is crazy..."

Lizzie paused mid-stride, dropped her bat and ran headlong towards the girls walking away from her. She pushed Amelia over. "I'm not crazy, don't call me that." Lizzie stood over the girl as she sat up and rubbed dust from her face and hair.

Amelia jumped up, her eyes blazing. She was at least a head and shoulders taller than Lizzie and three grades ahead. "What'd you do that for?" Amelia pushed her back and Lizzie stumbled but didn't fall.

"I told you not to call me crazy." Lizzie thrust her hands on her hips and scowled. The other girls, including her sisters, stood around watching to see yet another confrontation between the two.

Amelia thrust her own hands on her hips and wriggled her head in quick circles. "Crazy Lizzie, Crazy Lizzie," she chanted.

"Stop, Amelia." Sarah frowned.

"Crazy Lizzie, Crazy Lizzie," several of Amelia's friends joined in.

Lizzie's eyes blazed, and Hope observed her clench and unclench her fists. "Liz, don't. They aren't worth it." Hope touched her sister's arm.

"This doesn't concern you, Hope." Lizzie brushed off her sister's arm, took a step forward and slapped Amelia across the face.

"Lizzie!" Sarah gasped as Lizzie leapt on Amelia and pushed her to the ground, sat straddling her and began hitting her. Amelia shrieked and tried to push her away. Lizzie's younger sisters grabbed her arms and tried to pull her away, and the rest of the children paused their games and came running.

"Hit her, Lizzie." James Wood clapped his hands.

"Lizzie, stop, please." Hope was in tears.

Anna and Callie marched over from the spot under the tree where they'd been reading. They sighed and walked to Lizzie, physically hauling her off Amelia as they had done on several other occasions.

"Let me go!" Lizzie struggled against her sisters grip as Amelia stood up, and her friends helped her dust herself off.

"No, Lizzie, Pa said no fighting," Callie insisted.

"She's mean, she deserves it." Lizzie wriggled and pulled against her sisters, but they held her tightly.

Amelia scowled. "I told you she was crazy. Crazy Lizzie, you just proved to everyone here how crazy you are."

Lizzie shrieked and pulled at her sisters and other girls who tried to hold her back. At that moment, their teacher walked out. "What's going on here?" She scowled at Lizzie, and raised her brows. "What've you done now, Lizzie Morgan?"

Before Lizzie could speak, Hope turned to the teacher. "Miss Price, Amelia started it."

"I don't care who started it. Lizzie ought to know better than to finish it."

"But..." Lizzie clenched her jaw tightly against the retorts,

"Lizzie, you will stay after school every day this week and clean all the slates and chalkboards." Miss Price scowled at her and wagged her finger.

"What about her?" Lizzie gestured towards Amelia, who batted her eyelids innocently at the teacher.

"Now, Lizzie, you know that words are just words. No matter what they say, there is no excuse for violence. Now you have fifteen minutes of recess left. I suggest you girls go and play." Miss Price nodded to Amelia. "Miss Morgan, you come with me." The teacher grabbed Lizzie's shoulder.

Callie and Anna let go of their sister.

"Where're you taking her?" Callie demanded.

"To learn a lesson, she wants violence. I'll show her what happens when you're violent." Miss Price scowled.

"What're you gonna do?" Callie's lips trembled, and her eyes flooded with tears.

Miss Price spun on her heels and brought her face close to Callie's. She scowled at the girl. "If she insists on behaving like a boy, perhaps it's time we treated her like we'd treat a violent little boy." She dragged Lizzie up the stairs into the classroom and slammed the door shut behind her. Lizzie screamed and yelled at the teacher, trying desperately to pull away, but the teacher gripped her tightly.

"Oh no!" Callie bit her lip. "Lizzie isn't gonna like this."

"Neither is Pa." Anna grimaced.

"Maybe we should tell him…" Hope's voice was cut off by Miss Harper coming out of the junior class with the bell.

"Lizzie can fight her own battles. Come on, let's go to class." The worried frown on Anna's face suggested she knew this wasn't the end of it.

The girls turned towards their classroom and didn't see Lizzie fly out the back door and into the trees.

Anna walked back into the classroom, expecting to see Lizzie standing in the corner. *Lizzie spends a lot of time in the corner.* She grimaced and shook her head. But Lizzie wasn't in the corner. Anna scanned the classroom and frowned. Lizzie was nowhere to be seen. She mustered up all her courage and approached the red-faced teacher as she was hanging her strap back on its hook.

"Where's Lizzie?"

Miss Price turned and scowled at Anna. "Take your seat, Miss Morgan, before I give you a taste of what I gave your sister."

Anna gulped, and tears flooded her eyes. She bit her lip and nodded, and hurried to her desk. She didn't have the courage to defy the teacher like Lizzie did. She slumped into her desk and prayed fervently for her sister.

Lizzie thrust herself against a tree and sobbed, slapping the rough bark with her burning hands. She heard the bell ringing and waited until all the children were inside, then ran all the way to the lake and threw herself down at the picnic table. She buried her head in her arms and cried.

* * * *

Daniel hurried back to town. He was running late to meet Louisa for lunch. *She'll understand, a pastor must take the time to listen to his people when they're hurting. Widow Gibson needed a listening ear, such a tragic life to have no family at all...* His thoughts were brought to an abrupt halt by the sound of a child crying. He sped his steps, and as he came around the oak tree he noticed Lizzie and gasped loudly. "Oh, my heart." He fell into the seat next to her. "Lizzie, what on earth has happened?"

Lizzie sat up and showed Daniel her hands. Two red stripes covered each. "Ohhhhh." He pulled her close to himself. "Ohhhh, Lizzie." She sobbed against his chest. Fire began to rise in the pastor's cheeks. Daniel was a mild-mannered man, until someone hit a child, then he struggled to keep his anger at bay. He clung to Lizzie and seethed.

At last, Lizzie calmed a little, and Daniel stood and scooped her into his arms. Lizzie lay her head against his chest, and Daniel hurried her to the infirmary. "You're gonna be just fine, Lizzie." He kissed her hair and took off at a run. *I pity the person who dared to hit one of Adam's girls. Lord, please help him not to do anything that would threaten his job.*

"Owen," Daniel called from the doorway.

The doctor looked up from strapping Martin Ellis's leg. His mouth fell open. "Oh no! What is it?" He nodded to Martin. "You're good to go. Just keep the weight off it for a few days." Owen pointed to the crutch leaning against the bed.

"Much obliged, Doctor." The man hobbled out the door.

Owen ran to Lizzie as Daniel placed her gently on the bed. The doctor placed his hand on her shoulder and looked kindly at her. "What has happened?"

Becky hurried over and took Lizzie's hand to comfort the distraught girl. At Lizzie's wince, she looked down and gasped at the ugly red stripes. "Oh no, Owen." Tears flooded Becky's eyes.

Owen closed his eyes. "Ohhhh, Lizzie." He grimaced and gently stroked her hair.

Becky hurried to the corner, filled a basin with warm water, and snatched a rag from the pile. She ran back and began to gently soak Lizzie's hands.

Owen pulled Daniel aside. "What're we doing to do?"

"What do you mean?" Daniel stroked his beard.

"About Adam."

Daniel knitted his brows. "What about him?"

"If he gets his hands on the person who did this...." Owen shuddered. "Well, I don't know what he would do."

Daniel grimaced. "Me either. I will admit, that thought has crossed my mind."

"Do you want me to tell him?" the doctor offered.

"No, I'll do it. He's checking in on the trappers up the mountain this morning. I think I'll go to Katie. If anyone can soothe Adam's temper, it's her."

"Okay, I'll keep Lizzie here. Becky and I will look after her."

Daniel nodded. Walking out into the late fall sunshine, he was surprised to see Katie and his wife walking towards the café. He took a deep breath, whispered a prayer for wisdom, and hurried over to them.

"Daniel, Katie was in town. I hope you don't mind I invited her to join us." The serious look on his face frightened Louisa. "What is it?"

Daniel exhaled loudly. "I need to speak to you, Katie. It can't wait."

Katie's face fell. Her brother was seldom so serious. "What is it?"

"Not here. Come, we'll use Adam's office. You come too, Lou."

"Danny, you've got me worried. What's going on?" Katie asked once they were all seated.

He turned to look at his sister. "Lizzie's in the infirmary."

Katie sucked in a deep breath and stood to hurry to her.

"Katie." Daniel put a hand out to stop her. "She's okay. Owen and Becky are with her, but I need to tell you something."

Katie gingerly sat down. "I'm listening."

Daniel pursed his lips. "I found Lizzie at the picnic table by the lake in tears."

Katie frowned. "Why wasn't she at school?"

Daniel gripped both her hands. He took a deep, shaky breath. "She has two nasty red stripes on each hand. I believe the teacher struck her."

Louisa gasped, and her hand flew to her mouth.

Katie's face fell, and tears flooded to her eyes. "Who would do that? Who would strike a child?"

"I'm not sure. I imagine it's Miss Price, she's Lizzie's teacher and they've always been at odds."

Katie scowled. "She's always had it in for Lizzie. Ohhhh. I must go to her."

"Katie, before you do, what shall we do about Adam?"

Katie closed her eyes and shuddered. "He's not going to like this."

"Maybe we could keep it from him?" Daniel raised his brows.

She opened her eyes. "He'll find out when he sees her hands."

"Do you think he can control his anger?"

"I'll talk to him." Katie nodded. "It might pay for you to talk to Miss Price, before Adam does...." Katie grimaced. "I'm not sure what he'll say, he'd never strike a woman, but then no one has ever struck his child before, so I'm not so sure. If there was anything that would make Adam break his firmly held principles, it would be someone hurting his children."

Daniel nodded and looked up at his wife. "I'm sorry, Lou, I know I planned to take you for lunch, but I'm going to need an urgent meeting of the school committee. We can't have a tyrant teacher striking our children. We haven't had one so mean in a long time. Miss Fisher, the one you replaced, Katie, seems like a kitten compared to Miss Price."

Katie pursed her lips. "I never felt right about employing her."

Daniel shrugged. "It was out of my hands. She came with impeccable references. We've spoken to her a number of times about yelling at the children and keeping them back after class, or recess."

"Surely this is the final straw?" Louisa asked.

Daniel nodded and grimaced. "I just wish it hadn't been one of Adam's girls."

Katie squeezed her brother's hands. "Leave Adam to me. He's due home shortly. I'll talk to him. But first, I want to see Lizzie."

"Oh, my darling." Katie walked into the infirmary. Becky had the cool cloth against one of Lizzie's burning hands.

Owen paced back and forth, trying to calm himself. The thought of anyone ever striking a child was more than he could fathom. He strode over to talk to Katie. "She's okay, other than the bruises. She'll be in pain for a time, and those bruises will take time to heal, but they will heal." He clenched his jaw against his anger.

Katie nodded and hurried to Lizzie's bedside. She climbed up on the bed to take the girl in her arms and kissed her hair. "Darling, I'm so sorry."

Lizzie clung to her mother, and her tears came again.

* * * *

Adam grimaced as he rode down the mountain. He was earlier than he'd expected. It had been pretty straightforward in the end. Now he had a pile of paperwork to do. *You can't keep putting it off, Sergeant!* He scowled at the air. "I sure do hate filing reports, Eb. I wish you could do 'em for me." Ebony snorted and Adam laughed. "No, I wouldn't foist my tasks onto you." He entered the town and took a detour past the school. The girls would be at recess, and he always made sure to wave at them when he came past. Occasionally he stopped and joined in a ball game or a marbles battle. He sure did love children.

He slowed down as he passed. There was a ball game happening. He grinned. "I'll wager Lizzie is there somewhere." He spoke to his horse. But as he looked, he could see no one with auburn braids.

"Paaaaaa..."

Adam looked up abruptly and frowned. Anna ran headlong towards him. His gentle daughter was seldom so frantic, and it made his heart leap. He hauled Ebony to a stop and leapt off, falling to his knees before her. "Anna, what is it?"

Her eyes flooded with tears. "Pa, Lizzie's missing. I don't know where she went."

Adam scowled. "What do you mean missing? Isn't she at school?"

Anna swallowed, and her tears spilled over. Adam embraced her. "Darling, whatever is the matter?"

Anna pulled back, and Adam gave her his handkerchief. Her eyes grew wide, and her lips trembled. "Lizzie was fighting... with Amelia... and we tried to stop her..." Anna's breath came in gasps, and she struggled to get the words out. Overwhelmed, the girl burst into tears again. Callie noticed them at the side of the playground and ran over.

Adam stood up to talk to her. "Callie, do you know what this is about?" He took hysterical Anna in his arms again.

Callie bit her lip and nodded. Her eyes grew wide, and she couldn't keep the tremble from her lips or the tears from the corners of her eyes.

Adam squinted at her. "Callie Grace Morgan, I insist you tell me right now, what's going on here?"

Callie nodded and swallowed. "Teacher struck Lizzie." Her lip trembled.

Adam's eyebrows flew up. A fire rose in his heart. "What did you say?" The anger in her father's eyes frightened the fourteen-year-old.

"Pa, Lizzie was fighting with Amelia at morning recess, we pulled them apart, but Miss Price came out and hauled Lizzie away. She's awful mean. She slammed the door on us so we couldn't see what happened. All us seniors went to help in the junior class, but Anna told me when she got back to class, Lizzie was gone, and Miss Price was putting the strap back on the wall." Callie's voice faded out and her tears overflowed.

Adam brushed away her tears. He took a deep breath and closed his eyes. He exhaled loudly and set his jaw. "Where is Lizzie now?"

Callie shrugged. "No one knows, Pa. She must've run away."

Miss Price walked out and rang the bell. Adam clenched his teeth and tightened his fists. *Lizzie needs you, Adam.* A voice whispered in his soul. He exhaled loudly and embraced both girls. "Go back to class. I'll find her." His determined look sent a shiver through Callie. She nodded and grabbed Anna's hand. They hurried back to class. Adam watched them go, stood up and scowled. He clenched his jaw tightly. "How dare you strike my child," he said aloud, desperately fighting his urge to show Miss Price how it feels. *Never strike a woman.* He took a deep breath. *It's lucky for her she is a woman.* Adam clenched and unclenched his fists, took a deep breath and leapt on Ebony. *But for now, I have to find Lizzie.*

Adam galloped into town. His blood boiled, and his mind raced. He looked in all the places Lizzie liked to go. He couldn't find her. *Maybe she's gone home.* He turned towards the homestead.

"Adam." Katie had just stepped out of the infirmary. "Adam!" she called to him as he galloped past. He pulled Ebony to a stop and turned around.

"Katie. I have to find Lizzie. She's missing."

Katie lay her hand on Adam's knee and looked up at him. "She's in the infirmary. Daniel found her and brought her in."

Adam said nothing, he leapt off the horse, leaving her standing in the street and sprinted into the infirmary. Katie took Ebony's rein and led her to the hitching rail.

Adam fell to his knees by Lizzie's bedside, throwing his Stetson on the floor. "Lizzie, Darling." Lizzie threw herself in his arms. He held her, cradling her head and rocked back and forth. "Oh, my darling. I'm so sorry, Darling. I'm so sorry."

Owen and Becky observed the Mountie's clenched jaw and blazing eyes. He clung tightly to Lizzie and continued to soothe her.

At last, she sat back from him. "I'm sorry, Pa." She sniffed

Adam's face fell. "What on earth for?" He wiped away a tear from her cheek.

"I was fighting. Amelia called me Crazy Lizzie, over and over again. She wouldn't stop." Lizzie's tears came again. "It made me so angry I slapped her. I just wanted her to stop." Her lip trembled.

Adam closed his eyes. Lizzie may be impulsive, but she never lied.

"I pushed her to the ground and started hitting her. Anna and Callie pulled me off, and then Miss Price hauled me away and..." She stopped and turned her palms up to show him.

Adam gasped, and a sob escaped him. He lifted the small hands in his large ones. "Ohhhhh, my darling." His face curled up in pain. "Ohhh." Pain stabbed at his heart, and his blood began to boil again. He lifted both hands to his face and kissed them both, swiping his sleeve across his eyes. Katie joined him, kneeling beside him. She wrapped an arm around his waist. He looked at her and swallowed.

Adam looked back at Lizzie. He placed a hand on the back of her head and smiled kindly. "You don't have to be sorry, my darling. Fighting is wrong, of course, but no one should ever strike a child, not for any reason." His square jaw trembled with the effort of trying to control his anger. "You'll be okay, my darling. I promise." He embraced her again. "Oh, my darling girl. I'm so, so sorry." He kissed her hair.

"I'm okay, Pa. My hands hurt but I'm okay."

Adam stroked her cheek. "That's my brave girl." He kissed her hair again, then stood and turned to Katie. "I'll see you at home." He clenched his jaw, and his eyes blazed with fire. He strode out of the room.

"Oh no." Katie ran out after him. "Adam."

Adam stopped walking but didn't turn around. Katie ran to him and put her hand on his arm. "Adam..."

He turned around, fire burned in his eyes, and his face reddened. He clenched his fists tightly. "I won't abide someone striking one of my girls, Katie. I won't abide it, do you hear me!"

His stern voice and trembling lips frightened Katie. She put her hand on his cheek. "Anger only hurts you."

"I'm beyond anger, Katie. If that teacher was a man, I'd give him a taste of his own medicine." He exhaled loudly.

"What're you going to do?"

"I don't know yet." He gritted his teeth and walked away.

"Oh no." Katie hurried back into the clinic and petitioned her friends to pray with her. She had never seen him so angry in the entire time she'd known him.

Ten
There But For the Grace of God, Go I.

Adam galloped out of town. He wasn't going anywhere in particular, he just needed to think. "Lord, help me with this anger," he prayed earnestly. He rode for several hours and subconsciously made his way to the Price farm where Miss Adeline Price lived with her father. His blood began to boil as he approached, uncertain of what he would do or say. He leapt off his horse and strode towards the house. Raised voices coming from the barn stopped him. He silently walked towards the sound.

"...I don't care what you were doing, you're late. Do you think I wanna make my own supper?" Mr Price screamed at Adeline.

"But, Papa, I had a meeting, and I had to finish the grading..."

Adam heard a slap and a scream. Adeline flew back against the wall and hit her head. "You stupid woman, you're no better than your mother was. Useless. You wanted that job. You made me move to this godforsaken town and take on this pitiful farm so you could have the job you wanted." He hauled her to her feet and held her by the collar. "I ought to teach you a lesson about a woman's place."

"Papa..." Adeline cried. "I'm sorry."

Another slap and another cry. "I'll give you a reason to be sorry..."

Adam could bear no more. He strode in and grabbed Jim Price by the collar, yanking him away from his daughter. "Is this how you treat a woman?"

The man sneered. "She ain't a woman, she's my daughter."

"So? You shouldn't treat a woman this way." Adam looked towards Miss Price, her face was bleeding and eyes wide with fear. He was overcome with compassion for the teacher. "She doesn't deserve this."

"What would you know, Sergeant? She's useless, doesn't look after me, doesn't do what I ask, always off at the school. I ought to really teach her that a man is the boss, and she ought to do what I say."

Adam seethed and thrust the man up against the wall holding his collar tightly against the man's throat. "You can't treat her that way, Jim. She's your daughter." He choked on the word. "You should love her, not hurt her."

"What would you know? Your women obey ya. It must be nice having that red jacket – make people do as you say."

Adam tightened his grip. He pulled the man close to his face. "I would NEVER lift a hand to any of my girls, or any women, ever!"

"You just wait, Sergeant, wait till one of 'em disobeys ya. Be that feisty little redhead, I bet."

Adam's lip quivered as he desperately fought his anger. "No matter what my girls do, I could never raise a hand to them. That is not the way to deal with it. Force won't make them do what you want." He worked exceedingly hard to keep his voice calm.

Price sneered. "Like you're doing now?"

Adam pursed his lips, and pushed the man away. Mr Price fell into a pile of straw. Adam nodded and took a deep breath. "You're right. This isn't the way. But if you lay a hand on your daughter or anyone else again, I'm arresting you for assault."

"Huh, I got the law on my side, Sergeant. Law says she's my property. I can do what I like with her."

Adam shook his head. The law was so corrupt sometimes. "I'll find a way. Now go and cool off." Adam stood stoically and fixed his gaze on the man until he scrambled to his feet and slunk out the door.

He turned to Miss Price, who sat sobbing against the wall. He took a deep breath and noticed the red mark on the side of her face, and a small cut and streak of blood that ran down her cheek.

She sniffed and raised frightened eyes to him. "I suppose you're here to tell me off for striking your daughter."

Adam sighed deeply. He was surprised to find he was filled with compassion for her. He squatted down in front of her and lifted his hand. She flinched and covered her face. But Adam smiled and lay the hand gently on her shoulder. "Are you okay?" His voice was kind and gentle.

The woman snapped her head up, surprised at his gentle tone. She shrugged. "Just bruises, nothing I'm not used to."

Adam closed his eyes and sighed. He put his hand in his top pocket and pulled out his clean handkerchief. He lifted it to her cheek, and she took it from him and wiped the blood away. She passed it back to him.

"Keep it, Miss Price." He smiled kindly.

"Thank you, Sergeant."

"Come on. I'll take you to town. We'll get those bruises and cuts seen to." His eyes were kind and his smile compassionate.

She frowned and shook her head at his extended hand. "How do I know you won't beat me the second we get out of sight?"

Adam shuddered and gently touched her arm. "Miss Price, I would NEVER hit a woman or child, no matter what they had done. Women should be protected by men, not hurt by them." He gritted his teeth and the determination in his eyes let her know he was serious.

"I'm not sure I can stand. I sprained my ankle when I fell."

"Do you mind?" He gestured to her foot.

She shook her head, and lifted her skirts to expose her lower leg. Adam gently felt her ankle. The woman grimaced twice. "This is a pretty bad sprain." He smiled compassionately. "Come, I'll get you to the infirmary."

Before the woman could protest, Adam scooped her up in his arms and put her on his horse. Leaping up behind her, he put his arms around her to clutch the reins and headed to town. Neither spoke for the entire trip, but Adam's mind was busy. *This woman has suffered so much. How can I possibly be angry when she is acting the only way she knows? She's dominated by him, which explains why she dominates the children. Violence begets violence, after all.* He sighed as they entered town. *She needs our compassion and help, not our rage. Help me, Lord.*

Daniel walked down the street. The committee had unanimously decided the teacher needed to go. They'd had enough of her tirades, and now that it had escalated to violence, it was the last straw. They'd contacted her previous school and found out she'd left for the same reason. The good reference they'd given had been simply to get her out of their school. Daniel halted and paused, noticing Adam ride in with a very beaten and bruised Miss Price. The pastor's face fell, and his lip trembled. He closed his eyes and shuddered. *Oh no! Lord, I pray Adam didn't do that....* It broke his heart to even think that of Adam. He'd never dream of believing it, but then no one had struck his child before, and he'd never seen the Mountie as angry as he had been. He didn't know what Adam was capable of when someone he loved was hurt.

Adam approached and pulled Ebony to a halt. Daniel's eyes asked the question.

"Help me get her to the infirmary." Adam leapt off and hitched Ebony to the rail.

Daniel's wide eyes and grimace still held the question.

"I didn't hit her, Dan."

Daniel closed his eyes and exhaled loudly. "I'm glad to hear that."

Adam lifted the woman down and carried her into the infirmary.

Owen leapt up and gasped. "Adam?"

"I found Miss Price in this state; caught her father beating her." He closed his eyes and grimaced as though the very thought of it disgusted him. He lay her gently on the bed, and Owen hurried over. Becky noticed she had Adam's handkerchief in her hand. Adam raised it to her cheek which was bleeding again.

Owen hovered over her and began to assess her injuries. "Can you tell me what happened, Miss Price?"

She nodded sadly and smiled at Adam. "The Sergeant rescued me. Pa was on one of his rampages."

Owen could see old, partially healed bruises on her neck where her ripped collar had fallen open. He closed his eyes and gripped her shoulder gently.

"I'll take it from here, Adam. You go home to your family. Katie took Lizzie home about half an hour ago."

Adam nodded, tipped his hat to the woman and strode out. He walked into his office to find Dan standing inside, leaning against the wall.

"What are you doing here, Pastor?" Adam gritted his teeth.

"I came to check on you."

Adam's brows flew up. He thrust his hands over his chest and scowled at his friend. "I'm not impressed that you think I could hurt a woman, Daniel."

Daniel put his hand on Adam's shoulder. "Forgive me. I should've known better than to doubt you. I just knew how angry you'd be over what happened to Lizzie."

Adam gave his friend a resigned smile, gripped his shoulder and nodded. He walked to the coffeepot and poured two cups. "I've never been so angry in all my life! I was frightened at my own rage for a time. But there is one thing that I am just not capable of, it's hurting a woman or child." He gritted his teeth. "It just goes against every cell in my body."

Daniel nodded and stroked his beard. "I know, I really do know that. I'm sorry, Brother."

"I understand, Dan. I'd've probably thought the same if I were you."

"So why were you there?" Daniel gratefully received the coffee cup Adam passed him, and both men sat on either side of the desk.

"I'm not sure why I went there, what I planned to do. I think I just wanted to look her in the eye. I sure am glad I did go." Adam gritted his teeth. "To think of that man beating his daughter around like that, and it's obviously been going on for a long time. The poor woman was terrified of him. He was twice her size, and she had no defence against him."

"So what did you do?"

Adam grimaced. "Gave him a little fear, too."

Daniel raised his brows.

"I just pinned him to the wall and told him a few home truths."

"So, have you got over your anger at her?"

Adam thrust his arms over his chest and leaned back in his chair. "I'll never be okay with someone striking any of my girls or my wife." He gritted his teeth. "I would die defending them from harm, any woman or child for that matter." He sighed and ran his fingers through his hair. "But when I saw her in that pitiful state, that brute beating her around, I was filled with compassion for her. She's only acting from what she knows. Violence begets violence. We are all products of our upbringing after all."

"True, but you are nothing like The Commander."

Adam nodded, and his mouth curled up at the sides. "No." He paused for a moment and ran his fingers through his hair again. He took a sip of his coffee and placed his cup down. "But I could've been. I was pretty bitter and hurt when I first came here." He looked up at Daniel and grinned. "Then I met a mad red-headed pastor, and life changed for me." They both laughed. "Honestly, between the Lord, You, Katie, our family and friends, I'm so filled up with love and joy that I couldn't possibly be angry and bitter for long. If I'd been stuck with Delia and still in the darkness over my past indiscretions, my life would be so different. I might well have been like The Commander, perhaps even worse."

Daniel grinned. He leaned forward and gripped Adam's shoulder. "I'm glad to have been an influence on you, Adam. You're a fine man. Your compassion is admirable; you've had a huge influence in my life too. I'm a better man for your friendship." The two men nodded to each other and simultaneously took a slurp of their coffee. Daniel stroked his beard. "The school committee met to discuss Miss Price earlier."

"Oh?"

Daniel nodded and stroked his beard again. "We have unanimously decided to terminate her employment. We can't have a tyrant and a bully in our school."

Adam nodded and screwed up his face. "Is there no other option?"

"What are you saying?" Daniel tilted his head and furrowed his brows.

"Everybody can be redeemed. I didn't deserve the mercy I was granted. There but for the grace of God go I."

Daniel nodded again. "We are meeting with her this evening, if she's up to it." He glanced at the clock. "I need to go, Adam. I'm glad you've let go of your anger." He stood and strode out the door.

*   *   *   *

"Miss Price, I'm sorry to say, we are going to have to terminate your employment at Douglas Falls Public School." Mr Fox was reluctant to be the bearer of bad news, but as the head of the school committee and town council, the job fell to him.

Miss Price sat stoically in the front row of the church, her head down, desperately trying not to cry.

"Do you have anything to say..." Daniel stopped abruptly and looked up as the door swung open. Adam stood in the doorway, holding Lizzie's hand.

All faces held the question. Adam marched to the front with Lizzie in tow. "I'm sorry to interrupt your meeting, but my daughter and I would like to say something, if you don't mind?"

Daniel and the council members looked at each other and shrugged. The pastor nodded to his friend.

Miss Price shuffled nervously in her seat, refusing to make eye contact with Adam.

"Miss Price, I'm not okay with you striking my child. There is never ever an excuse to hit a child or a woman, not ever." He gritted his teeth tightly. Miss Price hung her head and scowled.

Adam's tone changed, and he smiled kindly. "However..." The woman looked up in shock, expecting his anger but was surprised to see kindness in his eyes. "I observed your father's treatment of you, and I know you have only been acting on what your upbringing has taught you to do. I know a bit about that. I too had a father who was a tyrant and a bully. He never struck me, but his words sure did. It's by the grace of God that I've been able to rise above that."

Adam paused, squeezed Lizzie's hand gently, then turned to address the council. "Gentlemen, my daughter and I have come to plead Miss Price's case and ask you not to terminate her employment."

All eyes widened. The teacher snapped her head up, and her eyes grew wide. Adam addressed her. "Miss Price, I've secured a place for you, should you want it, the small cottage next door to the Atkins place on the corner of Mainstreet. I'm prepared to fix it up for you free of charge so you can live there away from your father." He paused and then squinted at her. "I ask you to consider how you treat the children." He winked at Lizzie. "Love and kindness is much more effective than anger and violence. Now my daughter has something to say to you."

Miss Price nodded and bit her lip. Lizzie walked up to her. "Miss Price. I'm sorry for fighting. I know I'm not supposed to, but Amelia makes me so mad, and sometimes I feel like she's your favourite, but you don't see how mean she is to the rest of us at recess." She looked back at her father. "But I know that words are no excuse for violence, and I'm sorry. Pa taught me it's okay to defend yourself or to protect other people, and sometimes when you're doing that, you have to be tough because the people doing the hurting are tough. But if it's just words, we should find a way to love the person and pray for them, not be hateful towards them. I'm sorry, Miss Price." Lizzie threw her arms around the teacher's neck.

Caught off guard, the teacher sucked in a breath and returned Lizzie's embrace closing her eyes as she held the girl. Quite unaccustomed to such affection, she sniffed, smiled and lay her head against Lizzie's. Tears streaked down her cheeks. Lizzie pulled back from her, and the woman wiped at her tears and at last found her voice. "Thank you, Miss Lizzie, and I really am sorry that I struck you. I promise I won't ever do it again, to any child."

Lizzie smiled and hugged her again. "I forgive you, Miss Price." She stepped back. "Do you forgive me too, for fighting?" Sorrow was etched over the girl's face.

Miss Price smiled. "Of course, Lizzie." She looked up at Adam. "I thank you for your kindness, understanding and forgiveness, Sergeant." She stood and walked to him. "I'm sorry for striking Lizzie. I promise it won't happen again."

Adam nodded and squeezed the woman's arm. "Thank you, Miss Price. Would you take me up on the offer of the cabin? I think away from the tyranny of your father, you'll learn compassion and love instead of hate and violence."

She nodded. "But what about Pa? He'll be angry."

Adam smiled. "Your father left town about an hour ago. He's gone back to his brother's farm in Lethbridge."

Miss Price's face fell. "He has?"

"I suggested that maybe some time apart would be healthy, and you would be looked after by the town. Somehow he got the impression I'd be breathing down his neck and keeping my eye on him." Adam grinned and raised his brows. "I'm not sure why he thought that."

The men on the council chuckled, looked at each other and nodded. Mr Fox stood and came around from the table. "Very well, Miss Price, we will keep you on, but you must remember that our school values kindness and love, not violence and hate."

The woman's eyes shone, and her tears fell unbidden. "I understand, and I promise going forward, I will change my ways." She smiled at Lizzie. "Will you help me?"

Lizzie's face lit up. "Yes, Ma'am. Will you help me when Amelia calls me Crazy Lizzie?"

"Of course. I'm sorry, Lizzie, you most certainly are not crazy."

Daniel stood. "It seems there is nothing more to say. We will get the cabin ready for you by the end of the week. In the meantime, Miss Price, we'll find you a family in town to stay with and help you fetch your things from your father's house."

"That is most kind." The woman's lip trembled. Kindness was very unfamiliar to her.

*　　*　　*　　*

"You're an extraordinary man, Adam Morgan. To offer forgiveness like that. It was truly humbling." Daniel closed his Bible and sipped at his coffee. He sniffed and sucked in a deep breath. "That was better than any sermon I have ever heard."

Adam smiled. "I'm not extraordinary. I just know the mercy and grace of undeserved forgiveness and the chance to start over. If I'd not been granted such favour, I shudder to think where I'd be. I figured Miss Price deserves that too. The woman has been shown very little kindness in her life. How can a person grow up to be kind if they've never had any kindness offered to them? The more kindness we show her, the more she'll show the children."

Daniel nodded, sniffed, and swiped at his eyes. "I'm very moved by your example of humility and forgiveness, Adam. Perhaps you should be the pastor."

Adam grimaced. "No! You're much more suited to that task than me. How can I not forgive her, when so many have forgiven me?" A tight smile crossed his face, and tears rushed to the corners of the Mountie's eyes. "There, but for the Grace of God, go I! My mother used to say that all the time. Those who are forgiven much ought to forgive much."

Daniel merely nodded. "I've never heard such an eloquent and succinct sermon on forgiveness and grace. Yes, the Lord has forgiven us unconditionally for the sin and filth in our lives. How can we not turn around and offer the same forgiveness to those who have sinned against us?"

"In all honesty, it was Lizzie's idea to come to the meeting. When I told her about how Miss Price had suffered, she burst into tears and felt so much sorrow for her that she insisted we come and defend her."

"She's a remarkable little girl, Adam."

The Mountie nodded and smiled broadly. "Yes, she is, she's impulsive sometimes and rushes in headlong without thinking, but she has the kindest heart. Lizzie genuinely doesn't like to see others suffer. If she can do something about it, she will."

Daniel raised his brows. "I think there is a lot of her father in her. You're the same way, Adam."

"There but for the grace of God go I." Adam scratched his chin.

"And I." Daniel nodded and drained his coffee.

Eleven
Happy Birthday Rose

"Can you believe it's been two months since Christmas?" Alice commented as they trudged to school together on the last day of February.

"Yes, only four months to go." Sadie flung her satchel over her shoulder.

"I can't believe we are more than halfway through our teaching certificates." Mandy shivered and pulled her coat tighter around her shoulders. "I'm actually going to be a teacher."

"If we pass the boards." Rose rolled her eyes.

"You will." Alice squeezed her friend's arm. "You've got the highest grades of all of us."

They walked in silence for a moment and Rose sighed.

"Missing home?" Alice put her arm around her friend's waist

"Yeah, I guess."

"Missing Marcus, more like." Sadie grinned.

Rose smiled. "Yes, of course I miss him. But it's more than that. I'm missing all the family events and birthdays. Callie just turned fifteen, and I wasn't there to celebrate it. I missed Ma's birthday last year and Lizzie's, and Hope's and Anna's."

"And yours is in a few days, and you feel lonesome for them all?" Alice squeezed her arm.

Rose nodded and grimaced.

"I don't know what it's like to have a big family to be lonesome for." Sadie shrugged. "But I sure do miss my parents and my home. It must be even harder, especially having a young man waiting for you too."

"I know being here is the right thing for me. I'm certain it's where God wants me to be, and Pa says the sacrifices we make are worth it in the long run, so I'm happy to be here. It's just well...." Rose clasped the cameo at her neck that Marcus had given her and sighed.

"Hard when you've got people waiting for you back home you miss." Alice flashed her a sad smile.

Rose nodded again.

"Well, we will make your seventeenth birthday a day to remember for you, Rose. We'll spend it together, just the four of us. It's really helpful it falls on Saturday and we'll have a whole day to celebrate." Mandy squeezed her arm.

"What do you have in mind?" Rose squinted at her friend.

"I'm not sure yet, but we'll think of something. Leave it all to us." Alice winked at the other girls. They winked back at her.

Rose looked from beaming face to beaming face and squinted at them. "Oh, now I'm almost afraid of what you girls are planning."

"You should be." Sadie chuckled and gave the other girls a knowing grin as they followed Rose into their classroom.

* * * *

"Rose, look at all these parcels." Alice laughed as she helped Rose carry them to her room on Friday after class.

"I know. I can't believe it." Rose placed the parcels on her desk and swiped away a tear.

"It must be wonderful to know you are so loved." Alice grinned. "We'll leave you to your parcels." The three girls turned to leave.

Rose gripped Alice's arm. "Oh no, won't you please stay? It's always better when you have someone to share it with."

Alice nodded. The three girls sat around the room and cheered over each package as Rose opened them.

Rose gushed over the gifts, and through joyful tears, described each precious family member that had sent the gifts. There was a parcel from the Randalls, one from the Fergusons and another from her Coleman cousins.

The largest parcel came from her family. Her mother and sisters sent her mostly handmade gifts, clothing and things she'd need.

Even Lizzie, who hated sewing, had sat at the machine and created a simple but elegant new skirt for her older sister, in a soft pink crepe. Rose could see a lot of help from her mother, and few of Lizzie's characteristic rushed seams. She chuckled. "I'm so touched that Lizzie would do this for me." She smiled at Alice. There were long letters from each person, and she gasped as she opened a small parcel from her father; it was a pretty signet ring. "Oh, Pa." Tears washed down her face as she slipped the gold ring on her finger and admired the purple stone that sparkled in the lamplight.

Marcus's gift was tied up in brown paper and rawhide, and the girls laughed together, remembering Leo's reaction. "I'll wager Marcus did it deliberately." Sadie slumped down on the small trunk couch.

Rose untied the rawhide and carefully opened the paper. Alice took it from her and folded it carefully for reuse later. The heavy gift was wrapped up in a new white towel. "A thoughtful bonus. I can always use more towels." Rose unwrapped the towel, and all the girls gasped. "Oh, Marcus." She sniffed and wiped away a tear.

It was a small jewellery box that Marcus had obviously made himself. On the top was carved a rose, and Marcus had carefully painted it red. Rose grinned. She ran her hands over the delicate carving and then opened the box. "Oh, Marcus." Red velvet lined the inside and the top of the box was engraved with the verses from 1st Corinthians 13:4-8.

Love suffereth long, and is kind; love envieth not; love vaunteth not itself, is not puffed up, doth not behave itself unseemly, seeketh not its own, is not provoked, taketh not account of evil, rejoiceth not in unrighteousness, but rejoiceth with the truth; beareth all things, believeth all things, hopeth all things, endureth all things. Love never faileth.

They had shared the verses together many times as promises to each other in their growing courtship. Around the verse was engraved a rambling rose, which made Rose laugh. "Sometimes, when I get overexcited, and I chatter too much, Marcus calls me his Rambling Rose." The girls laughed.

Beneath the verse and the engraved rose was written.

Happy 17th Birthday, Rose.
With all my love.
Marcus.

Rose sighed and hung her head. Alice stood up to embrace her. "I know it's awful not being with them, but they all love you, so very much. Just look around at all these parcels. It has to be wonderful to know you are that loved."

Rose nodded and smiled. Sadie pointed at the open box. "What's in that envelope?" She grinned at the other girls. Alice and Mandy were clearly trying to stifle grins.

Rose squinted at them suspiciously, but the girls flashed her innocent faces. She shook her head and lifted the brown envelope. On the front was written, 'Rose,' in Marcus's handwriting.

She opened it expecting to find a letter from Marcus; instead, it was a small card. On the front, it simply had a golden rose embossed on it. She grinned. "I guess it's easy to buy cards with pictures of Roses on them, convenient when your girl is named Rose, I suppose."

"Open it, Rose." Mandy leapt up and down excitedly. She couldn't keep the secret much longer. She was bursting to tell her friend. Alice and Sadie glared at her, and she clamped her hands to her mouth but couldn't keep the sparkle from her eyes.

"What's going on you three?" Rose looked from face to face. All three girls refused to comment. She screwed up her face and opened the card.

Rose gasped. "Oh, Marcus." It was an invitation of sorts.

A carriage shall arrive for you at 6:00 p.m. out the front of the boarding house. Formal dress.

Rose shrieked. "Is that what you've been hiding? Oh, is Marcus coming for me?" Her eyes flooded with tears, and she held the card to her heart.

"You'll see." Alice wore a wide smile. "Just be ready, and it's formal dress."

"But I don't have a formal dress." Rose frowned, thinking of the few Sunday dresses she had in her wardrobe.

"Yes, you do." Sadie had slipped out to her own room and returned with the most beautiful dress Rose had ever seen. It was a pale lavender gown with a full skirt adorned with thousands of sparkling beads. It had short-capped sleeves and a scooped neckline.

"Oh, that's so beautiful, Sadie, but I couldn't ask to use your dress."

"It's not my dress, Rose. It's yours." Sadie beamed and held it out to her.

"That's too much. I can't let you do that."

"We didn't do it. Your father did." Mandy blurted out.

Rose screwed up her face. "Pa sent me a dress?"

Alice gripped her hand. "No, your pa sent us the money, and we chose it for you."

Rose smiled through her tears. "Oh, Pa, he's so thoughtful. I bet they conspired together. It's just like them." She grinned. "And they used my friends to make it all happen." She thrust her hands on her hips and feigned hurt. The three girls laughed heartily.

"They sure did. Swore us to secrecy too. It's been awful hard to keep your secret." Mandy rolled her eyes. "I've nearly blurted it out so many times, especially since you were so sad." She squeezed Rose's arm.

Rose hugged each of them. "Well, this is going to be a wonderful night, and I'm so grateful to you all. Where is Marcus taking me?"

"Nice try, Rose. We aren't telling you anymore." Alice shook her head. "Our lips are sealed."

"Alright, keep your secrets." Rose grinned and hurried off to get ready.

* * * *

Alice looked at her friend in the mirror and slipped her arm around her waist. "Oh, Rose, you look like Cinderella."

Rose's dark hair hung long, cascading down her back. Sadie had produced a pair of long, dangly, lavender-coloured earrings and a matching necklace that she had purchased at Adam's request.

They had also bought a matching silk shawl and new ivory boots. The folds of fabric on the full skirt hung beautifully and softly, with shimmering beads that sparkled in the lamplight. The girls had even applied a little bit of makeup and lip colour. The picture was quite breath-taking.

Rose's eyes shone, and she turned to embrace each of her friends. "Thank you, girls. I couldn't have done this without you."

"I told you it would be a birthday to remember." Alice winked at her.

There was a knock at her door. "Miss Rose, there's a carriage out front for you."

Rose opened the door. "Thank you, Mrs Green, I'll be right down."

The older woman put her hand to her face and gasped. "Oh, Miss Rose, you look quite beautiful. That young man of yours is gonna faint clean away when he sees you."

Rose blushed. "Thank you, Mrs Green."

The girls walked with Rose out to the waiting carriage. "Good evening, Miss Morgan." A footman in red serge stood before the open door.

"Constable Scott?" Rose grinned.

"Yes, Ma'am." He tipped his head. "I'm to be your driver for the evening."

"Can you tell me where we're going?"

Constable Scott reached his hand out to her and helped her into the carriage. "You'll see, Ma'am."

Rose nodded, took her seat, and grinned. *I can't believe all the fuss and all the expense Marcus and Pa have gone to, for my birthday.*

The trip was less was then ten minutes and they pulled up outside one of the most expensive restaurants in town.

The carriage door opened, and Constable Scott reached his hand out to help Rose down. Ensuring she was steady on her feet, he gave her his arm. "Miss Morgan, my orders are to escort you into the restaurant. Will you allow me?"

"Of course, Constable." She grinned and took his arm.

"Good evening, Constable, M'lady." The doorman nodded to them and opened the door. The Mountie led her inside, and there stood Marcus, wearing a fine new suit.

"Marcus." Rose longed to run to him and throw herself in his arms, but this was not the place. Instead, she grinned, and he took her hand.

"Thank you, Constable."

The Mountie nodded, turned abruptly and walked out the door.

Marcus took Rose's hand and kissed her cheek. "Happy Birthday, Rose." His shining eyes examined her and gave away his approval of her appearance. The server led them to their pre-arranged table, and Marcus pulled her chair out for her, kissed her on the cheek and took the chair opposite her.

"Oh, Marcus, this is all so lovely, but it's too much. I don't want you spending all your money just to say happy birthday to me. I'd've been happy with a picnic by the creek."

"I know, Rose, that's one thing I love about you. But I know how homesick and lonely you've been feeling, and your pa suggested I do something really special to show how much you are loved. They all miss you so much, and they helped me do this for you."

Marcus kissed the delicate white hand he held and looked deeply into her eyes. "You look absolutely breath-taking, Rose. I nearly passed out when you walked in just now."

"Oh, Marcus."

The whole evening was magical, and Rose was in a daze. They shared a romantic supper together, and Marcus was a true gentleman. He paid for the meal and walked her out. The carriage and its red-serge footman waited to escort them back to the boarding house.

Rose gripped Marcus's hand and climbed up into the carriage. "Where're you staying?"

"The boarding house again. Same room as last time."

"And how long will you be staying?"

"I have to catch Sunday's early train. I hate to miss church, but my boss only gave me one day off, so I need to be back for work on Monday."

"I'm just glad to have you here. I've been so lonesome for you and my family."

"I know, Rose. They all miss you terribly too. It broke their heart not to be with you for your birthday."

"I know, but it's much too expensive for my family to come here or for me to go home just for a weekend. I already feel bad about all the money you've spent." Her cheeks blushed red, and her eyes darkened.

Marcus squeezed her hand. "Hey, you must never feel bad. I want to give you the whole world, Rose. This is just the tip of the iceberg."

"You're the whole world to me, Marcus. You would be if you arrived with cheese sandwiches in tatty clothing." The shine returned to her eyes and she grinned.

"I know that. I just wanted today to be extra special. Since you live in the city for the moment, I thought we'd do it the city way. Of course, it'll be hard to compete with this birthday in the years to come."

"Oh, Marcus, I don't need you to. It's the thought that counts." Constable Scott pulled the carriage over in front of the boarding house, and Marcus climbed out first, and reached his hand up to help Rose down.

"Thank you, Constable, much obliged. I know this isn't usually in your job description."

Jonny took Marcus's outstretched hand and shook it. "When it comes to an officer's family, anything is in the job description. Happy Birthday, Miss Morgan." The Mountie tipped his Stetson to her.

"Thank you, Constable."

Jonny clucked to the horse and drove away.

Marcus put his arm out to her. She took it with a grin and allowed him to lead her. He paused in front of the stairs. "Before I take you up to your room, will you come to my room for a moment? I have a gift for you."

"You've done enough, Marcus. It isn't necessary for you to do more."

"It isn't really anything much."

"Okay, sure." She smiled, and he took her hand and led her down the hallway towards his room.

"I'm sorry my room is so dark and dingy. It's the catacombs for me." Marcus chuckled as he swung the door open.

Rose laughed. "It sure has that feeling about it. I'm glad my room is on the second floor and has a window to let light in. I feels like a dungeon down here."

He closed the door, wrapped his arms around her and kissed her deeply. When he pulled away, he put his hands on her waist and grinned. "I've been dying to do that all evening."

"Me too." Rose's cheeks reddened.

"Rose Morgan, you are so lovely. I can't believe how very blessed I am."

"Me too."

"That dress is exquisite."

Rose turned around, making the beads sparkle in the low lamp light. "The girls chose it for me."

"I know. They did an exceptional job."

"Oh, but it's so expensive."

"Hush, no complaints. You deserve to have at least one extravagant dress. You never know when you might need to be Cinderella."

"Like when my Prince Charming comes for me?"

"Exactly." He winked at her.

"So, was that kiss my gift?"

Marcus grinned. "Yes, but I do have a small gift for you."

"The jewellery box was enough. It's beautiful, thank you for all the work you put into it."

"It was my pleasure, Rose."

A wide smile crossed her face. "Awfully handy that your girl is named after a flower."

"Sure is. Suits her too. Roses are about the most beautiful flowers there are and the best smelling. Just like my beautiful girl." He stroked her cheek and winked at her, then pulled a small gift from his pocket.

It was a photograph her father had taken of the two of them on Christmas day. RNWMP officers were given cameras as investigative tools, and he'd taken many family photos with his. This one was of her and Marcus standing in front of the Christmas Tree. Marcus had made a small wooden frame for it.

"Thank you, Marcus. It's lovely."

"I have one exactly the same next to my bed, Rose. That was the happiest Christmas of my life."

"Mine too."

"Now, Miss Morgan, will you allow me to walk you to your room?"

"You don't want me in your room anymore?"

"It's not that. It's just that I know there are three girls up there who are dying to hear all about your night out with Prince Charming."

Rose laughed her musical laugh, and Marcus grinned. It was one of his favourite sounds.

They climbed the stairs, and Marcus remembered Leo. "I am so thankful Leo is not here this semester."

"Yes, it's nice not to have to look over my shoulder all day." She grimaced. "He really made me feel uncomfortable."

"Not as uncomfortable as I made him." Marcus sniggered.

Rose laughed in spite of herself. They reached her room, and Rose turned the doorknob to go in. Marcus put his hand on her arm. "Just wait a minute, Rose."

"What for?"

"Just before you go in, I just want to tell you I love you so very much." He stroked her cheek and kissed her.

Rose tilted her head to the side and squinted at him. "You're acting weird, Marcus. What's going on?"

Marcus shrugged nonchalantly. "Nothing. Can't a man just kiss his girl and tell her he loves her?"

Rose grinned. "Of course." She turned the handle, pushed the door open, and got the surprise of her life.

"Ohhhhhh," she gasped and put both hands to her face, and wept.

Sitting on the bed, at her desk, and on the trunk, were her parents and all of her sisters.

Marcus put his arm around her. She quickly regained her composure and ran to her father, who stood to embrace her. "Oh, Pa."

"Happy birthday, Darling," he whispered against her hair, his voice trembled as he kissed her.

"I can't believe you're here." Rose turned to embrace her mother.

"Happy birthday, Rose, Darling." Her mother squeezed her.

She hugged each of her sisters and sat down on the bed between her parents. Marcus leaned against the wall as there was nowhere left to sit.

"What're you all doing here?" Rose brushed at the tears forming in her eyes.

"Tomorrow is my daughter's seventeenth birthday, Rose. You didn't honestly think I was going to miss it, did you?" Adam put his arm around her.

"But in your letter, you said you couldn't make it."

"I know. Please forgive the untruths. We wanted to surprise you."

"Oh, Pa, this is the best birthday surprise ever."

"You look beautiful, my darling. How did Marcus manage to stay on his feet?" Adam raised his brows to Marcus.

The young man chuckled and thrust his hands in his pockets. "Wasn't easy, Sir. She took my breath away."

"I know what you mean, Son. She's beautiful, my Rosie." Adam winked at Katie. "Gets it from her beautiful ma."

Katie shook her head and grinned. "Adam." He still made her blush after eighteen years of marriage.

"Where are you staying, Pa?"

"The Grand Hotel just down the street. We thought you might like to stay with us for the weekend." He raised his eyebrows at her.

"But Marcus is staying here."

"No, I'm not." Marcus crossed his arms. "Mrs Green, just let me use the room to surprise you. I've got a room at the Grand as well."

Rose looked at them all, and tears flooded her eyes. "Pa, how can you afford all this? I feel bad you're spending all your money."

"I told you, Darling. I've kept every cent of the pay-out from the RNWMP to spend on my girls as you grow up."

"Pa." Rose hugged him tightly.

"Your ma and Callie packed you an overnight bag for the weekend, and you're coming to the hotel with us."

Rose tipped her head to the side and grinned at him. "Is that a command, Sergeant?"

"Yep." Adam winked at her.

"Well, then, I must obey." Rose grinned, added a few more items to the bag, and they headed for the door.

Their Mountie footman waited out front to escort them to the hotel. "Thank you, Constable Scott." Adam sat next to the young Mountie. Inside, the carriage was cramped. Hope sat on Marcus's knee, and they all squeezed in together.

The family entered the Grand Hotel, and Rose's eyes grew wide. Adam led her into their room and her mouth fell open. "This isn't a room, it's a suite."

"Yes. Your ma and I are in that room. Callie and you will sleep in the second room and the other four girls in the third room; there's a common area and our own bathroom through there."

"It's just about bigger than our house." Rose glanced around and drank in the lush surroundings. "At least before you extended it, Pa."

Adam nodded, lowering himself into the armchair. "Yes, and we have it until Sunday, so let's enjoy it."

"Yes, Sir." Her eyes glinted, and she ran and leapt onto the bed in her room.

"Still a lot of little girl in her." Adam chuckled.

Rose walked back out with shining eyes. "Where is your room?" She gripped Marcus's arm.

"Ground floor." He laughed. "It's the catacombs for me!"

"But you're most welcome up here with us, Son. In the daytime!" Adam furrowed his brows in a mock frown at Marcus.

"I understand, Sir." Marcus grinned.

* * * *

The weekend was over all too quickly. Constable Scott and another young recruit arrived in two cars to drive the family to the station.

Rose nudged Marcus, and he followed her gaze. Constable Scott's eyes danced, and cheeks reddened as he helped Callie into the car. Rose raised her brows when he lingered for a time before releasing her hand. Callie looked shyly up at him, and her own cheeks coloured. Marcus squeezed Rose's hand.

"Don't say anything to Pa." Rose mouthed to him.

Marcus winked at her and chuckled. "Don't worry, I won't."

Rose clung to her father. "I love you, Pa. Thank you so much for my birthday surprise."

"It's my pleasure, Darling. Your ma, your sisters, and I have been awfully lonesome for you, and we couldn't be apart on your birthday." He kissed her and turned to carry their cases to the train.

Rose turned to Marcus. "I'm really going to miss you. Thank you for my birthday surprises." She grinned.

"You deserve it all and so much more, Rose. I love you."

"I love you too. I can't wait to see you again."

"Me either." He looked around to see if her father was watching and kissed her gently.

Adam did see; he raised his eyebrows and shook his head nostalgically. Marcus released her, and they all headed for the train. Rose waited with Constable Scott. He tipped his hat at Callie, and she blushed as she got on the train. Adam caught that too and shook his head sadly. He knew it was only a matter of time before she too, caught the eye of a young man.

Adam sighed and ran his fingers through his hair as the train pulled out of the station. "I miss her already." He shook his head and Katie nodded her agreement

Twelve
Adam's Worst Nightmare

"Hey Phillips, what's your problem?" a man called across the bar.

"Shuddup! I aint got no problems," Phillips fired back.

"You was much nicer when you was a policeman!" The man approached Phillips and slumped into the chair opposite his friend.

"Yeah, well, I haven't been a policeman for eight years!" Phillips gritted his teeth and thumped the table. "Thanks to that no good Morgan."

"You been complaining about that family for years. Why don't you do somefin' about 'em or shut up. I been listenin' to you whine for too long."

Phillips sculled his whiskey and tapped his glass loudly to the bartender. The man walked over and slopped whiskey into the glass. "Leave the bottle."

The bartender nodded, placed down the bottle and walked away.

Phillips lifted the glass to his mouth, threw his head back and drank the whole thing in one go. He let out a loud sigh and thrust the glass on the table. Drops of whiskey ran down the sides of his mouth, and he swiped at his rough unkempt beard. "You know what, McDonald. You're right. It's high time I got my revenge." He squinted his eyes.

McDonald grinned. "What are ya gonna do?"

A maniacal smile crossed Phillips' face. "He's a family man. I'll attack his family. It'll be good to get that fickle woman back for ruining my career."

"What woman?"

Phillips slopped more whiskey into his glass. He was well on his way to being intoxicated. "Her, Morgan's wife, she's a pompous, self-righteous do-good!"

McDonald scratched his cheek and downed his own whiskey. "What's it got to do wif 'er? Fought you said it was that Morgan chap what got you fired?"

"You're an idiot, McDonald." Phillips slammed his hands on the table again. "They'd never've even found 'im alive if it weren't for her sticking her nose into Police business. She was way too high and mighty for her own good. 'E was dead and buried. She should'a just let 'em be dead and got on wif 'er life. She'd a got a pension for the rest of 'er life but no...." He flailed his hands in the air. "Had to go to that pompous Theodore Morgan. They all stick together in that family... I should'a known." He scowled.

McDonald nodded. "So whatya gonna do?"

"I'm gonna get to 'er, show 'er what I do to snitches. Shoulda done it years ago." The former Mountie's words began to slur. "And you're gonna 'elp me," Phillips sneered.

*   *   *   *

Phillips and McDonald hid in a cabin on the outskirts of Douglas Falls. They had to play this carefully, or they'd never get away with it. "You gotta go and snoop around, see what you can find out about the Sergeant." Phillips gave a mock salute.

"Why don't you do it?"

"Cause he knows what I look like, you idiot." Phillips slapped his friend across the back of the head.

"You was much nicer when you was the policeman and I was the criminal. You know if they catch us, you'll spend your life in prison." McDonald rubbed his head.

"I already live in prison." Phillips clenched his jaw tightly. "I was second in command, and they took it from me!" He thrust his hand in the direction of the town. "I've sat by and taken it for long enough. I'm gonna make him suffer. He should'a stayed dead!"

"Are ya gonna kill 'em?"

Phillips stroked his chin. "Nah, I'll go after his family. His wife and children. Got him six pretty little girls, I hear. Easy pickings. I'm sure we could have some fun with them."

"How are ya gonna get to to'em? He'll never let ya near 'em."

Phillips grinned. "Can't protect 'em if he's outta town, can he?"

"What do you have in mind?"

"I still know how to send a police message that he'll follow. I'll send it from that Ferguson chap he was in jail with. They were thick as thieves."

"How are you gonna do that?"

"You leave that to me, just go and find out all you can about the town, I need to know where he lives."

* * * *

"Excuse me, Sergeant?" The store boy marched into the café, letting the door slam behind him. Victoria scowled at him, and he grimaced his apology to her and headed towards Adam and Katie.

Adam squeezed his wife's hand and stood up. "What is it?"

"Mr Scott asked me to give you this, Sergeant. Says it's marked urgent." He passed the envelope to Adam, they nodded to each other, and the boy skipped out the door. Victoria shook her head at him as the door slammed shut loudly and the windows rattled.

Adam raised his brows to her and shook his head, giving her a sympathetic smile. He looked down, slipped the note out of the envelope and frowned.

"What is it, Adam?"

Adam looked back at his wife. "An assignment." He furrowed his brow.

"Oh no. Is it dangerous?"

Adam grimaced and shook his head. He sat back down. "No, it's just unusual."

"Unusual, how?"

"It uses an old code."

"Is it from HQ?"

"No, it's from Sam." He ran his fingers through his hair.

"Sam? Why would he send you on an assignment?" Katie tilted her head.

141

"I'm not sure. That's why it's unusual." Adam furrowed his brows and scratched his chin.

"What is the assignment? May I know?"

Adam frowned. He looked at the police code following the message. It was a sign Sam needed urgent help. "I should go and check this out, Katie. It might be nothing, but I don't want to waste time if he really needs me."

"Why don't you send a wire and check?"

Adam scratched his chin. "This code suggests utmost secrecy. If it's genuine, I don't want to risk interception, or waste any more time."

Katie stood up and gripped his arm. "I understand. I'll tell the girls, and we'll see you later." She smiled.

"I don't know when I'll be back, but I'll send a message when I know what's happening. I promise."

"I know, Adam, it's fine." They strolled out into the May sunshine. "Give Sam my love."

Adam nodded. She kissed his cheek. "I love you, Adam."

Adam cupped her cheek and flashed her a slow smile. "I love you more than I can ever put into words, Mrs Morgan." He leaned forward and kissed her cheek. "Tell my girls I love them."

"I will." She smiled and squeezed his arm.

He nodded, hurried across the road to his waiting horse, leapt on, and galloped out of town. He whistled to Jack and the husky leapt up from his spot, lying on the boardwalk and hastened to follow.

* * * *

Sam stood up abruptly when Adam walked in. "Sergeant?" He grinned. "What brings you here?"

Adam frowned. "You called for me, with emergency codes?"

Sam furrowed his brows and crossed his arms over his chest. "No, I didn't."

Adam pulled the telegram from his pocket and passed it to Sam. "If not you, then who?"

"This isn't from our station, Adam. You know we've recently updated all codes." Sam scratched at his chin. "What's going on?"

A frantic constable ran in. "Serge. There's an urgent phone call." The young man didn't stop to salute.

"Coming, Atkins." Sam turned to walk out.

"No, not you. It's for Sergeant Morgan. It's a Pastor Coleman on the line."

A foreboding feeling washed over Adam. "What is it, Atkins?" He followed the young constable out into the foyer where the telephone was.

"Not sure, Sir. He said it was a matter of life and death."

Adam grimaced at Sam and hurried to pick up the phone. "Daniel?"

Sam watched as Adam's face drained of all colour and his jaw clenched tightly. He put a hand to his face, gripped his temples, and his shoulders shook.

"How many..." His voice trembled. "Where's Katie?" Adam closed his eyes. He exhaled loudly and ran his fingers through his hair, his eyes widened and fire blazed in them. "Lizzie?..." Adam exhaled again. "Thanks, Dan. I'm on my way." Adam slammed down the phone and closed his eyes. His entire body shuddered and he leaned back on the desk. His face was pale, and his shoulders heaved as he took deep hulking breaths.

"Adam, what is it?" Sam had never seen such terror in Adam's eyes.

"My... my family..." His lips couldn't form the words.

"What about them?"

"Dan said..." He took a deep breath to calm himself, his lips quivered and his eyes blazed with fire. "...they're being held hostage, at gunpoint by two men."

Sam's mouth dropped. "What?" He closed his eyes and gripped Adam's shoulder. "How does he know?"

"Said Lizzie got home late and saw them through the window and hurried back to town to raise the alarm. I gotta go to them, Sam." Adam's whole body was on fire. He'd never felt such overwhelming terror and anger in all his life.

Sam grabbed his Stetson. "Atkins, you come on Sergeant's horse. We'll get there in half the time by car." He turned to the other young constable. "Hold the fort here, McLean. Get messages out to the nearby stations and HQ." The young man nodded and hurried out to do his bidding.

"Come on." Sam sped out the door and Adam hurried after him. They climbed into the car. Adam whistled to Jack, waiting on the footpath next to Ebony; the dog leapt in the back of the car. Speeding out of town as fast as he dared, Sam turned his head to look at his friend. Adam had his hand over his face. "Have faith, Adam, they'll be fine. We'll get to them."

Adam took a deep breath and clenched his jaw tightly. He gripped the car door so tightly his knuckles turned white. "Heaven help those men if they've laid a finger on my wife or any of my girls. I will kill them, Sam." His teeth clenched together as Adam's jaw and lips trembled. The anger in his eyes frightened Sam and he knew that Adam was serious. He merely nodded, unsure of what else to do.

"I mean it. One hair is touched on my girls, and I will put a bullet through the brain of both men. I don't care what happens to me."

Adam's expression caused Sam to shudder and step on the accelerator. *Lord, help us.*

* * * *

Katie had just arrived home with the two younger girls when Callie and Anna hurried inside. "Hi, Ma."

Katie looked up from her spot, preparing cookies and milk for the scholars. "Hi, girls." She smiled. "Where's Lizzie?" She tilted her head. Lizzie was always wandering off after school.

Callie rolled her eyes and placed her books on the table. Strolling to the kitchen, she reached for her apron, while Anna hurried to her room to change. Callie lifted the cups from the cupboard. "She just *had* to try out Simeon James' new fishing pole." She flashed her mother a wry smile. "Said she'd be right home afterwards. She even made me bring home her books." Callie gestured to the pile. "That girl." She shook her head.

Katie chuckled. "Oh, Lizzie. Well, she better be home in time to do her homework and chores, if she wants to play ball tonight with Andy...."

The sound of galloping hooves interrupted their conversation. Callie and her mother frowned, looked at each other and shrugged. Perhaps Lizzie had conned someone into bringing her home again.

Before either could contemplate it, hurried footsteps were heard on the stairs, and two armed men burst through the door. "Don't move!" One scowled.

Katie and Callie gasped. "What do you want?" Katie stepped in front of her daughter. The three other girls walked out of their rooms, all having changed into their working clothes. They screamed and McDonald stepped towards them with his gun. "Shut up that noise or I'll blow her brains out." He grabbed Hope and pointed the gun at her temple. Callie, Anna and Sarah trembled and clung to each other, their terrified eyes fixed on their mother. They nodded their understanding. Hope whimpered.

"What do you want?" Katie squared her shoulders, determined to show the men no fear.

Phillips walked to her and thrust his gun into her ribs. "Don't you recognise me, little lady? Guess you aren't so brave without the mighty Theodore Morgan to fight your battles."

Katie looked at the man and squinted. The colour drained from her face, and she gasped. "Phillips," she whispered as the realisation dawned on her.

He grabbed her roughly and gestured to both to step into the living room. Made all five sit down and kept both guns aimed at them. "Well, 'The Commander' ain't here to defend you now, and your husband is out of town, so it's just you and me and your lovely, girls, Mrs Morgan. Guess you ain't so clever with a gun in your face."

Katie grimaced and squared her jaw. "How do you know he's out of town?"

Phillips gave her a wide smirk. "How'dya' think?"

Katie nodded; he'd orchestrated it, which explained the strange message Adam had received. She looked the man directly in the eye and scowled at him. "You won't get away with this, Phillips. If you do anything to us, my husband will hunt you down and kill you. Of that, I am certain."

"Puh!" Phillips laughed and looked briefly at his colleague. "I'm not scared of him. He's nothing, was a coward back then, and still is." He lifted her chin and sneered at her. "You'll be dead long before he gets near here, and he'll never find me. I'm too clever. I've been looking forward to getting revenge on this family for a long time." He thrust the pistol against her temple.

Fear not, for I am with you. A voice spoke from deep inside her. She looked the man in the eye and clenched her jaw. No matter what happened, she would show him no fear.

"You took everything from me." He cocked the pistol, and the girls shrieked.

"Shuddup." McDonald cocked his pistol in Callie's face. The girls closed their eyes and clung to one another.

"And you left my husband to rot in an outpost jail. I'd say you got off lightly, considering you still have your life, Mr Phillips."

"I didn't even get my pension." He snarled in her face. "Had to get menial jobs just to keep food in my belly." He gripped her tighter and poked the pistol at her harder. "I will make your husband pay. He shoulda just died, and then we'd be done with all this.

"You and your suspicions, you couldn't just let the dead rest. You had to stir everything up. Well, I'm gonna take everything from you like you took everything from me." He pushed Katie roughly into the armchair, gripped Callie by the shoulder and hauled her out of the chair. He put the gun into her ribs and chuckled.

"First, we're gonna have some fun with your girls." He sniffed Callie's hair, ran his finger down her cheek and turned to glare at Katie. "And you will sit quietly. If you utter a sound, I'll blow her pretty brains out." He sniffed her hair again, closed his eyes and sneered. "Yes, so lovely." Callie shuddered. Terrified eyes fixed on her mother's. The younger girls wept silently, eyes wide, terrified. but they didn't make a sound.

Fear not for I AM with you. The voice in her heart encouraged her. God would save them. Katie fixed her eyes on Callie and gave her the slightest nod. Callie stopped trembling. Seeing her mother's courage gave her courage.

Phillips grabbed Callie around the waist and thrust the gun into her ribcage.

Terror gripped Katie's throat. *Please Lord, protect my girls.* Katie's blood boiled, and she leapt out of her chair. "Take me instead, Phillips. You can do whatever you like to me." She sucked in a breath and shuddered slightly. "But don't touch the girls."

Phillips scoffed at her; he gripped Callie tighter and moved the gun to her temple, laughing maniacally. The girl whimpered, closed her eyes and trembled. A light shone in Phillips' eyes. He threw Callie roughly down on the floor and she clambered up onto the seat with her sisters.

Katie stood stoically, refusing to show the man any of the fear that rose within her. She'd been a Mountie's wife long enough to know these men thrived on fear. If she could just keep him distracted and focused on her, she could at least keep the girls from the horrors. She would rather endure whatever he could think up to do to her, than watch it happen to her girls. Like Adam, she would protect them with her life if it came to it.

Phillips grabbed her by the shoulders. "That's a tempting offer, Mrs Morgan." He pulled her close, pressing his body against hers. He wrapped his arms around her and kissed her roughly. Katie's eyes grew wide and she turned her head away from him, praying earnestly the girls wouldn't do anything to upset him. They could see the terror in her eyes. At last, he pulled away. "Yes... I can have some fun with you, here in front of your girls." He stroked her cheek. "Give them a real education. That'll really get your husband back for what he did to me." He leaned forward and whispered in her ear. "Then, when I'm finished with you. You can watch while I do the same to all of your daughters."

Something occurred to him, and he frowned and looked around, gripping Katie's shoulders tightly. He scowled at her. "I thought you had six girls."

Katie began to speak, but Callie beat her to it. "Our older sister is away at college. And Lizzie is staying at a friend's place for the evening so they can work on a geography project," she lied. Her mother nodded her agreement.

"Yes, that's right." Katie smiled. "Lizzie is in town. She won't be back all night." She prayed internally that Lizzie would stay away. At least one of them was safe. She breathed a sigh of relief that Rose was away at college. This would bring back the terror of what had almost happened to her the night of the dance.

"Well, McDonald." Phillips grinned. "When we finish with these five, we'll go find the other two girls, and we'll kill them, both." He raised his brows. "I can't think of a better way to punish this family for what they did to me...." He whispered in Katie's ear, "Yes, I'm going to enjoy this." He leaned in to kiss her again, but she turned her head away. Phillips grabbed her chin in one hand and yanked her face back towards him. "You don't refuse me, Mrs Morgan, or we can do this the hard way." Clutching her chin tightly between his thumb and finger he kissed her roughly again.

"Mama," Hope cried out, her eyes flooded with tears. Phillips broke off the slobbery kiss and Katie grimaced. He turned to look at Hope.

"Shuddup, girl, or I'll forget about your Mama and start on you instead." The gleam in his eye made Katie shudder. *Please, Lord, not my girls, he can do whatever he must to me, but please, spare the girls.*

"It's okay, Hope." Katie tried to reassure her. "It's going to be okay."

Hope nodded sadly and her tears overflowed. Callie put her arms around her youngest sister.

McDonald thrust the gun at the girls. Internally he shuddered. He never imagined Phillips was capable of such cruelty. He'd gone along with it so far because the former Mountie had promised him a cut of the money he was planning to extort out of them. He sincerely hoped Phillips wouldn't carry through with his threats. He really didn't want to hurt anyone. He was a petty thief at the most. The menacing glare and evil smirk on his colleague's face frightened him. Glancing at Hope, he shuddered. She reminded him of his niece, Amelia. She was about the same age. He would try to find a way to stall Phillips and prevent him from actually hurting the girls.

*   *   *   *

Lizzie grimaced as she rode up onto The Rise. She'd borrowed Simeon's horse because she was very late. "Ma's gonna be hopping mad," she said to the horse as she approached the house. "What on earth?" She pulled Comet to a stop. There were two horses outside that she didn't recognise. She'd lived with her father for long enough to be cautious. Craning her neck, she stood up in the saddle and peered through the window. She could just make out two men. One had Callie in his arms with a gun to her head, he sniffed her hair.

"Ahhhh." Lizzie sucked in a breath, turning the horse as quietly as she could, she hurried into town.

"Uncle Daniel, Uncle Daniel." Lizzie leapt off the horse and bolted up the stairs of the pastorage. "Uncle Daniel."

Daniel leapt up from his chair where he'd been helping Emma with her homework. "What is it, Lizzie?"

"Two men..." she panted out. "With guns... at our house. They have Ma and the girls...." She got no further, bursting into tears.

"Oh no," Daniel exclaimed and wrapped Lizzie in his arms. "And your pa's in Pine Crest, your ma told me."

Louisa walked out of the kitchen. "You have to tell him. Get help, Dan."

Daniel pushed Lizzie away. "Stay here." His look meant she didn't dare disobey. She nodded and her lip trembled, running into Louisa's outstretched arms. "I will get help, you understand. Your family will be fine. I promise." He gritted his teeth.

After the incident with the teacher, he knew without a doubt that Adam wouldn't hesitate to kill these men if they hurt his family.

"What can we do, Pa?" Timothy asked.

"Pray." Daniel nodded and hurried out the door.

* * * *

Adam swallowed over and over, urging Sam to drive faster.

"I'm going as fast as I can, Adam. We'll be there soon." He waved his hands at the first few homesteads of the Douglas Falls township.

"Not soon enough." Adam seethed.

"Adam, you need to calm down. You know storming in hot-headed could mean someone gets hurt."

"I'm gonna kill them, Sam. I mean it." Adam clenched and unclenched his fist over and over.

"Adam." Sam raised his voice. It brought Adam's head up in shock. His friend seldom sounded as terse. Sam exhaled. "I know you're angry, and I would be too. But you have to keep your wits about you. You cannot risk your girls getting hurt. If you storm in there and open fire, who knows what could happen."

Adam closed his eyes and took a deep breath. "I don't know how, Sam. My whole body is on fire." He sighed and his voice trembled. "If anything happens to my girls..." An agonising groan came from deep inside him.

"I know, Adam. But remember, there is Someone who loves those girls even more than you do, and has promised to be with them. No matter what happens, God is with them. You have to hold onto hope." He echoed the words he'd used to keep Adam's spirits up in the Yukon prison.

Adam sighed loudly and ran his fingers through his hair, desperately trying to keep control of his feelings.

Thirteen
Whatever It Takes

Marcus wiped his brow and looked at the clock. He grinned, *knock-off time*. He placed his tools back in his wooden toolbox in the corner, dusted off his workbench and lay the chair he'd finished sanding in the back room, ready for varnish tomorrow.

He walked out into the shop. "I'm off for the night."

Arthur Campbell looked up. "Alright, Lad. You've done a fine job of those chairs."

"Yep, they are ready for varnish. Should be ready for Mrs Cole by the end of the week."

"You do good work." The master craftsman picked up the broom and began to sweep behind the counter.

"Thank you, Sir."

"You going to the Morgan's for supper again?" The man raised his brows knowingly.

"Sure am."

"How long before your girlie comes home?"

"Fifty-seven days." Marcus grinned.

"I'm surprised you aren't telling me the hours and minutes." The older man chuckled.

Marcus raised his brows. "I could, you know." He grinned. "I'll see you tomorrow."

"Alright." The man shook his head as the younger man fairly skipped out the door.

Marcus rode Dollar into town just as Adam and Sam pulled up outside the RNWMP office.

"Marc." Sam waved him over. The look on both Mountie's faces made Marcus's stomach churn. He'd seen that expression on

Adam's face once before, the night the men tried to hurt Rose. He shuddered and hurried over to them.

"What is it, Sergeant?" He looked from Adam's steely glare and tightly clenched jaw to Sam's stern face.

"Trouble at the homestead," Sam answered on Adam's behalf.

"What kind of trouble?" Marcus's face fell.

Dan came running out of the office where he was waiting, along with Owen, Andy and a group of the townsmen.

Adam acknowledged them with a nod.

"There are two men with guns at the homestead. They have Katie and the girls hostage." Adam's clenched his teeth tightly. "And I will do whatever it takes to save them. Whatever it takes." He hissed out a breath, clenched his fist and laid his right hand on his holster. His dark eyes were almost black.

Marcus gasped. "Oh no! What do you need me to do?" He echoed the sergeant's thoughts in his mind. He also would do whatever it took to protect Rose's family.

"I'll take charge." Sam gripped Adam's shoulder. "There are far too many emotions at stake." He glared at Adam. "Do I need to pull rank?"

Adam shook his head. He was much too angry to think straight. If he marched in there, it would certainly be with guns blazing. He needed Sam's cool head, and he was grateful for it.

"We can't go up there unprepared, and they better not know we're coming, or they might hurt the women." All heads nodded their agreement.

"Who are they?" Owen asked.

Daniel shrugged. "We don't know. Lizzie managed to get to me and raise the alarm. She saw them through the window, but they didn't see her."

"Brave girl," Marcus said aloud.

Daniel nodded. "She's at my house with my family. They're safe."

"We're wasting time; let's get up there," Adam hissed.

Sam put his hand on his friend's shoulder. "We need a plan and divine help." Sam raised his brows to the pastor.

Dan nodded and led them in a brief prayer.

"Now, here's the plan, Gentleman..." Sam began.

* * * *

Katie clenched her jaw and refused to show Philips fear. She communicated encouragement to the girls with her eyes. Twice when neither man was looking, Katie gestured with her head and eyes to the cellar door, hidden under the mat in the kitchen floor. Callie nodded. She got the message. If they got a chance, escape through the hatch and out the back door.

Phillips gripped Katie tightly and continued to torment her. He shoved the barrel of his gun roughly into her ribcage.

McDonald squirmed nervously, gulping over and over again. It seemed Phillips was really going to follow through on his threats. He kept his gun pointed at the girls but continued to hope he'd not actually have to use it. He had but two bullets and seldom cleaned his gun. He wasn't even sure it worked. His bravado crumbled by the moment.

Phillips slid his gun up to Katie's temple. He laughed maniacally as he felt her tremble. The terror in her eyes excited him. "I'm thirsty, Woman. Make me some coffee."

"Get it yourself," Katie threw at him.

"Ma." Callie exhaled. *She shouldn't taunt him.*

Phillips squinted his eyes at Katie and slapped her across the face. Katie clenched her jaw and desperately fought back the tears. A red handprint covered most of her right cheek, and his rough hands drew blood in two places.

Phillips gripped her chin in his thumb and finger. "I said, make me some coffee."

"No. I won't." Katie fixed her eyes on him, ignoring the blood running down her cheek.

He squeezed his thumb and finger tighter into her face and jabbed the gun into her temple. "I'll make you regret saying no to me, I promise you." He thrust Katie back into the chair and then turned to look at the girls. They trembled and wept. McDonald tried to gesture with his eyes for them to stop. Katie lifted her handkerchief to her face.

"Which one shall I pick?" Phillips taunted and leaned over to cup Callie's chin. He turned her face side to side and then moved to Anna, Sarah and then Hope. "Such sweet girls. Which one?" He stood and looked at them again. I do like a redhead." He smirked at Sarah and hauled her out of her chair. The girl shrieked as he thrust the gun at her temple.

"Leave her alone," Katie demanded.

Phillips spun on his heels to face Katie, holding the girl tightly at the waist. Sarah squirmed and tried to pull away. "Stop that squirming, Girl," he sneered and moved the gun to her chest instead. "I'll put two bullets through your heart. Be a shame to hurt a pretty little girl like you. How old are you, Girl?"

"T... t..." Sarah's voice faltered and she trembled.

"Stop, I'll make you coffee." Callie dared to stand up.

Phillips grinned, and shoved Sarah back into the seat, Anna and Hope wrapped their arms around her while she trembled.

"Glad one of you's got some brains. I need coffee, to keep up my strength. We've got a long night ahead of us, girls." He sneered at them all.

Katie looked at the girls, all eyes filled with unshed tears. She gave them all nods, trying to remain very calm. She never stopped praying.

Callie hurried to the kitchen to put the coffee pot on. Behind the counter, she filled the pot with water and walked it to the stove. She moved her foot, brushing aside the mat to expose the handle on the cellar door. It was little more than a finger-sized hole in a knot in a floorboard, cleverly disguised, but they all knew it was there.

"Hurry up in there, Girl." Phillips pointed his gun back at Katie's forehead. She continued to look him in the eye with her jaw set defiantly. It was important she keep his focus on her and not the girls.

I will do whatever it takes, bear whatever I have to, to keep my girls safe, she determined internally, but it didn't stop a tremble running through her.

"Come on,' Girl, I want my coffee," Phillips yelled at Callie again.

"I'm going as fast as I can." Callie grimaced. How could she find a way to slip into the cellar without being seen? If she did that, would he hurt her mother and sisters? She was conflicted. She pulled two cups down from the cupboard and glanced out the window. A soft gasp escaped her. Sam, Marcus, and two other men approached on foot, both with pistols raised.

Phillips caught the girl's gasp and looked up. He glared at Katie and strode to the kitchen to see what was wrong. Katie shuddered and fought the urge to wretch. She lifted a handkerchief to her bruised and bleeding cheek. Callie had to think quickly lest he look out the window. She turned abruptly with the coffeepot in her hand and spilled it down the man's trousers and boots. "Ahhhhhh." He hopped around as boiling water seeped through onto his leg. He scowled at Callie and lifted his gun to her face. "You did that on purpose." He grabbed her by her hair and marched her out to face her family. "Want me to show you what I do to women who defy me?" He pinned her against the wall with his body. "I show them who's boss." He thrust his gun into her temple and tore at the buttons on her blouse. Callie grimaced and turned her head away from him.

"Get off her." Katie leapt up. "I told you to take it out on me and not them." Her eyes blazed. She suspected he was merely grandstanding. If he wanted to hurt them, he'd have done so by now. Noticing a flash of red out the window, Katie caught Adam's eye through the glass. She closed her eyes and thanked God for sending Adam just in time.

Phillips dropped his gun to Callie's ribs and looked at her terrified face. He leaned in and sniffed her hair. Katie shuddered and glanced at him to make sure his back was still turned. McDonald had his back to the window, his gun aimed at the girls. Katie raised her brows at Adam, and he nodded to her; his dark eyes held both compassion and hatred. He looked up to see the man with his hands on Callie, and he could see the terror in his daughter's eyes. He fought the urge to storm in and put a bullet in the man's head. The look in his eye terrified Katie. She took a deep breath and doubled the prayers.

All heads snapped around towards a knocking on the cellar door. "What's going on up there?" a voice called.

Phillips stepped back from Callie. She fell to the floor in a heap of tears and snatched her torn blouse closed to hide her exposed undergarments.

Phillips strode to the kitchen and pushed the rug aside. "McDonald," he called. "We got us an intruder. Watch them. I'll see to this clever person." He bent down to lift the cellar door, his gun aimed and ready.

Katie ran to Callie. McDonald didn't try to stop her. Callie clung to her mother. "I'm okay, Ma," she whispered.

"Brave girl." Katie smiled and stroked her daughter's face. "Your Pa is outside." She mouthed.

Callie nodded. "I know." She mouthed back and gently touched Katie's bruised cheek. "Are you okay, Ma?"

"Yes, Darling, I'll be just fine, now that your pa's here."

Callie could see the relief in her mother's eyes.

"Come on out 'ere and face me, ya coward." Phillips put his hand down to the hole in the floor. Before he could open it, the trapdoor burst open, and Jack bounded out, leaping on the man and pinning him to the floor. He stood on the man's chest and a deep growl came from the dog's throat, he bared his teeth and brought his face close to the man's. His killer instinct had not diminished with age.

Daniel followed the dog out. Phillips slapped at the floor near him reaching for his gun. Daniel instinctively stomped on the man's hand.

"Ahhhhhh," Phillips yelled. "Get off me, Pastor." He kicked out at Daniel but missed. The pastor grimaced and drove his heel into the man's hand. "Ahhhh." The man squirmed.

Daniel stepped back. "I suggest you remain still. The dog's trained to kill. You move a whisker, he'll go straight for the jugular."

Daniel nodded to Adam through the window. McDonald still stood with his gun to the girls, frozen to the spot.

Phillips kept his eyes on the sharp teeth an inch from his face but didn't move. He could feel the dog's hot breath and drool dripped on his chin.

Adam burst in the door. "Pa!" Hope burst into tears. McDonald froze in fright his gun fell limp in his hand. Adam marched in and put both his pistols to the man's temples.

"Drop... your... weapon..." he spat through his tightly gritted teeth.

McDonald immediately threw the gun on the floor and raised his hands above his head. Sam and Owen ran in and grabbed McDonald, yanking his arms behind his back and marching him straight out the door. Adam walked over to the man on the floor in the kitchen.

"Heel, Jack." The dog barked once, growled at the man again and heeled obediently.

Adam stood over the man, grabbed his collar, snatched him from the ground and slammed him against the kitchen wall. He held his collar tightly in one hand and thrust the barrel of his pistol into the man's temple. He brought his own face almost as close Jack's had been and dark eyes reflected the hatred and anger he felt.

Phillips sneered. "Well, well, if it isn't brave Mountie Morgan."

Adam's face fell. "Phillips." He grimaced.

"Thought I'd come and meet your nice family." Adam tightened his grip on the man's neck. "I've been getting to know your lovely girls." He grinned maniacally.

"What do you want with my family?" Adam seethed, thrusting his pistol forcefully into his head, he cocked it, fighting every impulse to pull the trigger and empty all six bullets into the man's brain. It was the faces of his family watching on that stopped him. He couldn't do that in front of them.

"I didn't do anything. We were just getting acquainted." Phillips grinned. "You're wife sure tastes good; she's an excellent kisser."

Adam thrust his forearm into the man's throat and pressed as hard as he could. "I should've had them throw the book at you."

Katie shivered; she'd never seen so much hate in Adam's eyes before.

The man struggled against the arm across his neck, gripping Adam's forearm with both hands, trying to pry it off his throat. Adam pressed tighter. The man gasped for breath.

"Adam," Katie called to him. He turned his head to see tears streaming down her face. He noticed the bruises and scratches on her cheek and the terrified looks on his girl's faces.

He looked back at Phillips and released his grip slightly.

Phillips scoffed. "I knew it. You aren't the fearsome Mountie you make yourself out to be. Just a big coward like your father."

"The Commander is a better leader than you ever were."

Samuel marched inside. "I'll take it from here, Sergeant."

Adam looked the man in the face.

"You heard the staff sergeant; let me go. But I do so wish I could have finished what I started with your lovely girls. They smell so swe...."

Before he could finish, Adam raised his knee and thrust it into the man's groin and rammed his head into the rough boards of the kitchen wall. The man yelped in pain. Ignoring his cries Adam gripped Phillips by the collar, digging both thumbs as hard as he could into the man's neck. "Mention or even look at my wife or girls again, and I will kill you," he hissed through his teeth. "You have my word on that, Phillips. It won't matter where you go. I WILL find you, and I will kill you." Adam pressed his thumbs tighter, and Phillips struggled against him. Adam's jaws trembled with the effort of keeping his emotions in control.

"Sergeant!" Sam put a hand on Adam's shoulder.

Adam pulled the man off the wall and thrust him at Samuel. "You deal with this piece of filth before I do something I'll regret." Adam clenched his jaw.

Samuel marched Phillips to the door. Atkins waited in the car; Adam's horse was tied to the hitching post. Four men stood with guns aimed at McDonald's head as he sat in the back of the car.

"I'll take it from here, Adam." Sam paused at the door. "Phillips'll never see daylight again. I promise you that." Sam's tightened his grip on the man's arms. "You be with your family."

Adam nodded to Sam. As much as he longed to finish what he started, he looked at the terrified faces of his women all huddled together; Jack stood guard in front of them, his blue eyes fixed firmly on the crook, and his lips lifted in a growl, as Sam marched him out the door.

Marcus ran inside and closed the door. Daniel closed the cellar door. Adam paused for a second and hung his head. A loud sob escaped him, and he collapsed to his knees. Dan gripped his shoulder briefly and looked at Marcus. "Thank the Lord." Daniel exhaled loudly.

"Adam." Katie looked at him with tears washing down her cheeks.

He snapped his head up and sniffed back his tears. "Oh..." He leapt up and ran to the girls all huddled on the couch. "My darlings. My precious darlings." He shook as he cried out the emotion and anger he'd been holding in. He kissed each head. "I'm so sorry, Darlings, I'm so sorry." He trembled. "I'm so sorry," he repeated over and over.

Daniel and Marcus left the house to take care of Adam's horse.

At last, Adam gathered Katie in his arms and stood up, drawing her close to him. He pulled back from her and examined her with his eyes. There was a red mark and blood on her face, and her clothing and hair were dishevelled. He gently touched her cheek and then lowered his hand to the torn patch on her blouse. "Did he hurt you?" His voice was tight and strained, his eyes dark and brooding.

Katie shook her head. "No."

Hope spoke up from her spot in Callie's arms. "He forced Ma to kiss him. He had his mouth on hers, and he hit her, very hard and made her bleed," she cried.

Tears flooded Adam's eyes; he closed his eyes and swallowed back his scalding anger. Pulling his wife into his arms, he cradled her head in his hand. "Oh, Katie, Oh my darling. I'm so sorry. I'm so sorry."

Katie pulled back from him and looked up into his eyes. She put both hands on Adam's face and smiled. She brushed a tear from his cheek with her thumb. "I'm okay, Adam. He didn't hurt me, beyond a slobbery kiss and a few bruises." She lifted her hand to her injured cheek, closed her eyes and shuddered, thankful that Adam had arrived when he did. She raised her eyes to him again. "But I'd rather he did that to me than our girls."

He stepped away, turned his back and hung his head. "This is why Mountie's don't have families, I guess. I'm so sorry to drag you all into this."

"Adam." Katie's tone made him spin around and look at her. She thrust her hands on her hips. "You have no reason to be sorry. This is not your fault. If anything, it's mine. I'm the one who discovered the corruption in the ranks... and if you hadn't been married and had a family, you would've died in that jail. I'd rather bare up under a moment of fear than have you never come home to me." Tears streamed from her face. "All this is worth it, even the pain. It's worth it to have you here with us. We love you, Adam, and we're proud to be in this with you."

"Oh, Katie." Adam's tears overflowed, he lunged towards her and wrapped his arms around her. "I couldn't survive without you. When I got the message that armed men were in the house, I was crippled with anger and fear. I thought I was going to lose you all." His voice wavered and Katie felt his whole body shudder.

"You didn't, Adam. We're all still here." She stepped back from him. "But how did you know?"

He swiped his sleeve across his eyes. "Lizzie." He grinned and raised his brows.

"Lizzie?" all voices said in unison.

"Yes, she came home in a hurry, thinking she'd be in trouble for being tardy, noticed the men through the window and ran to get Daniel. He phoned the office in Pine Crest."

Katie grinned. "Lizzie." She shook her head.

"I sure do love my girls." Adam reached his arms out to all of them, and they piled into his embrace. He kissed each head again. He gestured to Callie's torn blouse, and his face fell. His jaw trembled again and he sniffed away a tear. He pulled her into his arms. "I'm so sorry, Darling."

"I'm okay, Pa. He just tore my buttons. He didn't hurt me."

Adam stood back, cupped her cheek and kissed her hair. "That's my brave girl."

They turned with a gasp as Lizzie and Daniel burst in the door. "Pa, Ma."

Adam ran to her and scooped her up into his arms. "Oh, Lizzie, my darling. You saved them all. You saved them."

"No, I didn't, I just hid at the Coleman's house like a coward."

Adam lifted her chin and kissed her forehead. "If you hadn't raised the alarm, it would have been hours before I got here. I wouldn't have been prepared and had the backup I had. Who knows what might have happened?" He shuddered. "I'm ever so grateful to you, my darling. You're a brave girl."

"Thanks, Pa. I was so scared. I thought they were all going to die. I don't want my sisters or Ma to die."

She embraced them all.

Adam dragged a feather mattress into the living room and placed it in front of the sofa before the open fire. He added pillows and blankets. Leaning back against the sofa they all cuddled together under quilts.

No one spoke. They just enjoyed being in each other's arms again. Adam kissed Katie's head that rested against his shoulder as she sat in his arms. "Thank the Lord you're all safe." He nodded and closed his eyes, grateful prayers ran through his mind. The family spent the entire night there, and eventually all the girls fell asleep.

Adam sat up in the darkness and tightened his grip on his wife, sleeping against his chest. He leaned down and kissed her head and stroked her cheek. He wiped away a tear. "Thank you, Lord, that my family is safe." He sniffed and looked at the faces of the five girls huddled together sound asleep. "There is no greater blessing. Thank You, Lord." For several hours he watched his girls sleep and cradled his beloved in his arms, there was nowhere else he wanted to be at that moment then right there with all his girls around him.

* * * *

Adam closed his Bible, and swiped at the tears that had gathered in the corners of his eyes. "I needed that, Dan. Thanks for praying with me."

Dan nodded and began to speak when they were interrupted by the shrill rings of the telephone. Adam snatched the receiver off the handle.

"Sergeant Adam Morgan...."

Daniel watched on, as he listened to Adam's side of the conversation and watched him run his fingers through his hair.

"Uncle..." Adam grinned. "Good to hear from you... Really?... That sounds like The Commander." Adam gave a strained chuckle and leaned forward to put his elbow on the table. "I'm not really surprised, and I can't say I'm sad, except I would've liked to have been there to see that." He clenched his jaw and sighed. "Yeah, I know. My hate only hurts me... Yeah, they're all okay. They are strong, brave girls.... Thank you, Sir. Yes, it's that good Morgan blood." He chuckled. "Thank you... yes, I'll let Sam know. Thank The Commander for me.... I'm much obliged."

Adam hung up the telephone and let out a deep sigh.

Daniel raised his brows and his face held the question.

"That was Sergeant Hudson, my uncle."

Daniel nodded. "I remember. What did he want?"

Adam grimaced. "He said he and The Commander visited Phillips in the county prison."

Daniel returned the grimace and sipped at his coffee.

"The Commander roughed Phillips up pretty badly. Beat him within an inch of his life... He died of his wounds in his cell. Pa got a reprimand from the RNWMP, but no one was overly concerned. I think The Commissioner thought Phillips had it coming."

"Oh." Daniel wasn't sure what else to say.

"The worst thing is I'm not sorry. I'm not a bit sorry. I'm just sorry I wasn't there to watch that man die." Adam clenched his jaw tightly and thrust his arms across his chest.

"Adam Morgan. I can't believe you'd say that. What happened to 'There but for the grace?'"

Adam closed his eyes and exhaled loudly. "I'm really struggling to forgive this time, Dan. Those men had my family at gunpoint. Phillips put his hands on my wife and girls..." Adam shuddered. "I can't shake this blind rage."

Daniel nodded. "Only prayer will help, leaving it to the Lord. He loves your family too, Adam. He was there with them, He kept them safe and that man didn't get to hurt them." Daniel gripped his friend's arm. "Adam, He never promises us that life won't be hard sometimes, and that evil men won't hurt us. But remember, if anyone knows the pain you're facing, it's God."

Adam nodded. "I know. I'm so grateful to the Lord that He protected my family. He kept the worst from happening. Katie told me she could hear God's voice and it kept her calm. You know that woman stared evil in the eyes and didn't even flinch." Adam grinned. "She's a heck of a strong woman."

Daniel nodded. "Yes, your love and the Lord's kept them going, Adam. Let go of the anger and the hatred, it'll just make you bitter, and that's not fair on your girls."

Adam closed his eyes and nodded. "You're right, of course." I'm glad I have you in my life, Dan. God knew how badly I'd need you. You are His hands and His voice in my life." Adam grinned at his friend. "I'm grateful to you. The amount of times I've relied on your level head, and your words of reason. I can never repay you for that, Friend." His voice trembled.

Dan gripped his friend's arm again. "Adam, you have no need to repay me. The love you have for my sister, and my nieces, all of our family is more than I can ask for. You've saved me a time or two, as well, remember. I'm grateful for you, Friend. In fact, I'm not afraid to say it. I love you, Brother."

Adam nodded, stood up, and the two men embraced briefly. "Will you pray with me, Dan, help me get over this? After this moment, I don't ever want to think about Phillips ever again, or have his name cross my lips. Pray that I can forgive and move on, and give my girls all the love and support that I can. That's far more important than holding a grudge."

"Absolutely, my friend. Shall we pray?" Daniel gripped Adam's shoulder, and the two men bowed their heads and petitioned the Lord.

Fourteen
Spring Break

Mrs Green knocked on the wall next to Rose's open door. "Miss Rose, I hate to interrupt, but there's a phone call for you."

Rose looked up from her desk and frowned. "It's not Thursday? Who is it?"

"It's your young man."

"But why is he phoning on a Tuesday?"

Mrs Green shrugged. "I dunno, Miss Rose. He sounded awful frantic."

"Thank you, Mrs Green." Rose hurried down the hall to the small alcove by the stairwell. She swallowed back the foreboding feeling and picked up the handset. "Hello?"

*   *   *   *

Alice walked past Rose's open door and saw her friend sitting on her bed hugging her pillow, with large tears rolling down her ashen cheeks.

She gasped and hurried in. "Rose, whatever is the matter?"

Rose looked up and her lip trembled. Alice thrust herself on the bed, and put her arm around her friend.

After a time, Rose sat back and dried her eyes.

"What's going on?" Alice's brow curled up in worry.

Rose managed a sad smile, blew her nose and leaned her head back against the wall. "I just got off the phone with Marcus."

Alice tipped her head to the side. "Why has that made you sad? Oh, Rose, did he break with you?" She gripped Rose's arm.

Rose smiled. "No, we're just fine."

"Oh, that's a relief, so what did he say?"

"Oh, Alice, my family was held hostage in their home by two men with guns. I'm just so relieved they're all okay."

"What?" Alice's hands flew to her mouth. "What do you mean held hostage?"

"Remember I told you my pa was falsely imprisoned?"

Alice nodded. "Yes, eight years ago."

Rose smiled. "The man who was responsible was dishonourably discharged from the RNWMP, and apparently, he's been nursing a grudge all those years. Evidently, he tricked my pa into being out of town and then stormed into the homestead and took Ma and four of the girls hostage." Her lip trembled, as memories of a similar situation in the barn entered her mind.

"Oh no, Rose!"

"Pa and Uncle Samuel got there in time, and they're all fine, thank the Lord." Rose sighed loudly. "But I'm just feeling so overwhelmed by it all. Marcus helped to save them." Rose couldn't help but smile at that.

"Of course he did. They're his family now too... Wait." Alice frowned. "Why only four of your sisters? I thought you had five."

Rose flashed her a sideways grin. "Lizzie has a habit of getting side-tracked. She was really late home from school; it turns out it's just as well she was. She saw the men through the window and was able to get help. I don't like to think about what might have happened if she hadn't." Rose shuddered again, and Alice squeezed her hand.

"Oh, Rose. I'm so glad they are alright."

"Marcus said he's never seen my pa so angry. He was genuinely frightened of what he might do. Pa said he'd do whatever it takes and I'm certain he would've."

"I'm surprised he didn't kill the men, based on what I know of him."

"I'm glad he didn't, for his sake. He'd've never forgiven himself. But I can imagine it was a struggle." Rose grinned. "It isn't a smart idea to pick on one of Sergeant Morgan's girls."

"No, I can imagine. You told me about the teacher striking Lizzie and how angry he was."

"I'm thankful that he has Uncle Daniel and Uncle Samuel to keep his temper in check." She laughed, but her eyes held great relief. "Alice, will you pray with me."

"Of course." The two girls bowed their heads and spent time in grateful prayer that Rose's family was safe and well.

*   *   *   *

Rose paced and fidgeted impatiently on the train platform with Constable Scott.

"They'll be here soon, Miss Morgan."

"I know. I'm just so excited that Marcus and Callie are coming to visit for the whole week of Spring Break."

Jonny's cheeks inadvertently reddened. Rose caught it and raised her brows; before she could comment, the train rumbled into the station.

Rose grinned as the Constable shyly greeted Callie and helped her to the waiting car, almost oblivious to Marcus and Rose's presence.

Dropping them at the boarding house, Constable Scott tipped his hat. "I'm happy to be your escort for the week, Ma'am." His words were aimed at Rose, but his eyes never left Callie's face.

Rose nudged Marcus again, and they both shook their heads.

Jonny watched as the three young people turned to enter the boarding house; he started the car and pulled out onto the busy street; carriages and cars shared the same road. "Lord, I sure would like to get to know Callie Morgan," he dared to say aloud. "I've never met a girl like her before. I know she's young; I'll bide my time." He sighed as his thoughts ran away from him and he dreamed of a future with her. But it seemed so impossible; they lived so far apart. He shrugged. *If the Lord wants it to happen, He'll make a way.* He vowed to leave it up to God. Still, he couldn't help but dream.

Adam lowered his newspaper and gratefully took the coffee cup from his wife's hand. He winked at her and looked at the mopey girls seated around the room. "Hey, why the long faces? It's Spring Break. You should be enjoying yourself."

Hope looked up and grimaced. "I miss Callie and Rose. It's not the same without them."

"I miss them too, Darling." Adam winked at his youngest daughter.

Lizzie put down her book an rolled her eyes. "Callie only left yesterday. You people are much too sentimental."

This brought laughter to the whole family. "We'll find a way to spend the days while school is out," Katie promised.

"Sure would be nice to do something as a family." Adam ran his fingers through his hair. "We could really use it after all we've been through."

"What do you have in mind, Pa?" Sarah stood to put her glass on the counter.

Adam gave her a sideways smile. "I'm not sure, Darling. Do you have any ideas?"

"We could put on a play?" Lizzie suggested.

Anna closed her eyes and shuddered. "I couldn't do that. All those people watching me."

Adam chuckled. "I think we can come up with something. I wish I could afford to take you all away for a vacation."

Katie reached over and gripped his hand. "We don't need a vacation, Adam. We had that when we went to Edmonton for Rose's birthday."

Adam nodded. "What do you think we should do?"

"We could have a picnic?" Katie suggested.

"Yeah." Sarah screwed up her face. "But we do that all the time. Can't we do something different?"

"Like what, Darling?" Adam placed down his empty cup.

Sarah shrugged. "I dunno, Pa. I'm sure we can think of something."

"We will," Adam promised, an idea forming in his mind.

*　*　*　*

Callie yawned loudly and plonked herself down on the chair before the mirror.

Rose slipped her nightgown over her head and chuckled. "It's been a long week. We've earned our sleep, that's for sure."

Callie brushed her long hair, peering at her sister in the mirror. "I think we walked all over Edmonton." She grinned.

"It sure was fun though. I'm so glad you're here with me." Rose took the brush from Callie's hands and ran it through her sister's hair as she had so many times before.

"I'm glad to be here. It was a great idea."

Rose yawned too. She grinned at her sister. "Oh no, it's contagious." They chuckled, put the brush away and climbed into bed. It was fun for Rose to share a bed with her sister again. It had been some time.

Despite their tiredness, they sat up talking late into the night. They talked about everything under the sun. Rose had never spent this much time with just Callie before, and it was wonderful. No younger sisters running in to ruin their conversations or the disruption of chores.

Rose gushed about Marcus and how lovely it was to be in love. After some time, she turned to her sister. "So, have any young men caught your eye?"

"No." The younger girl leaned back against the headboard, she bit her lip and lowered her head, but Rose could see the blush on her cheeks.

"Callie?" Rose grinned and put her hand on her sister's arm.

"Well... I dunno... I'm not sure I should say anything... We just met?"

Rose nodded and grinned. "Constable Scott?"

Callie's cheeks reddened further, and she smiled shyly.

"He's a wonderful man, Callie. He's been a good friend to me, and Pa likes him very much."

"He's older than me, and besides, I'm too young to be courting."

"True." Rose shrugged. "But there's no reason you can't get to know him more."

"Do you think so?"

Rose gripped her sister's arm. "Of course. Before you leave, ask him to write, there's no harm in that, is there? Maybe in a year or so, you'll be ready to court."

"But he lives so far away."

"Callie. If God wants it to happen, He'll make it happen. You just have to trust Him!" Rose squeezed Callie's arm again. "I wasn't expecting Marcus to come into my life, but God orchestrated it; He will for you too. I'm sure of it."

"You're right." Callie smiled. "Besides, I'm much too young yet, and I doubt the constable would be interested in the likes of me."

Rose screwed up her face. "And just why not, Callie Morgan?"

"I'm not like you, Rose. I'm not a teacher or a confident speaker. I'm shy and homely."

"Stop that, would you. You're a wonderful girl, Callie, and Constable Scott or any other young man would be lucky to have you on their arm. Marcus told me he thinks you're pretty great, and I know for a fact there were at least two boys in the youth group back home that think you're special. I wasn't going to tell you this, but the way Constable Scott was looking at you tonight, I'd say he thinks you're more than just special. You're a great catch. You're so talented at cooking and sewing just like Ma. You're a beautiful singer. You're plucky and strong. I think you'd make an ideal Mountie's wife."

"You're just saying that."

"No, sisters are always honest, remember? If anyone is going to tell you a harsh truth, it'll be a sister." Rose grinned.

"Do you really think so?"

Rose reached for her hand. "Callie, I really do. Of all my sisters, you're the most like Ma."

"But you're the teacher."

"Yeah, and that's where our similarities stop. I'm not a great cook like you. I do okay, and I'll be able to cook and sew for my family someday, but when you whip up a meal, it's better than a restaurant. I never could get my gravy to set like yours." Rose chuckled. "And your cookies. I don't know what you do differently, but they always melt in my mouth. You sew beautifully, just like Ma."

"So I'm little better than a housewife." Callie grimaced and hung her head.

"Well, is there anything else you'd rather be?"

Callie sighed. "I don't really know. When I try to imagine my future, I see myself as a wife and a mother."

Rose smiled and gripped her sister's hand. "Then be the best wife and mother you can be. There is no shame in that, Callie Morgan. Ma doesn't work anymore, leastways outside the house."

"Yes, but she did. She was a teacher and a fine one too. I don't have that kind of confidence."

"Callie, some man, maybe Constable Scott, maybe someone else, is going to fall head over heels in love with you someday, and you will be everything to them. They will love you for exactly who you are, for all the amazing things you CAN do and not for the things you can't."

Callie nodded.

"Believe in yourself." Rose leapt up and pulled her sister out of bed; she lifted the lamp and carried it to the mirror. "Look at that girl there." Rose pointed to Callie's reflection. "She is so beautiful. Callie, your green eyes are so striking. You have Ma's long dark hair. That smattering of freckles is very becoming. Your figure is lovely, and you're a very beautiful girl. Marcus told me that he saw several young men notice you on the train. He got a little protective actually.

"Someday, someone is going to fall in love with that beautiful girl there, and I can't wait for us to be wives and mothers together. And you'll be a good one. I just know I'll be coming to you to swap recipes or to help me with the canning."

Callie blushed. "Thank you, Rose. I've never really seen myself as anything much. I'm not nearly as beautiful as you."

"Oh, stop, Callie. Can I tell you something? I've always been jealous of you."

Callie smirked and knitted her eyebrows. "Of me? Why?"

"Because, look at your flashing green eyes, mine are dull and brown, and yours are bright and shining. You have perfectly shaped lips, and I have a crooked smile. Your hair is so beautiful and shiny, and you never seem to struggle with the frizz like I do." Rose laughed.

"But Rose, you are so beautiful. On your birthday, when you wore that lavender dress, you looked like a princess. Marcus told me he nearly fainted because you were so beautiful."

Rose shrugged. "And yet all I see is my flaws, just like you. But do you know what my friend Alice said to me last night?"

"No." Callie shook her head.

Rose led her back to their bed and they snuggled under the blankets. Rose put her hand on Callie's shoulder.

"Alice said you and I are so alike that she could have mistaken us for twins. She told me she'd never seen two more beautiful sisters in all her life."

"Really?"

"Remember, I said I wouldn't lie to you? You just need to find that beauty in yourself, and whether you work like I plan to or go on to be a wife and mother or do both; you are going to be wonderful at it, and there is no shame in either, Callie. I can't wait to see what your future holds, Sister. I'm very proud of you, and I love you so much." Rose kissed Callie on the forehead.

"I love you too." Callie grinned. "What would Pa say if I started courting a Mountie?"

Rose rolled her eyes and giggled. "I'm not sure. It would take some getting used to for him, that's for sure."

They laughed together, and both yawned. "Well, Sister, let's get some sleep."

* * * *

Katie wiped her hands on her apron and hurried to answer the knock on the door. "Daniel?"

"Hi, Sis." He bent down to kiss and embrace his sister.

"What're you doing here, Danny?"

"I've come to kidnap you."

Katie's brows flew up in question.

"I've been sent by Adam to collect you and the girls."

Katie glanced at the clock. "But it's near suppertime. Where're we going?"

"Don't worry about supper; everything's prepared for you. All you need is your coat. I've got the doctor's car out front. I expect you and the girls to be in it in five minutes." He raised his brows in mock sternness.

Katie thrust her hands on her hips and squinted at him. "Daniel Coleman, what's going on?"

Daniel chuckled. "Nope, not telling, now get the girls and your coats and get in the car. You have four and half minutes." He affected his big brother voice.

"What's Adam up to?" Katie persevered, pursing her lips.

Daniel gripped her arm and smiled kindly. "Trust Adam, Katie, you know he'd never do anything to hurt any of you. He's got something wonderful planned for you all." He raised his brows then. "Now you have three minutes."

Katie grinned and ran down the hallway to get the girls.

Daniel pulled over to the side of the road in the car. "I'm afraid I have to blindfold you all from here." He turned off the car and exited.

"What?" Katie frowned.

"Trust me, you're gonna love it, but Adam wants it to be a surprise, so I'm going to lead you there, but you need to be blindfolded."

"We trust you, Brother." Katie and the girls looked around and shrugged at each other.

They walked single file holding hands, following Daniel. It was only a short distance, and Daniel stopped them all. He guided the girls to stand next to their mother in a line. Katie could smell fish cooking and heard the crackling of a fire. "Where are we, Danny?"

"Okay, take off your blindfolds."

The four girls and Katie lifted the rags over their heads and looked around. Mouths fell open and eyes grew wide. They looked at each other incredulously.

"What is this?" Katie finally found her voice.

Adam stood with his arms folded under a wide canopy of trees. A pile of feather mattresses lay side by side, with quilts and pillows. A fire burned nearby with fish cooking over it. A line of lanterns skirted each side of the small campsite.

Adam grinned and walked slowly towards his family. He gave Daniel a nod. "Thanks for kidnapping my family for me."

"My pleasure, have a good time." Daniel squeezed his sister's arm and walked away. They heard the car start and drive away.

"What is all this, Pa?" Hope asked.

Adam cupped her chin. "I thought we'd sleep under the stars tonight. What d'ya think?"

All faces lit up. "Really, Pa." Lizzie grinned.

"Really, Darling." He looked up at Katie and her eyes sparkled. "What do you think, Ma?"

"Adam, this is wonderful. Last time you took the children camping, I missed out. I was pregnant with Sarah at the time."

Adam put his arm around Katie and kissed her. "Well then, it's been far too long, and I'm thrilled to have my wife with me this time."

They walked towards the mattresses. "This is wonderful, Adam, such a beautiful, tranquil spot." Katie looked over the small stream. Jack lay sleeping next to the fire and Lizzie hurried over and stroked his head.

"I'm glad, Darling. I've been setting this up for two days, and I'm glad the weather is pleasant."

"I've never slept outside before." Katie grimaced as Adam sat down on the mattresses and she joined him.

He put his arm around her, as the girls began throwing sticks for Jack. Adam tilted his head to the side. "Never?"

Katie shook her head. "Never, I was a city girl, remember?"

"Not even on the farm?"

"No." She chuckled. "But I can't wait."

"You aren't scared?"

Katie leaned her head against his shoulder. "I'm never scared when you're with me, Adam."

Adam swallowed and kissed her hair. "I'll always do my utmost to keep you safe, Katie." He sighed.

Katie sat back. "Adam, you aren't to feel bad. It's not your fault that evil men tried to hurt us. They didn't get to, because you saved us, like you have so many times before."

"I know, Katie. I just wish there was a way I could guarantee you're always safe. I worry about you all.

"We're just fine, Adam. Now let's get on with enjoying ourselves. What do you have available to make for supper?"

"I have it under control, Katie. I've got our supper ready. You get the evening and morning off."

Katie raised her brows. "You cooked?"

Adam chuckled. "Don't look so scared. I can cook a bit, you know."

Katie tried to keep her face straight. "I will reserve judgement, Husband."

Adam shook his head. "Trust me."

Katie's face became serious. "I always trust you, Adam."

He kissed her again and then stood up to join the girls in their game. Katie sat and watched while they played tag and splashed in the shallows of the river. She shook her head and brushed away a tear. Adam was such a wonderful father, so devoted to his family. Spending time with his girls was never a chore for him. She laughed heartily as the wet dog shook all over them and the girls grimaced and chased him around.

Katie leaned back in Adam's arms and watched the girls sleep in the flickering light of the lanterns. "This is so wonderful, Adam."

Adam sat with his long legs stretched out, leaning back against the large pine tree. Katie sat across his legs, her head on his shoulder. He wrapped his arms around her and kissed her cheek. "It's wonderful having you in my arms out here in the great outdoors, enjoying God's creation."

"Thank you for this. It's just what we needed."

"If only Callie and Rosie were here, it would be perfect."

Katie nodded. "Yes, but it's as perfect as it can be."

They sat in silence for a time, both alone with their thoughts. Adam grinned and brushed his wife's cheek. "I love you, Wife, do you know that?"

Katie turned in his arms to look at him. "I do know that. I feel your love every day."

"Good. I'll keep on telling you. I love you more than I ever thought possible. It's like you fill my soul somehow. Does that make sense?"

"Yes, that's how I feel, too. I remember when I thought you had died, that I could still feel you deep in my soul. Like you were still a part of me even though you were dead, at least at that time you were."

Adam squeezed her. "I still can't believe you went through that. It broke my heart when I was in the jail and I heard they'd had funerals for us." He sighed and laid his head against hers. "It was so hard to think of you moving on, learning to live without me. To think of my girls hurting so much and having to grow up without me. My thoughts often ran away with me, and I'd imagine the years to come and another man walking my girls up the aisle, loving them, and holding you in his arms as you slept."

Katie sat up incredulously and her face fell. "Another man?"

He shrugged. "Yeah, I assumed you'd remarry, eventually. I was so jealous to think of another man being there for my girls, and them forgetting me...." Adam stopped abruptly as a tear ran down Katie's cheek. "What is it?"

Katie raised her hand to his cheek. "Adam, I could never love another man, not even if you had really been dead. I would've lived the rest of my days alone rather than let another man into my life.

176

It would be treasonous to my heart. You fill every inch of me. I remember saying this to Jo, she was worried I'd remarry and they'd have to move out. I told her it would be the ultimate betrayal for me to do that. I admire Louisa, but I would rather die myself than love another man. I will love you till my dying breath, even if you've been dead and buried for fifty years."

Adam sniffed loudly and looked into her eyes. Cupping her cheek, he leaned in and kissed her. Katie put her arms up around his neck, and they prolonged the kiss for some time.

Then she lay her head on his shoulder and snuggled back against him. "Thank you, Katie." His voice shook. "I feel the same; my soul began to atrophy in that prison, away from you all. If it weren't for God and Sam, I would've died there, and not because of the conditions. I would've died of a broken heart."

"Oh, Adam." Katie sighed. "Thank you for this time. It's so wonderful. We all love you so much."

Adam grinned then. "So, how was supper?"

Katie sat back and tapped her chin. "I give you a passing grade, Husband."

Adam furrowed his brow. "Just a pass?"

Katie chuckled. "Well, since you are the teacher's pet, I think I can confidently give you an A+. Your fish, potatoes and vegetables were delicious."

"I'm glad. Well, shall we turn in?"

"Yes." She smiled. They stood, kissed each sleeping face and climbed under the covers fully clothed. Katie lay with her hands and head on his chest, they slept between the girls, and Jack stood guard. Adam would not sleep that night. He'd never let himself fall asleep and put his girls at risk. Instead, he'd enjoy lying with his wife in his arms and spending the night looking at the stars and counting his many blessings.

"That was the best Spring Break ever, Pa." Lizzie grinned as they unpacked the car.

Adam winked at her. "I'm glad you enjoyed it, Lizzie Girl."

"If only Callie and Rose were here, it would've been perfect." Anna lifted out two feather pillows and walked towards the house.

"Yes, I agree. Callie and Marcus will be back tomorrow." Adam lifted his elbow to Katie to escort her inside. "Did you have a good time, Wife?"

"Very much, Adam. It was wonderful to spend time outside together. Thank you."

"Thank you, Wife. My soul is dancing a jig. You all bring me so much happiness and love; it's refreshing and restoring and makes me strong."

"Me too, Adam. I feel like I could fly."

"Really?" He raised his brows. "I think I can oblige that."

Katie frowned and then shrieked as Adam lifted her up in his arms and carried her inside. He placed her down on her feet and kissed her.

She laughed and shook her head at him. "Sergeant Morgan, you are incorrigible."

"True, that's why you love me." He winked at her.

She chuckled and hurried into her kitchen to prepare the noon meal.

*　*　*　*

Constable Scott arrived early to escort Rose, Marcus and Callie to the train station. Rose observed the Mountie carefully and came to the conclusion that he did have feelings for Callie. He tenderly touched her arm and smiled at her as he said goodbye, and Rose could see the light in his eyes. She grinned. *They're well suited.* But she would do no matchmaking and wouldn't say anything to Jonny. It was up to the Lord, and He'd orchestrate the events if they were meant to be.

Rose clung to Marcus and Callie for the longest time until the conductor made the last call. Rose and Jonny waved until the train was out of site.

Jonny opened the car door for her, then walked around to take the driver's seat. "Thanks for inviting me along this week, Miss Morgan. I've enjoyed it."

"My pleasure, Constable. You're good company." Rose touched his arm affectionately.

"You too, Miss Morgan and your Marcus is a fine man."

"I think so." She grinned.

"Your sister is great too." He tried to sound nonchalant but failed miserably. "Is she still at school?" He blushed slightly, and Rose grinned. She had been right. He did have feelings for her.

"Yes, she has one more year after this one."

"What does she hope to do when she leaves school? Does she want to be a teacher like you?"

"Nah, not Callie. She's not sure yet, but she does know in the future, she'd love to be a wife and a mother. She's already a fine cook and seamstress." Rose hadn't meant to talk her sister up that much and had got a little carried away. She blushed slightly.

Jonny Scott grinned. She sounded like the perfect woman to him. He tried to keep his voice casual and not give away his feelings. "Well, I found her to be a bright and clever young woman. I'm sure whatever she does, she'll be good at it." He failed at sounding professional, but Rose pretended not to notice.

"Thank you for the ride home, Constable."

Jonny pulled the car up to the curb outside the boarding house. "It's my pleasure, as always, Miss Morgan. Enjoy starting school again. Only three months to go now, I believe?"

"Yes." She grinned. "I like studying, but I'm looking forward to going home."

"I can imagine. Any job prospects yet?"

"No. It's not looking like there will be anything available at home." She shrugged and grimaced.

"Oh no." Jonny's tone was compassionate and caring. "So what will you do?"

Rose sighed. "Pray, I guess." She lifted her shoulders sadly. "God has it all in hand." She tried to reassure herself.

"Yes, He does. I'll pray for you."

"Thank you. I'll see you at church on Sunday." Rose exited the car.

Jonny nodded and grinned at her. "Yes, I'll be there. Good day, Miss Morgan." He tipped his Stetson to her.

"Good day, Constable Scott." She waved and headed into the boarding house.

Fifteen
Congratulations, Miss Morgan.

"Three months to go!" Rose sighed as she climbed the stairs. "And then what?" Alice and Mandy already had schools lined up. Sadie was waiting to hear back from two jobs. But Rose had absolutely no prospects. A tear ran down her cheek as she entered her room. She slumped into her chair.

She simply couldn't imagine living in any other town than Douglas Falls. She'd applied at Pine Crest too, but Alice had been offered the one position there, given it was her home town. Rose was delighted for her friends, and she really hoped that Sadie would get the job she had her heart set on too. But she worried for herself.

The school at Douglas Falls had two classes, but neither of the teachers was planning to leave anytime soon. Rose didn't want either of them to lose their jobs so she could get one, but she longed to go back to Douglas Falls. She couldn't bear the thought of moving to another town and being so far away from her family. This year had been hard enough.

There were six jobs going in Edmonton schools and many more in other parts of the territory. If she wanted to go further west, she could get a job easily, but none of those places were Douglas Falls, and that was where her heart was. It was the only place in the world she wanted to be. She sighed loudly and prayed again.

She prayed every day that the Lord would make a way where there seemed to be no way. She trusted Him, but waiting on Him was so difficult. She talked to her pa and Marcus about it on the phone many times as the semester continued on, but none of them had any advice for her, except to pray.

She knew her parents would support her no matter where she went, but the thought of being away from Marcus and her family for another year was torture. She sighed. "Oh Lord, please show me the way." She shrugged and pulled out her book to continue her study.

*   *   *   *

The semester wound to an end. All that was left was to submit a paper, wait for her final grades and then she would graduate. "And then what?" Rose sighed as she waited for the phone to ring. Every other person in her class had a job, except her.

Graduation was Friday morning, and then she'd go home. As much as she longed for home, she also dreaded it. Going back there as a graduate would be wonderful. "Oh, but what if I can't get a job? I'll just be an overqualified store clerk?" She sighed again. The shrill ring of the telephone made her jump. She hurried to answer it and shared her fears with the man she loved, sobbing on the phone to him.

"I'll have to go back to working in the store, I guess."

"But, Rose, you're meant to teach. It's who you are."

"Then I'll have to leave Douglas Falls." She sobbed. "I couldn't bear that. My family is there."

"I know, my darling. But if you do leave, I'll come with you. I can get a carpentry job anywhere."

"I just couldn't, Marcus. It's been so lonesome here away from my family."

"But you'd have me. I'll be your family."

"It wouldn't be the same. We aren't married."

"We could get married."

"Marcus, that's not the right reason to get married, and you know it."

"I know." He sighed, out of ideas to encourage her. "God will work out the details."

"I know He will, Marcus, and it's sinful of me to fret and despair, but I can't help worrying that all this sacrifice and cost to my pa has been a waste of time."

"He doesn't think that, Rose. He wouldn't even if your fears come true."

Rose just sighed.

"I have to go. I'm sorry. I know things are tough for you, but they will work out. I know it. I'll be praying that your examination results are good, and I'll see you on Thursday, and Rose, just think, on Friday, you'll be a teacher!!"

"A teacher with no students."

"Hey, you don't know that. A lot can happen over a summer. Try to enjoy your last days at college."

"I will, Marcus. I'm sorry for despairing. I love you."

"I understand, Darling. I love you too."

* * * *

"This is the last time I have to wait for the train." Rose beamed.

Constable Scott squeezed her arm. "This time, when your family leave, you get to go home with them."

"I want to thank you, Constable. I know Pa meant for you to be my protector, but you've also become a good friend."

"Thank you, Miss Morgan, it's been my pleasure. I'll miss you."

"I'll miss you too. And won't you please call me Rose?"

Jonny chuckled. He nodded slowly. "Of course, Rose, if you'll call me Jonny."

"Certainly, Jonny."

They had no more time for conversation as the train approached and the whirlwind of greetings began. Rose observed the shy glances between the young Mountie and her sister as she climbed down the steps. His eyes sparkled, and his cheeks flushed. Callie looked shyly up at him as he put his hand out to help her down. Both gulped as a current passed through them for the short time they touched. He let go of her hand as she stepped out onto the platform, nodded to her and turned to help Anna and Hope who alighted next.

Rose embraced each of her family as they exited the train. She found herself being held in Marcus's arms again and his relief was evident all over his face. Relief that they didn't have to miss each other anymore.

He released her, and there was barely time to take a breath before her cheek was leaning against red serge. The strong arms of her father wrapped around her.

"Pa, I've missed you."

"No need to miss us anymore, Darling." He kissed her hair. "You've done it. You've finished, and I'm so proud of you." He released her and kissed her cheek. Her ma claimed her next.

"Darling." Katie held her grown-up daughter. "Well done."

She embraced each of her sisters while Adam greeted Constable Scott. He reached out to shake the younger man's hand. "Thank you for looking out for my daughter, Constable. It's been comforting to know a fellow Mountie is here watching over her."

"It's been my pleasure, Sir." Jonny's eyes roamed to meet Callie's. He couldn't help but smile. Somehow she seemed even more beautiful to him. Perhaps absence really did make the heart grow fonder. Adam followed his gaze and grimaced when he saw the constable smile and the blush on Callie's cheeks.

Another young Mountie, Constable Jackson, walked over to help get all the people and luggage to the hotel.

Adam noticed Jonny in an animated conversation with Callie and frowned. Did he notice sparks there? He sincerely hoped not! He wasn't thrilled with the idea of his daughter marrying a Mountie and going far away from him. He wasn't worried about any of his girls not being up to the challenge. They were strong, brave, and courageous girls. But the thought of one of his girls being far away was horrifying to him. He sighed.

"What is it, Husband?" Katie gripped his hand.

"I think that Mountie has his eyes on my Callie." He grimaced.

"Do you think so?"

Adam nodded. "I don't blame him. She's beautiful." His voice trembled slightly.

"It'll be okay, Adam. She's very young yet, and in no hurry to leave your home."

"I thought that about my Rose, and I won't be able to keep her for much longer, I'm sure of it." He shook his head sadly.

"It's going to be okay. Just trust God."

"I do, Katie. That's the only reason I can keep going." Adam laid his head on his wife's.

Constable Scott pulled up at the hotel.

"Thanks for your help, chaps." Adam nodded and shook hands with the two constables after they'd placed the last of the luggage in the suite.

"Again, it's our pleasure, Sergeant. We'll be back on Saturday to take you all the train." Jonny smiled, and his eyes turned to Callie again. He blushed, tipped his hat to her and left the room. Adam shook his head and closed the door on the two men.

Katie ordered everyone tea and coffee, and they all sat down to enjoy the warm muffins that came with them. Adam placed his cup down and raised his brows at Rose. "Are you going to open that envelope or not?"

"I'm too nervous." She grimaced.

"You've already passed the year with excellent results, Darling." Adam beamed in pride. "I'm sure you've done very well in your exams. But whatever the result, we are proud of you."

"A kiss for courage." Marcus kissed her on the cheek and squeezed her arm.

She grinned. "Alright." She took a deep breath. "Here we go." Rose looked around at the smiling faces of her family for courage. She opened the envelope and pulled out the piece of paper it contained. "I can't look. You look." She closed her eyes tightly and shoved the paper at Marcus.

Marcus chuckled. He took the paper, read it, and grinned. Then he folded it back up and put it in his pocket.

"Well, Marcus, what does it say?" Adam squinted his eyes at the young man.

"Oh, she got ninety-two percent," he said nonchalantly and then grinned at Rose. Everyone cheered.

"Oh, Rosie." Adam hugged Katie and Sarah, sitting on either side of him.

"Ninety-two percent?" Rose asked incredulously. "That can't be right."

"It is. I knew you'd ace it, Rose. You're so brilliant."

"Thanks, Marcus." He embraced her and kissed her on the cheek.

Adam sniffed and Rose looked up and ran to him. He stood to take her in his arms. "Rosie Girl, I'm so proud of you." He spoke into her hair. "You've done so well."

"What good is it, if I don't have a school to teach at? I'll just be an over-qualified store clerk." Her voice trembled.

"Hey, that's not going to happen, Darling. I know it."

She pulled back from him and tears flooded her eyes. "How do you know? How can you know that for certain? Every single person in my class has a teaching position for after they graduate, except for me. Ninety-two percent and straight A's are meaningless if I can't teach." Her tears overflowed down her cheeks. A loud sob escaped her lips. She ran to the bedroom, threw herself on the bed and sobbed.

Adam turned to Katie. "I'll go to her."

She gripped his arm and nodded. "Have you got the letter?"

He patted his breast pocket and nodded. Adam walked into the room and sat on her bed. He placed his hand on her hair and talked to her softly. "Rose."

She sat up and threw herself in his arms. He wrapped his arms around her and held her tight as she cried as he had so many times before. It was never a chore for him. He'd hold her for just as long as she needed. At last, she was cried out, and he released her, reached into his pocket and pulled out his handkerchief. She dried her tears and blew her nose.

"Pa, I'm a failure."

"Rose Katherine Morgan." His voice was stern. She looked up at him in surprise. He so seldom spoke to any of his girls that way. "I will not have anyone, least of all you, call my Rosie a failure. That couldn't be further from the truth." His eyes became misty as he stroked her cheek. "I am so proud of you, of all you've achieved. Ninety-two percent in the teaching board exam, straight A's in your college exams. Rose, you're exceptional."

She shrugged. "But if I can't teach, then what's the use?"

He grinned, pulled the envelope out of his pocket, and passed it to her. On the front was written: "Miss Rose Morgan."

"What is it?" She frowned and reached for it tentatively.

"Open it." He raised his brows and grinned.

She opened the envelope and read the letter. She gasped and turned to her father with shining eyes. "I don't understand. How is this possible?"

"Come on, let's go out there, and I'll explain it to everyone." He grinned and hugged her again. "I'm so proud of you. Congratulations, Miss Morgan." He kissed her on the forehead.

"Oh, Pa. I can't believe it."

"Shall we go tell that lot out there?"

She nodded her head and smiled.

"Family." Adam got their attention. "I was going to wait until after she graduated to give Rose this, but now seemed a better time. Rose, please read your letter."

She stood next to him, and he put his arm around her as she read with shining eyes and trembling lips.

"Dear Miss Rose Morgan.

Thank you for your application letter you sent us in March of this year. We apologise for not replying sooner. We had to wait until we were certain of our role for next year. As you know, Douglas Falls is growing rapidly, and next year we will be expanding to three classes. Therefore, we wish to offer you the position of teacher for the grade 5-8 children beginning in September, provided you pass the teaching board examinations. Please reply as soon as possible should you choose to accept this offer. Congratulations on your graduation.

Yours sincerely,
Mr James Fox, Mayor
Douglas Falls.

"Oh, Rose!" Marcus gasped, leapt up and ran to embrace her. "I'm so proud of you."

"I'm going to be a teacher. I'm going to be a teacher." She sobbed in his arms.

"I knew you would, Rose. I'm so happy for you." Marcus closed his eyes and sighed in relief. He released her at last and kissed her cheek.

Her mother embraced her. "Ma, I got a job. I'm going to be teaching at Douglas Falls, just like you."

"I'm so proud of you, Darling."

Each of her sisters embraced her excitedly.

At last, Rose sat back down beside Marcus. She turned to her father again. "I still don't understand, Pa. How did you get hold of this?"

"The mayor approached me on behalf of the teaching committee. He said he wasn't sure whether to post it to you here or at home because he didn't know when you were coming home. I asked him if I could deliver it to you, and he whispered to me what it was. You've worked so hard, and I'm thrilled for you, following in your Mother's footsteps."

"Thanks, Pa."

"I'm so proud of you, Rose. You're going to be a wonderful teacher. I just know it. I can't wait to see you in action." Marcus held her tightly and kissed her forehead.

*   *   *   *

Rose grinned as they drove onto The Rise. "Home," she said wistfully. "I've missed this place so much." The pastures were covered with wildflowers, and birds flittered in the trees. It was a beautiful, warm summer's day. She drank in the familiar sights and smells that she'd longed for so many times.

Rose gasped as they drove up towards the house, and colourful bunting welcomed her home hanging from the trees outside. Standing beneath the banner was a crowd of people, food and drinks set up. The Randalls, Colemans, and Fergusons all gathered around, as well as most of the townsfolk. They drove up to cheers and cries of, "congratulations" and "welcome home graduate."

"Pa, what's this?" Rose looked around.

Adam grinned. "Your Uncle Daniel's doing."

"You deserve it, Rose." Marcus squeezed her hand. "They're all so proud of you."

Daniel walked over to the car, opened the door and helped Rose out, he wrapped his arms around her. "Congratulations, Rose, I'm so proud of you."

"Thanks, Uncle Danny." She embraced her Aunt Louisa and was soon hugging the entire town, or so it seemed. Once the greetings were over, Mayor Fox wandered over to her and asked if she'd received their offer.

"Yes, Sir, and I'm delighted to accept."

"That's wonderful news, Miss Morgan. You'll be an excellent teacher."

It was late in the afternoon before the last person left, and Rose was finally settled back in her bedroom. She sat on her bed and sighed. She reached for her old rag doll and held her to her chest. "Molly, so much has happened, and I'm so glad to be home. I'm a teacher. I'm actually a teacher."

"Yes you are, my darling." Adam grinned at her from the doorway, his eyes shining with pride. "I'm so glad to have you home with us again. It's not been the same without you."

"Me too, Pa. It's so beautiful and peaceful here. I could happily live up here on this hill for the rest of my days. It's the only place I ever want to be. I can't believe God worked it out so I could teach here."

"He always works things out, Darling."

"I know, and I'm so grateful. This is what I always dreamed. I can't wait for September."

"Just enjoy your summer, Darling. School will start soon enough." He winked at her and placed her case in her room.

Sixteen
Double Engagement

"Andy, your Amy is just lovely. I'm so glad I finally get to meet her." Rose smiled at her cousin. They took a few peaceful moments away from the rabble to catch up. "I can't believe you've been courting nearly six months."

Andy blushed and looked across the flower-covered pastures. A wide grin crossed his face and a twinkle entered his eyes. "I think she's pretty great."

Rose tipped her head to the side and flashed him a smile. "Do you have any plans?"

"Well, since you asked, yes, I do!" He couldn't keep his cheeks from colouring.

"Good for you, Andy. I look forward to hearing about them."

"All in good time, Rose. I wonder which of us will be first to get engaged." He raised his brows at her.

"Don't be absurd, Andy. It's obviously going to be you."

"Don't be so sure. Marcus isn't going to want to wait too long, now that you're home."

"We haven't been courting very long."

"Nearly a year." Andy raised his brows.

"Yeah, but we've not actually seen each other very much in that time."

He flashed her a knowing grin. "We'll see."

Rose sighed, she hadn't given any thought to getting engaged, but now that Andy was making plans, she started to dream. *Maybe Andy is right. Maybe Marcus will propose soon.* She grinned and her cheeks coloured. "What would my pa say?"

Andy chuckled. "He'd say yes, after he stopped crying. He's awfully tender-hearted when it comes to you girls."

Rose shrugged. "I guess having six daughters does that to a man. Imagine what he'll be like when it's Hope's turn."

"I can understand. I'm quite sure I'd be the same. I feel strongly enough about my sister. I can't imagine what it would be like with my own daughters."

"Do you and Amy hope to have a family someday?"

He blushed again. "We haven't really talked about it much, but I do know she likes children."

"Does she have any siblings?"

"She has a younger sister, but it's just the two of them."

Their conversation was interrupted by Marcus and Amy approaching. "There you two are." Marcus passed Rose a cup of coffee. "I was beginning to worry. Thought I might have to call a search party."

Rose nodded her thanks and took a sip of the coffee. "I just wanted to catch up with Andy. We've not talked in a long time. I was telling him how nice it was to finally meet you, Amy. I've heard so much about you." Rose smiled at the lovely, gentle, blonde girl.

"Thanks, Rose. I've been dying to meet you, too. Andy read me all your letters. Your life in the city seemed so interesting."

"That's because I only told Andy the interesting parts. I'm sure he didn't want to hear about all the mundane things. I saved them for Marcus."

"Lucky me." Marcus gave her a mock frown. Rose swatted at him, but he caught her hand, kissed it, and remained holding it.

Rose curled her face up at Marcus and turned back to Amy. "So, are you working?"

"Yes, that's how we met, actually. I'm a teller at the bank, and Andy works at the feed and grain store. He comes in every week to bank the cheques, and...." She shrugged. "We just started chatting, and then he asked me to supper." Amy smiled shyly up at Andy, who winked at her and took her hand.

"That's great." Rose beamed. "Do you enjoy working there?"

"Yes, very much. There are only three women working at the bank, but Mr O'Neil, the bank manager, told me I've got an excellent head for numbers. Which is strange because I never did very well in mathematics at school."

"I'm sure you did better than you thought, Sweetheart." Andy squeezed her hand.

"So, Andy, you ready for a rematch?" Marcus drained his cup and raised his brows at his fiend.

"You're on, Marc. If you're ready to lose again."

"Those are fighting words, my friend." Andy winked at Amy and headed inside to get the checkerboard out.

Amy smiled shyly, and Rose put her arm around the girl. "It's so lovely to get to know you, Amy. You are just as lovely as Andy described you to be."

"So are you."

"Walk with me to get the eggs? It looks like Lizzie got distracted, as always." Rose chuckled, watching her sister stepping up to bat in the baseball game; the egg basket discarded off to the side.

Rose and Amy walked the short distance to the chicken coop, taking a slight detour to pick up the discarded basket.

"So I bet you're glad to be home." Amy fell into step with Rose.

"Yes. It's been nearly three weeks now, and it's so wonderful. This is my favourite place in the world, up here on The Rise." Rose swept her arm around, gesturing to the scene before her.

"It is beautiful. I can see why you like it. Too bad you'll have to leave soon."

"Why?"

"When you and Marcus get married."

Rose's eyebrows flew up. "Oh, I guess I hadn't thought of that. It's a ways down the track. We aren't even engaged, so I think it'll be some time before I have to worry about that." She shrugged.

"I don't think so. Marcus hasn't been able to wipe the grin off his face since you got home."

Rose blushed.

"He missed you so much, Rose. He moped around most of the time. We'd go out for supper, and he'd just sigh and look off into the distance. Andy said he understood and he'd feel the same way. They're best friends, you know?"

"Yes, I know they have been since school. They were both a grade ahead of me." Rose placed the warm eggs in the bucket that Amy held out to her.

"I hope you do get engaged soon, Rose. It's so exciting. Andy can't wait for Marcus to be married to his cousin."

"Well, I can't wait for you to be married to my cousin either." Rose placed the last egg in the basket. "Wouldn't it be lovely? I hope when that does happen, we'll live close by. I sure would enjoy having a married friend like you. And with our men being best friends, it would be wonderful." Rose took back the basket, put it over her arm and led Amy out of the coop.

"I was thinking the same thing. I admire the friendship your parents have with Andy's folks and the Randalls, and Fergusons. I hope we get to have that someday."

Rose placed the egg basket down, flicked the latch to close the gate and lunged to embrace Amy. It caught her off guard, and they both laughed. "Me too." Rose scooped up the eggs, and they fell into step together.

"I'm glad. I just knew that you and I would be friends. Andy told me so much about you. He told me you two have always been very close."

"I guess we are. We're the oldest two, and we sorta grew up together."

"I love being a part of this family. Everyone has been so welcoming."

"Marcus feels the same way."

* * * *

"I'm excited to come and stay over with you tonight Amy, we'll have so much fun." Rose gripped her friend's arm as the two young couples walked to town.

"I can't wait, I don't like to be home alone. Ma and Pa will be gone two days and I'm glad I'll have you with me." Amy smiled.

Andy squeezed her hand. "I'm glad too, I feel much happier knowing you aint gonna be there alone. I'd stay over myself if I had to."

Amy gasped. "Andy!"

Andy chuckled. "I just mean so you're protected and not scared, I'd sleep on the front porch, not in the house, you know I'd never do anything to tarnish your reputation."

Amy gripped his arm and smiled. "Thank you. I appreciate your care for me. We'll be just fine."

"Well I can't wait to see what the two of you will cook up for us tonight."

Rose grinned at Marcus. "Typical of you to think of the food."

Both men chuckled as they approached the store.

"See you soon, Darling." Andy winked at Amy.

Marcus squeezed Rose's hand. Both women took their baskets from their men and hurried up the stairs.

Andy and Marcus watched them until they were in the store then headed for the saloon.

"So, did it arrive?" Andy raised his eyebrows as they sat down at the table with glasses of sarsaparilla.

"It sure did. Picked it up this morning." Marcus grinned.

Andy nodded. "When are you gonna ask her?"

Marcus shrugged. "Not sure, gotta talk to her pa first." He grimaced.

"Yeah, that's not an easy conversation. I'm dreading talking to Amy's pa, too."

"Amy's pa isn't a sergeant." Marcus smirked.

"No, he's a farmer, but it's still his precious daughter."

"I know. It's not easy when a man only has girls. Sergeant Morgan's about the most protective father I've ever met."

"Yeah, but he loves you, Marc. You're like a son to him."

Marcus grinned. "I hope to make that official soon."

Andy slapped him on the back. "Don't wait too long, Brother."

"You can talk, Andy. You've had your ring for about four weeks. When are you going to ask Amy?"

"I'm trying to pluck up the courage. Well, if truth be told, I have to save first. I've nearly got enough for a small home. But the ring set me back some." Andy screwed up his face.

Marcus sighed. "I know what you mean. I have enough saved for a small place, but I don't want some tiny little house on the other side of town. I've been looking at a plot near the Randall's home. The old Grant Estate, but I doubt I could afford it."

"I know that block. The house is pretty dilapidated."

"That's okay. I plan to build her a new house anyhow."

"I wish I could build. Might be easier to purchase land without a house. Ma and Pa will help me, but they don't have much either." Andy grimaced.

"I imagine not. Ministers don't exactly make much."

"No, but I'll be fine. I can take care of Amy once we have a home. My wages are good, and she gets a good wage at the bank too."

"Does she want to keep working after you're married?" Marcus drained his glass and signalled to the bartender for more. The man nodded, put down the glasses he was cleaning, fetched the blue bottle with the brown liquid, and headed their way.

Andy shrugged. "I don't know. These are things you tend to talk about once you're engaged." He nodded to the bartender, who signalled to ask if he wanted a refill. The man slopped liquid in both glasses, fetched the two coins off the table and walked back to the bar.

"Well, Brother, we'll work it out. I don't think I can wait much longer. I need to marry that woman." Marcus grinned.

"I completely understand. I need to marry Amy too. I can't wait to see what they're cooking us tonight. We're lucky men, Marc. Our ladies sure can cook." Andy lifted the glass to his lips.

"They sure can. A wonderful blessing."

"So when are you going to talk to her pa?" Andy asked again.

"Very soon. I hope to be engaged before she starts teaching."

Andy grinned. "I look forward to it, Marc."

"What about you?"

"You've inspired me. I think I'll go visit William and Elizabeth when they return from Pine Crest."

"Attaboy Andy. You won't regret it."

"Unless he says no!" The young man grimaced.

"He won't. Bill loves you. Besides, who wouldn't want their daughter to marry the pastor's son."

Andy laughed. "I guess. But I'm no pastor myself. I have a hankering to farm someday."

"Perfect, tell Bill that. Maybe you'll farm with him when you marry his daughter. He doesn't have any sons to pass the farm to."

Andy grinned and nodded. That had never occurred to him.

"Just think, my friend, by the end of the week, we could both have permission to marry our ladies." Marcus raised his brows.

"Or both have been turned down." Andy gave a mock scowl.

Marcus grimaced. "Let's pray the opposite happens."

Andy nodded. "I hope it works out for both of us. Sure would be nice to have another married fellow around to talk to when I need it. Well, someone my own age."

"Be nice to have a close family nearby like your family and Rose's have."

"I was thinking that too. Amy and I have talked about how good that would be."

Marcus grinned as the women stood at the doorway. Both men jumped up.

"Check in with you Saturday, Brother." Andy slapped his friend on the back, flashed him a toothy grin and headed out the door.

Both men took the baskets from the women and offered their arms, the four fell into step back towards the Louis farm.

*　*　*　*

Three days later, Marcus excused himself from work early. He walked home quickly, washed up, and got out of his work clothes before heading for town. He spent the entire walk planning what he was going to say. Pausing outside the RNWMP office, he took a deep breath, and tried to keep his hands from trembling. He knocked at Adam's door, and poked his head in, relieved to find the Sergeant at his desk.

Adam looked up and grinned. "Marc, come on in."

Marcus took another deep breath to control his swirling feelings. He walked in. "Good afternoon, Sergeant. I... uh wondered if I... I might have a conversation with you."

"Certainly, Marcus. Would you like some coffee?" Adam gestured to the empty chair. "Rose brought me a batch of cookies this morning. Applesauce. They're nearly as good as her ma's. Would you like some?"

Marcus nodded and grinned. He loved Rose's baking. The Mountie stood and walked to his small counter in the corner. He paused as he reached for two cups. He took a deep breath, and closed his eyes, steeling himself with a quick prayer, certain he knew what was about to come.

Right about the same time Marcus left work, Andy walked out of the feed and grain store. He'd also taken the afternoon off. The two young men had planned together, to face it at the same time, each taking comfort from knowing the other was in the same predicament.

Andy walked the few miles out of town towards the Louis homestead. He took a deep breath, whispered a prayer for courage and knocked on the door.

"Good afternoon, Andrew. Won't you come in?" Mrs Louis smiled at him. Andy grinned and followed her inside. Amy's parents were the only ones who ever called him Andrew. He was just Andy and always would be.

"Would you like some lunch, Son? There's plenty," William offered.

"No, thank you. I've eaten, but some coffee would be great if you don't mind, Mrs Louis."

"Of course, Andrew. I'll be right back." She hurried to the kitchen.

William put down his fork. "What brings you out here in the middle of the day?"

Andy took a deep breath as he sat down opposite Mr Louis. "I hoped I might have a word with you, Sir."

Mr Louis nodded knowingly and exhaled loudly. "I'll have a cup of coffee too, Darling." He grinned sheepishly towards his wife. She placed the cups and two large slices of almond cake on the table before them, then left the room with the excuse that she needed to return to her sewing.

* * * *

Adam sat down and poured the coffee. He handed Marcus the cookie dish, and they both sat in silence for a few moments. Marcus took a cookie and ate it hurriedly. He swallowed several times and wrang his hands together.

Adam could bear it no more. "Just say what you came to say, Marcus. Don't make me agonise over this any longer than I have to." Adam's eyes were misty, and his voice trembled.

Marcus nodded and reached for his coffee cup. Adam braced himself, and Marcus cleared his throat. "Sergeant Morgan, I've come to ask for your permission to marry Rose."

Adam closed his eyes and sighed. When he opened his eyes again, they were damp with unbidden tears. "I've dreaded this moment since Rose got home. I knew it would come sooner or later." He ran his fingers through his hair and tried desperately to keep his tears from running over.

Marcus nodded. "I wanted to wait until I had something to offer her. You know I'm qualified now. I have enough money saved for a small parcel of land, nothing like yours, but I hope to buy the small block just up the hill from the Randalls. The old Grant estate and then save to build her a house. I plan to provide for her, Sir."

Adam sat back and crossed his arms over his chest. "There's more to being married than just providing, Marcus."

"I know that, Sergeant. I plan to devote myself to making Rose happy for the rest of my days. I'm deeply in love with her, Sir. I'd give my life for her in a heartbeat, if it were required of me. I want to give her the world and everything in it, and live for her and with her for the rest of my days. If you'll let me."

Adam curled up one side of his mouth. "Marcus, I'd be proud to have you marry my Rose," Adam choked out.

"Really, Sir? I thought I'd have to fight harder than that. I know how you feel about her."

Adam took a deep breath. "I've had a feeling this was coming for some time now, so I've been preparing for it. I hate to lose her. She's my greatest treasure and the apple of my eye." Adam sniffed and ran his fingers through his hair, again. "But you're a fine young man, and I've seen how hard you've worked and how you've loved her and supported her. I know you two will be happy together. I can't come between true love even though it hurts me. It's a father's duty to raise his girls to leave his home for their husband's. It sure doesn't make it any easier though." He shook his head.

Marcus's smile stretched from ear to ear. "Sergeant Morgan, you've just made me the happiest man alive."

Adam sighed and nodded. "I know how it feels to have the love of a good woman, Son. It makes you feel weak and strong at the same time."

"It sure does."

They both stood. Adam walked around the table to embrace Marcus. "I'll be proud to call you son, Marcus."

"Thanks, Sir. I'm proud to be joining your family. It's the finest I know."

"Thank you, I think so." Adam grinned. "And to be worthy of one of my girls, you have to be one of the finest men I know, or you'd never've made it past my doorstep." Adam raised his eyebrows, and Marcus knew he was serious.

"I won't take that lightly. As soon as Rose says yes to marrying me, I plan to go and put a deposit on the land."

"When do you plan to ask her?"

"This evening. I want to take her out for supper, with your permission."

"Of course, Marcus. Promise you'll come by the house afterwards. It's too great a secret to keep for too long."

"We will. I have to bring her home anyway, Sir."

"Marcus."

"Yes, Sir?"

"Don't call me sir."

Marcus grimaced. "Yes, Sergeant."

Adam nodded. "Now get out of here before I change my mind."

"Of course." Marcus grinned and skipped out the door.

Adam sat back on the edge of sighed loudly.

"What about your Rose?" Daniel stepped in.

Adam shook his head. "You always did have the most uncanny timing, Pastor. You seem to always turn up just as I become introspective."

"It's a gift." Daniel chuckled. "Now, what about Rose?"

Adam raised his eyebrows and smiled wryly. "That young man who just skipped out of here just asked for her hand in marriage.

Daniel's grin disappeared. He sat back on the desk next to the Mountie. He put his hand on his friend's shoulder. "My commiserations, Brother. That can't have been easy."

"It wasn't, but how can I deny a love like that? I was just as hopelessly in love some years ago, and you didn't deny me."

"My sister wasn't seventeen though."

"No, and I wasn't eighteen, but I don't think age matters so much. Their love is obvious and true, and I can't get in the way of that. I do hope they'll wait a while though." He sighed.

"Well, I'm proud of you, Adam. The first one has to be the hardest, surely."

"I dunno." Adam shrugged and shook his head. "I'm not sure it'll ever be easy."

Daniel slapped his friend on the back and chuckled.

* * * *

"Mr Louis, Sir." Andy took a deep breath. "I've ah... come to ask your permission... to marry Amy."

William Louis chuckled. "I figured as much, Son."

"Well... what do you think?" Andy scoffed internally. He'd spent the entire walk working out what to say, and now he felt tongue-tied.

The older man stroked his beard. He tilted his head to the side and squinted at the boy. "What are your plans, Andrew? How do you plan to support my daughter?"

"Uh, well... I have enough saved to purchase a small piece of land. My friend... Marcus... Marcus Murray, he's gonna help me build when I can save enough money. Course he'll... be building a house of his own too," he stammered. He took a deep breath to calm his nerves. *Come on, Coleman, Pull yourself together!* He scolded himself and continued. "I plan to save enough money to get a farm of my own one day, Sir. A lot like yours. My birth father was a farmer, and I hope to follow in his footsteps."

Mr Louis grinned. He'd hoped that would be the case. Andy had spoken about wanting to farm before. He hoped to persuade the boy to work alongside him on his farm.

"That won't be necessary, Son. I've been planning to expand for some time but haven't had the manpower. Evans has offered me his block three times now. It borders us just here to the north. That's his homestead. You can see it just a few hundred yards from here. It's a pretty little house. His wife passed a while ago, and they had no children. He's planning to head into the mines if he can sell." The farmer smiled. "I've been knowing for a time you'd be coming here asking for my Amy's hand, and I been thinking if we was to pool our money and purchase the Evans property together, you and Amy could live right there, and you could start farming right away with me, if that's what you want."

Andy thought for a moment and grinned. "Are you saying yes to me marrying your daughter, Sir?"

"Yes, Son. I thought I said that. You'd be a fine son-in-law; already been a big help to me many times. I'd be right glad to be sharing my farm with you. And Andrew, in the future, it'd be yours and Amy's when we're dead and buried; for you to raise your family on." The man chuckled at the shocked look on Andy's face. "I don't mean to get ahead of you, Lad. And I'm not planning your future for you, but I been thinking on it some. I don't have me any sons, you see. It seems to me that you're a mighty fine lad. You have excellent character, and you're from a good family. You do right by my Amy, and you make her happy, so I'd be most happy for you to marry my daughter, even if you don't want to live next door and farm."

Andy grinned. "Thank you, Sir. Thank you so much. I promise you, I'll love your daughter for the rest of my life, Sir. I'll do everything I can to make her happy. As for the farm... it sounds like a dream come true, but I'd want to talk to Amy about it. Can we have some time to talk it through?"

"Of course, Son." William stood and Andy followed suit. "Welcome to the family." He shook Andy's hand and gripped his shoulder. "Ma'll be right excited. We both think you're a fine chap. When you gonna ask her?"

"Tonight over supper at the café."

"Alright, we'll see you afterwards then." He shook the young man's hand.

"Very well, Sir." Andy grinned and promptly left. As soon as he was out of earshot of the Louis farm, he leapt in the air just as high as he could and whooped, thrusting his fist in the air. "Yaaaahooo."

Just as he approached town, he spotted Marcus coming out of the RNWMP office. He wore the same wide grin, and Andy knew he'd got the same answer. Andy whooped again, and Marcus spotted him and ran towards him. "Well?" Andy asked just so Marcus could say it.

"Got his blessing." Marcus grinned. "You?"

"Yep, and he offered me to work with him on the farm."

Marcus raised his eyebrows. "Wow, that's big. Are you going to accept?"

"I'll have to talk to Amy about it first."

"I'm happy for you, my friend."

"And I you, Marc." They slapped each other on the back

"Tonight?" Andy grinned.

Marcus nodded. "Yes, you?"

"Yes! And I can't wait."

"They are going to be so excited to be getting engaged on the same day."

Andy grinned. "Best of luck to you."

"And you, Andy."

They turned and walked in opposite directions. Andy leapt in the air again and shouted, "Yes!" Marcus chuckled. He felt like doing the same.

* * * *

Andy and Amy were the first to arrive. Victoria seated them at the back of the cafe where the lamplight was low. They sat and chatted happily. From Andy's seat, he could see Marcus and Rose walk in and take their seat nearer the front. The women had their backs to each other, both totally unaware of what was happening. Marcus caught Andy's eye as he seated Rose, and they gave each other the slightest of nods.

Dessert reached both tables almost simultaneously. Andy couldn't wait any longer. He put down his spoon, reached for Amy's hand, and looked her in the eye. "Amy, I love you so much. I have for some time, and I know you love me too. I'm not one for big speeches; I just want to say that you make me so incredibly happy." He stroked the delicate white hand and lifted it to his lips. "I feel like the most blessed man alive because you love me, and I want to spend my life making you happy." Amy's eyes flooded with tears. He let go of her hand, slid out of his chair, pulled the ring box from his pocket, and knelt in front of her. He held her hand and looked up into her glistening eyes. She gasped and bit her lips together, her breath coming in small gasps.

"Amy Evelyn Louis, will you marry me?" His voice trembled, his eyes searched hers, full of hope.

Amy nodded and reached her arms out to him. "Yes, of course I will, Andy. I love you too."

Andy drew her into his arms. "I'm the happiest man alive, Amy." He kissed her gently and returned to his seat, took her hand, and slipped the ring onto her finger. He lifted the hand to his lips and kissed it. Amy admired the beautiful ring

"Do you like it?"

"Oh yes, it's beautiful, Andy. Thank you. You make me so happy." Tears rimmed her eyes, but she wore a wide smile.

"What are you grinning at, Marcus?" Rose tilted her head to the side. The little scene across the restaurant had caught his eye.

"I'm grinning, Rose, because you make me so happy." He lifted her hand and kissed her fingers. "I never imagined I'd ever be this blessed that I'd get to hold the heart of a woman as remarkable as you. You are everything to me, and I love you more than life itself."

"I love you too, Marcus."

Marcus opened his jacket and pulled out a small box. Rose gasped. "Marcus." He stood up and walked around to kneel before her as Andy had done. He reached for her hand. Rose held her breath, tucking her lips under. Her spare hand flew to her face.

"Rose Katherine Morgan." He grinned. "I have loved you for a long time, and I will for the rest of my days. You are the most important person in my life, and I want to spend my days serving you and devoting my life to making you happy, because you make me incredibly happy. More than I ever thought possible. I want to give you the world and hold you in my arms for the rest of my days. Will you be my wife, Rose? Will you marry me?"

"Oh, Marcus! Of course, I will. I love you so much." She was not a bit concerned about the eyes around her. He slid the ring on her finger, and kissed her, taking her in his arms.

"Rose, you don't know how happy you've made me."

"Yes, I do, because you make me feel the same way," she said against his shoulder.

Marcus sat back up in his seat and held her hand. Rose admired her ring. It had a diamond with small green stones that ran along the top of the band. "It's so beautiful, Marcus. Green is my favourite colour."

"I know, that's why I chose it. I'm sorry to say the stones aren't real." He grimaced.

Rose smiled. "I don't need real stones. This is beautiful, and I love it. Thank you."

"Come on, let's go tell your parents." He grimaced. Rose chuckled. As they stood to leave, she kissed him on the cheek.

Andy and Amy met Rose and Marcus by the door. Both couples held hands and all eyes sparkled. As soon as they stepped outside, Rose and Amy looked at each other, and both at the same time grinned and said, "We're engaged." Both gasped, chuckled and hugged each other tightly.

"Oh, Rose, I'm so happy for you."

"I'm happy for you too, Amy."

"I can't believe we got engaged on the same night." Rose turned and screwed up her face at Marcus, squinting her eyes at him. "Did you two plan it that way?"

"Yep!" Andy slapped Marcus on the back. "Was good to have another chap going through the same agony as me." He chuckled, and Marcus grinned and nodded his agreement.

Both girls laughed. "We should have a combined engagement party too," Rose suggested.

"Oh, I'd love that," Amy responded.

While the girls gushed together, the two best friends patted each other on the back, then thought again and changed to a warm embrace. "Congratulations, Friend. She's a good woman."

"So is, Amy. I'm happy for you both, Andy."

"Well, I best get my fiancée home." Andy gripped Amy's hand.

She shrugged her shoulders and beamed. "Fiancée."

"Me too." Marcus reached for the hand that wore his ring and, lifting it to his lips, he kissed it. "Fiancée." He winked at her and they parted ways.

* * * *

"Andy, your place is closer than mine. Shall we tell your folks first?"

"You don't mind?"

"Of course not."

They changed course, and headed to the pastorage. Andy opened the door. His parents and siblings were seated in the lounge. Daniel was reading to them from a book of Bible stories. He looked up as the door opened.

"Sorry, Pa, we can't stay." Andy's face lit up. "We just wanted to tell you that, well... we're engaged."

"Oh, Son. Congratulations." Daniel discarded the book and stood to embrace him. He released his son and put his arms around Amy. "You are most welcome in our family, Amy. I'll be proud to have another daughter."

"Thank you, Pastor."

Louisa hugged them both. "I'm happy for you two."

After hearty congratulations, Andy escorted Amy back to her parent's house. While they walked out of town in the evening sunshine, he discussed her father's offer. "What do you think?"

"Do you want to farm, Andy?"

"You know I do. It's always been my dream. Working at the feed and grain store is only temporary to make some money. I thought it would be years before I could get a farm of my own, but this way, I can farm with your pa, right away, and we can work to pay off the land and extend the house."

"And I'd be right next door to Ma and Lydie."

"Does that mean you want to?"

"Oh yes, Andy. I never dreamed we'd get to live on a farm. I thought we'd have to live in town. This is so much better than I could have imagined."

"Yes, and it's not so far from the land Marcus hopes to purchase for Rose."

"I'm so excited, Andy. Our future looks so bright."

*   *   *   *

Adam paced nervously in front of the fire. *What's keeping them?* He'd told Katie that Marcus was planning to propose tonight, but now he was nervous. This was much harder than he thought it would be. He stopped pacing when he heard the wagon pull up and footsteps on the stairs. He took a deep breath and stood to wait for the couple to walk in, crossing his arms over his chest. Katie was knitting before the fire; she looked up at Adam and chuckled.

The door opened, and Katie immediately laid her knitting aside and stood with Adam, awaiting the inevitable announcement. Adam put his arms around Katie for support and sucked in his breath. His eyes already misting over.

The young couple entered with shining eyes and glowing faces. Marcus carefully shut the door, then reached for Rose's hand. Rose took the lead. "We're engaged."

Adam exhaled. "Oh, Rosie." His lips trembled.

Katie grinned and ran to embrace her daughter. "Congratulations, Darling. You look so happy."

"We are, Ma."

The girls all jumped up, squealed and danced around happily.

Adam approached slowly and wordlessly took Rose in his arms while Katie moved on to Marcus. He tried to swallow back his emotions, but his voice quivered as he held her. "Rose, my darling, I'm happy for you."

"Really, Pa? I thought you'd be sad."

"Oh, I am. I'm sad for me but happy for you. My loss will be Marcus's gain."

"You'll never lose me, Pa. I'll always be your girl."

Adam tightened his grip and kissed her hair. "I know, Rosie, but it won't ever be the same now. You're Marcus's not mine anymore! But I'm glad, Daughter, that you've found a good man." He stood back and looked at Marcus, gripping his arm. "A fine man to share your life with." Marcus gulped. Adam's faith in him meant everything.

"You wouldn't have let me marry just any man."

"That's for sure." Adam grinned, and winked at her. "It's a father's duty to make sure his girls are in good hands, and with Marcus, I know you are." He embraced Marcus briefly, leaving his hand on his shoulder. "Look after her, Son." He sniffed back his tears. "She's my pride and joy."

"I know, Sergeant. I will. You have my word that I'll treasure her for the rest of my days."

"You'd better. I am a policeman, you know." Adam raised his eyebrows at Marcus. "I carry a gun."

Marcus nodded, "I'm aware." He grimaced, and both men chuckled.

"Ma, Andy and Amy got engaged tonight too."

"Really?" Katie grinned. "You'll have to have a shared engagement party."

"Amy and I have already talked about that. It would be wonderful."

They sat down, and Katie provided them all with coffee. After some time, Adam looked at Rose; tears brimmed his brown eyes, and a wry smile crossed his face. He was trying hard to swallow back his feelings but failing miserably.

Marcus put down his coffee cup and gripped Rose's hand. "So, I've talked to Rose as we rode here. I showed her the piece of land I'm looking at, and she's happy with it." He chuckled. "I think I'll go to town tomorrow and put an offer on it."

"Don't do that, Marc."

Marcus frowned and looked at Adam. "Why ever not?"

"It's not close enough." Adam smiled wryly.

"Pa, it's just down the road. It's the closest parcel of land for sale in the whole town." Rose frowned at him.

"Not close enough." Adam shook his head.

"I'm sorry. I don't understand." Marcus grimaced.

"Son, when I first bought this parcel of land as a single man, I did it with my future family in mind. I always wanted a large family, and that dream came true. I have eight acres here, and I'm not a farmer. I have no desire to farm this land, and it was always my dream to cut it up for my children, should they want to live here too. Now it's up to you, but I'm offering you an acre of your own up here on my land."

Rose's eyes lit up, and tears streamed down her face. "Pa, do you mean it? We could live up here on The Rise?"

Adam reached across to brush Rose's cheek. "Darling, nothing would thrill me more. If, one day, there are six more homes up here, that would be beyond my wildest dreams. I know not all of my girls and their husbands will want that, but those who do, I want them just as close by as they want to be.

"Growing old here with my girls and their families all around, grandchildren running across the acreage, that would make me the happiest man alive. There's plenty of space, and that was why I built such large stables a ways back from the house, so they'll service the whole property."

Marcus was stunned. "We couldn't ask you to do that. I have the money to purchase a property."

"Then purchase mine, Marc, if that's what you want. You can choose any plot you want. I'll give you a good price for it, and the title will be yours. How big was the plot of land you were looking at?"

"Less than half an acre."

"Well, this is better. But I won't force you to."

"Oh, Marcus, could we." Rose gripped his arm, her pleading eyes locked on his. "I can't imagine living anywhere other than The Rise."

"Well, I don't see why not, but I'll expect to pay for it, Sir. We aren't asking for charity."

"I respect that."

"Oh, Ma. I can't believe it. We'll be close by. Are you sure, Marcus? If you don't want to, the land down the hill will be just fine."

Marcus reached for her hand and grinned. "I can see how happy it'll make you to be up here with your family, and nothing makes me happier than knowing you are happy. It's fine by me. We can go for a ride tomorrow and choose a spot."

"I already know which spot I want."

"You do?" Adam and Marcus said at the same time and chuckled.

"Mmhmmm." Rose nodded. "The far acre overlooking the valley and the small waterfall. There's a large tree stump out there and a grove of trees; it's so beautiful. I could sit there and stare at that view all day."

"The far acre it is," said Adam. "We'll finalise the paperwork tomorrow, Son, and you can start planning your house. I'd be more than happy to help you build it, when I have time."

"That all seems settled. I really wasn't expecting this." Marcus laughed.

"Why wait? Let's go look at it now." Adam looked at his wife, and she nodded. They climbed aboard Marcus's wagon and headed for the far acre, pacing out the plot of land, approximately an acre, and Adam suggested a price. It wasn't nearly what the land was worth, but he insisted he wouldn't take a cent more, and they should save their money for their home.

Marcus and Adam shook on it. "We'll be delighted to have you both nearby." Adam reached for Rose. "I couldn't be more thrilled, Darling. It's a little easier to give you up knowing you'll be close by."

The young couple walked around the intended spot for their home, and Adam turned to his wife. "Katie, just think, in the future, our grandchildren will come running across the acreage and straight to our house. To think we'll have them right up here with us, just whenever we want to see them." His eyes sparkled his joy.

"You're getting sentimental in your old age, Husband." Katie laughed.

"I know." He nodded and grinned. "I would love it if all our girls lived all around up here."

"Like some kind of community."

"Morgan Estate!" He grinned. And they all laughed.

"I want a porch to look out over this beautiful view." Rose gushed. "Although it will be awfully hard to get any work done when I've got this to distract me."

"Well, we best get back before we completely run out of daylight." Marcus placed the last rock on the corner of the house site. "We have plenty of time for this, Darling." He kissed Rose on the cheek.

Seventeen
New Semester

"Are you ready for your first day, Rose?" Marcus escorted her from the livery to her classroom. He opened the door for her and followed her in. There, on her desk, was a large bouquet of late summer wildflowers and a note.

Rose grinned at Marcus and kissed him on the cheek. She opened the envelope and gasped. "Oh, Marcus."

"Well, will you, Miss Morgan?"

"Will I accompany you to supper at the cafe tonight? Let me just check my schedule?" She raised her eyes and screwed up her mouth teasingly. Her expression changed to a wide smile. "Of course, Marcus, I'd love to."

"I'm so proud of you, Miss Morgan. You're going to be an amazing teacher. These fifteen learners are so blessed to have you."

"I'm nervous, Marcus. What if I'm no good?"

Marcus reached for both of her hands and looked her in the eye. He kissed her deeply. "That's not possible, Rose. You're a gifted teacher, and you're going to be wonderful. Remember how well you did with all the children when you were studying?"

"That's different. I always had experienced teachers with me. Now I'll be on my own, and these fifteen children's education is solely in my hands. Not to mention that I have Hope and Samuel in my class."

"Rose, I believe in you, Darling. I sure wish you were my teacher growing up. I'd've paid attention for sure."

"No, you wouldn't have. You're easily distracted, Marcus."

"I'm distracted by you." He winked at her and kissed her cheek.

"Marcus, the children will be here shortly." Rose's face reddened.

"I know." He stepped back from her and squeezed her arm. "Have a wonderful day, Rose. You'll be amazing. I know you will. I'll be praying for you." He brushed her cheek, and turned to leave. "I'll be back after school to pick you up."

"Thanks, Marcus." Rose turned to write, 'Miss Morgan,' on the blackboard. Marcus paused at the door, watched her as she wrote sums, and grinned. She already looked the part.

* * * *

Marcus took a swig of lemonade and smiled at Rose. He reached across the table and squeezed her hand. "So tell me all about you first day, Miss Morgan."

Rose's eyes lit up. "Oh, Marcus, it was wonderful. They're such dear children. Hope was funny. She kept forgetting to call me Miss Morgan and called me Rose at least four times, Samuel too. They'll get used to it. They were all so keen to learn, and they're bright and fun. Marcus, I really feel like I can actually do this."

Marcus gripped her hand. "Of course you can, my darling. I saw the excitement on their faces and a couple of the boys admiring you. I'll have to keep my eyes on them!" He squinted his eyes and pursed his lips.

Rose chuckled, and he winked at her.

"I can't believe I'm finally a teacher. I never thought I'd ever truly get here."

"Of course you would've. You're the most determined and talented woman I know."

"Having your support means the world to me. I couldn't do this without you."

"Of course you could, but you'll always have my support, no matter what." He kissed her hand.

"Thank you, Marcus."

* * * *

Superintendent Oliver Michaels sipped at his coffee. He looked up at Adam and nodded. "You were right to call me here. I agree with your assessment. This job is getting too big for one man, Sergeant. Even the two of us have been run off our feet for the last week."

Adam put his own cup down on his desk. "Yeah, I can't get over how much Douglas Falls has grown since I arrived."

"More people move west every day."

Adam nodded. "So you'll get me a man?"

"I'll find you the right man. I think it would suit an officer with a little bit of experience rather than a brand new recruit."

Adam nodded. "Have you heard from my father recently?"

The older Mountie shook his head. "I've not had an update recently. Last I heard, he was at Athabasca, checking up on operations there."

"Any closer to getting him to retire?"

The older Mountie grinned. "Not any time soon, Sergeant." He mounted his horse, and Adam saluted him, which he returned. "You'll be hearing from me soon. I'll get you the right man."

"Much obliged, Superintendent."

* * * *

Rose walked into the livery to see Marcus preparing Buttercup. "Marcus, I can saddle my horse you know?" She thrust a hand on her hip and gave him a mock scowl.

Marcus tightened the girth and looked up at her. "I know that."

She raised her brows in question.

He walked to her and took both hands in his. "I just like to serve you, Darling. Please don't see it as me thinking you're incapable and I need to do it for you. I'm pretty certain you don't need me at all." He grimaced and then gave her a wide smile and stroked her cheek. "I serve you because I want to. I love you, Rose. You're my most precious treasure, not in an inferior kind of way, in a valuable way."

Rose stood up on her toes and kissed his cheek. "Thank you, Marcus."

"You're welcome, Ma'am." He chuckled and returned to finish with Buttercup. "So, how was your day? Did Marty Rogers and Jonny Cook give you trouble today?"

Rose rolled her eyes and grimaced. "Those boys spend more time in the corner than they do at their class work. The worst part is Marty has a shameless crush on Hope and torments her with gifts. Every day he asks if he can walk her home and carry her books."

Marcus frowned and looked up at her. "What did she say?"

"She scowled and stamped her feet at him, and declared, 'My Pa's a Mountie, so you have to leave me alone'."

Marcus laughed at all the antics. "You know any boy that wants to court Hope will have to get past me first."

"You're so protective." Rose grinned as she followed Marcus out, leading the two horses. They both paused as a Mountie rode up. Rose's mouth dropped open. "Constable Scott, what brings you here?" She grinned.

"I've come to take up my new posting."

Rose and Marcus looked at each other.

"You're the new constable in Douglas Falls?"

"Yes, Miss Morgan." Jonny dismounted and removed his Stetson.

Marcus stepped forward. "Good to see you again, Constable. Welcome to Douglas Falls."

The Mountie nodded his head and grinned. "Looks like a nice little town."

"It is, Constable, and full of wonderful people." Rose smiled.

Jonny was unable to hide the grin as he thought of the joy of living in the same town as the lovely Callie Morgan. "Do you have any idea where your father is, Miss Morgan?"

"In his office, I imagine. His horse is here, so he's not out on patrol." She gestured into the livery towards Ebony.

"Could you point me in the right direction?"

"I'll walk you there if you like?" Rose looked to Marcus.

"Good idea, Rose. I'll bring the horses over. Leave your books and I'll bring them."

"Thank you, Marcus. Right this way, Constable. So, how did you end up on this posting?"

Jonny fell into step with her. "I requested it when I saw it was available, and I jumped at the chance to work with your father. I found him to be an honourable and dedicated Mountie and well...." He stopped. Rose's raised eyebrows told him she knew there was more to it than that.

"And you hoped you'd get to spend more time with Callie?" Rose gave him a knowing grin.

The Mountie blushed deeply. His face almost matching his red serge jacket, and he began to stutter. Rose laughed and put her hand on his forearm. "Relax, Constable. Your secret is safe with me."

He calmed a little and grinned. "I admit I think your sister is pretty great, but she's young, and I won't pursue anything. Besides, your pa would never give his lovely daughter to the likes of me!" He shrugged.

"You never know, Constable. Just bide your time and be there for her. Let Pa see your character."

"Thanks, Rose. I really meant what I said though, about wanting to work with the sergeant. If I get to spend time with Callie, it's a bonus."

"That's a great attitude. I'm glad you're here. It's Edmonton's loss though, Constable." She squeezed his arm again.

"Thank you, Miss Morgan."

"Can we not be so formal? I feel like you're one of my students. And we're friends, aren't we, Constable?"

"Of course, Rose. And please just call me Jonathan, or Jonny if you like."

"Which do you prefer?"

"Well, most of my friends call me Jonny, but it doesn't seem fitting for a Mountie. My uncle always called me Jonathan James when I was bad."

Rose chuckled as they approached the office. "I like Jonny. I think it suits you, Mountie or not."

"Thank you, Rose, and I see congratulations are in order?"

"Congratulations?"

"That's an engagement ring, is it not? I assume you and Marcus are engaged?"

"Yes." Rose smiled and poked her head around the door. "Pa, the new Mountie is here."

Adam looked up from his desk and grinned. "Excellent, I've been longing for some help for a long time." He stood up and walked over to greet the Mountie. "Welcome, Constable... Scott!" His face lit up. "You're my new man?"

"Yes, Sir, at your service." Jonny saluted Adam.

Adam frowned and waved away his hand. "No need for that, Constable. I'm glad to have you here in Douglas Falls. Thank you, Rose, for bringing him."

"Just returning the favour, Pa. He did it for me many times."

"It was my pleasure, Miss Mor... Rose." Jonny nodded to her.

"Well, this is your quarters, Constable." Adam gestured around the room. "Doubles as our office and jail. It's not uncommon for a country office, and sometimes you'll have less than savoury roommates, I imagine. I'm sorry, it's likely much more primitive than you're used to."

"It'll be fine, Sergeant."

"Well, I'll give you a tour of the town, and I insist you dine with us tonight. Rose, will you let your ma know we'll have a guest, please?"

"That's kind of you, Sir." Jonny blushed slightly.

Rose grinned at him and nodded to her father. "Marcus is here to ride home with me, Pa. I'll see you for supper."

"Alright, Darling." Adam embraced Rose and kissed her cheek as he always did.

Rose turned back as she walked to the door. "It's wonderful to have you here, Jonny."

"Thank you, Rose."

After a tour of the town, Adam led Jonny towards the homestead and showed the younger Mountie around his land, and to the far side of the acreage to see Rose and Marcus's home in progress.

"It's nice they'll be living up here with you, Sir."

"Yes, I hope all my daughters and their husbands will want to live up here eventually. I couldn't bear any of them living far away, but I know I can't keep them all. I bought this land though, so they'd at least have the option."

Jonny stored that information away in his heart. He sure wouldn't mind living there with Callie one day. But he was getting way ahead of himself. She wasn't even sixteen yet, and he was twenty. He had to tread carefully, or he'd never get a chance with her. He was determined to build a friendship with her and let the Lord lead.

The two Mounties released their horses to pasture and headed for the house.

"Constable Scott, it's wonderful to see you again." Katie welcomed him with an embrace.

"Thank you, Mrs Morgan. Your husband invited me to supper, I hope it's not an imposition."

"Absolutely not. You were so kind to our Rose when she was in Edmonton, and you're welcome at our supper table any time you like, Constable. We enjoy company very much, don't we girls?"

"We sure do." Anna grinned. Lizzie just shrugged. Callie shyly watched the scene from the kitchen. She blushed as Jonny caught her gaze. She couldn't believe that Constable Scott was the new Mountie that would be working with her pa. *Chalk one up to answered prayers.*

Adam gave thanks for the meal and Katie began the questions. "So, where did you grow up, Constable?"

Jonny put his fork down and smiled at Katie. "Please, Ma'am. It's just Jonny tonight. I'm out of uniform. I grew up in Calgary."

"A city boy, eh?" Katie chuckled.

"Somewhat, Mrs Morgan." He grinned, and Katie liked his easy, confident manner. "But I've always had dogs, and I really enjoy working with horses, so I'm not completely unprepared for life on the frontier."

"I'll teach you how to milk Daisy if you like," offered Lizzie.

"I'd like that, Miss Morgan." He grinned at her.

"Why did you become a Mountie?" Marcus sipped at his coffee. "Was your father a Mountie too?"

"Actually, my uncle was. I never met my father, he passed away before I was born," Jonny said matter-of-factly. "My Uncle was stationed at the training camp for a time."

Adam's head snapped up. "What's his name?"

"Superintendent Paul Stewart."

"Superintendent Stewart is your uncle?" Adam paused with a forkful of beans halfway to his mouth.

"You know him?"

"Yes, of course. I was raised at the training centre for a time. My father is Assistant Commissioner Morgan. He was Superintendent Morgan then."

"Really?" The young man's mouth dropped open. "I remember him well. He made us all call him Commander, and he was...well...." Jonny paused.

"Needlessly cruel?" Adam chuckled.

Jonny smiled and nodded. "I like to think of it as character building, Sir."

Adam nearly spat out his potato as he laughed. That was one of his father's favourite phrases at the academy. "It's not harsh. It's character building."

"Well, it's a small world, Constable." Adam took a long slurp of his coffee. "Unfortunately, in the Police Force, I can't shake the name Morgan. Everyone knows The Commander."

"Yes." The younger Mountie swallowed his mouthful. "I never would've picked you were his son, though. I might've been too afraid to come if I'd known that, but didn't already know you."

"The Commander and I are nothing alike, except in looks. He's mellowing a bit in his old age, but he's still The Commander at heart."

"So, were you posted to Edmonton, or did you request it?" Rose asked.

"It was my first posting. I really didn't want to be a city constable though. I may have grown up in the city, but joining the Mounties was my way to get out of that environment and have more opportunities, and I always wanted a frontier posting."

"I'm not sure we're really frontier anymore. Douglas Falls is growing all the time." Rose laughed.

"Yeah, I'll admit it's bigger than I expected."

"It's still a great town though, full of wonderful people," Callie entered the conversation shyly.

"Yes, it is, Miss Morgan," Jonny replied with a slight blush to his cheeks as he looked at her, and then he quickly added. "As far as I know. I'm still getting to know the place."

"Well, we're very happy you're here, Jonny. It'll be nice to get more time with my husband." Katie put her hand on Adam's arm. He winked at her and covered her hand with his, giving it a squeeze.

"I'm happy to be here, Ma'am."

"Can we please dispense with the ma'am? You make me feel old. Just Katie is fine."

He nodded.

Jonny thrust himself on his bed and placed his hands behind his head. "I think I'm going to like it here." He grinned into the semi-darkness. "Thank you Lord, for bringing me here."

Eightteen
Courting Callie

"Can you believe it? All these years later, and now two of you are about to have married children?" Becky smiled at Katie.

"I know. I can't believe I'm thirty-eight years old." Katie grimaced. "I don't feel nearly that old. Certainly not old enough to have a married daughter. And I'm definitely not old enough to be a grandmother in the not-too-distant future."

"By next Christmas, she could well be expecting." Jo raised her brows at Katie. "You got pregnant straight away."

"Oh, imagine that. Adam would be a mess!" Katie chuckled.

Louisa laughed. "He sure would. What if Rose's first child turns out to be a girl?"

"Poor Adam." Becky laughed.

"You know you could be in the same situation, Lou. Are you ready to be a grandmother too?" Katie raised her brows.

Louisa's face dropped, and she gulped. "I hadn't thought about it, but yes, I guess that's a likelihood for me too. Daniel would be delighted."

"Let's not hurry the children though. One thing at a time. Dealing with my daughter getting married is bad enough." Katie gestured over to the young Mountie. "I have my suspicions that Callie won't be far behind." The women observed Jonny grin at Callie, his eyes sparkling. Her cheeks reddened.

"What does Adam think about that?" asked Jo. "Samuel would have a fit if Esther married a Mountie."

"I don't know really. I know that Adam thinks the world of Jonny, and he knows the two have eyes for each other, but Callie doesn't turn sixteen for a few weeks, and he's made absolutely no moves towards anything other than a friendship. But then he's been kind to all the girls." Katie reached into her basket for another ball of yarn. "I don't think Adam even wants to consider the possibility of another daughter courting. Least of all, to a Mountie who could take her off to anywhere."

"I can imagine." Becky looked wistfully at her young daughter. "I don't know what I'd do if Kate went away."

"Well, we can't keep them forever." Katie gave her friend a compassionate smile. "No matter how hard it is. We have to let them go."

"By the way, did I tell you? Jamie's planning to join the force when he turns eighteen."

Louisa looked at Jo. "He's going to be a Mountie?"

"He sure is. Just like his pa." Jo smiled proudly.

"How does Samuel feel about that?" asked Becky.

"Delighted but scared for him at the same time. He's only too aware of the dangers, but Jamie is strong and bright and Sam thinks he'll make an excellent Mountie," Jo replied.

"That'll be hard, Jo. I don't envy you. I guess I should be glad I don't have any sons to go off to the Force." Katie grimaced.

"But it looks like one of your girls might marry one. I'm not sure that's any easier. Samuel dreads the thought of Esther marrying a Mountie. She's almost fifteen now, you know." Jo grimaced.

"Fifteen!" Louisa shook her head. "Where did that time go? I'm still getting used to my Emma being fourteen."

"They grow up so very fast, don't they?" Becky added.

"Sergeant, I believe that young Mountie has his eyes on your Callie." Owen chuckled and lifted his cup to his mouth. The snow had stopped falling, and the winter sun shone. The four patriarchs of the family retreated to the front porch of the Morgan's home.

"I'm trying not to notice, Doctor Randall. Why do you have to keep pointing these things out to me? Can't you just leave a man to his denial?" Adam leaned back against the porch rail and grimaced. He put his coffee cup on the railing and ran his fingers through his hair.

The other three chuckled.

"How do you feel about that, Adam?" Samuel raised his brows.

Adam took a deep breath and exhaled loudly. "Not a whole lot I can do about it, I don't suppose. If they fall in love, I can hardly stop them. Although I do worry about my girl marrying a Mountie."

"I admit it's my biggest fear with Esther. She's fifteen now, and the young men are starting to notice her. I don't blame them; she's beautiful." Sam twisted his mouth to the side and groaned. "One of my young recruits had his eyes on her the other day, and with her brother going into the Force, I'm afraid she's got red serge fever. I wouldn't be surprised if she did marry a Mountie, but I'd hate for her to go far away from home with some young recruit."

"I guess you two understand better than most the dangers of being a Mountie. Imagine then how your own wives fear. Would you have wanted them not to marry you for that reason?"

Adam threw his friend a mock grimace. "Pastor Coleman, you're much too logical and pragmatic for your own good. Now, I beg of you, could you just be on our side for once?"

Sam lowered his coffee cup. "Besides, Pastor, your daughter is nearly fifteen. What if she ran off and married a Mountie?"

Daniel's face fell, and his grin changed to a frown. "I have tasted my own medicine, gents, and it's bitter. Let's not joke about this anymore. I vote all our girls just stay as they are right now."

"Here, here!" Owen nodded, thinking of his own daughter.

"At least none of us have it as bad as the old serge!" Sam laughed. "He's got six pretty girls and has to go through this six times." He slapped Adam on the back.

"Enough of the 'old' there, Samuel. As hard as it is, it's worth it. They are some pretty exceptional girls." Adam's eyes shone.

"I agree!" the other three said in unison, the men were proud and protective of each other's children.

"Hey, I just thought of something. With two weddings in July, you two men could be grandfathers before long. Who knows, we could be anticipating them this time next year!" Owen raised his brows.

"'Gramps!' has a nice ring to it, don't you think?" Sam slurped nonchalantly at his coffee. Adam and Daniel frowned.

Adam groaned. "Oh, don't joke chaps. I'm not ready for that yet. It's bad enough knowing I'm going to have a married child soon."

"I know what you mean," Daniel agreed.

"I'd not get too cocky, Sam. Jamie's nearly eighteen. You know it's not far off for him, and then it'll be Tim and the twin's turns. It'll happen to us all before you know it." Adam shrugged.

"Hmm, Not too soon, I hope." Owen's grimace changed to a frown. "Sure would love those grandbabies, though."

*   *   *   *

Adam was on edge, he had been since Callie turned sixteen. He knew that at any moment Jonny Scott would be asking to call on Callie. He sighed as he rode to the school to greet his girls.

In some ways, he wished Jonny would just get it over and done with and put him out of his misery. And yet he hoped for Callie's sake he'd at least wait until she finished school.

In the meantime, he'd enjoyed getting to know Jonny. He found him to be an honourable and dedicated young Mountie and a fine Christian man. He had to admit he'd be a good match for Callie, and if he was honest, he'd be proud to have him as a son-in-law.

He chuckled at himself. He truly wanted his girls to be happy. He really would never deprive them of a good godly marriage. He knew first-hand how wonderful it could be, and he really did want that for his girls. If they found worthy men, he'd certainly give his blessing, wholeheartedly. He just felt sad for himself because he'd miss them. And his greatest fear with Callie falling for Jonathan Scott was that he'd get a new posting and take his daughter far away.

Adam sighed again as he pulled up outside the school. He dismounted and stood out front with the other parents, and leaned against a post to wait. From his vantage point, he could see Rose in her classroom, handing out papers and stopping to talk briefly to each child. He smiled at her dedication and care for her students. She placed a hand on a young boy's shoulder and gave him an encouraging smile.

"She's quite a woman." Daniel spoke from behind him. On Mondays, the two men took their children and the Randall children out for an ice cream. Daniel smiled, he noticed Adam's wistful look. He knew it was going to be tough for him to give up Rosie in a few months' time.

"Yes, she is, Dan." The Mountie grinned. "Two months, and she's no longer mine."

"I know, Brother." Daniel patted him on the back. "Then it won't be long for that one either." The bell rang and Callie headed towards them.

Adam sighed. "No, it seems not." He grimaced.

"Has Jonny asked to come calling yet?"

"No, not yet. I think he might be waiting until after graduation."

"Wise," said Daniel. "She's very young, and he's twenty now, isn't he?"

Adam just nodded.

"How do you feel about it?" Daniel watched as Callie stood at the edge of the playground to wait for her younger sisters.

"Resigned." Adam grinned, and then became serious. "Truthfully, I think they'll be a good match. It's a bit hard to give her up to a Mountie. I'm afraid he'll take her far away."

"It's a possibility, but it is even if she marries a farmer, you can't keep them forever." He smiled at his fifteen-year-old daughter as she approached.

"Hi, Pa." Emma walked with her younger brothers, Jack and Samuel.

"Hi, Darling, ready to go?" Daniel reached for her books. Emma smiled and gave them to him.

Anna, Lizzie and Sarah ran up to Adam. As usual, he embraced and kissed each one. Callie walked a little slower holding Hope's hand. Adam stacked up all their school books under his arm as Timothy ran over with the Randall twins and their little sister. The two men led all the scholars to the ice cream store. They passed the RNWMP office just as Jonny was arriving back on Major. Adam grinned as Jonny and Callie caught each other's eyes and blushed. He grimaced internally. *No, I can't keep her forever.*

* * * *

"Well, it's time." Jonny took a deep breath and dismounted off his horse. He was determined today he would talk to the Sergeant about courting Callie. He was deeply in love with her and longed to be able to court properly.

Adam was finished for the day and about to leave, he locked his desk drawer and stood to rinse his coffee cup.

Jonny stepped in and began unbuttoning his red serge jacket. "I'm glad you're still here, Sergeant." He thrust his coat on the hook. "I was hoping I could speak to you."

Adam closed his eyes and sighed as he turned to place the coffee cup back on the shelf. *It's time.* He took a deep breath and braced himself for the inevitable. "Certainly, Constable. What can I do for you?"

"Well, actually, it's a personal matter, Sir." Jonny sounded a lot more confident than he was.

Adam nodded and turned to lean against the counter. He ran his fingers through his hair, folded his arms across his chest and raised his eyebrows in question.

Jonny took a deep breath. "It's probably no surprise to you, Sir, that I'm rather fond of Callie." A wide smile crossed his face.

Adam chuckled. "I'd say a good deal more than fond, Jon."

Jonny blushed and stepped closer to Adam. "Well, if I'm honest, Serge, I'm in love with her." The young man's eyes sparkled.

Adam flashed the constable a wry smile. "I'm well aware."

Jonny nodded, he knew he'd not been good at hiding his feelings.

Adam continued. "I've been expecting this for some time. Just say what you have to say, Constable. Put me out of my misery." He grimaced.

Jonny nodded again. "Very well. I want to ask your permission to call on Callie."

Adam smiled, stepped forward, and slapped Jonny on the back. "And you have it."

"I do?"

Adam sighed. "Yes, I can see the love you have for each other. How can I refuse it?" He shook his head comically.

"Thank you, Sir." Jonny grinned.

"Not so fast, Scott. This comes with one condition." Adam's eyes grew stern.

All colour drained from Jonny's face and his smile faded quickly. "Which is?"

Adam grinned. "That you'll always trust her. She's stronger than you think, and women are more than able to handle the life of a Mountie. Never doubt her, and you'll have a fiercely supportive ally in her. And if you hurt her...." He raised his eyebrows and meant to continue.

"Let me stop you there, Sergeant." Jonny looked Adam in the eye and held his chin up. "I love Callie. I'd never dream of hurting her, and I can assure you I'm in this for life."

"Good." Adam waved away Jonny's hand and embraced him briefly. He released him. "I know Mounties don't usually hug each other, but you're not just a Mountie to me. You're like a son, if I'm honest. I welcome you as a part of our family. Look after my daughter, Jon."

"I will, Sir, and by the way, I have no intention of moving away from here. I won't be seeking new orders any time soon."

"You know as well as I do that you don't always have a choice."

Jonny nodded. "I know, Sergeant, but if it's in my power to do so, I plan to stay."

Adam nodded and patted Jonny on the back, turned, and strode out. He leapt up on Ebony, nudged her into a gallop and shook his head as he hurried home.

* * * *

Jonny laid the picnic blanket beneath the large oak tree and seated Callie. He reached for the basket, placed it between them and sat down opposite her. He took a deep breath to try to calm his swirling nerves and pounding heart.

Callie smiled shyly at him as he sat down, her own heart racing, suddenly acutely aware of his every movement.

Both knew the relationship was changing, and they sat silently for a while, both contending with their deepest thoughts. Callie lowered her eyes, feeling Jonny's deep blue eyes exploring her face. She blushed deeply and swallowed.

Jonny took a deep breath. "Callie."

She lifted her eyes to him. "Yes." The intensity of his gaze made her tremble.

"You look very beautiful today. That yellow dress is lovely."

"Thank you," she managed, her cheeks deepening to a dark shade of crimson.

"Did you make it?" He was a bundle of nerves, trying to build up the courage to say what he really wanted to say.

"Yes." She nodded.

"You're very talented." Jonny swallowed. "I have a gift for you."

She lifted her eyes to his. "You do?"

"Mmmhmm, to say congratulations for graduating today."

"What is it?" She could barely get words past her throat. The air was thick with their awkwardness.

"Here." He handed her a small box. She opened the lid and gasped. It was a beautiful silver bracelet with sunflowers and her name engraved on the top.

"It's beautiful. Thank you." Callie swallowed. Her hands shook as she lifted it out of the box.

Jonny smiled. "Here, let me help you." He held her hand. Callie closed her eyes and gulped; lightning sparked through her body as their skin touched. He slipped the bracelet on her wrist. "There you go." He didn't let go of her hand. Callie's eyes remained tightly closed, her cheeks warmed, and her heart raced. He lifted the soft white hand and kissed it.

She lifted her eyes to his and smiled. He took a deep breath. "Callie, I want you to know that this bracelet isn't just for congratulations."

She gulped again. "It isn't?"

"No, it's also a promise."

"A promise of what?" Callie couldn't keep the tremble from her voice.

Jonny took a deep breath and chuckled. It went some way towards lightening the mood.

Callie smiled. "What's so funny?"

"Nothing, really. I just didn't imagine this being so tense and awkward."

Callie smiled. "Me either. Why can't we just be ourselves? We're friends, aren't we? We can usually talk about everything."

"I guess that's the problem. I suppose we're both aware that things are changing, and well... Oh, I'm just going to say it. I was wondering if you'd let me call on you." He exhaled as if relieved to finally get that out.

She blushed deeply and looked shyly at him. She bit her lip and nodded. Her green eyes sparkled.

"That makes me so happy, Callie." He kissed her hand again. "I know you're nervous and uncertain, Callie. Truth be told, I'm nervous too. This is new to me, but we'll take our time. We'll work this out together. All I know is I want to be with you." He tucked a stray curl behind her ear. She closed her eyes and trembled at his gentle touch. She opened her eyes, and they shone brightly.

"Trust me, Callie. I'll never do anything to hurt you, and we'll take it slowly. Will you trust me?"

Callie swallowed and smiled shyly. She found her voice at last. "Of course, I trust you, Jonny. I'm just... it's all just very new and a little bit scary for me."

"I know. But you do have feelings for me?" His blue eyes searched hers eagerly.

She smiled and nodded.

"Do you love me?" he dared to ask.

"I don't know."

He grinned and kissed her hand. "That's okay. These things take time. You'll know soon enough. In the meantime, I'll be here whenever you need me."

"I know."

"I don't mind waiting, as long as you need me to. We should go. Your parents will be expecting us for supper." He reached out his hand to her, and she took it and stood up.

He paused for a moment and held both of her hands. They looked into each other's eyes. Jonny bent his head down and kissed her cheek. She closed her eyes and blushed again. When she opened her eyes, he was ginning at her.

"What?"

"I was just thinking how very blessed I am. The most beautiful girl in town has agreed to court."

"I'm sorry I'm so shy and awkward." She dropped her hands and walked away from him to stare at the water.

"Callie." He chased after her and cupped her chin. "You don't have to be sorry. I told you, this will take some getting used to for both of us. The start of a courtship can be awkward, but we'll work it all out. The most important thing is we'll work it out together. I'm okay with that. I'll wait ten years if you need me to. Do you believe me?"

She nodded and smiled. "Thank you for being patient with me and for this beautiful bracelet."

"You're most welcome, Callie. It's not what it should be, but we'll get there."

"Oh no, it's very beautiful. It really is. Sunflowers are my favourite. You're most kind." She was beginning to relax. Standing up on her toes, she kissed his cheek, and looked him in the eye shyly. "Thank you."

Jonny grinned, glad to see she was becoming more comfortable with him. He wrapped his arms around her and held her close to himself. She relaxed into his arms and pressed her cheek against his red-serge-covered chest. All her nerves and fears faded away as he held her. He sighed happily and leaned his head against hers. There in his arms, she felt so safe, so protected, and so loved. She didn't ever want to leave.

Jonny's heart was doing somersaults. There was no more wonderful feeling to him than holding Callie Morgan in his arms.

He'd wanted this for a long time. He closed his eyes and savoured the moment.

When he finally released her, he saw the shine in her eyes and the smile on her lips. She looked at him with such adoration and trust that it almost made his knees buckle. He grinned at her, and then regaining his composure, he gave her his arm, and they headed back to their horses to go and face her family.

Nineteen
The First Wedding

"Oh, my Rosie girl. I can't believe tomorrow you'll be a married woman." Adam's voice trembled. He stroked Rose's cheek and winked at Callie. The rest of the household was sleeping.

"Pa, I'm so nervous. I'm not sure I know how to be a wife. What if I let him down?"

Adam reached for both girls' hands. He smiled and looked from one face to the other. "My darlings, I want you to know something about men. We aren't interested in having some perfect little housewife to cook, clean, and sew for us. What we want... no... that's not right. What we need, is simply the love of our wife. Her undying support and love. Knowing she's waiting, ready with an embrace or a kiss, makes a man feel strong and proud.

"That other stuff... that's a bonus. I'm blessed that your ma is an excellent cook, seamstress and housekeeper, but you know what? None of that would've mattered to me. If she burned our supper every night and made me wonky clothing, I wouldn't have minded one bit. It would be worth it for the love and support she gives me."

The two girls smiled, and Adam rubbed both soft hands with his thumbs and continued, "Rose, tomorrow you're getting married, and Callie, I know I can't keep you for long either, but I want you to know that as hard as it is for me, this is right. Women and men are made to leave their parents' homes and join together to make their own families. Oh, I'll miss my beautiful girls terribly, but I'm also very proud of both of you and the men you have chosen to spend your lives with." Callie blushed a deep red. "I know it's very early days for you, Callie, but you and Jon are well-suited, and I know you'll be together in the future. You've both found excellent men, and I couldn't be more delighted for you." He leaned over and kissed both girls' cheeks. He fixed his eyes on Rose and lifted a hand to her cheek. "There's nothing more wonderful in life than a godly marriage."

Both girls nodded, Rose stood and walked around the table. Adam stood to embrace her, holding her tightly to his chest, cradling her head, knowing he'd not get this privilege as much as he once did. Tomorrow she'd be in Marcus's arms and not his. He kissed her hair. "I love you so very much, Rosie. I'm really going to miss you, Darling."

"I love you too, Pa."

Adam opened an arm to Callie and she leapt up to join the hug. He held them and kissed both heads. "Oh, my darlings, my beautiful girls. I love you both so much." They stayed in their huddle for some time before Adam reluctantly released them, and walked them to their bedroom.

"Goodnight, Pa."

"Goodnight, Darlings, sleep well." He kissed each on their hair again and closed the door. Leaning back against the door he paused for a moment and sighed. That was the very last time he'd get to kiss his Rosie goodnight. He closed his eyes and shook his head.

Adam sighed as he strode into his room and prepared for bed. "Katie, releasing those two from that embrace was one of the hardest things I've ever had to do. I wish I could keep them and hold them all, just as they are, forever." He sighed and climbed into bed next to his wife. "But it's the right thing to do."

Katie lifted a hand to his cheek. "You still have me, Adam. I'm not going anywhere."

Adam grinned and pulled her into his arms. "I know Katie, and that's why I can even do this. It's you that gives me the strength and courage." He kissed her and pulled her close.

* * * *

The first of July arrived in beautiful sunshine, and the pastureland up on The Rise was alive with brightly coloured flowers, just as Rose had hoped. Adam had cut the grass to make a wide aisle, lined on each side by lanterns.

Marcus and Andy shuffled nervously on the small platform Adam had built under the ancient oak. Daniel stood with them,. The arch was made from twisted vines and the girls had decorated it with flowers and ribbons.

Friends and family began to arrive and took their seats on the logs Adam and Marcus had placed in rows.

Jo and Becky snuck over to the house.

"Hi, ladies." Adam gave them both a nervous smile.

"Hi, Adam." Jo embraced the Mountie. "How you holding up, Pa?"

He embraced Becky, and grinned. "It's not easy." He stepped back and fastened the blue and yellow belt of his dress uniform.

"Well, you look the part, Sergeant." Becky gripped his arm and nodded to Mr Louis sitting on the couch, swallowing over and over.

"We thought we might sneak in and see the brides." Becky grinned.

Adam nodded and gestured towards the bedroom, then resumed his nervous pacing.

Becky and Jo knocked on the bedroom door and poked their heads in the door. "Oh, Rose, Amy, you look so beautiful."

"Thanks, Aunt Jo," Rose grinned. Her face beamed and her eyes sparkled. Louisa and Amy's mother buzzed around Amy and Lydia's dresses.

"Well, I think we're ready." Tears flooded Katie's eyes as she gave Rose's full skirt one more adjustment.

"We best get back to our husbands." Becky nodded to Jo. The women embraced and kissed the brides-to-be, then hurried from the room.

Mrs Louis and Katie handed their daughters their bouquets and headed out into the living room, followed by two shy brides.

Adam took one look at Rose, and his eyes flooded with tears. He sucked in a breath and shook his head. "Oh, my Rosie." He was much too overwhelmed by her beauty and presence and the enormity of what the day was that he could say little else.

"Pa." She clung tightly to him.

"I love you, Rosie Girl. I'm so happy for you, Darling." He unashamedly let his tears fall.

"Why are you crying, Pa?" Rose asked as he released her.
"Because I'm going to miss you, but Rosie, my darling, you are glowing. You're so beautiful, and your eyes are shining so." He brushed her cheek. "You look happy, Daughter."

"I am, Pa, I really am, I can't wait to marry Marcus, I love him so."

"Then...." Adam sniffed and gave her a wry smile. He kissed her forehead. "I'm happy for you."

Mr Louis was a much less emotional man. He simply embraced Amy and kissed her on the cheek. His eyes expressed to her what his words could not.

At last, the two fathers stood on the deck with their daughters on their arms. They watched as Callie and Lydia made their way up to the archway and stood with the men there. Jonny grinned as he watched Callie, with her skirts swishing around her legs. She looked so beautiful in her lilac dress carrying a bouquet of wildflowers, with flowers in her hair and her eyes shining. He sighed and smiled. He hoped that one day she'd be the one in the white dress, and he'd be shuffling nervously at the front.

The harpist began to pluck out the bridal march, and the audience stood as the two men with their daughters on their arms came around the side of the house, and all eyes swung to them. Mr Louis led Amy up the aisle first.

"Are you ready, Darling?" Adam's voice trembled.

Rose nodded and fixed her eyes on Marcus. Adam began his slow walk sucking in deep breaths, trying very hard to stop himself from openly weeping.

They reached the front and Daniel looked at the two brides. With a shaky voice he asked, "Who gives these women to be married to these men?"

"I do." Mr Louis said and passed Amy's hand to Andy. The young man's eyes fixed on Amy and he grinned so hard his face hurt.

Adam swallowed back the tears. "I do." He shook his head and kissed her on the cheek. She smiled at him. "I love you, Pa."

"Oh, I love you too, Darling." He winked at her and passed her hand over to Marcus. The young man nodded and Adam gave him a slow nod in return; a message of honour and respect passed between them.

Both fathers stepped over to join their wives, and Adam clung to Katie as he watched his precious daughter marry the love of her life. He sighed. Being a father to girls was such a blessed joy, but it was ever so hard to give them up. He exhaled loudly.

Katie squeezed his hand. "It's okay, Husband."

Adam put his arm around Katie's waist and squeezed her. "I know, Katie, but look how happy and how beautiful she is." He sucked in a breath and Katie reached up to brush a tear from his cheek. He caught her hand and gripped it tightly, as always drawing support from his wife.

Daniel's voice wobbled, and he exhaled loudly. "Ladies and Gentleman, it gives me great pleasure to present to you, Mr and Mrs Andrew Coleman." He gripped the shoulders of the young couple and waited for the applause to stop. He nodded to Rose and Marcus. "And Mr and Mrs Marcus Murray."

Adam shook his head slowly and clung to his wife.

The ceremony ended and women produced picnic baskets and blankets. Families took their places under the oak and two blissfully happy couples walked from person to person, greeting each and receiving hearty congratulations.

Adam led the couples over to the large oak that bore his and Katie's faded initials. They added their own initials to what would become known as 'the wedding oak.'

At last the meal was packed away and the young couples stood with their families gathered around. Daniel led the family in prayer for the newlyweds.

Amy and Rose embraced each other, promising they'd have the other couple around once they had settled into married life.

Katie embraced her married daughter. "Oh, Rose. This was a beautiful day. I'm so happy for you, Darling."

"Ma, thank you for all you've done."

"It's my pleasure. I'm going to miss you, Darling." She squeezed her daughter.

"I'll miss you too, Ma."

Katie kissed her then and put her arms out to Marcus. "I finally have a son. Welcome to the family, Marcus."

"Thank you, Mrs Morgan." Marcus kissed her cheek.

"Marcus, we're family now. Please just call me Ma."

"Thanks, Ma." He nodded, gripped his bride's hand and winked at her. "Ready to go, Mrs Murray?"

"Mrs Murray!" Rose gushed. "Yes, I'm ready." Marcus led her to the gig. Adam held the horses and swallowed over and over again. Marcus lifted his hand to shake Adam's.

Adam hesitated, swallowed and shook his head, lunging to embrace the young man. "Son, family doesn't shake hands." He lingered in the embrace. "I'm proud to welcome you to our family, Marc."

The two men nodded to each other and Marcus climbed up on the gig to wait. Adam looked at his married daughter, his eyes glistened with tears and his lips trembled. He lifted a hand to her cheek. Wordlessly he gathered her into his arms and held her tightly, thinking back to all the years he'd held the precious girl, from the very first moment when she was born under a tree, to the tears he'd wiped when she was a girl, her graduation, college and everything in between, and now she was a married woman. He reluctantly released her and grinned through his tears. "Rosie, Darling, I love you so very much. I'm happy for you both, and I will miss you so."

Rose smiled and kissed him on the cheek. "I love you, Pa. I'll always be your little girl, I promise."

"I know, Mrs Murray." He gave her a rather wobbly smile. With his arm around Rose, he turned to look up at Marcus. "Take your wife home now, Son. We'll see you for supper later in the week."

"Thank you, Pa." Marcus put his hand out to help Rose up into the gig. Adam lifted her by the waist and put his arm around Katie, sniffing back his tears. He lay his head on Katie's as they watched their daughter embark on her new life with her new husband.

"She's not mine anymore!" Adam gulped in his breath. "But I'm happy for them, Katie. He truly is the right man for our Rosie." He smiled as he watched them pull up outside their new home. Marcus leapt down from the gig and helped Rose down, picked her up in his arms and carried her up the stairs and through the door. Adam squeezed Katie again. "Well, Wife, let's go home." Arm in arm, they walked back to their home and prepared for supper.

Adam was quiet all evening. Several times during supper, he put his fork down, looked around and sighed. He felt like the sun had gone out of his home. Katie noticed he was very attentive to all the girls but Callie in particular. He looked at her, and his eyes became hazy. It was as if he was determined to make the most of every moment he had with them before he lost them too. The entire family was sombre that evening. But by morning, they were all back to normal, especially when the new Mr and Mrs Murray came over to get their horses and stopped in for coffee.

Adam and Katie stood on the porch as they farewelled their newly married daughter. "They're so comfortable together, Katie, like they've been married many years."

"Yes." Katie grinned. "It's beautiful to see. I know another couple who were just like that."

"You do?" Adam grinned.

"Yes." She stood up on her toes to kiss him, and slipped her arms around his neck. "I remember thinking on our wedding day I could never be more in love with you, and how I couldn't wait to spend the rest of our lives together."

"And what a life it's been so far, Wife." He stroked her cheek.

"Yes, but I was wrong about one thing."

Adam tipped his head to the side. "What's that?"

"I love you now even more than I did then. I love you more and more every day."

He kissed her deeply and wrapped her in his arms. "Me too, Wife. So no regrets then?"

Katie lay her head against his chest and relished being held by him. "Absolutely none, Husband. Marrying you was the smartest thing I ever did. I hope that Rose and Marcus are as happy as we are after they've been married nineteen years."

Adam squeezed her and lay his head against hers. "They will be."

"How do you know?"

"Because like us, they're soulmates. Their marriage is ordained by God. There is no coming between a love like that."

Katie nodded and they stood for a moment holding each other before returning indoors to their family.

* * * *

"So Andy, you two as happy as we are?" Marcus asked as they walked to the barn; leaving the women in Rose's kitchen preparing supper.

"It's pretty amazing. Been the best week of my life." Andy grinned. "I feel like I'm dreaming, having that woman there with me. I still pinch myself."

"I understand. I was happy before in my blissful ignorance. Now I can't believe I was ever able to live without her." Marcus opened the barn door.

"I don't know what I'm going to do when Amy goes back to work in a few weeks' time." Andy grimaced. "It's gonna be awful hard to let her go."

"I know what you mean. At least I get the whole summer before Rose goes back to school."

"Busy working wives. How very modern of us." Andy chuckled. "I don't mind, really, I'm very proud of her, and I want her to be happy. It's just, I'm going to miss her. I kind of like being with her all the time."

Marcus slapped his friend on the back. "I understand completely, Friend." They both filled their arms with firewood and headed back towards the house.

"How's it going for you two?" Rose pulled the coffeepot off the stove and passed it to Amy to pour into cups.

"Wonderful! Andy is such a wonderful and attentive husband."

"I know what you mean!" Rose moved over to strain the beans. "I can't believe I ever coped without Marcus."

"I miss him when he's gone."

Rose nodded. "I understand. I never imagined I could ever be so happy. I do miss living with my family, but this is so wonderful, and I wouldn't have it any other way." Rose blushed as Marcus and Andy entered with an arm full of firewood each.

Marcus winked at Rose and dropped the wood in the basket by the fireplace. He leaned over the kitchen counter and kissed his wife. "Something sure smells good, Mrs Murray."

"It's just a pot roast, Marcus."

"I love pot roast." He grinned.

Not to be outdone Andy kissed his own wife. "Can't get enough of you, Mrs Coleman." Amy blushed, and grinned and kept right on mashing.

"You two go and sit down. We'll bring the supper over in a moment." Rose smiled.

"Yes, Ma'am." Marcus winked at her again and followed Andy to the table.

"I hope you and Rose will join us for supper next week?" Andy squeezed his wife's waist as they sat in the living room after supper.

Marcus looked at Rose and she nodded. "We'd love to," she answered on their behalf.

"Let's do it every week!" Amy blurted out. "We could alternate homes."

"Absolutely. Thursday nights can be our supper nights." Rose's face beamed.

"Great idea." The men nodded to each other. Andy and Marcus began a conversation about farming, and the two women headed to the kitchen to finish up the dishes.

Twenty
Samuel

Adam pulled the paper from his typewriter and stood to file it. He closed the filing cabinet and grimaced as the door and windows rattled in the swirling storm. "I'm worried about the girls in this storm."

Jonny looked up from the report he was reading from headquarters. "They're at school, aren't they?" He glanced at the clock.

"Of course, but it looks pretty set in. I think I'll leave early and make sure they get home okay."

"I understand. Do you want some help?"

"No, between Rose's horse and mine, we'll get them all home. You should stay here in case there are any problems in the town. I'll come right back once I'm sure they're all safe." He stood and reached for his hat.

"I understand, Serge. I plan to escort Callie home later too." Jonny grinned.

Adam opened the door, turned and raised his brows. "So, just like every other day then?"

Jonny chuckled.

Adam clicked his tongue to signal to his new dog, Honey, wrapped his thick coat around himself tightly and shivered. It was blowing a gale and looked to be getting worse. He hurried to the livery and saddled Ebony and Rose's horse, Buttercup. Leading the two very reluctant horses towards the school he tethered them under the shelter of the tree, with Honey standing guard. He stood to wait for the girls, in the newly built foyer with other parents.

Adam embraced each of his girls as they left their classrooms. He was never ashamed to hug or kiss his girls in public. They never rejected his hugs either, nor did they feel uncomfortable with their father's displays of affection. Let others look and laugh, it was much more important to Adam that his girls know how much he loved them, than what others thought of him. If they thought him soft or weak, then so be it. In truth, most of the community found it endearing. Adam had repeatedly proved his strength and trustworthiness as a Mountie, and they loved that he had a gentle and caring nature with his children.

The girls waited while Adam went for Rose. He came out arm in arm with her, only to see Marcus coming their way as well. He'd had the same thought as Adam.

"Hi, Marc. I hope you don't mind me escorting your wife." Adam chuckled as he released Rose and handed her books to Marcus.

"Course not, Sir. I appreciate it, actually." He nodded and took his wife's arm.

"I'm glad you're here. That gives us three horses, and we need to get home before the snow gets too heavy."

The girls wrapped their coats tightly around themselves and made their way out into the snow. Hope climbed up in the saddle in front of Marcus and Lizzie behind Rose. Anna and Sarah sat front and back of Adam, and they all hurried home through the falling snow.

At last, Adam had all the girls warming themselves in front of the fire. Katie brought them hot chocolate and cookies and then embraced her husband. "Thanks for bringing them all home. I was worried about them all walking in this storm."

"Of course, Katie. I would never leave them to walk home in this weather. I wish I could have spared them the trip at all." He squeezed his wife and kissed her hair.

"You can't change the weather, Adam."

"I'm sorry I have to go back again, Katie. I've got at least a couple of hours to work...." his sentence was cut off by Jonny bursting through the door; he hadn't even stopped to knock.

"Sergeant." He ran to where they were standing.

Adam released Katie and turned towards the younger Mountie. "What is it, Constable?"

"It's Sergeant Ferguson, Sir."

"Sam?" Adam frowned. "What about him?"

"Mrs Ferguson phoned to say he's missing. He was doing a prisoner transfer from Moose River south to Spruce Valley. He was supposed to be gone two days at most. It's been four, and the young constables have been unable to locate him."

Adam turned to look at Katie. She placed her hand on his arm. "Go, Adam. You have to find him."

He raised his brows. "I don't know how long I'll be. It's hard going in the snow. I'll take Honey; I just hope she's ready for this."

"It's fine; you have to go. You have to find him. For Jo." Katie grimaced, thinking of the worry her friend must be feeling. "He'd do it for you. We're fine here, I promise. I'm glad you'll have Honey with you. I feel better knowing you have her keen ears and eyes on the trail."

Adam kissed Katie and embraced her and each of the girls. "I'll be back as soon as I can, and I'll get word to you if I can. I love you all very much, my darlings." He buttoned up his coat while he spoke, snatched his Stetson from its hook, shoved it on his head and stomped out the door behind Jonny.

*   *   *   *

Adam took the time to make phone calls to Jo and the RNWMP office in Pine Crest. He needed to be as informed as possible. He discovered the prisoner was the infamous Terrance 'Buffalo' Jones.

Buffalo Jones was a ruthless outlaw who terrorised the North. He seldom ran with a gang, but had many friends just as evil as he was, and wouldn't hesitate to kill any man who got in his way.

He'd tortured and killed four Mounties before they managed to catch him just north of Moose River. It was decided not to leave the job to the young constable, but instead to get two sergeants from the nearby stations to accompany the prisoner. So Samuel and Sergeant Michael Turner from Walkers Rise were given the job. It had been several days, and there was no sight nor sound of the two sergeants or The Buffalo.

Two of Sam's young constables had gone looking for their sergeant, taking the route that the sergeants would have taken. Unable to find them, they knew they needed Adam.

Adam sighed and picked up the phone. The operator patched him through to Jo.

"Adam, oh thank the Lord. Sam's missing. I'm so worried."

"I know, Jo, I promise you, I'll find him."

"Thank you. I'll forever be in your debt."

"No debt needed, he'd do the same for me. Katie sends her love and prayers, she's sorry she can't get to you because of the blizzard."

"I know, thank you, Adam."

"I'll find him, don't worry."

"Thank you." Adam could hear the tremble in her voice.

* * * *

By nightfall, Adam and Jonny reached the old Buckner Cabin on the outskirts of town. It was too dark and stormy to keep going, even with lanterns. They spent the night in the cabin, tethering the horses in the single stall in the small barn. Honey laid beside the fire. They took time before turning in to make a plan. Pouring over maps of the area, they planned out their route.

"Given the reputation of The Buffalo, I'd imagine he had people waiting to rescue him."

Jonny scratched his chin. "Do you think the two sergeants were ambushed?"

"I'd imagine so. Sam's a fine Mountie; he wouldn't have gone easily."

"What are their chances, Serge?"

Adam closed his eyes and gritted his teeth. He looked sternly at the younger Mountie. "I refuse to even entertain the thought until I know otherwise. He is alive and well. We've both been through worse and survived."

Jonny nodded. He knew the story of Adam and Samuel's time in prison in the Yukon. "Do you think we need reinforcements?"

"Maybe, but in the meantime, we have one distinct advantage."

"What's that?"

"I know these areas well. If they're around these parts, I'll find them. Besides, we have Honey. She's an excellent tracker."

"You're right, Serge. Honey'll find 'em."

"I just hope she's had enough training. She's already three years old, but for two of those years, she didn't do much more than sit by the fire and chase squirrels."

"You've worked with her extensively, Sir. I'm sure she'll be fine."

"I just wish her first real test wasn't so serious. I sure wish this storm would stop." Adam ran his fingers through his hair.

"Serge, I think we should pray."

"Good idea."

The two Mounties spent time petitioning God to watch over Samuel and Sergeant Turner wherever they were and for help to find them before it was too late. They prayed for protection and divine intervention.

The two Mounties left before the sun was even up, the storm had stopped but the trail was covered in deep snow, and Honey was unable to find a scent. They trudged on following the trails they'd marked on their maps. "This snow really doesn't help."

"It's not too deep."

"Deep enough to cover any footprints though." Adam sighed. "This isn't going to be easy."

They spent the entire day checking all the little trails and huts within a ten-mile radius. It was slow and frustrating, but they persevered. "I will not stop until I find my friend." Adam ran his fingers through his hair as they pitched their tent in a clearing under a wide canopy of trees where there was minimal snow.

"What if it takes weeks?"

"Then it takes weeks."

"What about your family?"

Adam closed his eyes and sighed, he sat down before the fire Jon had made and handed his cup out for Jonny to fill. "I hate being away from them. But I know they're safe." He sipped at the hot liquid and draped his arms over his raised knees. "There are plenty of people around that'll check in on them. Marcus, Daniel, Owen.

Sam needs me, he's my best friend, and I have to find him. No, he's more than just my friend. He's my brother. He's saved my life more than once, and I owe him this. I owe it to Jo and his children."

"You know he could be dead already." Jonny was not trying to be hurtful, just honest.

Adam sighed again and stared at the flames. He lifted his coffee cup to his mouth. "I admit that might be a possibility, especially given the conditions. I refuse to despair though. He never gave up on me in that jail, and I won't give up on him. I'm taking him home to his family, dead or alive!" Adam was almost shouting when he finished. He clenched his jaw and then sighed. "Sorry, you don't deserve my anger, and it won't help anything. I'm just so frustrated at our lack of any sign of them."

"It's quite okay, Sergeant. I understand."

It was another whole day of searching before they found anything. Around midday, on the third day they headed down their umpteenth trail for the day, when suddenly Honey took off barking. The two Mounties hastened their horses and followed the dog. "Serge." Jonny pointed to a figure on the ground, half-covered in snow some metres ahead of them dressed in red serge.

"Ohhhhhh." Adam gasped, and hastened Ebony. Before he even got off his horse, he could see the person was dead and the sleeve bore the bars of a sergeant. He dismounted quickly and knelt down in the snow. "Please, no." He furiously pushed the snow off the face and sighed in relief. "It's not Samuel. This must be Turner."

"We have to be close." Jonny dismounted. He gestured to Honey, who was sniffing around, ears pricked up, hunting for any signs. The two Mounties wrapped Sergeant Turner's body in a blanket and moved him to the side of the road. They'd come back later and take him home, but for now, they had to find Samuel.

"Honey," Adam called, leaping back on his horse. He headed off after her down a trail into the woods. If The Buffalo was still around, she might alert him, and they could all be in trouble. He called out to the dog, and she heeled when he called. Adam dismounted and tethered his horse to a tree. He instructed Jonny to follow quietly, bade the dog to stay and hoped she'd oblige.

Up ahead, they could hear voices arguing. Adam gestured for Jonny to go around and approach from the side. They could both just make out smoke in the distance.

Jon nodded and moved to do Adam's bidding. The sergeant cocked his rifle, and headed towards the small clearing in the woods. From behind a tree, he could see two men sitting on makeshift seats on either side of their campfire, arguing loudly.

"Why are you keeping 'em, Buffalo?"

"He could come in handy. Besides, the sergeant and I have a relationship. It's a game we likes to play." He kicked out at the tied-up Mountie next to him. The red-serge-covered man was motionless, and Adam couldn't see if he was alive or not. He did notice rips in Samuel's clothing, and it looked like one of his legs was at a very unusual angle. He lay face down with his arms tied behind his back.

Catching a flash of red on the other side of the clearing, Adam signalled for Jonny to stay where he was. The two outlaws were armed, and he'd have to play this carefully. He moved around a little further so the fire was no longer between him and Samuel. He strained his neck to get a glimpse and try to assess his friend's condition. *Lord, let him be alive.*

Adam observed the scene carefully. A wide canopy of trees made a sheltered clearing and the men had pitched their tent where there was little snow. A billy boiled over the fire and some RNWMP tinned rations warmed nearby. Adam caught Jonny's eye and made the motion of a horse. From his vantage point, Jonny could just see a group of horses tied up in the distance behind the men. He signalled to Adam that there were four.

Adam gestured towards them. Jonny nodded his understanding. He made his way silently around to the horses and released their tethers, slapped them on the back, causing them to whiny in fright and hurry away.

"The horses." One of the bandits leapt up. "They're loose." Both men were distracted for a moment, and Adam stepped out of the clearing and shot one in the leg. The man fell to the ground screaming. The Buffalo snatched up his rifle and pointed it at Adam. Jonny stepped out with his rifle raised.

"You can't shoot both of us, Buffalo." Adam taunted him, walking closer with his pistol aimed right at the man's head.

"No, but I can take out this one." The Buffalo sneered and rolled Samuel over with his foot. Adam heard Sam groan and breathed a sigh of relief. *He's alive.* Buffalo aimed his rifle square at Samuel's chest and scoffed. "Put down your weapon, Sergeant, or this one is dead."

The man on the ground clutched his leg and continued screaming.

The Buffalo growled at his friend. "Stop that noise, Charlie, ain't nothing but a flesh wound. These cowards in red serge wouldn't actually hurt anyone. They're yella!"

Adam slowly advanced.

"I wouldn't if I were you, Serge." The Buffalo dug his rifle into Samuel's ribs. "I'll blow his stomach out through his back."

"And you'll be dead before your bullet hits him, Buffalo."

"You won't shoot me. Mounties are too nice."

Adam scowled at him. "Try me."

Charlie stopped his screaming, gritted his teeth and clutched his bleeding leg, wincing in pain, oblivious to Jonny sneaking up behind the Buffalo. Adam frowned, and Buffalo noticed his expression quickly change. Jonny put his rifle up to Buffalo's head and cocked it. "Drop your weapon!"

The Buffalo smirked and lifted his own rifle in the air, firing aimlessly towards Adam, who dove out of the way. The bandit turned quickly and took a shot at Jonny, catching him in the leg. Jonny fell to the ground as blood flowed from his wound. Buffalo spun to aim at Adam again, but he was nowhere to be seen.

"That's right. I knew you were a coward, Sergeant. I got two of your men here dying, and you ain't even got the guts to stand your ground," he yelled into the woods. Adam crept silently around the side of the clearing. The Buffalo pointed his rifle towards the woods. His friend groaned on the ground in pain, and Jonny, ignoring his own pain, stretched his arm out for his rifle. The Buffalo turned, and stamped his foot hard down on Jonny's wound. The Mountie cried out in agony. The Buffalo snarled and scoffed. "Do you like that? Your sergeant is long gone, Constable, and you're gonna die out here, with this sergeant." He kicked out at Sam again.

The barrel of a gun nudged the back of the outlaws head. "You were told to drop your weapon, Buffalo."

The Buffalo smirked. "Whatcha gonna do, Mountie? I know you're honour bound and won't kill me. It's not the Mountie way!"

"Is if I'm defending myself." Adam nudged the man's head again.

A movement caught Adam's eye. Sam opened his eyes and grinned. While Adam taunted the Buffalo he reached for Jonny's discarded rifle.

Adam lowered his gun, and The Buffalo turned around. "I knew you didn't have it in ya. You're yella!" Buffalo raised his gun and thrust it into the Sergeant's chest. Adam didn't flinch. He fixed his steely glare on the man and clenched his jaw. A gun cocked behind them and the Buffalo flinched as a gun rammed into his temple. Adam raised his brows and a voice said, "Terrence Jones, you're under arrest. Drop your weapon and turn around with your hands up."

Buffalo spun around. "But, but, but, you're...." he stammered and threw his weapon to the ground. Samuel stood on his one good leg with Jonny's rifle pointed at the Buffalo's face.

Adam cuffed the man, and Sam painfully helped him to bind both men then collapsed to the ground again.

"Honey." Adam whistled and the dog bounded into the scene. "Guard." Honey gave him to quick yips and fixed her blue eyes on the crook. "If you move she'll go for the throat," he warned. The Buffalo looked at the bared teeth and folded back lips of the dog and grimaced. "Sam, hold tight. I'll set your leg, but if Jon loses any more blood, he's gonna die."

"Help me up. I'll help you." Adam put his arm around Sam and helped him stand, hop over to Jonny and sit next to the younger Mountie.

"I need my kit. Put pressure on his wound; and I'll run for my horse," Adam yelled over shoulder as he ran.

Sam put as much pressure as he could on the young man's leg wound, ignoring the agony in his own. Adam galloped into the clearing leading Jonny's horse behind him. He leapt off, grabbed his saddlebags and ran over to help Jonny. Together the two men stitched up his wound.

"That's the best I can do for ya, Lad." Adam grimaced as he bound the wound tightly.

Sam nodded. "He'll make it, Adam."

"He has to. My daughter'll never forgive me if he doesn't survive."

Sam nodded.

"Now I'll set your leg."

Sam reached for a nearby twig. "Do it, Adam." He put the stick in his mouth and bit down.

Adam placed both hands either side of the broken leg. "Ready."

Sam nodded and put his hands back on the ground behind him.

Adam grasped the leg and pulled quickly.

"Arrrrgh!" Sam cried out and spat out the twig.

"All over, Sam. I'll get something to splint that leg."

Sam exhaled and inhaled loudly through the pain. "Thanks, Adam." Sam nodded gratefully.

* * * *

Adam stroked the head of the husky in his lap and stared at the fire. Sam and Jonny lay sleeping in the tent behind him, and the two bandits were bound and lying beside the fire. Adam sighed. *Lord, somehow I have to get all four men home on two horses. I could use your wisdom here.*

He sipped at his coffee, buried his hand in the long honey-coloured fur of the husky, and turned his thoughts towards home. He longed for Katie and his girls, and knew Callie would be beside herself in worry about Jonny. He knew without a doubt that Rose and Marcus would be visiting with them all. Adam nodded and grinned. Marcus would take responsibility for the family in his absence, of that he was sure. *Thank You, Lord, that there are so many people to watch out for my family.*

That was a small relief, but he longed for them all the more. He shivered, moved closer to the fire, and pulled his blanket around his shoulders.

"Thank you, Lord, I'm bringing home two wounded colleagues, not two fallen heroes." It shocked Adam to realise just how scared he'd been when Jonny had been shot. It occurred to him that the young man mattered a great deal to him. More even than a much-appreciated colleague, more like that of a son.

He drained his cup and ran his fingers through his hair. "Honey, my girls sure made good choices in the men they love. I couldn't have chosen better myself."

There would be no sleep for Adam that night, he dared not let himself close his eyes for long. As soon as the first fingers of light swept across the sky, he was up. Leaving Honey to guard the campsite, he walked a little way into the woods and set to work cutting down a branch. Returning to his fire, he regained his seat and fashioned a crude crutch for Samuel.

He woke Sam. "Sergeant, I'm gonna need your help. We've gotta get these men on horses and back to Douglas Falls so I can get someone to come get them. I just wish we had more horses."

"Where are our horses?"

"I'm not sure. Jonny let them all go. They could be anywhere."

"Phoenix wouldn't have gone far. He won't go further than he has to."

"I'll go for a short look around and see if I can find them."

"I'll get some coffee on and see if I can't rustle up some beans for breakfast." Sam hopped with the help of his crutch towards Adam's bag.

Adam was surprised to find Phoenix and Sergeant Turner's horse, Flash, grazing just a few metres into the trees. He breathed a sigh of relief and issued up a short prayer of thankfulness that the two Mountie horses hadn't run away. They'd been trained to stay nearby even after being spooked. He led them back into the clearing. Sam was stirring a small tin of beans and spoon-feeding the two bandits, propped up against a tree stump. He replaced their gags as Adam approached. "Can't bear to hear what they have to say."

"Good thinking." Adam nodded. "I found the horses, just as you said. These men's horses are long gone."

"Mountie horses are well trained." Samuel hopped over to pet his horse, Phoenix. "Faithful to a fault."

"Yes, more reliable than most men. Let's get Jon up, and then we'll get these men back to the iron bars hotel."

Sam hobbled behind Adam to the tent and they woke up Jonny, and helped him out of bed. The two Mounties assisted him to the fire and gave him a plate of beans. The young man sweated from the pain in his leg, but managed a few bites of the beans. Adam and Sam strapped the two bandits to the back of Sergeant Turner's horse.

"Did you find the Sergeant?"

"Yes." Adam frowned. "We'll collect him on the way back."

"He died saving my life." Sam choked back his emotions.

"What happened?" Adam helped Jonny up on Major. They tied his hurt leg into the stirrup, and he winced in pain. "Sorry, Son, can't risk you falling out."

Sweat ran down the Mountie's ashen face. "I can make it, Serge." He nodded and prepared to leave.

Samuel took a deep breath. "The one called Charlie was waiting in the trees. We had The Buffalo bound and sitting on the horse. Charlie leapt out, dragged me off my horse and knocked me out. He freed The Buffalo, and held the Sergeant and me at gunpoint when I came to.

"The Buffalo started to beat me just for his own amusement. He stood on my leg and snapped it. Aimed his rifle right at my face and told me to beg him to live. I didn't give him the satisfaction. Sergeant Turner knew I had a family. He could see that Buffalo was about to shoot me, so he punched Charlie in the face, knocked him to the ground, leapt up, and dived over me, taking the bullet on my behalf. The man saved my life." Sam gulped.

"He's a hero. We'll see to it he gets a hero's burial." Adam gripped his friend's shoulder and helped him onto his horse. "You lead. I'll bring up the rear. You okay, Constable?"

"Yeah." Jonny gritted his teeth.

"You have to, Jon, my daughter'll never forgive me if you don't."

"You aren't scared of her, are you, Serge?" Jonny chuckled despite the pain.

"Absolutely. Aren't you?"

"Terrified, Sir!" Adam smirked and they headed for home, stopping to pick up the Sergeant's body. By late evening they reached Douglas Falls. They pulled all the horses up to the RNWMP office, and Samuel painfully helped Adam get the two men into the cells, untied their bounds and locked them in. "Get comfortable, Gentlemen. This is your home until backup arrives."

"Much obliged, Sergeant," the Buffalo scoffed.

Adam leaned against the wall while the doctor went to work, but he was anxious to get home. First, he had messages to send and Sergeant Turner's body to deal with. He sighed, he longed for his wife and daughters, but duty meant he had to do right by his fellow Mounties.

"You can go, Adam. I've got it from here," Owen offered. "You did a good job of the constable's wound and setting the sergeant's leg. They'll both recover fully. Go back to your family, Adam. I know you'll be anxious to see them."

"Thanks, Doctor, but I need to stay so I can make an accurate report."

"Go, Sergeant, there's nothing more you can do for us," Sam insisted. "I need you to send a wire to Jo."

Adam nodded and turned to leave. He headed to the RNWMP office and made some phone calls, first letting HQ know about Sergeant Turner and requesting an escort crew for the two men. He sighed, knowing full well he'd have to babysit them tonight and still wouldn't be able to go home.

"Jo." Adam's voice held deep relief.

"Adam, did you find him?"

"Yes, he's in our infirmary."

"Oh no," came her voice over the crackly line. "What happened?"

"He has a broken leg but the doc says he'll make a full recovery."

"Thank you, Adam, thank you for finding him."

"Jo, there was no way I was coming home without him."

"Thank you." She sucked back a sob. "I'll be over as soon as I can."

"Very well. I must get back to them."

"Thank you. It means so much to me that you found him."

"Of course, Jo, there was no way I wasn't going to find him." Adam managed before hanging up the phone.

"Pa." Callie stormed into the office. "Where is he, Pa?" She threw herself in Adam's arms.

Adam closed his eyes and wrapped his arms around her, relishing the moment to hold one of his precious girls for even a moment. "Callie, what are you doing here? How did you know we're home?"

"Vinnie came to tell us. Ma is most anxious for you to be home."

"I know, Darling." He kissed his daughter on the hair. "But I have to babysit these two." He gestured to the jail.

"How's Jonny?".

Adam gripped her shoulder. "He's injured, Callie, he was shot."

Callie clasped her hands over her mouth, and tears sprung to her eyes. "No!"

"He's going to be okay." Adam embraced her tightly. "He's strong and courageous. He was shot trying to apprehend these men. They're dangerous and had already killed one Mountie and injured Sam. Jon's a hero, Callie."

She grinned, stepped back from him and wiped his eyes. "I know, Pa." She hugged him again. "Can I go and see him?"

"Sure, Darling, Doctor Randall is with him now. Don't stay long though. You need to get home before it gets too dark."

"I know. I just missed you both. You've been gone five days."

Adam embraced her again and she ran from the room.

"Jonny!" Callie fell into the chair next to his bed.

"Oh, Callie." He put his arms out and embraced her. They kissed gently and she wept.

"Oh, Jonny, I missed you."

"I missed you too, Darling, but it was thinking of you that helped me through the pain."

"Pa told me you were shot."

"It's just a flesh wound. I'll be okay."

"Oh, I'm so sorry."

"Hush, I'll be okay." He smiled and squeezed her hand.

They sat together chatting for a few hours. Callie brought him a meal from the café, and they ate together.

Jo hurried into the infirmary. "Sam."

"Jo." Sam put a hand out to her. "My darling."

Jo ran to him and they clung to each other. "Oh I'm so sorry about your leg."

"I'm going to be fine. Thanks for calling Adam, Jo. He saved my life."

"I knew he'd find you. I knew he'd not stop until he did."

"He's a good friend."

Sam turned to the young constable. "Thanks, Sullivan. I appreciate you bringing my wife over."

"You're welcome, Serge."

"Go and relieve Sergeant Morgan. He needs to go back to his family."

"Yes, Sir." The young man nodded, turned on his heels and walked next door to Adam's office. "Sergeant Morgan?" He poked his head in the door.

"Constable Sullivan, what brings you here?"

"I escorted Mrs Ferguson over, Sir. I want to offer to guard the prisoners for you so you can go home, Sergeant."

"That's kind of you, Constable." Adam didn't labour the point; he was most anxious to get home. He stood and shook the young man's hand. "I'll see you in the morning."

"My pleasure, Sir." The young man took a seat at the desk.

Adam strode into the clinic. Jo leapt out of her chair, ran and threw her arms around him. She kissed his cheek. "I'll never be able to thank you enough."

He squeezed her tightly and kissed her hair. "There's no need, Jo. He's saved me more times than I can count." The relief in his voice was evident.

"Still, you brought him home to me, and from what he tells me, he'd be dead if you hadn't found him."

Adam released her and gave her a nod and a relieved smile.

"Adam, you need to go home to your family. Constable Sullivan can watch the jail." Sam sat back against the wall with his arms crossed.

"I will. I just wanted to check on you."

"Well, you have. Now go home." Sam raised his brows at his friend.

"Yes, Sir." Adam saluted Sam and hurried out.

Sam shook his head and turned back to his wife.

*   *   *   *

Katie was sitting up in bed, with her Bible open on her lap. She didn't hear Adam enter the room.

"Katie."

"Adam, you're home." Katie leapt out of bed and threw herself in his arms. "Oh, I've missed you so."

"It was only five days." He smiled as he held her and kissed her firmly. He took a deep breath and held his wife close, as always drawing strength from her.

"Five days feels like forever. Even one day apart is too many, Husband." She kissed him again.

"I'm exhausted, Katie. I'm so glad to be home with my girls."

At last, she was lying in bed, encircled in his arms, her cheek against his chest. He kissed her head.

"I missed you. I was sitting out there in the wilderness, and all I could think about was you and the girls."

"We missed you too, and we prayed for you all. Oh, Adam, I'm so relieved Samuel is okay."

"Jo's with him now."

"Good. She's the best nurse he needs. How's Jonny? Vinnie said he was shot?"

"He's going to be fine, Katie, any longer and he would've died."

She pulled back from him and stroked his cheek in the semi-darkness. "But he didn't, and he's going to be fine."

"When I thought he might die, I couldn't help thinking of Callie and how much she'd hurt. I realised something."

"What's that?"

"I love that lad. He's the right man for our Callie, and I know he'll be a worthy husband to her. He was a hero out there. I'll be recommending him for a promotion."

"But that means he could end up being posted elsewhere."

"I know."

"And take Callie with him."

"I know." He sighed. "But they need each other, Katie. She was the reason he survived. It was for her. I'd rather know they had each other and were far away, than watch my daughter suffer for even a moment at his loss."

"You're a good man, Adam Morgan. Perhaps they won't post him elsewhere, for some time at least."

"I hope not, but I've made my peace with it. If they go, it will be with my blessing. That goes with all our daughters. I know I can't expect to keep them all with me forever."

Katie kissed him. "You're a wonderful father, Adam willing to sacrifice your own happiness for theirs."

"My highest calling is my duty to my family, Katie. I have to because I love them."

"I know you do, and I love you too."

He nodded and pulled her close. "I love you, more than life itself. You are my strength."

"Now you need to sleep, Adam."

"Goodnight." He kissed her head as she snuggled closely into him and they fell into a deep and contented sleep.

Twenty-One
Anniversaries

Adam sat on the bed in the cell with Jack's head in his lap, Katie sat beside him and both stroked the furry head. The girls gathered around.

"I'm here with you, Boy." Adam spoke to his faithful friend. "It's alright." The dog partially opened sad eyes and let out a single whine. Adam stroked his head again. "It's okay, Boy." Adam buried his hands in the dog's thick fur as he breathed his last.

Katie lay her head on his shoulder. "I'm so sorry, Adam."

The girls all said their goodbye's and Adam sniffed away a tear. "I'm glad he's not hurting anymore."

Katie squeezed his arm. "He was a good friend."

Adam nodded. "And colleague."

"Sorry, Pa." Callie stood and leaned forward to embrace him.

Adam lifted a hand to her chin. "Thank you, Darling. I'm sorry this is overshadowing your birthday."

Callie smiled. "It's not, Pa. We celebrated this morning. And we are all together to remember Jack, he's been with us girls for our entire lives."

Adam swiped a sleeve across his eyes. "Thank you, Darling."

"Want me to bury him, Serge?"

Adam looked at Jon. "I'll need your help to dig the hole, the ground is pretty frozen."

"Rest easy my friend." Adam placed the dog in the hole. "You served well." He stood and gulped back a tear as Jonny and Marcus shovelled dirt over him.

Adam put his arms around Katie and Rose. He lay his head against Katie's. "I'm sorry I'm so sentimental over a dog. You probably all think me a little soft in the head." He grimaced.

Rose squeezed his arm. "Pa, you aren't soft in the head. Jack was more than a dog to you. He was a colleague and a friend. We all loved him."

Adam nodded and kissed Rose's hair. "Yes and he guarded your cradle when you were a baby, he's saved my life on several occasions. I saw him as a Mountie just as much as I am."

"Like with Bear and Midnight." Katie gestured across to the two plaques Adam had put up for the animals who'd served with him."

"Fallen heroes." Adam nodded and squeezed them again. "Well, we better get back to our birthday celebrations." He winked at Callie.

With one last look at the grave they turned and followed Adam and Honey from the plot behind the RNWMP office, climbed on the wagon and headed for home.

* * * *

Spring came early that year, exploding all at once in vivid colour. The meadows, roadsides, and pastureland abounded with wildflowers and new life.

"Such a beautiful day to celebrate." Jo grinned as they all picnicked below the trees on The Rise.

"Yes." Katie squeezed Adam's arm. "We have lots of birthdays to celebrate."

Adam winked at her. "As much as I hate the reminder that I'm getting old, it is nice to celebrate all the birthdays. Thank you, ladies, for this wonderful meal."

The women nodded and turned to their handcrafts.

"Dan, Adam, come on we need more men to make up our team." Sam lifted his bat over his shoulder and gestured towards the diamond.

Adam looked up at Sam. "Coming, Sergeant. We'll prove to these young'ns there's a lot of life left in these old bones." He kissed Katie's cheek, winked at her and leapt up to join the game.

They divided the teams and the game began, with fourteen-year-old Lizzie in the midst; despite her cumbersome skirts, she kept up with them all.

The women called the game to a stop by banging on a pot. Coffee and muffins were laid out and the family in various places with their cups. Marcus drained his cup and called out to silence the gathering. He stood up and helped Rose to her feet. "Everyone, Rose and I have something to tell you."

Adam and Katie stood by the table. The Mountie gasped, and slipped his arm around Katie. He held his breath while they spoke.

Rose's eyes misted over and she looked at her parents. "Pa, you're going to be a grandpa."

Adam exhaled deeply and squeezed Katie ever so slightly. There was a pause, a brief silence, and no one moved. Then Adam ran headlong towards his daughter and hugged her tightly. "Oh, My Rosie Girl! I'm so happy for you, Darling." He kissed her on the forehead. He released her and embraced Marcus. "Congratulations, Marc."

"We're due around the first of November, Pa." Rose grinned.

Adam embraced her again and kissed her hair. "A new baby for Christmas." He beamed. "I can't think of anything sweeter!"

"Oh, Darling, I'm so happy for you." Katie clung to her daughter. Rose and Marcus received congratulations from the entire crowd. After some time and many well wishes, the noise died down, and everyone turned back to their coffee.

Amy nudged Andy, and he stood up and got everyone's attention. "Hi all, not to try to steal Rose and Marcus's thunder, but we, ah, also have an announcement."

Daniel and Louisa gasped while Rose beamed. She and Amy had whispered their good news to each other earlier.

"What are you saying, Son?" Daniel, squinted at Andy. "You two aren't expecting too, are you?"

Andy grinned and wrapped his arms around his wife. "Yes, Pa. We're due right around the first of November also."

Another round of congratulations ensued. Rose, Amy, Marcus and Andy held each other for some time, delighted they'd get to share this experience.

"Imagine if we had our babies on the same day too." Rose laughed.

Daniel and Adam embraced each other. "Looks like we're both going to be grandparents at the same time, my friend. Who'd've thought twenty-two years ago when we first met that we would not only be brothers-in-law someday but grandfathers together!"

"Can't think of a better chap to share it with." The Mountie grinned, and the two men slapped each other on the back. Samuel and Jo, and Owen and Becky came to congratulate them also.

"You don't look old enough to be a grandfather, Serge." Sam gripped his friend's shoulder.

"Don't joke, Ferguson. You won't be so far behind."

"None of mine are even courting, Morgan."

"It'll happen soon enough."

* * * *

"We've been banished here and told we aren't to go back until six. The men are planning an anniversary supper for us." Rose grinned.

"That's so lovely. It'll be wonderful." Katie refilled the coffee cups.

"I hope my kitchen isn't being destroyed." Rose grimaced.

"It'll be fine, Darling," Katie reassured her.

"That's easy for you to say, Ma. What if it was Pa and Uncle Danny?"

Katie looked across at Adam, reading his newspaper. Her face fell and she screwed up her mouth comically. "I guess I would be just as anxious." She winked at Adam and whispered loudly. "Your pa isn't much of a cook."

Adam smiled and shrugged. "I wish I could say it wasn't true, but your ma is right. That's why I'm so grateful for you, Darling." He stood and walked over to kiss his wife.

"That doesn't really give me any confidence." Rose grimaced.

"That's why I suggested your place." Amy chuckled.

"Hmmm, I thought we were friends." Rose gave her friend a mock scowl.

Anna spoke up then. "Jonny, when does Callie get home? I thought she was coming with you?"

"Anna, she'll be here soon." Jonny tried to give Anna signals to say nothing. Callie was over at Far Acre helping the two men prepare the meal for their wives, and they didn't want Rose and Amy to know. Rose caught the exchange between the two and smiled. If Callie was at her house with the men, all would be just fine. Callie was more than capable of organising them.

Just before six o'clock, Callie came home and entered nonchalantly. She greeted them all and received Jonny's kiss. "Oh, hi Rose, hi Amy, I didn't know you were here?" She turned to Jonny. "I'll just go change. I'll be right back."

Jonny nodded.

"Well, it's nearly six o clock, Amy. Shall we go?" Rose stood.

Amy placed her coffee cup down and stood. "Yes!"

"Happy Anniversary, ladies." Adam embraced Rose and kissed her hair. I can't believe you've been married a whole year, you too, Amy. And both of you have a little one on the way. We're so thrilled for you."

"Thanks, Pa." Rose returned her father's kiss and reached for her shawl and basket.

Arm and arm they walked up the stairs and knocked on the door.

Marcus opened it and welcomed them both in. Both men reached for their wife, with loving kisses and hugs. They led the women to the table, lit with candles and flowers in the centre. They walked to the kitchen and returned with plates of beefsteak and vegetables. The meal was delicious and the women were pleasantly surprised.

"And now for dessert." Marcus winked at Rose, stood and cleared their plates and he and Andy hurried to the kitchen and came back with big slices of cake. Callie's contribution was confirmed when the cake came out with Callie's signature cherry sauce.

"Thank you, Marcus. That was a wonderful evening." Rose snuggled into her husband's arms, leaning back against him on the chaise. He laid a hand on her gently rounding abdomen and kissed her hair.

"It was our pleasure, my darling. Andy and I wanted to make our first anniversary special for the two of you. You bring so much joy to our lives, and we wanted to show you just a small glimpse of what you bring to us." He chuckled. "We're just sorry we aren't better cooks."

"I'm glad you had Callie to help." Rose chuckled.

"Us too." They sat for a time, just enjoying each other's company.

"Well, should we turn in, Husband?"

"Great idea, Wife." Marcus stood and took Rose in his arms. "Happy Anniversary, Mrs Murray. This has been the best year of my life."

Rose gushed. "Happy Anniversary Marcus, it's been the best year of my life too. And it's just going to get better." She lay a hand on her abdomen.

Marcus put his hand over hers and kissed her gently. "I can't wait." He winked, scooped her up in his arms and carried her to their bedroom.

*   *   *   *

Adam laid down the blanket, sat with his back against the ancient oak. He gestured to Katie to join him. She eagerly sat down and leaned back into her husband's arms.

He wrapped his arms around her and grinned. This was still his very favourite thing in the world to do. Just hold his wife in his arms. Second to that was holding his girls. There was nothing that thrilled him more, no greater tonic to his heart. He took a deep breath and sighed contentedly. "Can you believe we've been married twenty years, Katie?"

"It feels like just yesterday."

"But so much has happened. What a twenty years it's been."

"I know. Six children and a grandchild on the way."

"Yes, Darling. We've certainly had some good times since we got married." Adam kissed her hair.

"And some not so good." Katie closed her eyes."

Adam nodded and squeezed her slightly. "I'm sorry." He sighed. "Thinking I was dead must've been awful for you all, worse even than losing our baby. At least we could bare that together."

"You'll never know how horrible it was, Adam. Learning to live without you was the most awful thing I've ever faced. But it was nothing compared to what you went through in that jail."

Adam nodded. "Yeah, but you never gave up on me. If it wasn't for your tenacity, contacting The Commander and forcing him to listen, Sam and I would likely have died in that place."

"As soon as the horse turned up, I knew it wasn't Midnight. I knew you weren't dead."

"I'm glad you are the way you are, Katherine Morgan. You've saved my life many times over." Adam kissed her hair.

"And you've saved mine, Adam. We're even."

"It's not a competition. I could never ever repay all the incredible things you've done for me. I love you so very much, more and more every day. You are the most amazing woman I've ever met, from stitching me up, to ordering around The Commander." He grinned. "I can't believe I got to marry you. I never imagined I could be so blessed."

"Me either, Adam. You were the man of my dreams."

"You weren't the woman of mine," Adam smirked.

Katie turned in his arms to look at him. "I'm not?"

Adam grinned at her. "I could never have dreamed up such an amazing woman. I really thought if I did marry, it would be to someone like Delia, and I'd live in an unhappy marriage all my life."

"I'd forgotten about her." Katie grimaced.

"I'll never forget, because then I might risk taking advantage of what I've got, and I never want to do that. I have the most amazing wife and six beautiful, talented daughters. I couldn't be happier, Katie. We have amazing friends and family and a wonderful home. Really, Mrs Morgan, it doesn't get better than this."

"Wait until November. It just might?"

Adam grinned. "You're right. I can't wait to hold my grandchild, Katie. Rose is going to be a wonderful mother."

"Yes, I agree, Husband. I can't believe I'm going to be an old grandmother."

Adam kissed her cheek. "Not old, a beautiful young, sprightly grandmother. How amazing to have our grandchildren living right there on our land, and to have them while we're young and can enjoy them."

"It'll be wonderful for sure."

They sat quietly for some time, enjoying holding each other until Katie broke their silence. "Adam, this is still my favourite place to be in the whole world, right here in your arms."

He squeezed her tightly and rested his cheek on hers. "Mine too, Darling. I'll never tire of holding you or our girls. God gave me broad shoulders and long arms for a reason."

"I know, Adam. You're a wonderful husband and father. We're so blessed to have you."

"I'm the lucky one, Katie. I'm nothing without you. Honestly, I'm only the husband and father I am because of the wife and mother you are."

"Here's to another twenty years."

"Make it fifty. I plan to grow very old with you, my darling."

Katie smiled. "I don't want this day to end."

"Me either." He sighed. "But sadly, anniversaries don't mean whole days off."

"I know, they aren't always even pleasant."

Adam frowned as he helped her to her feet. "Really? Which one has been unpleasant?"

"The one where I was told you died."

Adam stopped in his tracks, placed the blanket on the back of his horse and turned to her. "That was on our anniversary?" He put his hands on her elbows.

"Yes, our ninth."

"You've never told me that before. I'm so sorry, Katie."

Katie smiled and put a hand on his cheek. "It's fine. It turned out to be okay. You're here now."

"Yes, I am." He grinned. "And nothing can spoil this anniversary."

They mounted their horses and headed towards town, continuing their conversation as they rode. Both snapped their heads up as Jonny came galloping towards them. "Sergeant. Serge, you have to come quickly."

Adam hastened his horse to meet him. "What is it, Constable?"

"There's an urgent telephone call for you, from Mountie HQ."

Adam frowned. "What could be so important?" He turned to Katie. "I'm sorry, Darling."

"It's fine, Adam. Go."

"Meet me at the office. I'll ride home with you afterwards."

"Alright." Katie gave him a smile.

He winked, tipped his Stetson at her and galloped off with Jonny. Katie followed at a much more leisurely pace.

Adam sat at his desk on the phone with a deeply furrowed brow. He looked up, noticed Katie and beckoned her in. The look on his face made her heart lurch and she hurried over and put her hands on his shoulders.

"Are you sure?" Adam listened for a time. "Thank you, Uncle." Adam's voice broke. "I'll get there as soon as I can. Goodbye."

Adam hung up the phone and buried his head in his hands. He began to sob. Katie wrapped her arms around him. It took a lot to make her strong husband cry. Finally, he regained his composure and gestured to Katie to climb up on his knee, and he put his arms around her and lay his cheek against hers.

"What is it, Adam?"

"The Commander." His voice trembled.

"What about him?"

"He's dead, Katie."

"Oh, Adam. I'm so sorry." Katie put her arms around his neck.

Adam squeezed her and drew strength from her support.

"What happened?"

"He died saving two children from a burning house. The superintendent said a gang of whiskey runners were trying to extort information out of the father, but he wouldn't tell them what they wanted, so they burned his home, not realising he had two small children."

"Oh." Katie lay her head on his shoulder. "How awful. Did the children survive?" She shuddered.

Adam nodded. "The Commander entered the burning building and managed to hand the two children out the window to one of his constables. Then when he tried to get out, the whole building came down on him."

"Your father died a hero, Adam. He saved those two children."

"I know. I'm proud of him." Adam nodded and ran his fingers through his hair.

"So when is his funeral?"

"They have to get his body back from the Northern Territories, so it could be more than a week."

"You're going then?"

Adam nodded. "Will you come with me?"

"I wish I could, Adam, but I have a household to run."

Rose clung to Marcus, and Callie clung to Jonny. The family took the news pretty hard. Adam recounted the story of how he saved the two small children. "So being a hero runs in your family, Pa!"

Adam cupped Hope's cheek. "I'm not a touch on The Commander, Hope. He's always been very strong and brave."

"So are you, Pa."

Adam smiled and kissed her hair.

Anna tipped her head to the side. "Are you going for the funeral, Pa?"

"Yes, I plan to. I'll leave tomorrow." Adam turned to look at Jonny. "Constable, the town'll be in your hands. Sam's on alert should you need him."

"I'll take care of the town, Sergeant, don't worry," Jonny reassured him. Adam gave him a grateful nod.

"Are you going to go with him, Ma?" Lizzie queried.

"I don't think so." Katie shrugged. "You all need me here."

"I can look after the younger girls, Ma." Callie eyed her sisters and they nodded their agreement.

"I don't need looking after!" Lizzie scowled and thrust her arms over her chest.

Callie grimaced at her. "Well, at least I can cook for you all."

Adam slipped his arm around Katie's waist. "That's right, Katie, Callie and Anna are more than able to take care of things here. Rose and Marcus are right next door. Why don't you come with me? I sure could use your support."

"I'm not so sure. We've never left them alone for this long before."

"Ma, you should go." Rose squeezed her arm. "We can check in on them."

"I'll check in on them!" Marcus eyed her. "You'll rest up and look after that baby, Mrs Murray."

"Are you sure you can do it?" Katie looked at all the faces.

"Of course, Ma," Callie insisted. "I'll get some time off work, stay home and look after the place. It'll be good practice for...." She blushed and looked shyly at Jonny. "...my future."

Jonny grinned and winked at her, then turned to look at Adam. "I'll check on them too, Sergeant."

"Of that, I am quite certain." Adam raised his brows.

"Would you like us to stay with you?" Rose offered. Marcus frowned.

"No, I think I'll be okay." Callie smiled at her sister.

"We'll be just across the acreage." Rose gripped her sister's hand.

"That settles it, Wife. You're coming with me. It'll be like a second honeymoon."

"We never even had a first." Katie laughed.

"I know we're going for a tragic reason, but we'll try to make it a holiday too, Darling. You're long overdue for a break."

Twenty-Two
Farewell Commander

"Don't worry about home, Katie. They'll be just fine." Adam leaned back against the plush velvet seat of the train.

"I know. Callie is more than capable of running the household and looking after her sisters."

"Then what is it?"

Katie shrugged and gave him a sideways smile. "I just miss them. I've never been away from them for so long before."

"It's only been half a day so far."

"I know, but I miss them."

"Truth be told, so do I." Adam grinned. "But it's wonderful to have my wife here with me. It's quite a privilege, you know."

"Oh, Adam."

"It's true. Mounties don't normally get to bring our wives when we travel."

"This is different. It's your father's funeral."

"I know, but we must also take some time to see the city before we head west to HQ. You've never been to Calgary, have you?"

"I passed through on the way to your funeral, but I haven't seen the city."

"Well, I'm glad I get to change that. Calgary is a beautiful city. There's lots to show off."

"Sounds wonderful, Adam." Katie snuggled into his arms.

* * * *

"You're not the boss of me, Callie Morgan." Lizzie stamped her feet. An exasperated Callie tried to get the stubborn fourteen-year-old to go to bed.

"I am while Ma and Pa are away. Nine o'clock has always been bedtime. You don't hear Anna, Sarah, or Hope complaining."

"You aren't bossing them around." Lizzie pouted and stamped her feet again.

"Lizzie, do as your sister says," Jonny added, with just a tinge of authority in his voice.

"Hmmmphf, it's not fair. Everyone is picking on me." Lizzie scowled and stormed off to her room.

Callie and Jonny looked at each other and laughed. "Stubborn girl." Jonny shook his head.

"Thanks for sticking up for me, Jon." She kissed him on the cheek.

"Always! That's one thing I can promise you, Callie. I'll always stick up for you, my darling. And might I say, you're doing a wonderful job."

"Thanks, Jonny. Ma and Pa have only been gone two days. I'm not sure I'll cope."

"All I know for sure is you're going to be a great mother someday." He winked and brushed her cheek. Callie blushed. "Though I sure hope our children won't be as stubborn as Lizzie."

"Our children?" Her cheeks grew a bright scarlet.

"You know I plan to marry you, Callie Morgan. We'll have our own family someday."

Callie gulped and turned away to carry their coffee cups to the sink. Jonny frowned and followed her. "Callie?"

She hung her head and sighed. "Hey, Callie, look at me. Don't you want to marry me someday?"

"Of course I do. I just get so scared when I think about it."

"Scared?" Jonny flicked the towel from the hook to dry the cups she was washing.

Callie stared intently at the sink, trying to distract her mind. "Yes." She nodded and sighed. "I don't know how to be a wife and a mother. I can't even get my sisters to listen to me."

Jonny reached over, took the dishcloth from her and placed it on the countertop. He put his arms around her waist, and she lifted hers around his neck. He smiled kindly at her and kissed her forehead. "Callie, you are getting ahead of yourself, my darling. All I know for sure is that you'll be a wonderful wife and an excellent mother one day. I'm not worried even a bit about that. But if you must know. I'm scared too. The important thing is we work it out together."

She smiled and nodded. "I need to finish these dishes."

"Yes, Ma'am." He released her, and they completed the task.

"I should probably turn in now, Callie."

"Okay, thanks for checking in on us."

"It's my pleasure." He grinned. "It is my job, you know."

"Is it now, Constable? Is that the only reason?" She pretended to pout.

He gave her a slow wide grin. "Well, there is a beautiful young woman here that might just encourage me to visit more frequently."

"Really?"

"Yes." He kissed her on the cheek. "Now, goodnight, Miss Morgan. I'll see you tomorrow."

"See you, Jonny.

*   *   *   *

Katie sipped at her coffee and hoisted her stockinged feet up onto the couch in their hotel room. "I wonder what the children are doing right now."

"They'll have just had supper, and Callie will have two of her sisters cleaning up, no doubt." Adam sipped his own coffee.

"Do you think that Mountie is there with them?"

"Oh, I know he is. I have a feeling he'll be there most evenings."

"Checking on our daughters."

"And one in particular." Adam grimaced.

"Do you think that he'll be asking for her hand soon?"

Adam sighed. "It wouldn't surprise me. I sure hope he'll agree to living up on The Rise. I so need my girls close by."

271

"You said you'd be supportive if they left town, Adam."

He grimaced. "And I will. I'd just prefer it is all."

"Has your father's body arrived yet?"

"They expect it to arrive at HQ tomorrow."

"And your sister?"

"She's coming tomorrow also. Her husband and children are staying behind, though."

"That's a shame, but at least she's coming."

"Of course, we have to farewell The Commander. I imagine he'll get quite a send-off."

"What day is the ceremony?"

"HQ said it would be Wednesday."

"In two days." Katie sighed. "Then we can go home."

"You anxious to get back, Wife?"

"Oh, Adam, I love being here on holiday with you. We've never got to have a holiday together all on our own. But we've been here four days now, and I miss them all."

Adam chuckled and squeezed her hand. "I know, I do too. I hope Callie is managing. Lizzie can be awfully stubborn."

"It'll be good practice for her. She'll be a wife and mother soon enough."

"I don't doubt that, Katie. She'll be wonderful. You've trained all our girls well."

* * * *

Adam stood by his father's grave with his arm around his wife and his sister. He sniffed back his tears, and the two women cried openly.

The Assistant Commissioner approached Adam and the two saluted each other. The older man handed Adam The Commander's Stetson and medals. He nodded to Anna and then turned abruptly and walked away. The funeral was over and the crowd dispersed, leaving Adam, Katie and Anna standing before the mound of dirt.

Adam passed the medals and hat to Katie and embraced his sister.

"I'm glad you're here, Adam." Anna clung to her brother.

"Me too, Anna."

"You're the last remaining Morgan." She stepped back from him.

Adam closed his eyes and ran his fingers through his hair. "Don't put that pressure on me, Sister."

"A shame you only had girls. The Morgan name stops with you."

Adam sighed and walked away from her, between the Mountie graves, careful not to stand where any of his fallen colleagues lay.

"Adam, don't walk away."

He spun on his heels to look at Anna. "Don't say that about my girls."

"What did I say?"

"I'm proud of them. I'm glad all my children are girls. I wouldn't change it for the world."

"I didn't mean anything by it. I just think it's a shame there are no more Morgans, that's all."

Katie followed silently behind them.

"Anna, the Morgan name means nothing. I couldn't care less about it carrying on!"

"Are you ashamed to be a Morgan?"

Adam sighed and ran his fingers through his hair. "Of course not," he said a bit more gently.

"Then why are you getting so worked up about it?"

"Alright, if you must know, I am sad the name finishes with me, but I can't do anything about that, and I'm not sorry all my children are girls."

Anna gripped her brother's arm. "I'm not either. They're wonderful girls. I'm sorry I upset you. It was just an observation. I know you feel that you have big shoes to fill."

"I'm not The Commander. I don't crave the power and recognition like he did."

"I know, but you do know he was proud of you."

"Sure found a funny way to show it."

"He did in his later years."

"Occasionally, but how do I know that's how he really felt."

"Excuse me, Sergeant Morgan," came a voice from behind him.

Adam turned and saluted the man. "Uncle, what can I do for you?"

Sergeant Hudson looked at him and his eyes offered sympathy. "Nothing at all, Adam. I have something for you. Your father wrote it some time ago and asked me to get it to you should anything happen to him."

"Thank you, Uncle, give Aunt Carla and the children my love."

"I will." Adam saluted him again and the older man nodded, turned abruptly and walked away.

"I have to go, Adam. My family is expecting me back." Anna gripped his arm.

"I wish we had more time." Adam gulped and wrapped his sister in his arms.

"Me too."

He kissed her hair and released her. "It's good to see you, even under these circumstances. Do you need a ride to the train station?"

"No, thank you. I have a carriage coming for me."

"Okay, Sister. I do love you, you know."

"I love you too, Adam. It's just the two of us now." She kissed her brother's cheek, embraced Katie, and walked away.

Adam watched her go and sighed. Katie stood next to him, and he put his arm around her. "I miss her, Katie."

"I know you do."

"I miss our girls more though. Maybe it's time to go home."

"Yes, but first come with me."

She led Adam by the arm towards the other side of the Mountie cemetery. Katie walked down the rows to a certain headstone and stopped.

"What is it?" Adam looked around and frowned.

"This is where we stood."

"Where who stood?"

"Jo and me, when we thought you and Samuel were dead."

"Oh, Katie." Adam put his arm around her.

"Your father stood with me. And he cried for you, Adam. Real tears. He hurt so much for you, and he told me how much he loved you."

"Funny, he never really told me." Adam creased his lips up into a sideways smile.

"He was a proud man, but I know how much he loved you and how proud he was of our girls."

"I know." He looked up at the graveyard and hugged Katie tightly. "I'm sorry you had to go through all this, thinking we were dead." The shadow of that time would always haunt Adam.

"It's okay, you're not dead, and that's all that matters. You get to watch your girls grow up and have their own families."

"Oh, I miss them so, Wife. Come on, let's go home."

"You need to read your letter."

"Not here."

"Okay."

*   *   *   *

Adam sighed and leaned his head against the wooden wall of the train. "Two days, Katie. In two days, I get to hold my girls again."

"I know, but right now, you can hold me?"

"With pleasure, Mrs Morgan." He put his arms around her and kissed her cheek.

"Ah, my favourite place." She snuggled back against him.

"Mine too. I'm sorry we didn't get much time together. I promised you a second honeymoon."

"Don't be sorry, Adam. Wherever we are together is a honeymoon for me. I love you so much."

"I love you too, Darling. Thank you for being here for me. I needed your strength to make it through." He hugged her tightly and kissed her. Leaning back against the leather seat, he sighed contentedly and closed his eyes.

"Adam."

"Yeah."

"Are you going to read it?"

"Mmmhmmm."

"When?"

Adam sighed. "I don't know."

"What's the hesitation?" Katie leaned forward and turned to look at him.

"I don't know." He shrugged. "I guess I feel if I read it, I'll be putting him to rest."

"I think I understand. As long as you don't read it, it's like he's still alive, and there's still something to anticipate."

"It sounds foolish, I know."

"No, it's not foolish. It's the last piece of your father."

"You always understand me, Katie. And you give me strength. Even the strength to face whatever this holds." He pulled the letter from his coat pocket.

"Are you sure? I thought you might prefer to read it alone?"

"Yes, I couldn't bear to read it without you. In fact, I was hoping you would read it to me?" He raised his brows in question and held the envelope out to her.

"Certainly." Katie tore open the envelope and pulled out the letter. She leaned back against her husband, and he leaned his head against hers. She began to read.

Adam, my son.

> *If you're reading this, I'm no longer with you. I only hope I died in service to King and country, and you can be proud of me. I know I didn't spend much time telling you my thoughts when I was alive, and I hope this letter changes that.*

> *I want you to know I'm proud of you, Son. You're a fine, brave Mountie, and I've been impressed with your career, your promotions and even your choice not to take a promotion after your time in prison. You've earned many accolades for your service, and Canada is lucky to have you serving her.*

> *But Adam, I'm not just proud of you as a Mountie. I'm proud of you as a man, as a son, as a husband, and as a father."*

Adam sniffed back his tears and Katie briefly gripped his hand and then continued.

"You've become an excellent man. You faced the consequences of your actions early in your career with maturity. You came through a harrowing ideal with strength and honour. I know a lot of that had to do with your Katie. She's a fine woman, and together you are a remarkable team.

I told you it was foolish to marry and that she'd never cut it as a Mountie's wife, but she's sure proved me wrong over and over again. The way she fought for the truth after facing your death with strength and tenacity was something that most men I know would not have been able to face.

Together, you're a force to be reckoned with, and I'm so proud of you both. And then there are those beautiful girls you have. Nothing in this world makes me prouder than those six incredible young women. Katie apologised to me at your funeral for not giving you any sons, to carry on the Morgan name, but I'm not at all worried about that. Just raise those girls to be strong, tenacious women like their mother, and I'll rest peacefully in that knowledge.

Adam, I'm proud of those girls, especially your Rosie. She's the delight of my life. Be the father and grandfather that I never was. I'm sorry, Son. I know I was tough on you, and I know that I was woefully inept as a father. The truth is I was scared of my emotions. I didn't know how to love you the way I should. Despite me and my shortcomings as a father, you're a wonderful, loving, and supportive husband and father and everything I wish that I was.

Promise me you'll look after your sister. I've left all that I have to your girls, as Anna and her husband are independently wealthy and have a lot more than I do. I know that you wouldn't want the money, and it isn't much, but I want my granddaughters to have a piece of the Morgan legacy for what it's worth. Kiss them all and embrace them on my behalf.

Please don't mourn for me. I lived a good life, and I go with no regrets. I look forward to seeing your mother again, and I promise we shall watch over you all, and those precious girls.

I was always proud of you, Adam. Other than your ma, you were the greatest joy of my life. I know you think I loved your younger brother more than you, but that wasn't true, not at all. You were the *most like me, and that frightened me. But now I know you weren't like me at all. You're a far better man than I ever was. You aren't afraid of your feelings, and I've always admired you for that.*

I love you, Son, more than I can ever put into words. That won't change, even after I'm gone.

Your father,

Teddy 'The Commander' Morgan.

Adam clung to Katie tightly, and sniffed back a tear. "Thanks Katie, I'm glad you're here with me to share this."

"You're welcome. Those are pretty special words."

Adam nodded and swallowed the lump in his throat. "I never knew he felt that way. He never said much to me. Only told me he was proud of me a few times."

"But now you know he always was. He was just so afraid of his feelings. He's right, Adam. You are a wonderful man."

"And his words about you are all true."

"Oh, Adam." They shared a heartfelt kiss.

"I love you, Mrs Morgan."

"I know. I love you too."

"I can't wait to get home to my army of girls." He squeezed her.

"Me either."

Twenty-Three
Jonny and Callie

Adam looked up from his typewriter as Jonny walked in. "Hi, Serge." He hung his Stetson on the hook.

"Constable." Adam wound the sheet out of his typewriter and placed it on the stack of papers. "How'd you get on at the Williams estate?"

"Fine. Mrs Williams is beside herself. She's had a hard time of it with her husband dying, and now someone has stolen her gold necklace. It was a family heirloom."

"Any leads?"

"Some. I'm working on it."

"Good. You'll get there. Just work the process."

"I will. Any coffee on?"

"Yup, just made a new pot."

"Can I get you a cup, Serge?"

"Yes, and there's a parcel of Callie's raisin cookies too."

The young Constable grinned. "My favourite."

Adam smirked. "I expect that was why she brought them by."

Jonny brought the coffee over, filled Adam's cup, and offered the older man a cookie. Adam nodded his thanks. "Jon, take a seat. There's something I want to talk to you about."

"Sure, Serge. Is everything okay?" Jonny slipped into the chair opposite Adam.

"You tell me?" Adam folded his arms across his chest and leaned back.

Jonny squinted at him and scratched his chin. "I don't understand. Have I done something wrong?"

"Not wrong, exactly. I just don't understand what you're waiting for?"

"Waiting for, Sir?"

"Yes, what's the delay? Have you changed your mind?"

Jonny screwed up his face and shook his head. "Sergeant, I'm really not following you."

Adam took a long drink from his cup, placed it down, and leaned his elbows on the desk. "I thought you loved my daughter?"

Jonny's face lit up and his eyes sparkled. "I do, Sir, with everything I am."

Adam raised his brows. "Then what are you waiting for?"

"What do you mean?"

"I've been expecting you to ask for her hand for some time now. I'm just curious as to why the delay?"

Jonny turned a deep shade of red and stammered for a moment. Finally, he took a deep breath. "I've been meaning to for some time, Sir, but I guess... well... I was worried you... would be concerned that she was too young."

"She'll be eighteen in January. Would you marry before then?"

"I don't imagine so, Sir."

"Then she isn't too young."

Jonny grinned.

Adam took another mouthful of hot coffee, sat back in his chair and ran his fingers through his hair. He folded his arms across his chest again. "I'm listening now, Jon." He raised his eyebrows.

Jonny took a deep breath and grinned. "Well, Sir. I really do want to marry your daughter. She's everything I want in a wife. I've watched her the last week, while you were away, and she's incredible, Serge!" His eyes shone, and he wore a wide grin. "I want to spend the rest of my life trying to make her happy. There's nothing I'm more sure of in this world."

Adam nodded and waited with his eyebrows raised and a wry grin.

Jonny took another deep breath. "Sergeant Morgan, Sir. I'd like your permission to marry Callie." He was unsuccessful at remaining stoic; a broad grin crossed his face.

Adam paused, took a deep breath, and stood. He came around to the front of the desk, and motioned for Jonny to stand up. He embraced the younger Mountie and then released him, and with his hand still on Jonny's shoulder, he grinned. "Of course, Jon. I'll be delighted to welcome you as a son."

"Thank you, Sergeant Morgan. This means the world to me. I was going to come to you, this week, I really was. I have the ring ready and waiting. I was just plucking up the courage."

"I'm sure you were, Constable. I'm really not as scary as you think." Adam chuckled.

"Not scary, Sir, just very protective of your girls."

"A man with six daughters has to be. I'd not let just any man within a mile of my girls. You know that." Adam's face reflected his seriousness.

"I take that as the highest compliment, Sergeant."

"You should, Jon." Adam knitted his brows and held the younger man in a steely gaze giving Jonny no doubt that he meant his words. "Letting my daughter marry a Mountie is not something I really desired to do, but I can't deny the love between you two. I can't come between a love so strong and fierce as yours."

"Thank you, we have your example, Sergeant. Your marriage is an inspiration to us both. You have my word that I'll love and cherish Callie until my dying day."

"I know you will, Son. I'd expect no less. If I didn't think you were worthy of my daughter, the answer would be no."

Jonny nodded in understanding.

Adam returned to his seat and refilled both coffee cups. He sat down and took a deep breath. They drank their coffee in silence for a time. "What plans have you made for a home?"

"Well... If you mean how will I provide for Callie? I don't have all the details worked out... I'd really like her to be a part of the decision-making. But I have some money saved, enough for a very small house."

"Do you have any places in mind?"

"I've seen a few places for sale in town, but I really was hoping for a place closer to your home. Callie would be lonesome for her ma and sisters, so I'd love her to live as close by as possible."

"How about right next door?" Adam grinned.

"What're you saying, Sergeant?" Jonny slurped at his coffee.

"I'm not sure if you're aware of this, but I have promised one acre of my land to each of my daughters, should they want it. Nothing would please me more than to have all my girls and their families living around me. It was why I bought the large piece of land in the first place. It's up to the two of you, but give it some thought."

"I don't know what to say, Sir."

"I would expect you to pay something towards it, Constable. A man needs to pay his own way for his family."

"Of course! I would insist on doing so."

"Well, it's up to you both. You could choose one square acre anywhere on the land you like."

"That's quite an offer."

"What do you think? Brave enough to live next door to your in-laws, Son?" Adam smirked.

Jonny chuckled. "It's up to Callie, Sir. First, I have to get her to say yes to me."

"She will. That girl is fiercely in love with you, Jon. I can see it in her eyes."

Jonny grinned. "Well then, Serge, if you don't mind, I don't want to waste another minute. I think I'll go and see if she's ready to leave and escort her home."

Adam sighed. "Good idea. I expect you to bring your fiancée to supper tonight."

"I will, and thank you."

"You're most welcome." Adam gripped his shoulder again.

Jonny entered his little room in the back of the office, opened the top drawer, and took out the ring. He walked back out into the office and looked in the mirror on the wall, and tried to tidy his wayward hair, but it wouldn't budge. "Do I look okay, Serge?"

"It really doesn't matter to me how you look, Jonny. I wouldn't marry you." Adam chuckled and wound another page into his typewriter.

Jonny grinned, "Not even if I gave you this?" He showed Adam the ring."

"Tempting!" Adam grinned. "But still no!"

"Oh well, just as well for you, I prefer Callie anyway, Sir." The young man snickered.

"Me too, Jon."

Jonny grinned. "I'm relieved. I doubt this dainty ring would suit you anyway, Sir."

Adam flashed him a sideways smile. "I'll see the two of you at supper time."

Jonny grinned, reached for his hat, and ran out the door. Adam chuckled, stood up and stretched his back. There was no way he was going to get any more work done today, so he tidied his desk, reached for his hat and jacket, and headed out the door. He strolled to the livery in the bright sunshine and shook his head when he saw Jonny and Callie gallop off in the direction of the waterfall. He sighed and hastened his steps to the livery.

"Eb." He stroked the horse's sleek neck. "That was my beautiful daughter, and she's getting engaged. I'm thrilled for them. I really am. I want them to be married, they're perfect for each other, and Callie's happiness is all I want. But it hurts! I sure am gonna miss my precious girl."

The horse whinnied slightly as if in support of the Mountie. He patted her neck and nudged her into a canter. "Let's go home, Ebony."

* * * *

"What's going on, Jonny?" Callie squinted at him as he helped her from the horse.

"I'm just fine. Why do you ask?" He swallowed and tethered both horses to the tree.

"You seem very nervous. The spontaneous ride to the waterfall. It's just unusual, is all."

"Well, there's a reason I asked you to come up here with me, Callie." He held her hands and looked deeply into her eyes.

"What is it?"

"You know I love you."

"Yes, of course. I love you too, Jonny."

He grinned. "It always thrills me when I hear you say that."

Callie blushed.

Jonny brushed her cheek and became very serious. "I mean it, Callie. I love you. I love you with all my heart, and I will go on loving you until my final breath."

"Oh, Jonny."

He kissed her gently. "You're my whole world. You're everything I want in a woman. You make me so happy, and I plan to spend the rest of my life making you happy, if you'll let me."

Callie blushed deeply. "What are you saying?"

He grinned and knelt down, reached into his jacket, and pulled out the box. Callie gasped and her eyes flooded with tears.

"I'm saying that I want you to be my wife. Will you marry me?"

Callie grinned and nodded. "Of course I will, Jonny. Of course, yes."

He stood up, and kissed her deeply. They both eagerly prolonged the kiss. He held her with her cheek against his red serge jacket, his strong arms wrapped around her, and she felt utterly content.

Finally, he released her and slid the emerald ring on her finger. "Oh, Jonny, it's so beautiful."

"Not as beautiful as you, Callie Morgan." He leaned in and kissed her again.

"Oh, Jonny." She stood encircled in her fiancé's arms, watching the cascading water in front of them.

"Callie, are you really sure?"

She stood back and looked at him. "Sure about what?"

"Marrying me?"

"Of course. I've known for a long time I want to marry you. How can you ask me that?"

"But I'm not an ordinary man, Callie. I'm a Mountie."

"I know that, Silly." She frowned

"A Mountie's life isn't easy, Callie, and it can be hard on a woman...."

"Let me stop you right there, Constable Scott." Her voice was sterner than she meant, and she fixed determined eyes on his. "Don't you think I'm fully aware of how hard it can be? I've watched my ma for my whole life. I remember when we all thought Pa had died. I was six years old, but I remember it like it was yesterday. Ma ached for Pa, wept for him, and stood by his graveside. I've seen her long for him when he's been away. I've seen the fear and uncertainty she's faced, and we've talked extensively about what it's like to marry a Mountie.

"She told me she doesn't regret any of it, not for a moment. That loving Pa is worth all the hard times. You know he left on assignment five days after their wedding, and she thought he'd died even back then. She told me that if five days was all she ever got, it would still have been worth it, and she still would've married him all over again, even knowing the outcome.

"She chooses to make the most of the time she has rather than dwelling on what she doesn't have. The love my parents have is so strong, pure, and unbreakable, and that's what I want, Jonny. I'm under no illusions that it'll be easy, and I know sometimes you'll be in danger. I won't be thrilled about that, but I love you, and I'll always love you." She smiled and walked to him, placing her hand on his cheek. "So Jonathan James Scott, Yes, I'm sure. I've never been so sure of anything in my life."

Jonny grinned, reached for her hand, and brought it to his lips. "I'm so glad, Callie, because I don't think I'll survive without you by my side."

She reached for his hand. "And it's where I'll always be, right by your side, forever. You have my word."

"And you have my heart."

"You have mine too."

He grinned and kissed the hand that wore his ring. "You make me so happy. I can't believe how very blessed I am."

"Me too, Jonny."

"Now I must take my fiancée home to her house for supper."

"Oh no, what's my pa going to say? He won't be thrilled at one of his girls marrying a Mountie." Callie grimaced.

"He'll be fine. He already knows."

"He does. You asked him?"

Jonny grinned. "In a manner of speaking, he asked me?"

"He asked you? What, to marry him?"

Jonny laughed out loud. "No, of course not. He just asked me why I'd put off asking to marry you for so long. I guess he knew I was planning to."

"He did. Maybe he's trying to get rid of me?" She smirked.

Jonny put his arm around her. "Of course not, he just knows we're meant for each other, and he doesn't want to get in the way of that."

"Sounds like you two planned it all out."

"Of course not. This was my plan, he just gave me a little nudge."

"Well, I'm glad." Callie squeezed his hand as they walked towards their horses.

"You know what else he told me?"

"No."

"That we could live up on The Rise if we want to like Rose and Marcus. We can choose a square acre anywhere we like."

"I know. He's as much as told us all we can do that. I think he'd like us all close by, but there's no pressure, and I know that."

"Well, what do you want to do?"

"I just want to be where ever you are. We can live in the Mountie office if you like?"

Jonny screwed up his nose; he'd seen the longing look in her eyes. "No way, you deserve so much better than that. I couldn't ask you to live like that."

"Well, what do you have in mind?"

Jonny grinned and squeezed her hand. "I want to live on The Rise with your family."

Callie's face lit up. "Oh, Jon, do you really mean that?"

"Of course, I love it up there, and I couldn't take you away from the family you love."

"What if you get a new posting?"

"We'll deal with that when the time comes. In the meantime, we'll live up on The Rise with your family, with our family." He blushed.

She threw herself into his arms and kissed him on the cheek. "Oh, Jonny, thank you."

Jon tilted his head and grinned. "Why do I get the feeling you already know the exact spot."

"Because I do, I've been dreaming for some time, Constable."

Jonny grinned and stroked her cheek. "I can't wait to see it. Your pa will let me pay it off and offered it at a very generous price."

"That's wonderful news." She put her arms up around his neck and kissed him deeply.

He stood with his eyes closed for a moment and shook his head. "Don't let go of me, Callie. I think my knees are going to collapse!" He chuckled and then opened his eyes.

Callie blushed and grinned at him. "Come on, let's go home." Jonny helped her up on Maisy and mounted Major. He clucked to the horses, and they galloped off towards The Rise.

* * * *

Callie and Jonny burst through the door. Adam stood and grinned wryly. "Ma, Pa, we're engaged," she gushed.

"Oh, Callie!" Katie ran to hug them both. "I'm so happy for you, Darling." She kissed Jonny on the cheek and hugged him. "I'm so pleased to welcome you to the family, Jonathan."

"Thanks, Mrs Morgan." He beamed.

Adam stood back and watched the celebrations. He leaned against the wall with a sly smile on his face. After all her sisters had congratulated her, Callie walked shyly over and stood in front of him. He stood with his arms crossed over his chest and a bemused look on his face.

"Pa."

Adam's smile disappeared, and his lips quivered. His eyes filled up with tears. He took a deep breath and lunged to hug his daughter. "Oh, Callie, I'm so proud of you and so happy for you both."

"I love you, Pa."

"Oh, I love you too, Darling." He kissed her on the forehead. Jonny walked over and Adam released Callie. He embraced Jon. "Well done, Son. I'm proud to welcome you to the Morgan family."

"Thanks, Serge." His eyes sparkled. "I promise I'll take care of her."

"You'd better." Adam grinned, but his steely eyes belied his words. "I'm an expert marksman."

"I'm aware, Sir." Jonny nodded. Adam gripped his shoulder to let him know he was mostly joking.

"And, Pa, we want to live on the acreage." Callie grinned.

Adam took a deep breath and smiled. "I'm glad, Darling. Any idea where?"

"Yes, I know the exact spot."

Adam raised his brows. "You do?"

She nodded.

"Care to show me?" Adam looked across at Katie. She nodded to let him know they had time before supper.

"Let's go." Callie led them on a a goose chase, riding around and around, laughing and grinning.

Adam called out to her, "Callie, where is this spot?" He grinned.

She led them to the block near the Murray's home. "Right here. I want my house right here to overlook the valley, and it's only a short distance from Rose and Marcus."

"It's a beautiful spot." Jonny put his arm around her. "Good choice, Darling."

Rose walked out of her house to collect the eggs and waved at them. "Rose." Callie waved her over.

Rose placed down her egg basket and put her head inside to tell Marcus where she was. He came out with her and they walked over. "What's all this?"

"This is where I want to have our home." She grinned at Rose.

Rose screwed up her face. "Your home? What are you saying?"

Jonny walked up then and held Callie's hand. "We're engaged."

"Oh, Callie!" Rose embraced her sister. Marcus grinned and reached out to shake Jonny's hand.

"Well done, Constable. Welcome to the family." Marcus gripped the Mountie's shoulder.

"Thank you, Marcus. I'm proud to be joining the ranks."

Rose reached up to embrace Jonny. "Oh, Jon. I'm so happy for you both. It'll be wonderful having you so close by." Stepping back, she gripped Callie's arm. "This is a good spot, Callie. It would've been my second choice."

"I love it here. You can see the whole valley down below and the mountains in the distance." Callie beamed.

"And you're close enough for us to walk over to each other." Rose squeezed her hand. "It'll be so lovely to raise our families here together." She placed her hand on her growing stomach.

Callie blushed, and so did Jonny.

"First things first." Adam gave them a mock scowl. He walked up behind them with a grin.

"How are you coping, Pa?" Rose gave her father a kind smile.

Adam sighed. "It's never easy, Rosie." He slipped his arm around her waist and kissed the side of her head. "But watching you all grow up and have families of your own is a privilege, even though it sure is hard to let you go. But I see how happy you and Marcus are. How can I deprive you of all of that."

They all nodded, and Marcus patted Jonny on the back. "Let me know when you have your house planned out. I'd be happy to help build it."

"I'll help too," offered Adam.

"Thank you both. I'm not nearly as talented with wood as you are." Jon gave them a wry smile.

"It's a pleasure," Adam and Marcus both said at the same time.

Callie turned to Marcus. "How long do you think it would take to build the house?"

"About three to four months, depending on the weather, maybe a few months more if we get too busy. Why? Are you anxious to get married?" Marcus raised his brows.

"Well, no, I just need time to make all the things we'll need." Callie blushed.

"You'll have our house looking like a home in no time, Callie," Jonny squeezed her hand.

She smiled at him.

"When do you think you'll get married?" Rose rubbed her abdomen again, leaning back against Marcus. Her back and ankles ached.

"We don't know yet, but I was thinking maybe March or April?"

"Sounds great. I'm confident we can have it done by then," Marcus assured her.

"Wonderful. I can't wait to be married." Callie beamed and Rose hugged her sister again.

Twenty-Four
Two Babies and a Ball

"Forty-two. I'm forty-two! Face it Sergeant, you're married to an old woman." Katie frowned.

"Pshaw, Katie. You're still young and beautiful." He reached for her and kissed her deeply.

"Thank you, Husband. Still, I feel old. Thank you for a wonderful birthday celebration." She put her arms around his neck and kissed him deeply.

"You're most welcome, Katie. You deserve so much more than that."

"Oh, Adam. You're the most thoughtful man."

"November is a tough month for me. Your birthday and Hope's then, Lizzie's."

"I can't believe she's going to be fifteen in a week and a half."

Adam gave her a sideways smile and shook his head nostalgically. "I know, our girls are really growing up."

"Yes, I'm still coming to terms with Anna turning sixteen a few months ago." They stood staring into the fire together.

"She's so enamoured by that beautiful black horse you bought her."

"Trixie." Adam grinned. "She's a beauty, that's for sure." Katie nodded. Adam tightened his grip on her. "We sure have amazing girls, Wife. Can you believe Callie is getting married, and Rose will be having her baby soon?"

"Yes, poor Rose, she's very overdue."

"Well, first babies are often late."

"Just think, any moment now, we'll be grandparents."

"Daniel too. I can't believe Amy is late too. Do you think they'll have their babies on the same day?"

Katie laughed. "They got engaged on the same day and married on the same day, so I don't see why not. It sounds like something God would do."

Adam nodded and grinned. "Yes, it does." Adam chuckled and pulled his wife into his arms and pulled the covers up over them both.

"What on earth?" Adam sat bolt upright. Someone was pounding on the door. Before Katie could even respond Adam was out of bed and pulling on his trousers. He tucked his nightshirt into them and flicked his jacket from the hook, thrust it over his shoulders as he ran and opened the door.

"Hi Vincent, is it Rose?"

"Yes." The young man smiled. "Rose is in the clinic. Baby's coming. Amy's there too with Andy."

"Thanks, Vinnie, we'll be right there." Adam grinned.

* * * *

Adam paced nervously in the small waiting room. Every seat was taken and Herbert, Mr Louis and Daniel stood leaning against the wall.

"Wouldn't it be wonderful if our first grandchild shared my birthday?" Katie grinned. Louisa gripped her hand.

Dan grinned. "The two cousins could share the same birthday."

"I know it's wonderful, Danny." Katie stood to hug her brother.

A half hour before midnight Marcus walked into the room with a bundle in his arms. His eyes brimmed with tears, but he wore a wide smile. Adam clung to Katie and held his breath.

Marcus walked over to them standing next to his parents, and they all looked down at the little pink face. "I'd like you to meet your granddaughter, Lily Katherine Murray." His voice trembled.

Adam released his breath. "Oh, Rosie." He swiped at a tear and touched the little face. "She's so precious, Marcus."

"She sure is." The proud father sucked back the tears. "Pa, I can't believe you went through this six times. I already feel like I'm going to burst my buttons."

Herbert nodded and patted his son on the back. "Can I hold her, Son?"

"Sure." Marcus grinned and passed the little girl to his father.

The farmer nodded and a wide smile crossed his face. "Hi, Miss Lily, you're a beauty. She looks like her ma, Marc."

"She sure does." Marcus' face hurt from the wide smile.

His mother claimed the little girl. "My granddaughter." She smiled, and kissed the wee face.

Katie put her arm around Connie. "Isn't she precious, our shared grandchild?"

"Yes." Connie kissed the little face. "I'm not sure I want to share though. She's my only baby girl."

Katie took the wee girl, kissed her, then handed her to the Mountie.

Adam sniffed back his tears and kissed the little head. "Hello, Miss Lily. I'm your Grandpa. I love you so much, Darling Girl." Finally and reluctantly, he gave her back to Marcus, who introduced the little girl to the others in the waiting room.

Adam and Katie tiptoed in to see Rose. "Oh, my Rosie, you're so amazing, Darling." Adam kissed his daughter's hair.

"Thanks, Pa. I'm so happy."

"You should be, Darling." Katie squeezed her arm. "You have a beautiful little girl."

"Did you see her?"

"Yes." Adam's voice caught in his throat. "She's perfect. She looks just like you did when you were born."

Marcus walked in carrying his newborn daughter. "This little girl needs to eat."

"We'll leave you to it, Darling." Katie kissed Rose.

Rose called to their retreating figures. "Hey, Pa, has Amy had her baby yet?"

Adam turned back at the doorway and shrugged. "Not as far as I know."

"All in good time." Marcus grinned down at the little girl.

"Happy Birthday, Ma." Rose smiled.

"Lily and I share a birthday. It's very special."

"Yes, it is." Marcus kissed the baby and handed her to Rose, as Adam and Katie made their way back to the waiting room.

Nearly half an hour later, a beaming Andy walked out into the waiting room carrying his own baby. Again they stood to attention, and it was Daniel and Louisa's turn to hold each other in anticipation. "She was incredible, Ma. Amy, she did so well." His eyes sparkled.

"Yes, she did. And who is this little one?" Louisa patted her son's back.

"Sorry." He grinned and fixed his eyes on his father. "This is your grandson Jesse Daniel Maxwell Coleman."

"Awwww, Son." Daniel sniffed away a tear. "He's a beauty, and I'm honoured you gave him my name."

Andy passed the boy to his mother, and Daniel embraced his son.

"Of course, Pa. I'm proud to be your son and I hope my son grows up to be like you."

Daniel sniffed back a tear and squeezed his son tightly. "I'm proud of you both, Andy. You're going to be a wonderful father."

Andy enjoyed his father's embrace. "Thanks, Pa, I've had a good example."

"I love you, Son." Daniel stood back from him. It had never made a scrap of difference to him that Andy wasn't his flesh and blood. He was the child of his heart and that's all that mattered.

"Andy, what time was he born?" Katie asked.

Andy paused before leaving the room. "Five minutes to midnight." He smiled.

"They do share a birthday!" She gasped.

"Rose has had her baby too?" Andy grinned.

"Yes, a little girl." Adam's face lit up in delight.

"Awww, Amy'll be thrilled." Andy took his son and headed back to his wife.

Daniel shook his head and gripped Adam's shoulder. "Can you believe we're grandparents? I've never felt anything so exhilarating in my life. Only my wedding day and the birth of my own children matches this."

"They're quite something." Adam returned the gesture. "I'm rather in love with that little girl." He grinned.

"They sure are," Mrs Murray added. "I can't believe I finally get a little girl. I can't wait to make little dresses for her."

"She'll be the most loved baby in Douglas Falls," gushed Katie.

"I'm not sure, Sister. I think my little grandson might give you a run for your money." Daniel beamed in pride.

"Now, now, you lot." Owen walked into the room. "There's plenty of love to go round. No need to brag. They're both perfect, beautiful babies."

*　*　*　*

Katie looked up from her baking as the door opened. Adam walked over and embraced his wife. He kissed her and stood back with a wide grin on his face. Katie squinted at him. "What are you smirking about, Sergeant?"

"I have a surprise for you, Wife." He kissed her again.

"Oh?"

He pulled two small green slips of paper out of his pocket and handed them to her. "Two tickets to the Mountie Christmas Ball. I promised to take you all those years ago remember, last time it was in Edmonton, and then we couldn't go?"

"I remember. I was expecting Lizzie and feeling very unwell. I was really looking forward to it too."

"Well, it's in Edmonton again this year, and I want to make it up to you."

"Really Adam? It sounds wonderful."

"It will be, and I'll be escorting the most beautiful woman in the world."

"Oh, Adam." He still managed to make her blush even after all these years. "That was a long time ago. I'm an old woman now."

"No, you aren't, Katie. You're older, but you're still the most beautiful woman I've ever met."

"Thank you, Adam, but I'm not a stitch on our lovely girls." She nodded to Callie, cooking with her sister Anna. Both had rosy red cheeks from the heat.

"They certainly are beautiful, Katie, all six of them, but you're the most beautiful. They get their beauty from you." He grinned at her, cupped her cheek in his hand and looked at her intensely. He leaned in and kissed her, prolonging it for a time. None of the girls batted an eyelid. They were used to seeing their parent's affection for each other. It was good, and showed how a loving Christian marriage should be. It's what each of them aspired to be like when they were married.

Katie stepped back from Adam. "Are you going, Callie?"

Callie put down her dishcloth, walked out and shrugged. "I'm not sure, Ma. Jonny hasn't mentioned it."

Adam stepped over and cupped his daughter's chin. He grinned and his eyes twinkled. "Well, two tickets came in the post for him as well. So unless he's planning to take someone else, it would appear you're going, my darling!"

"Eeeee." Callie raised her shoulders to bury her neck and grinned.

"You're so lucky, Callie." Anna sounded wistful as she stirred the gravy. "You're engaged to a handsome Mountie. I wish I could go to a ball, just like Cinderella." She swooned and spun around in the kitchen with the gravy spoon in her hand, dripping gravy across her sister's apron. Callie frowned and reached for the dishcloth to wipe it off.

"I hear that Esther is going with the young Mountie she's courting." Katie walked away from Adam to help her daughters in the kitchen.

"Constable Fraser." Adam folded his arms across his chest.

"So, are Sam and Jo going?"

"Not this year. Sam will patrol both towns while we're away. One of his constables will stay over for the two nights. I told him I'd watch out for Esther on his behalf."

Katie nodded in agreement. "Well, I look forward to going with you, nonetheless, Sergeant."

"Me too." He winked at her and headed down the hallway to wash up.

* * * *

Callie and Katie were adding last-minute touches to their dresses and preparing for their trip. Anna hovered over them, obviously envious about going to the ball. She sighed over their dresses and their new boots. "I can't believe you get to go in three days." She sighed. "I wish I could go to a ball." Anna waltzed around with her arms in the air holding tightly to her imaginary prince.

Adam walked in the door and straight to the kitchen. He embraced and kissed his wife as always. "You're so beautiful, Mrs Morgan, have I told you that lately?"

"Yes, Adam. You're not so bad yourself."

He grinned and kissed her again. "Thank you." He slipped an arm around her waist and lifted the other, leading her in a waltz around the kitchen, unable to drag his eyes from her face. "I can't wait to take you to the ball and show you off to all my colleagues." He flashed her a sideways grin.

"I was thinking you should take Anna."

Adam stopped the waltz and frowned at her. "You don't want to go?" He sounded almost hurt.

Katie put a hand up to his cheek and smiled at him. "Oh, of course I want to go. I just know how much it would mean to Anna."

Adam leaned in and kissed her again. "I want to take my wife, so no arguing."

She lay her head against his chest and he wrapped his arms around her. They swayed in time to the music in their minds. Adam lay his head against hers. "I love having you in my arms, Katie, I love dancing with you."

"Me too."

"I can't wait to show you off at the ball."

"Oh, Adam."

He chuckled and kissed her hair. Their pleasant moment was interrupted by their scholars marching through the door.

* * * *

Katie stood up from up from her sewing and stretched her back. "I'm going to go and fetch the eggs, Callie. I might take a short walk. I need to loosen my tired old muscles."

"I'll come with you, Ma." Hope jumped up from her spot in the corner where she'd been reading. "I've had enough of staying indoors."

"I'd like that, Darling. Get your coat."

"Can we bring Honey?"

"Yeah, we won't go far, and she's been a bit stronger lately. Her paw is healing after that run-in with the racoon. I'm sure she'll be fine."

Hope did up her coat and clicked her tongue at the dog. Honey stood up from her spot by the fire and followed them.

They walked straight to the chicken coop, and Katie stayed outside with Honey while Hope collected the eggs. Hope hurried over to the house and passed the eggs to Callie. Running back out, she made her back to her mother.

"Where shall we walk, Darling?" Katie reached her hand out to Hope.

The little girl took her mother's hand and screwed up her mouth. "Ummm, in the woods, there's no snow in there, and it'll be warmer."

"Great idea, Darling." They chatted happily as they walked towards the stand of trees. Honey plodded along happily behind them, often stopping to dig at the snow and sniff around the trees.

Before too long, the dog began to limp on her sore foot, and Hope started to shiver. "I think it's time we go home." Katie gripped her daughter's hand tightly, and they turned towards their home.

As they walked up the small slope on the way out of the woods, Honey ducked in front of Katie on the trail of some scent. Katie tried to swerve out of the dog's way and stepped on a tree root, wrenching her ankle and falling to the ground.

"Ma." Hope knelt beside her mother, with furrowed brow and anxious eyes. "Ma, are you okay?"

"Yes, Darling, I'm fine. I've just sprained my ankle is all. I think I'll need help getting to the house." Katie winced in pain and clutched her ankle tightly.

"I'll get Callie."

"Thanks, Darling. I'll be fine waiting right here. Honey'll stay with me." She put her arm around the husky, and the dog sat down next to Katie on guard duty.

Hope ran back towards the house. As she came out of the woods, she saw Jonny galloping up to the house. "Jonny." She changed direction. "Jonny, you have to help."

He dismounted, threw Major's rein over the hitching rail, and ran towards Hope. "Hope?" He knelt before the girl and wiped away a tear from her cheek, gripping her shoulders supportively. "What is it?"

"It's Ma. She fell." fell, and his eyes widened. "What do you mean? Where is she?"

"In the woods."

"Show me." He reached for her hand, and she led Jonny into the woods to where Honey was standing guard. Katie had her boot off and her sore foot resting on the tree root that that she had tripped on.

Jonny's heart flew to his chest. "Mrs Morgan, are you okay?"

"Yes, Jon, but I've sprained my ankle quite badly. Look, it's already swelling."

He gently touched her ankle, and she winced in pain. "That's a pretty severe sprain, Mrs Morgan. I best get you back to the house. We need to elevate and strap that ankle."

"I'm afraid I can't walk."

"Not a problem." The Mountie scooped up Katie in his strong arms, careful not to hurt her ankle further. Hope held her discarded boot and followed with Honey walking slowly to accommodate her steps.

Jonny walked carefully and slowly out of the woods.

At that moment, Adam rode up over The Rise and gasped. Fear stole his breath. He hastened his horse, and skidding to a stop he leapt off. He touched her arm and grimaced. "Katie, what's happened?"

"I'm fine, Adam. I just sprained my ankle in the woods."

"Oh, Darling." Adam frowned.

"Honey tripped her, Pa." Hope scowled at the dog and wagged her finger at her.

"Hope, it's not Honey's fault. It's just an accident," Katie reassured her.

Jonny walked up the stairs. Adam opened the door and pulled up the footstool in front of the comfortable armchair, so Jonny could place her down.

"Ma. What happened?" Callie ran to her, and the other girls gathered around.

"I just sprained my ankle. I'm okay."

Adam knelt before her, gently examining the injured foot. "I'm going to need you to remove your stocking so I can see what's going on here."

Jonny stood up and walked to the kitchen to help Callie and Anna continue the supper. Katie looked around, lifted her skirt, unhooked her stocking, and removed it, quickly dropping her skirt again. Hope held it for her while Adam strapped her ankle tightly. "How's that, Darling? Not too tight?" He looked at her with deep worry in his eyes.

"It's fine, thank you, Adam. I'm sorry."

"Hey, what are you sorry about?" He stroked her cheek; his eyes full of compassion and love.

"I won't be able to go to the Mountie Ball. You said it'll be at least a week before I'm up and around again."

"It's fine, Darling, we don't have to go. It's much more important that you're well."

Katie put her hand on Adam's cheek. "Adam, you should still go."

Adam frowned. "What? Don't be silly. I'm not going to go on my own?"

"I wasn't suggesting you go on your own." She smiled and glanced at Anna, who was setting the table.

"I think I should just stay and take care of you."

"Adam, I sprained my ankle. I'm not sick. I'll be fine, and in a few days, I can get up and about again with help. Lizzie, Sarah, and Hope are more than able to help me with the housework. You'll only be gone a few days. Besides, Sam is counting on you to watch over Esther."

"Are you sure, Darling?"

"Yes, of course. It would mean ever so much to Anna."

Adam grinned at her and kissed her cheek. "I'll talk to her." When he was certain Katie was comfortable, he stood and walked up to Anna, who was placing food on the table.

"Anna, Darling?"

"Yes, Pa."

He frowned deliberately and scratched his chin. "I have rather a conundrum I wondered if you could help me with?"

Anna put the last fork down, looked up at him, tilted her to the side, and frowned. "If I can, Pa."

"You see, with your ma's ankle the way it is, she won't be able to go to the Mountie Christmas Ball, and I couldn't possibly go alone. I was wondering if you might know of anyone that would like to come with me?" He smiled and stroked her cheek, raising his eyebrows.

Anna shrieked and threw her arms around his neck. "Really, Pa, I can come with you?"

He wrapped his arms around her and lifted her off the ground. "Nothing would make me happier, Darling. If I can't take your ma, then taking my beautiful daughter will be a real honour." He released her and revelled in her shining eyes and glowing cheeks.

"Oh, Pa, thank you, thank you so much." She stood up on her toes to kiss his cheek and put her arms around his chest.

Adam chuckled and kissed her hair. "You're welcome, Sweetheart. I always love the chance to take my girls out."

Anna ran to her mother. "Are you okay with that, Ma?"

"Yes, of course, Anna, it was my suggestion."

"Oh, Ma. I don't have a dress."

"You could wear mine. We can adjust it to fit you."

"Ma, your beautiful new gown? I couldn't."

"Why not?" asked Callie. "It'll look beautiful on you. You've always looked lovely in lilac."

"Are you sure, Ma?"

"Yes, Darling, of course. Callie and I will modify it for you tomorrow to your tastes. I really want you to wear the lilac silk. You'll be the belle of the ball."

"You will be, Darling." Adam put his arm around Anna and winked at her. "All the other chaps will be jealous of my lovely partner."

* * * *

"Keep your eyes on my daughter, Sergeant." Sam chuckled and kissed her hair.

"Paaaa." Esther rolled her eyes at him. Constable Fraser smirked.

"I will, Sam. You have my word." He patted his friend on the back.

Sam laughed outright. "You might have to keep your eyes on Anna too. There'll be plenty of young eligible Mounties who'll notice a beautiful girl like her." He nodded towards Anna, laughing with Jonny and Callie.

Adam's face fell, and he groaned. "Ahhh, Sam, don't even joke! One daughter marrying a Mountie is enough."

* * * *

Three Mounties waited in the living area of the suite in the hotel in freshly laundered dress uniforms. Each man held a small buttonhole of store-bought flowers for the young lady they would be escorting.

The bedroom door opened, and the three ladies walked out. Three men's faces dropped at the sight of the beautiful women who stood before them. Ben Fraser grinned at Esther in her lemon-coloured dress. "Esther, you look beautiful." He walked to her and presented her with the flowers for her buttonhole.

"Thank you, Ben." She blushed and reached for his arm.

"Callie Morgan. You take my breath away!" Jonny grinned. "I sure would like to marry you!"

"I'm sorry, Constable, I'm already engaged." She laughed as he pinned the flowers on her lapel.

Adam stood back and grinned. "Anna, you are so beautiful, Darling. You look just like your mother, and that dress it's very lovely."

"Thank you, Pa. Thank you so much for bringing me."

"Of course, Darling." He kissed her cheek and presented her with a flower too. "You make me look good."

The hall was a swirl of red serge and women in colourful dresses. Almost as soon as they entered, a voice called from across the room, "Esther!" A Mountie ran headlong towards her. Constable Fraser grinned, and after the man released Esther, he reached his hand out to shake his hand.

"Jamie. Good to see you, Constable."

"You too, Fraser. I heard you're courting my sister." He smirked. "I can't believe Pa agreed to letting a lout like you court Esther." He slapped the man on the back.

Ben grinned back at him. "Careful, Constable, I've got a whole year on you!"

"Still just a Constable though." Jamie grinned.

"So, Constable Ferguson, do you have a young lady?"

"Sadly, no, I haven't been blessed yet. At least here, I can hope to dance with a pretty girl."

Jamie turned to talk to the others who walked up to him then. "Constable Scott, good to see you again."

"Constable Ferguson, you remember Callie."

"Yes, of course. Good evening, Miss Morgan. I hear you two are engaged now. Congratulations."

"Thanks, Jamie. You don't need to be so formal. It's just Callie."

"I know, when I'm in uniform, I tend to be more formal. Just comes with the serge, I guess." He laughed at himself.

"Good evening, James." Adam put his hand out to the young constable and squeezed his shoulder.

"Sergeant Morgan." The young man returned Adam's handshake.

"Your parents send their love. They wanted to come, but your pa is taking charge of both towns. Sent Ben here on his behalf."

Jamie smiled. "And you to chaperone, right?"

Adam nodded. Jamie turned to see the young lady standing next to Adam. He gulped and grinned. "Anna Morgan? That can't possibly be you."

She blushed. "Of course it is, Jamie, you know me."

"I knew little Anna, but this beautiful young woman I don't recognise." Jamie's heart began to beat a little faster, and his eyes sparkled. He felt the skip to his heart and inhaled sharply. He hadn't expected such overwhelming feelings to wash over him for a girl he'd known all his life.

Anna could feel his adoring eyes on her. She blushed and lowered her head. Adam noticed the shine in his eyes and shook his head slightly. *I knew bringing my daughter was a bad idea.* He smirked.

"Would you allow me to get you some punch, Miss Morgan?" Jamie blurted out.

"I'd love that." He nodded to her, grinned and skipped off to oblige without finding out if anyone else wanted anything.

Adam frowned, and Jonny grinned. He knew exactly what Constable Ferguson was feeling. His own heart had skipped a beat the first time he'd met Callie. These Morgan girls were really something special; they had a presence about them that rendered a young man unable to breath effectively. He chuckled at Adam's forlorn expression and guided Callie across to the punch stand.

"So, is it all you expect it to be?" Adam whisked Anna onto the dance floor.

"Oh, it's even better than I thought, Pa."

The waltz finished, and Jamie skipped back with two glasses of punch, and the two young people chatted happily. A wide grin crossed the younger man's face, and it never left for the entire evening.

Adam crossed his arms over his chest and grimaced. He shook his head again and smirked. When Samuel had told him to keep an eye on the young men with their eyes on Anna, he hadn't expected it to be Sam's son he needed to keep his eye on.

Anna finished her drink, and Adam was just about to invite her back out to dance when Jamie approached him. "Might I have a word, Sergeant Morgan?"

"Certainly, Constable. What can I do for you?"

"Um, well, I'm sure this is a bit unorthodox, Sir, but I was wondering if, well, you'd be okay with me escorting Anna for the rest of the evening?"

Adam's brows flew up. "You would deprive me of my partner for the night?"

"If that's okay with you, Sir?" Jamie grinned.

Adam sighed loudly and curled up his face into a rather wonky grin. "If it's okay with Anna, then it's okay with me." He ran his fingers through his hair and shook his head as Jamie skipped away.

Jamie took Anna's hand and spoke to her. She nodded excitedly at him and looked over at her pa. He gave her a nod and a rather uncertain smile. She grinned and then excused herself from Jamie for a moment to come over to Adam.

"Do you mind, Pa?"

He raised his brows and gave her a sad smile. "Yes, I mind. I mind having some other man whisk away my daughter. But you go, Darling. Have a good time."

"Thank you, Pa." She grinned and stood up on her toes to kiss him on the cheek.

"You're welcome, Darling. Just don't forget your old pa."

"Never, Pa." She embraced him briefly. Adam kissed her on the forehead, and she hurried back to Jamie. Adam made his way to a seat at the side of the room, and sat back and watched his two beautiful daughters being whisked around the dancefloor with two young Mounties. He sighed and grinned nostalgically.

* * * *

"Well, Sam, I've brought your girl back safe and sound."

"I knew you would, Adam. I trust they behaved themselves?"

"Your daughter did. Not too sure about your son though." He grimaced.

Sam frowned. "What does that mean?"

"That rascal son of yours has eyes for my Anna." Adam raised his brows, and a slight mist formed in his eyes.

"What?" Sam grinned.

"He asked me if he could escort her for the evening. Stole her right out from under me, and then, of course, he stuck around the rest of the time we were in Edmonton. Just before we left, he asked my permission to write to her. He's gonna fall in love with my Anna and take her far away, isn't he?"

Samuel grinned and slapped Adam on the back. "And just think, Friend, if that did happen, we'd have shared grandchildren."

Adam smiled in spite of himself. "Yeah, but he'll end up in the North Country, and we'll never get to see them."

"I think you're getting a little ahead of yourself, Sergeant. Still, I can't think of a better girl for my James."

Adam took a deep breath. "Yeah, I guess you're right. Not too sure about his parents though!" He grinned, and his eyes twinkled.

Samuel smirked. "You'll keep, Morgan!" He laughed.

"Well, we better get home, Sam."

"Thanks for looking after Esther, Adam."

Adam gripped Sam's shoulder. "Of course, Friend. You'd do the same for my girls."

"Yes, I would." Sam's voice was sincere.

* * * *

That evening over their mother's supper table, the two excited girls described the ball in living colour. Adam sat back and grinned. He was glad they'd enjoyed themselves so much. He'd been so honoured to show off two of his girls at the ball. Anna had turned many heads, and so had Callie, for that matter, but she and Jonny only had eyes for each other.

"Oh, it sounds so wonderful," Sarah gushed. "I wish I could've gone."

Lizzie rolled her eyes.

"Can I go next year?" Hope asked.

Adam grimaced. "Not until you're least twenty, Darling." He winked at Katie.

Katie laughed.

"Why, Pa?" Hope cocked her head to the side.

Adam's face grew wistful. "I don't want all my daughters falling in love with Mounties."

"What's wrong with loving Mounties?" Callie squeezed Jonny's arm.

"Nothing at all, Darling." Adam smiled. "It's just that I know that Douglas Falls won't need any more Mounties for some time, and that would mean them moving away for his posting. I'd be awfully sad not to have my army of girls nearby. I know I can't keep you all forever, and if you do move away with your husbands, you'll, of course, have my blessing, but I'll be awful lonesome for you."

He raised his eyebrows and sighed. "I miss Rose so much, and she lives next door. Callie will be leaving us soon, and I dread it, and seeing Anna dancing with Jamie at the ball made me think I'll be losing her soon." He finished with a loud sigh and his eyes brimmed with tears.

"Pa, you're so sentimental sometimes." Lizzie rolled her eyes again.

Adam reached out to stroke her cheek. "I can't help it, Lizzie. I have a beautiful wife and six amazing daughters. How can I not be sentimental, when young men have their eyes on my girls?"

"Well, you don't have to worry about me, Pa. I'll never marry!" The auburn-haired fifteen-year-old grimaced.

"Don't say that, Lizzie. One day some young man will catch your eye."

"Yeah, but I'll never catch their eye, Pa. No one wants to marry someone like me. Men want sweet, beautiful girls like Callie and Anna, not ugly tomboys like me!" She dropped her fork and hung her head.

Adam put his own fork down and leaned across to lift Lizzie's chin. He looked intensely into her eyes. "You are not ugly, and you're not a tomboy. You're Elizabeth Anne Morgan, and you are beautiful. You have the most amazing hair and eyes. You're tenacious and stubborn and so very talented."

He smiled at her and looked her right in the eye. "Do you know what I love about you? You aren't afraid to get dirty. You love to climb trees and fly kites. You fish and play baseball with the best of them. But, Lizzie, you're also beautiful, soft and feminine, and those traits together are so attractive to the right man. Someday some young man is going to be absolutely enamoured by you, and you'll love him fiercely.

"Please don't ever say you are ugly or put yourself down, Lizzie. It breaks my heart to hear you say that. No, you aren't an ordinary girl." Adam stroked her cheek and grinned, his eyes full of love and joy. "You, my darling, are extraordinary, and I can't wait to see what you do with life and who you become. You can do anything you set your mind to, and of all my daughters, you are the one I know will make a great difference in this world."

Lizzie's green eyes were large and brimmed with tears. "But you have to say that. You're my Pa."

"I don't have to." Jonny stood up and walked around the table to kneel down before her and took both her hands in his. She turned to look at him. "Lizzie, your pa is right. I, too, think you're an extraordinary woman, and you'd never be suited to an ordinary man like me. The man that falls in love with Lizzie Morgan will be an extraordinary man, of the highest character because, that's what you have." He kissed her on the forehead and walked back to his own chair. Callie grinned at him and squeezed his hand.

Lizzie sniffed back a tear and swallowed to try to regain her composure. She did not like public displays of emotion.

"Lizzie, I wish I was more like you." Hope squeezed her sister's hand.

"What? No, you don't, Hope. You're so lovely and sweet. Why would you want to be like me?" Lizzie rolled her eyes.

"Because you can talk to anyone and be instant friends, Liz. You're so brave and confident and wonderful." Hope was the only person who ever got away with calling Lizzie 'Liz'. If anyone else tried, Lizzie would scold them.

"She's right, Lizzie," Sarah offered. Callie and Anna nodded their agreement.

Lizzie smiled. "Thank you." Her lips trembled in uncharacteristic humility.

"We all feel that way, Darling," Katie encouraged her. "I wish I had some of your boldness too."

"Really, Ma?"

"Really, Child."

"And you think one day a man could really love me?" Lizzie lifted wide eyes to her father.

"Absolutely, a wonderful man. I'd never let just any man marry my Lizzie. He's going to have to be special indeed." Adam gave her a determined grin.

They continued with their meal, and the friendly chatter resumed. Although nothing more was said to Lizzie, she stored away her family's words in her heart and began to start believing them.

Twenty-Five
Jamie

The first Christmas with two new grandchildren was blissful. The two grandfathers rocked their month-old grandchildren as the family gathered.

Jamie got two weeks leave to come home for the Christmas break.

The two older Mounties enjoyed the growing friendship between Jamie and Anna. It was very new, but it was obvious they were very comfortable with each other.

Jamie brought Anna a cold drink and sat down beside her on the couch. She blushed shyly, and he squeezed her arm.

Adam noticed the little scene, looked at Katie and shook his head sadly. Katie squeezed his arm knowingly. Adam smirked.

"What's so funny, Sergeant?" Sam perched on the armrest of the chair next to Jo.

"I was just looking at those two and thinking one day you and I might be fighting over grandbabies."

"You're getting ahead of yourself again, Adam. They aren't even courting yet."

"Am I? I see how they look at each other." He frowned and shook his head. "It seems rather inevitable to me." He finished with a wistful sigh.

Samuel laughed and slapped his friend on the back. "I can't think of a better family for him to marry into, should it come to that."

"I'm not sure I can handle two daughters being married to Mounties." Adam shook his head sadly.

"At least they've grown up knowing what to expect. Nothing should come as a surprise to either of them," Jo added.

Adam nodded thoughtfully and ran his fingers through his hair. "Jamie plans to go North, doesn't he? It's a primitive place. I fear for Anna."

"You don't think she can handle it?" Katie frowned at her husband.

"Oh, she can handle it for sure. It just could be pretty lonesome."

"For her or for you?" Sam lifted one eyebrow.

Adam ran his fingers through his hair and gave his friend a nostalgic smile. "For both of us, I guess. If it comes to that, I sure will miss my girl."

"You know they can't all live up here on The Rise with you, Friend."

"I know. Sure would be nice though." Adam sighed.

"You're a remarkable man, Adam. I've never known a man so attached to his daughters."

Adam shrugged, and a wide smile crossed his face as his eyes shone. "They're the ones who are remarkable, amazing girls, all six of them." His eyes travelled from face to face of each of his girls around the room, their eyes sparkled with love and joy.

*   *   *   *

Adam pulled a piece of paper from his typewriter and sighed. Laying it aside he reached for the updates from HQ. He grimaced. *When I finish this paperwork I'm going to phone HQ and ask for a new recruit. If only I could ask Jamie to stay on. It's been a huge help having him on over Christmas. But I can't ask him, he wants to go north!* Adam shrugged and ran his fingers through his hair.

"Sergeant Morgan." Jamie walked in the door.

Adam looked up and rubbed his stiff neck. "Hi, James. Did you look in on the trappers?"

"Yes, Sir, I believe it was just a misunderstanding."

"Oh?"

"I spoke to the two men. It seems a wolf took the animals from the trap, and not the neighbour."

Adam smirked. "They are prone to jumping to conclusions."

"I gathered that, Sir." Jamie bent down to pat Honey, who was, as always, sleeping by the fire. "Your dog is beautiful, Serge."

"Yes."

"Have you taken her on the trail?"

"A few times. She helped me when I found your pa. I'm thankful to have her by my side. I personally believe all country Mounties should have a husky, especially sole officers. She's mighty good backup."

"I can see why, Sir. We'd have no use in the city."

"Well, my dogs have saved my life on a number of occasions. I'm glad to always have one, and to protect my family." He nodded across to a photograph on the wall. My first dog, Bear, died saving Katie's life. He'll always be a hero to me."

Jamie nodded. "Serge, I wondered if I might talk to you for a moment."

"Certainly, Constable. What's on your mind?"

"Actually, Sir, it's a personal matter."

Adam smiled. "I see." He gestured to the chair opposite his desk.

Jamie sat down and gratefully accepted the cookies and coffee Adam offered him.

"Mrs Morgan sure is a good cook." He grinned.

"Yes, she is, but Callie made these. I believe they were intended for that other constable, but he's not here, so he'll never know." Adam grinned. "Now, what can I do for you, Constable?"

"Well, Sir, I'm not sure where to start." He gulped and scratched at his hair just above his ear.

"I imagine you're here to talk to me about my sixteen-year-old daughter!" Adam raised his brows, sat back in his chair and folded his arms.

"Yes, Sir." Jamie's cheeks coloured slightly, and a crooked smile crossed his face.

"What is it you want to say?"

Jamie swallowed and took a deep breath. "Well, it's obviously clear to you that I have feelings for her, Sergeant Morgan."

"I got that impression, James."

"It's early days, Sir. She's only sixteen, and I know I don't live nearby, so asking her to court would be futile."

Adam nodded.

"Sir, I'm in a bit of a quandary. I sure would like to pursue a relationship with Anna. She's quite something." Jamie grinned and his eyes sparkled.

Adam gave him a sideways smile. "Yes, she is."

"You've already given me permission to write to her, but I was wondering if perhaps it would be okay to at least ask her to wait for me. I plan to ask for a transfer, if not here in Douglas Falls, then a town nearby."

"I thought you wanted to go further north." Adam squinted at him.

"I considered it, Sir. But my heart really lies on the western frontier. The longer I'm away, the more I miss home. Being here reminds me of just how much. I've greatly enjoyed working with you and Constable Scott the last few days."

"James, I hope you aren't planning to make that decision just for Anna."

"No, Sir, I wouldn't dream of it. Even before the Mountie Ball, I found myself longing for the wide open spaces out here."

Adam nodded slowly. Unfolding his arms, he ran his fingers through his hair and sipped at his coffee. Both men sat silent for a time. "Jamie, for what it's worth, I think you and Anna would be good together, and I've been most grateful to have your help the last week. I'll miss you when you're gone. I'm starting to think I might need another young, energetic Mountie around here. I'm beginning to feel old."

"No, Sir, you have many good years ahead of you."

Adam chuckled, "Thank you, Constable."

Jamie grinned. "Pa's the same though, likes being able to leave some of the more energetic jobs to the younger chaps."

"It sure would be good to have more time with my family." Adam's eyes grew dreamy.

"I'm sure." Jamie nodded and reached for another cookie. Shoving the whole thing in his mouth, he chewed it up and swallowed it quickly. "Sergeant, if you do take on another officer, would you consider me?"

Adam smiled. "Of course, Jamie, but it isn't up to me. Mountie HQ has the final say."

"I know. I can only apply and hope, Sir."

"I'll put in a request. I sure could use another man."

"And Anna?"

Adam sighed loudly and shook his head. "It pains me to say so, but, yes, Jamie, you have my blessing to ask Anna to wait for you." Tears flooded the corners of the Mountie's eyes.

Jamie flashed him a toothy grin. "Thank you, Sergeant." He leapt up and skipped out the door.

Adam chuckled and sighed deeply. He shook his head and turned back to his stack of reports.

* * * *

"Anna, I've brought you something."

"You have? Whatever for Jamie? It's not my birthday."

Jamie took a deep breath. "It's well... A promise..."

"A promise of what?"

"Us."

"Jamie Ferguson, speak plainly. You asked me to go for a walk with you after supper, even though it's freezing out here." She chuckled and rubbed her mittened hands together. "You said we'd be quick, and now you're speaking in riddles."

Jamie chuckled. "I'm sorry. I'll get to the point. I have to leave tomorrow, Anna. I'm expected back in Calgary by Monday."

"I know." Anna hung her head.

"I wish I could ask you to court."

"Me too." Anna's voice was quiet and shaky.

He stopped walking and turned to look at her. "But I can ask you to wait. Will you?"

"Wait for what?" She blushed.

He reached for one hand and kissed it. "For me. I plan to get a transfer. If not here, then close by. The Sergeant said he'd put in a request for a new officer. I'm going to apply. I promise to wait for you. There isn't anyone else I want to court."

"Of course, I'll wait, Jamie. But what if you can't get a transfer, or it's years away?"

"We'll cross that bridge when we come to it. All I know is you're the girl for me." He smiled and brushed her cheek. "As soon as I can, I want to be in a position to be able to court properly. In the meantime, I want you to wear this." He handed her a small cloth bag.

Anna opened it and lifted out a small necklace with a star on it. "Oh Jamie, it's lovely." She pulled it on over her head and lifted her hair over it. Holding the star in her hand, she lowered her eyes to admire it.

"It isn't much. I just thought maybe the star would remind you that when you look up at the stars at night, you might remember that I'm looking at the same stars, thinking of you." He gestured to the array of stars in the clear winter sky above them.

"Jamie Ferguson, that is much too sweet. I thank you." She stood up on her toes and kissed him on the cheek.

Jamie grinned. "Well, if it gets that response, imagine what it will be like when I give you a ring someday."

Anna bit her lip and her cheeks coloured. "You'll have to wait and see, Constable."

Jamie laughed, delighted that she was comfortable enough to tease him. "You're right, of course, Miss Morgan." He kissed the hand he held one more time. "We best get back. I've kept you out here in the cold far too long." He offered her his arm, and she reached for it gladly.

"Thank you for this necklace, Jamie. It's quite lovely."

"You're the lovely one, Anna." He opened the door for her and bid her goodnight.

Jamie galloped back to the Mountie office, whistling a tune the entire way. His heart danced and his eyes shone brightly. It wasn't a courtship, but knowing that Anna would be here waiting for him would be such a joy.

Building began in earnest again on Callie and Jonny's home, and they eagerly looked forward to their spring wedding. The women worked hard to add all the soft furnishings.

Jonny helped Callie to hang the fluffy curtains in the windows, and stepped back off the chair. He looked around their living room. "You've done a wonderful job, Callie. Our house looks beautiful."

"You built it. I just did some sewing." She shrugged.

Jonny squeezed her arm. "It's those touches that make it a home, Darling." He wrapped his arms around her waist. "I can't believe in just a weeks' time, you'll be my wife, Callie."

"I can't wait to live here with you, Jonny."

"Me either, Miss Morgan. It sure will be better than living in the jail." He kissed her and then released her. "Just the one last curtain?"

"Yes." She pointed up at the final window.

He swiftly hung the last curtain and then he stood back from the job. He turned to her and shrugged. "Well, Darling, our home is complete."

"It's so wonderful. I can't believe it's ours. Thank you for building this for me."

"Oh, Callie, this is nothing compared to what you do for me. I'll never be able to repay you." He brushed her cheek with his thumb.

"You do, Jon, every day."

They shared a sweet kiss then Jonny raised his brows and smiled at her. "I have another surprise for you."

"You do?" She frowned and tilted her head.

"Mmmhmmm, I've been paying it off for some time, and I'm so glad it's ready for you in our new house."

Callie looked around. "What is it?" She noticed nothing new or surprising.

"Follow me." He grinned, reached for her hand and led her to the spare room. "Over there."

Callie gasped, and her hands flew to her mouth. Tears sprung to the corners of her eyes. "Jonny! Oh, I can't believe it, my own sewing machine?" She threw herself in his arms and kissed him. "Thank you." Her eyes sparkled.

Jon squeezed her tightly and drank in her scent. "You're most welcome, Callie. Consider it a wedding present."

"You're so thoughtful, Jon, but you shouldn't have spent all that money. It wasn't necessary."

Jonny grinned and brushed her cheek. "Callie, my darling. It's worth every cent, just to see that look of joy on your face. Besides, I know how much you love to sew, and, I plan for us to have lots of babies for you to sew for." He winked at her as she ran her hand down the shiny wood of the new machine.

She lowered her eyes and blushed. "Jonny."

He reached out to her and lifted her chin. "Don't you want a family, Callie?"

"Oh, yes, you know I do." Her eyes shone.

He embraced her and cradled her head in his hand. "Good, because I don't have much of a family, and I hope to have a whole passel of children one day, Darling. Nothing would thrill me more!"

She stood back from him and grinned. "What if you end up with six daughters like Pa?"

His face dropped, and he gulped. His eyes widened. "Six girls." He curled his face up into a rather uncertain grin. "I'd be delighted." He smiled, leaned in, and tucked a stray curl behind her ear. "Especially if they're anything like their beautiful ma."

Callie blushed again. "Jon, we should be getting back to Ma and Pa's for supper."

"First things first, I want to hang our sign."

"What sign?"

He reached for a parcel wrapped in fabric. "Marcus made us this."

Callie unwrapped the ribbon and ran her hand across the carved wood. "Scott's Acre," she read aloud. "Jonathan and Callie Scott."

Callie clapped her hands together. "Ohh, it's wonderful. Scott's Acre, I like it. Now we have Morgan's Acreage, Far Acre and Scott's Acre all up here on The Rise."

"Yes, I like it too." Jonny grinned and took it from her. "Let's go hang it."

They hung the sign on a post at the entrance to their land and then kissed. Callie chuckled and they stood hand in hand looking back at their new home. She lay her head on Jonny's shoulder. As if he sensed her thoughts, he said, "One week, Callie."

"Mrs Jonathan Scott," she whispered.

Jonny squeezed her. "That sounds pretty good to me." He led her back towards her parent's home.

Twenty-Six
Fear

Lizzie looked up from the potatoes she was peeling. "Ma, when's Pa going to be home?"

"I'm afraid I'm not sure, Darling. It'll be in time for the wedding though, Callie" She smiled to reassure Callie, who was working alongside her. "He'll be here." Katie gripped her daughter's arm.

"I hope so, Ma. I know he took this assignment so Jonny wouldn't have to."

"Yes, just on the odd chance that Jonny wouldn't have made it in time. But your pa will be here, Callie, it's escort duty. He's only supposed to be gone until Friday."

"Oh, Ma, what if he isn't? It'd be just awful not to have Pa there for my wedding."

Katie put down her knife and put her arm around Callie's waist. "He told me if the worst does happen and he doesn't make it in time, you're not to postpone on his behalf. He would not be happy knowing you aren't happy, Darling. As much as he'd love to be here and he'd regret missing it, he said absolutely not to miss out on his behalf. He's already prepared Samuel to take over the honours of walking you up the aisle if he can't make it, but rest assured, he'll do everything he can to be here."

"I know, Ma." Callie nodded but tears ran down her face. Katie squeezed her waist supportively.

"What time will Jonny be here?" Lizzie tried to change the subject.

"Not till just before supper. He's got a lot more work to do with Pa away." She wiped her eyes.

"So he won't be here for our noon meal then?"

"Not today, Ma."

Lizzie put the potatoes aside to be baked later for their evening meal. She wiped her hands on her apron and walked to her mother. "Ma, do you need me for anything else?"

"Why?"

"Since it's Spring Break, I thought I'd go fishing."

Katie smiled. "Sure, Lizzie. Just be back by three."

"Ma, do you need anything from the store?" Callie finished her task too and removed her apron. "I've gotta go by there to meet Hope at the ice cream store."

"No, thank you, Darling. I'm going to have a cup of coffee then get to my sewing." Katie reached for the coffee pot.

"Okay, Ma. I'll be home in time to help you finish preparing supper. Lizzie, do you want a ride to town?"

"Sure." Lizzie grinned, delighted not to have to walk.

Lizzie climbed up behind her sister with her fishing pole and pail tied to the saddle. "Come on, Lizzie, sit still," Callie scolded. Lizzie squirmed and wriggled. It bumped the saddle and made Callie feel like she was going to slip. She was relieved to finally drop Lizzie at the pond and head into town.

Callie sat down on the seat outside the ice cream store to wait for Hope. The clock on the bank chimed out the half-hour and Callie frowned. Hope was running very late. She had so much work to do for the wedding, but her sister had begged her to take her for an ice cream cone. The younger girl been visiting with her best friend, Hettie March, and Callie promised to take them both to the store. Now they were nearly an hour late. She needed to get home soon.

"I can't wait all day," Callie fumed aloud, glancing up at the clock. She stood to leave and paused when she saw Hettie running around the corner.

"Callie. I can't find Hope." The little girl had quivering lips and a look of panic in her eyes.

Callie reached her arm out to the girl's shoulder to try to comfort her. "What do you mean you can't find her?"

The girl sniffed twice. "We were playing up by Skippers Ridge, and I turned around, and she was gone."

Callie sighed; it was like Hope to get caught up in exploring and lose track of time.

"I think I know where she is, Hettie. You wait here. I'll go and get her." Hettie sat down on the chair and waited. Hope was usually just hanging in a tree trying to find bird eggs or chasing a butterfly. She was likely playing in the meadow or the trees around Skippers Ridge. That's where Callie found her last time. She sighed, and wished Jonny wasn't out of town, checking on the outlying homesteaders. She mounted Maisy and cantered off in the direction of Skippers Ridge.

"Hooooope," she called as she approached the clearing; riding close to the tree line, she continued to call out. "Hooooope." She yelled as loudly as she could, but there was no sign of her. She rode further up the ridge. "Surely she hasn't come this far? Hoooooooooope," she called again. "Oh, where could she be?" Callie scowled.

"Maybe she's gone into the mine." She spoke to the horse again. "I found her there once before, Maisy. She'd chased a squirrel into the mine and tried to catch it, got her foot caught and Pa had to pull her out. Oh, that girl." Callie chuckled in spite of herself. "I don't really have time for this." She grimaced.

She dismounted from Maisy at the mine entrance and threw the horse's rein over a sapling. "Stay there, Girl." She patted the horse's silky neck.

Callie left Maisy eating grass and walked into the mine entrance. "Hope, Hope Morgan, are you in here?" There was some light, although the deeper in she got, the less light she had. Callie thought she heard a movement down the left-hand shaft a little way, it was a fair way in, but she headed towards the movement. "Hope, is that you?"

The vibrations from her footsteps and her voice rattled the precariously placed, rather rotten, boards above and stones began to fall from the ceiling. She put her arms over her head and waited for the rumble to stop. "Hope are you here?"

Callie froze. A loud rumble and crack pierced the air, dust and rocks rained down on her. The last thing she remembered was a splitting pain in her head and then the world went black. A cloud of dust emitted from the mine. Maisy reared in fright, snapping her tethered rein, she galloped in the direction of town until she calmed and headed for a meadow of lush grass..

*　*　*　*

Hope wandered into town. She grimaced as she heard the clock on the bank chime out the hour. "Oh no! Callie is going to be hopping mad, and Hettie!"

Hope didn't mean to wander off; she just found animals and nature so fascinating. She'd been chasing a butterfly, trying to watch how it flew and changed direction in the wind. It was so beautiful, and she just lost track of where and when she was.

She paused and gasped, a loud rumble stopped her in her tracks. She turned to look in the direction it came from, noticing a billow of smoke. Someone was blasting nearby. She frowned and hurried towards town.

Hope made it to the ice cream shop more than an hour late, it was nearly time for lunch, and she was sure Callie had just brought Hettie an ice cream, and they'd both gone home.

"Why do I get so side-tracked by animals?" Hope scolded herself, "Callie's gonna be steaming!" She grimaced.

Hope shrugged and started walking towards home. She met Lizzie carrying her fishing pole, and bucket with six fish tails sticking out. "Hi, Lizzie, looks like you caught lots."

"Yep. Catfish, yum!" Lizzie held up the bucket and grinned. "Hey, where's Callie? I thought she was with you?"

Hope shrugged and seemed contrite. "I was late. I bet she came home without me."

"She's gonna be mad at you, Hope."

*　*　*　*

Jonny wound the last piece of paper out of the typewriter and filed it as per protocol. He'd finished much earlier than he expected. He cleared his desk and hurried off to the bathhouse to

322

get cleaned up. Perhaps he could spend an hour or so with his fiancée before supper.

He bathed and cleaned himself up, buttoned on a freshly laundered red serge and headed for The Rise.

Katie answered his knock. "Good evening, Jonny."

He nodded and smiled, looking around. "Where is Callie?"

"She hasn't returned." Lizzie shrugged.

Jonny frowned. "What do you mean?"

"We assumed she was with you?" Katie furrowed her brows. "I can't think of another reason she wouldn't be home when she said she would."

"I thought she was meeting Hope for an ice cream; I saw her as I headed out of town; she said she'd just dropped Lizzie at the lake, and she was headed to the store to meet up with Hope. She asked if I'd join them, but I had to head out of town to check on some homesteaders and then file some paperwork."

"Where could she be?" Anna walked out of the kitchen to join the conversation.

"I'm sure she's fine." Katie tried to reassure the others, but the fear rose in her own mind. *I sure wish Adam was here.*

Jonny frowned. He gripped Katie's arm. "I'll find her. I'll see if Marcus can help."

"Where will you look for her?"

"You could ask Hettie? She left before me for town, and she might have seen Callie."

"Thank you, Hope." Jonny cupped her chin and winked at her. He fixed his eyes on Katie and gave her a reassuring smile. "I'll find her, I promise."

Twenty-Seven
A Perilous Rescue

Jonny squatted down before the little girl and put a reassuring hand on her shoulder. "Hettie, did you happen to see Miss Morgan this afternoon? I heard she was going to meet you and Hope at the ice cream store?"

"Yes, I told her that I couldn't find Hope. Sometimes she wanders off. Miss Morgan went to look for her."

"Where were you playing?" asked Marcus.

"I told Miss Morgan we were playing up at Skippers Ridge." Tears rimmed her eyes again. "Hope was chasing butterflies." Hettie shook her head and burst into tears. "I'm sorry, I didn't know Miss Morgan was missing."

"It's okay, Hettie." Jonny squeezed the girl's shoulder. "You've been most helpful."

Marcus and Jonny took off in the direction Hettie had suggested. About a mile and a half out of town, Marcus spotted her horse. "Constable, Isn't that Maisy?"

"Yes." Jonny changed direction and headed for the grazing horse. He leapt off Major and grabbed Maisy's rein. "It's broken. She must have pulled loose."

"Maisy is not usually a flighty horse. Something must have spooked her."

"Marc!" Jonny's face fell as he recalled something. "Hope said she heard dynamite nearby. You don't think someone's been blasting? That would cause Maisy to spook."

"Why would they? The mine's been out of action for nearly twenty-five years, and the only quarry is some ways south of here. We'd not hear an explosion from here." Marcus frowned.

"Then what do you think....Ohhhhh!" A thought occurred to Jonny, and he leapt back on Major. Leading Maisy behind him, he galloped towards the old mine.

"What is it?" Marcus called out and followed.

As they approached, they could see that there had been a cave-in. Dust and debris littered the entrance, now completely sealed off with a wall of rocks. A piece of Maisy's rein was still attached to the sapling outside. "Oh no!" Jonny leapt off Major and reached for the small piece of leather. "Oh no." He fell to his knees.

Marcus leapt off his horse and gripped his shoulder. "It's going to be okay, Jon."

"How can you be sure, Marc? If she's in there, under all that rubble...." He couldn't even finish his thought.

"Jon. Look at me. I know you're worried." Marcus raised his eyebrows. "But you have to be strong. If Callie is going to have any chance at surviving this, you have to lead, okay? We need you. Now, I'll start hauling these rocks out. You ride into town for reinforcements."

Jonny took a deep breath and shrugged his shoulders. He stood up. "You're right. We need help." He leapt on Major and headed for the town at a gallop. He almost knocked over Daniel as he rounded the corner into town.

"Wooow there, Constable. What's going on?"

Jonny skidded his horse to a halt. Daniel reached for the reins of the heaving horse. "You have to help, Pastor. It's Callie; she's trapped in the old mine. We need help to get her out." The Mountie's eyes were wide and his voice trembled.

"Ohhhhhh." Daniel took a deep breath. "What do you need me to do?"

"Round up as many men with shovels and pitchforks. Get some wagons out there. It's going to be dark soon. We have to get her out."

"Right, I'll get lanterns and as many men as I can, too. We'll get her out, Son. She'll be fine, I promise."

"Thanks, Pastor." Jonny nodded and galloped away.

Daniel sprinted the rest of the distance to town and to the general store to raise the alarm.

Jonny arrived back at the mine and leapt off his horse. Marcus was hauling out a rock. By now he had a small pile he'd removed. "Are reinforcements coming?" He dropped the rock outside the mine with a loud sigh.

"Yep, I bumped into Pastor Coleman. He's rounding up men and shovels." Jonny tethered his horse and headed into the mine to help.

Men and wagons began to arrive and there was a whirl of activity. Jonny took charge, organising the people gave him a way to feel useful. By imagining it was someone else he was rescuing, he was able to swallow back his fears and set his mind on the task at hand.

He gave directions and drove the action. It was laborious work, but the men persevered.

Katie and a group of women arrived at the mine with hot soup, bread and coffee to keep the men going.

The men, led by Jonny and Marcus, hauled out the rocks. Many needed to be broken up or pried out with tools. They had a growing pile but still had not broken through.

Anna and Lizzie ran from man to man with buckets of water and ladles; keeping them hydrated was essential.

The sky began to darken, and they still hadn't managed to make an opening in the rock wall. Jonny whimpered and put his hand to his face.

Owen paused and walked to the man. "Jon." He placed his hands on the Mountie's shoulders and shook him. "Jon."

Jonny looked up at him and sniffed.

"Jon, you can't lose it now. We need you to direct us. You breaking down will not help Callie."

"What if she's dead? It's been hours." His voice trembled.

"What if she's alive, Jon? Standing here and feeling sorry for yourself won't help her. Now, pull yourself together and lead the men. For Callie." Owen looked him in the eye.

Jonny nodded slowly. "You're right. Thank you, Doctor."

Owen nodded. "Come on." The two turned and headed back for another stone.

"What I wouldn't give for Adam to be here right now.".

"I know what you mean." Daniel put down his coffee cup and squeezed her hand. "You stay out here, Katie. Keep feeding the men who come out. We need them all strong. It's the best thing you can do, keeping everyone's spirits up. I'll head back in to help."

"I'm so worried, Danny."

Daniel put an arm around her and kissed her hair. "God's in control, Katie. No matter what happens." Katie caught the slight tremor in his voice.

"What if she dies and Adam isn't here? He'd never forgive himself."

Daniel embraced her tightly. "Let's not make trouble, Katie. Let's just focus on getting her out." Daniel released her.

Katie wiped her tears, nodded, and headed back to the wagon. Serving the food would help her keep her mind off the situation.

Hope and Sarah clung to each other and cried. "It's all my fault. She went after me. What if she dies and doesn't get to have her wedding?" Hope sobbed into her sister's chest.

Jonny overheard the girl and gulped. "Please Lord. We need a miracle." He paused for a moment, squared his shoulders, drank in the Lord's peace and hurried back into the mine.

As darkness closed in, the men had to work by lamplight, making the task a lot more difficult. Women and children still sat around outside. Hope and Sarah huddled together on the back of the wagon, both asleep under a blanket. Becky and Louisa did all they could to keep Katie's spirits up but from time to time, they would notice her hang her head and sob.

A rumble emanated from inside the mine and rocks rained down on the men. Hopes fell as they fled from the entrance.

Jonny fell to his knees. "Noooooo. Please, no." He trembled as the fear overrode his Mountie resolve. Marcus gripped his shoulder.

"We're through." Vinnie's voice rang out. The cave-in had dislodged some of the higher rocks that they were trying to penetrate through. Two tumbling rocks had fallen and opened up a gap. "I can see her."

Jonny leapt up off his knees, sniffed back the emotion and ran to help. "Callie." He pushed his way to the front. He lifted his lantern so he could see through the hole that Vinnie and three others were working to widen. "Callie." Miraculously there was a only a single beam lying across her. She wasn't buried in rocks. Jonny could see a beam of light coming in from a ventilation shaft above; at least there was oxygen.

"Let's widen this gap, I have to get in there." His cool head and Mountie training kept him calm. "Callie, I'm coming. I'm here." He hauled out a large rock and passed it to a man behind him who removed it from the mine. Three more large rocks and he could just squeeze through. He ran to her and yanked the beam off her, throwing it aside. "Callie, Darling, I'm here." He knelt beside her and felt her pulse. "Oh, praise the Lord. She's alive." He buried his head in his hands for just a moment, breathing a sigh of relief.

Sighs and exclamations of relief could be heard from all those peering in.

Jonny looked up. "She's weak. I need the doctor."

"Pa." Vinnie ran to his father who was just rehydrating outside. "Pa, Constable Scott is with her. She's alive, but he needs you."

"I'm coming, Son." Owen turned to Katie and embraced her briefly. "She'll be okay. I promise. Vinnie said she's alive. You have to have hope." He snatched up his kit and ran for the mine.

"I know, Owen." Katie nodded to his retreating figure and the tears ran down her face. She clung to Lizzie, and Daniel came over to them.

"Let's pray." Those around linked hands and bowed their heads, and the pastor led them in fervent prayer.

Owen climbed through the widened gap in the rocks and carried his bag and lantern. He sat down next to the Mountie holding the delicate hand of the ashen Callie.

"She's alive, Doc," the Constable managed through trembling lips. "She's appears to have at least two broken ribs.

The doctor nodded and knelt over Callie to do his assessment. "I agree. I don't believe she has a head injury, but I can't be sure. Normally I'd not suggest to move a patient, but we have to get her back to the clinic." With one eye on the creaking rafters above, he added, "And quickly."

Owen took control, Jonny was much too overwhelmed at seeing the woman he loved lying there lifeless and hurt.

The Mountie gently brushed her hair off her forehead and kissed her cheek. "You're going to be okay, Darling. I promise. You're going to be okay, and we're going to get married just as soon as you're well again."

"Jon, we need to get her out of here, but we can't risk hurting her further and one of those ribs puncturing a lung."

"We could fashion a stretcher." He forced his foggy brain to focus.

"Good idea."

Jonny stroked the pale cheek. "I'll be right back, my love." He headed back through the gap in the rocks. The timbers creaking as he climbed through. "Please, Lord, hold it back till we get her out."

He ran out to where the men were still hauling out rocks to expand the opening. Some were drinking water to rehydrate. "We need planks, ropes, and a sack. We need to make a stretcher."

Men bounded away to do his bidding and were soon back with the supplies he required. They fashioned a makeshift stretcher. Daniel ran to him. "Can I help, Jon?"

"Yes, come on." Jonny grabbed the stretcher and ran inside. Daniel followed him in, and they crawled through the opening in the rocks. "You two men stay out here," Jonny ordered two of the workers. "We'll pass her out to you."

They heard a loud creak above them, and dust and stones rained down on their heads. The two men and the doctor covered their faces. "We have to get her out of here fast," called Daniel.

"Lay the stretcher over here." Owen gestured. Daniel and Jonny followed his instructions, and they worked together to get Callie onto the stretcher as carefully and gently as possible.

She groaned in pain as they lifted her. Jonny sighed.

"It's a good sign," Owen said. "She's starting to come round. Then we can assess the full extent of her injuries."

"Jonny, we've gotta go! This whole place is going to come down!" Daniel gripped his arm, and they hastened to the hole.

They passed Callie on her stretcher through the gap in the rocks to the waiting men. "We've got her, Doc." One man nodded to him.

"Get her out," Jonny called as Owen crawled through the gap. The men hurried off towards the mine entrance with the stretcher.

More creaking, and the mine shook as another rotten beam splintered, the heavy rocks above it barely held in place. "Go, Owen. She needs you." The Mountie handed the doctor's bag through the gap.

The mine continued to creak. "Come on, Pastor." A man reached his arms through the hole to Daniel. He put his arms and head through the gap, and they yanked him through. "It's coming down."

"GO!" Jonny put his arms and head through the hole. "Go!" The men ran towards the entrance, and a cloud of dust burst out behind them as they collapsed outside, heaving in fresh air.

"Noooo!" Katie leapt up to look towards the entrance as the area shook and the mine collapsed. "Nooo!" Tears sprang to her eyes, and she held her breath. Daniel and the two men stamped out into the sunlight, heaving huge breaths and coughing on the dust.

Daniel turned and covered his face with his arm. He yelled into the dust cloud. "Jonny."

Katie and the girls stood with their hands to their faces, desperately hoping the Mountie would emerge. The dust cloud settled, and there was no sign of Jonny. Daniel gazed into the darkness, his eyes burning and blurred with tears and dust. "Jonny." He sighed loudly as he heard a cough. Jonny lay near the entrance coughing on dust, pinned under a fallen beam. Daniel and Mr Johnson quickly lifted it away. He was unhurt, and they helped him to his feet. He staggered out of the mine, and Anna ran to him with cold water.

Oblivious to his dusty and soiled state, Katie threw her arms around him. "Oh, Jonny, I was so worried."

He pushed her away from him and nodded. Rubbing the dust out of his eyes. "Callie?"

"She's alive. The doctor's with her." Katie pointed to where Owen was tending Callie on the back of the wagon.

"That's all that matters." Jonny sighed.

"You matter too, Jon." Katie gripped his arm.

Jonny fixed his eyes on Katie in the dull lamplight. "Ma'am, I'd willingly give my life to save hers." He gulped down the glass of water and slumped down onto a rock, buried his head in his hands and sobbed out his gratefulness to the Lord.

Twenty-Eight
A Wedding Delayed

It was late that night when Callie woke up. Katie slept in the next door recovery room. Jonny had taken a few naps in his chair, but he refused to leave her side. Every groan from her stabbed at his heart. She started to squirm and groan and toss and turn. Jonny leapt up to fetch Owen. "She's waking up, Doc."

Owen followed the Mountie to her bedside. "Callie, can you hear me?" He patted her cheek and squeezed her arm lightly.

Callie opened her eyes and groaned. "Jonny."

"Shhh, it's okay, Darling. You're going to be okay." He squeezed her hand.

"The mine." She gasped. "Hope!"

Owen assessed her visually, relieved to see she seemed to have no serious brain injuries.

"Callie, Hope is just fine." Jonny brushed the hair off her face. "You're going to be just fine too."

"Oh, Callie, Darling." Katie walked in. She took the chair next to her daughter's bed.

"Ma." Callie reached out to her.

Katie leaned over and kissed her forehead. "I'm so glad you're awake, Darling. We were very worried."

"I'm sorry, Ma."

"Hush, Callie, you have no reason to be sorry. You were only thinking of your sister."

"Pa?"

"He's not home yet, Darling."

Callie nodded sadly.

Owen took over. "Callie, how are you feeling?"

"It hurts so much, Doctor." Every breath was painful.

"I know. I'm afraid it will be for a time. You have two broken ribs and a nasty gash on your head. You're going to be sore for some time. I'll give you something for the pain, and then you should really try to get some sleep. The more you sleep, the more your body will heal."

She nodded. Owen had Katie help him hold her head up, and she was able to drink the painkiller and the water offered. "Sleep now, Callie." Jonny kissed her hand.

"Stay with me?" Her green eyes pleaded with him.

"I'm not going anywhere, Darling." He gave her a reassuring smile. Callie closed her eyes again. Her body was exhausted because it was putting all its energy into trying to heal. She was soon asleep again.

*   *   *   *

Adam sat by the campfire and stared blankly into the flames. The young Mountie put down his coffee cup and looked up at him. "What's eating you, Serge?"

Adam frowned and sighed. "My daughter is getting married in the morning, and I'm not going to make it back in time."

The younger man's eyes widened, and he nodded slowly. "I'm sorry, Serge."

"It's not your fault. You didn't break the wagon wheel or cause the endless delays." Adam sighed and ran his fingers through his hair.

"You should leave, Sir. Our duty is done."

"Can't do that, and you know it. I have to get the wagon repaired and back to the station at Moose Creek. Have to complete my orders."

"Well, for what it's worth, I'm sorry. I never understood why they'd send a sergeant on this type of assignment anyway."

"The assignment was actually for the young constable I work with, but I volunteered to take it."

The constable slurped at his coffee and furrowed his brows. "I don't understand. Why would you if there was a risk of you not making it back for your daughter's wedding?"

Adam gave him a wry smile. "The young constable is the groom."

Constable O'Connor chuckled. "Now I understand."

Adam shrugged one shoulder and took a large gulp of coffee. "Well, it'll be well after nightfall tomorrow, at the earliest, that I make it home, and they'll be married by then. It's the second biggest regret of my life." He closed his eyes and sighed again.

"Can I ask what your biggest regret is, Sir?"

Adam stared into the fire again, took another slurp of coffee, and rested the elbow of the arm that held the cup on his raised knee. His eyes grew far away. "I wasn't home for the birth of my youngest daughter."

The young Constable nodded. "How many children do you have, Sergeant?"

Adam snapped out of his reverie and looked up at the young man. "Six." He gave the young man a wide smile, reached into his top pocket and pulled out a photograph of his family.

"All girls?" The constable frowned.

Adam nodded. "Yes, my army of girls."

"I'm sorry."

Adam gazed at the young man across the fire. "Whatever for?"

O'Connor shrugged. "No sons, Sir."

Adam grinned. "I'm not sorry. Not one bit! They're incredible girls, all of them. I wouldn't trade a single one of them for a son."

"You didn't want boys?"

Adam sighed. He got this question a lot. He drained his coffee cup and placed it down beside him, lifted his other knee and hung his arms over both. "I would've been just as happy to have sons, but I have no regrets about having six daughters. And I don't feel cheated for not having had boys. Those girls are my pride and joy. I also have one granddaughter." He beamed.

"Well, you must be enjoying the peace and quiet and a break from them, Sir?"

"Not at all. Every moment I'm away from them makes my heart ache. Apart from holding my wife in my arms, there is no greater feeling than having one of my daughters throw herself in my arms, wrap her little arms around my neck, kiss my cheek and say, "I love you, Pa'." Adam choked on those words. "I can't get enough of my girls. I miss them when I'm not with them."

"You seem like a devoted father and husband. How do you do it?"

"Oh, it's easy to be devoted when they're as amazing as they are. My wife is incredible, talented, and beautiful."

O'Connor observed the shine in the older Mountie's eyes and the twitch to his lips as he spoke of her. "That's not what I mean, Sergeant. How do you manage the life of a Mountie with family life? Isn't it a struggle constantly choosing between duty and love?"

Adam shook his head. "No, because it's not a choice. Love always comes first. My wife and my girls will always be the most important priority of my life."

O'Conner lifted the coffee pot to Adam in question. "But you're here now, missing your daughter's wedding?"

Adam nodded and held his cup out for the constable to fill. "Doesn't mean she's not important to me. Her love and support mean I can do my duty. If I didn't have that, I wouldn't be able to. Even missing Callie's wedding, she knows she has my love first and forever."

"Remarkable, Sir. I thought it couldn't be done."

Adam caught the wistful look in the younger man's eye. "Do you have a sweetheart, O'Connor?"

The young Mountie blushed. "Back in Turners Creek, where I live, there's this beautiful girl who I've taken out a number of times, but nothing serious. I didn't think she'd be able to handle the life of a Mountie's wife."

Adam laughed out loud. "I'll tell you what my wife told me before we even started courting. If you think a woman can't handle it, you'd be underestimating her. I don't like what Katie's had to face, and no doubt it'll be challenging for Callie in the future too." He paused and ran his fingers through his hair. He nodded and looked the young man in the eye. "But I'm a better man, and a better Mountie, because of her. I can't do it without her. I'm so glad I let her make that choice, and she's proved to me time and time again, that she's much more capable and strong than I am. She even stitched me up one time." He grinned.

O'Connor tilted his head. "Stitched you up, Sir?"

Adam removed his boot, lifted his trouser leg and pushed down his stocking so Constable O'Connor could see the long purple scars running down his calf. "Stitched me up."

O'Connor raised his brows. "What happened?"

"Tangled with a black bear."

The young man's eyes grew wide. "Oh, you're lucky to survive."

"Wasn't luck. It was God and Katie that saved me, but she's handled more than that. Strongest person I've ever met." He grinned. "She'd've made a good Mountie!"

O'Connor chuckled. "Sounds like it, Sir."

"So, O'Connor, don't let fear stop you from having the happiness and joy a wife and family bring you. It'll only make you a better man and a better policeman."

"Thanks, Sergeant. I'll think about it." His eyes glowed with hope.

"What's her name."

"Mary-Anne." O'Connor's face twitched into a smile as he thought of her.

Adam smiled and nodded.

*   *   *   *

Callie glanced up at the clock, and then a tear ran down her cheek.

"Hey, what is it, Darling?"

"We should be sitting down for our wedding lunch right now!"

He grinned. "That's what you're eating."

"How can you be so blasé about it, Jonny? We're missing our wedding, and it's all my fault."

Jonny lifted her face and smiled at her. "It's far more important that you're well, my darling. I told you I'd wait as long as it took for you, and I mean that."

"You don't mind?"

He gave her a mock grimace. "Oh, I mind. I should've been married to you by now." He sighed. "But, Darling, when I saw you in that mine, I thought I'd be standing beside your graveside, not your hospital bed, and I greatly prefer this." He brushed back some hair off her forehead and bent down to gently kiss her. Pausing just above her, he smiled and held her gaze. "So I'll not begrudge the delay, Callie. I'd rather you were alive and we never married than you died and I never got to see your smile again."

"Oh, Jonny, I love you so."

"I love you too, Darling." He lifted the hand he held to his lips.

"At least now I know that Pa won't miss our wedding."

"That's true."

"Thank you for saving my life, Constable."

"You're most welcome, Miss Morgan. It's my pleasure."

Twenty-Nine
Married At Last

Late the following afternoon, Adam rode into Douglas Falls, exhausted and frustrated. The trip had taken so much longer than intended. Everything that could delay them, had! He sighed and hastened his horse, anxious to be home.

He was devastated to have missed Callie's wedding. "But at least I know they're happy. That's what really matters," he told his horse. He'd thought about his family as he rode home from Moose Creek. He didn't end up leaving until sunup that morning. He had to sign off the assignment and was obliged to report to headquarters, but the phone line was down due to a storm. He had to wait for a telegram to come back, releasing him from the assignment.

Before he could go home, he'd still have to stow the wagon and file some paperwork. He removed his Stetson as he rode and ran his fingers through his hair. He just wanted to get home to be with his girls. He smirked as he thought of the young constable who couldn't believe a man could love spending time with his children, especially his girls.

Perhaps he was abnormal in that respect, but all he knew was he loved those girls and Katie more than anything in the world, and not being with them was agony.

Adam sighed as he pulled up to his office. It would be several hours before he'd get to go home. If he didn't do this work now, he'd have to leave his girls again and come and do it later. Adam tethered Ebony outside the office and headed inside.

He froze as he entered the office, furrowing his brow tightly; he lifted a hand to ask what Jonny was doing there.

"Sergeant." Jonny stood to attention. "Welcome home."

"Thanks, Jon." Adam squinted. "I didn't expect to see you here. I thought you and my daughter would be staying in for a few days, newlyweds."

"Um, Sir. The wedding didn't happen."

"What do you mean it didn't happen?" Adam's face contorted into a tight frown and his eyes lit with fire. "You better not've changed your mind."

"Never, Sergeant!" Jonny looked Adam square in the eye.

Adam exhaled, threw his Stetson on his desk and walked to the counter at the back of the room to get himself some coffee. "I told you both not to wait for me. You should've gone ahead."

"We would've, Sir, but there were... um... extenuating circumstances." Jonny grimaced.

Adam reached for the coffee pot and poured himself a cup. "Please explain." He ran his fingers through his hair, leaned back against the countertop, took a long slurp of the rather stale coffee, and looked at Jonny expectantly.

"Sir, there was an accident..." he began and explained all that happened.

Worry and pain etched all over Adam's face. "Where is she now?"

"Next door in the infirmary, sleeping! I took the time while she was asleep to catch up on some paperwork. They promised to come and get me when she wakes up."

"Well, I'm not waiting." Adam drained his coffee cup, thrust it into the basin and headed for the door. He hurried next door into the infirmary. "Katie."

She gasped, discarded the small garment she was making for Lily and leapt out of her chair. "Oh, Adam." She threw herself into his arms. "I'm so glad you're home."

"My love." He closed his eyes and held her tightly, cradling her head. "I've missed you so!" He leaned his head on hers and kissed her hair, drawing strength from her. He released her and kissed her deeply. Then he turned to Callie and exhaled loudly. "How is she?"

"She has two broken ribs, scratches and bruises, but thankfully no head injuries. Owen said she'll make a full recovery but will be in bed for several weeks."

"Oh, my darling." He leaned over and kissed Callie's forehead, then sat down next to her on the chair and stroked her cheek. "Oh, my baby girl. I hate to see her like this, Katie. It breaks my heart. I'm sorry I wasn't there when you all needed me." He closed his eyes tightly and rebuked himself.

"Adam, it's not your fault." Katie knelt next to him. "You can't be everywhere."

"I should be here when my girls need me, Katie." He gritted his teeth.

"She had Jon. He found her and got her out. She has Jon now too, remember." Katie touched his stubbly cheek.

"Yes, I know!" Adam took her hand from his face and kissed it. "I'm glad she has Jon."

"Adam, she's going to be okay." Katie brushed a lone tear that ran down his cheek.

"I know she will, Katie. I just can't bear to see my girls hurt and not be able to help. It touches me so."

"You're a good man, Adam Morgan. Our girls are so blessed to have such a brave, loving man in their lives." She kissed him on the cheek.

Jonny entered. "Any change?"

"No, she's still sleeping, Constable." Adam nodded to her.

Jonny sat down beside her bed on the other side.

"Jon, I wanna thank you, Son."

"What for, Sir?"

"For saving her life."

"Sergeant, there was no way I wasn't going to get to her. I would've dug her out with my bare hands if necessary. Nothing would've stopped me from getting to her."

"You put your life at great risk, from what I hear."

"I'd give up my life a hundred times over to make sure she's safe." He stroked her forehead as he did. "I love her."

"I know." Adam nodded. "I'm sorry your wedding was delayed."

"I'm just glad she's okay, Serge. When I saw her lying in that mine, with the beam over her, I thought I'd lost her, and for a moment, my heart felt like it'd been torn from my chest." He closed his eyes and took a deep breath; opening them again, they sparkled. "I'd happily wait a lifetime just knowing she's alive and well. I wish it was me suffering rather than Callie. I should've known she's too strong and determined to keep down."

Adam flashed a sideways smile. "She's a Morgan, Son!"

"That's for sure." Jonny grinned.

"Pa?" Callie woke up. Katie leapt up to get Owen from the next room as per his instructions.

"Oh, my darling." Adam kissed her forehead and gripped her hand. "I'm sorry I wasn't here, Darling. I'm so sorry."

"Pa, it's okay. I'm okay."

He stroked the pale cheek. "I know, Darling, thanks to Jon. He's a good man. I'm sorry you missed out on your wedding day."

Owen entered the room and smiled at her. "How are we today, Callie? You've had a good long sleep."

"It still hurts a lot, Doctor." She groaned as she lifted her arm.

"It will for several weeks."

Adam looked up at Owen. "When can she go home, Doc?"

"I'm hoping tomorrow, but she'll need to keep those ribs strapped up for four weeks. It's not a major break. They'll heal if they are kept still and not aggravated." Owen mixed up the painkillers and helped her take them. "No more exploring mines, young lady."

Callie grinned. "I won't, Doctor, I promise. How long until I can be up and around? We have plans to make?" She smiled and reached her hand out to Jonny.

"I'd say four more weeks at least."

"I'm sorry, Jonny. We should have been married by now. I'm sorry we're going to have to wait, but I want to be well and whole so I can make a home for you."

"Hey, Callie." He cupped her cheek. "It's quite okay. I'll wait forever if you ask it of me." He leaned in and kissed her.

Callie smiled her thanks at him and put her hand on his face.

* * * *

Adam and Jonny carefully helped Callie up into the wagon. Jon wished he could scoop her up and carry her in his arms, but she was in too much pain for that. He climbed up in the back of the wagon with her and held her gently against him as Adam carefully drove home.

Jonny put one arm around her. "I love you, Callie Morgan."

"I love you so much, Jonny. I can't wait to marry you."

"Me either, and we will just as soon as you are well. I promise." He kissed her cheek.

"I never thanked you, Jon." Callie turned to look at him.

"Thanked me for what?"

"For saving my life. I was so scared when I heard the timbers break in the mine. The last thing I remember before everything went dark was that I wished you were there with me." She shuddered.

"I'm here now, Darling, and I'm not going anywhere."

The family fussed around Callie, 'helping' to get her in a chair. Lizzie laid a blanket over her.

Hope sat in the corner, eyeing Callie and sniffing back the tears that threatened to escape. She swallowed over and over again. At last, they had Callie comfortable. Dr Randall had said she could be up for a few hours at a time each day as long as she didn't overdo it.

Jonny tucked her in gently and kissed her on the cheek tenderly. "Are you comfortable, my darling?"

"Yes, Jonny, I'm fine." His eyes said he didn't believe her. "Really, I am." She grinned and touched his cheek. "So you can stop the fussing."

"I'll never stop fussing over you, Callie. It's my job."

"Not yet, Son. She's still mine for a few more weeks." Adam chuckled and cooed to Lily in his arms.

"You almost sound glad the wedding didn't happen, Pa." Rose smiled at him.

"No, I'm not glad. I'm sad Callie didn't get her day as planned, but I'm not sad that I didn't miss it after all. There are silver linings to all clouds. We get at least four weeks more of our precious Callie before she leaves our home for good. I was devastated when I thought I wouldn't be there to see you off, Darling." He stroked the cheek of the wee baby.

"Silver linings." Katie squeezed her husband's arm.

*   *   *   *

The family routine began to happen all around Callie. She spent a lot of time in bed but was able to be up for more and more time. The pain lessened a bit each day, and she continued to get stronger. She chaffed at not being able to help her ma and sisters with many chores, although she was able to occasionally peel carrots or wipe some dishes, until the pain got too much.

Jonny made sure she followed the doctor's orders. Everyone fussed around her and helped her fill the time. Except for Hope, she was sullen and withdrawn and couldn't look Callie in the face.

Three weeks after the accident, on a Saturday evening, Callie was sitting in the chair by the fire doing some mending. It hurt, but she had to do something. She didn't like having idle hands.

Sarah challenged Jonny at checkers. Lizzie, Anna and Katie were finishing up the dishes, and Adam read his newspaper. Hope was slumped in a corner on the small couch trying to read.

Adam observed her over his newspaper. The little girl swallowed repeatedly and took shy glances at Callie. She sighed and stared at her page. Adam lowered his paper. "Hope, Darling, come to me."

She put her book down and walked over to him. He patted his knee, and she climbed up. He put both arms around her and kissed her hair.

"What is it, Pa?"

"I just wanted to kiss you, Darling, and tell you that I love you."

"I love you too, Pa." She wrapped her arms around his neck. He squeezed her and inhaled deeply, prolonging the hug.

"Oh, my sweet girl. I love your hugs, thank you."

"You're welcome, Pa." She sat back and looked at him.

He brushed her cheek. "Now, what's troubling you, Daughter?" His caring dark eyes searched her young face.

She hung her head and sighed. "It's nothing."

He lifted her chin. "Darling, your feelings are never nothing. They matter a great deal to me. If you hurt, I hurt, Hope. Now, tell your Daddy what's bothering you."

Hope burst into tears and wept all over his red serge jacket. He held her and stroked her hair, lying his head against hers. "Hope, Darling. It's okay." He whispered encouraging words to her and waited patiently for her to stop crying. "Oh, Sweet Girl, it's okay, my darling." Adam passed her his handkerchief, and helped her wipe her eyes. "Now, what's hurting you?"

She looked over at Callie and grimaced. "It's my fault. I ruined everything, and Callie nearly died, and it's all because of me."

"Hey now, what's this?" Adam furrowed his brow. Everyone in the room turned to listen to the conversation.

"If I hadn't gone off chasing butterflies, Callie wouldn't have had to come looking for me, and she wouldn't have been in the mine. She wouldn't have got hurt, and she wouldn't have missed her wedding."

"Is that why you've been so sad? Why you've refused to do all the things you've loved, and why you've been sitting around moping?"

She nodded, and her wide, sad eyes brimmed with tears. "I don't deserve to have any fun. That's what got us in this trouble, and Callie can't have fun, so why should I? She can't even have her wedding." Hope's lip trembled.

"Oh, Hope." Callie sniffed away a tear. "Come to me, Sister."

Hope looked at her father, and he motioned her over to Callie.

Callie patted her knee and Hope climbed up.

"Be careful." Jonny raised his brows.

Callie put her arms around Hope and kissed her sister on the forehead.

"Hope, it's not your fault. It was an accident, and you mustn't blame yourself."

"But you're hurt, and you nearly died, and your wedding."

"I'm healing, and I'm very much alive, and the wedding will happen soon. You don't have to feel bad about it, Hope. It wasn't your fault. I'm fine now, and I'm happy."

"Really?"

"Yes, Darling, and you can't stop having fun because of me. You got carried away chasing the butterfly because of your love for all God's creatures, and I love that about you. Perhaps you'll be a veterinarian someday and help the animals you love. I'm not angry or upset with you."

"But, why not?"

"Because that wouldn't achieve anything. I'm alive and well. Remember when Pa told you about how he wasn't here when you were born because he was in jail?"

"Yes."

"Well, I remember him telling me that he refuses to be angry. Not at the people who put him in jail, not at anyone. He said being angry only hurts the person who is angry. He was just so happy to be home with us that he chose love instead of anger. Hope, I love you very much, you are my dear sister, and I can't be angry with you."

Hope forgot about Callie's sore ribs and threw her arms around her sister's neck. Callie grimaced but hugged her sister back.

"I love you, Callie, and I really am sorry. Please forgive me."

Callie tightened her arms around the little girl. "I love you too, Hope, and there is nothing to forgive."

She pulled back from Callie. "Your wedding is going to be wonderful. I can't wait to be a bridesmaid."

"Me either, Hope."

Jonny knelt at Callie's feet during the whole exchange, and Hope climbed down off her sister's knee and threw her arms around Jonny. "I'm sorry, Constable Scott. I'm sorry Callie got hurt and you couldn't have your wedding. Please forgive me."

Jonny closed his eyes and squeezed the girl. "Hope, of course I forgive you, Darling. It's okay, Callie is going to be just fine, and then you'll get to be her bridesmaid just like you wanted."

"I can't wait." She grinned at Jonny and put her arms around his neck. "I'm going to like having another brother."

He beamed at her and kissed her forehead. "I can't believe I get to have such lovely and beautiful sisters. I'm very proud."

Callie stood in front of the mirror in her room with Rose and her mother on each side of her. "Callie, Darling, you look so happy."

"I am, Ma. I can't believe my day has finally arrived, and I get to marry Jonny, even if it is six weeks later than we planned."

"You look so beautiful, Callie." Rose slipped her arm around her sister's waist and kissed her temple. "You did a wonderful job of your dress."

"Thanks to Ma's help."

"It's my pleasure, Darling." Katie squeezed her waist.

Callie's dress was white satin with layers of lace and small flowers all over it. She wore her dark hair down over her shoulders and her eyes shone brightly.

Her sisters and mother gathered together to help the bride prepare. Adam waited in the living room, and Marcus stood with Jonny under the oak, waiting for the bride to arrive.

"Are you ready?" Anna looked beautiful in her pale yellow dress. Her three younger sisters wore matching yellow dresses.

"Yes, I think so." Each woman embraced the bride, and Lizzie passed Callie her bouquet of flowers.

"Are you ready, Pa?" Rose gripped her father's arm.

He gulped, nodded, and put his arm around Rose as Callie walked out into the room on her mother's arm.

Adam smiled at Katie, and his eyes swung to Callie. Tears filled his eyes as he reached his arms out to her. "Callie, Darling, you are absolutely radiant."

She walked into his arms. "I'm so happy, Pa."

"And I'm so happy I didn't miss this. When I thought I hadn't been there to walk my beautiful daughter down the aisle, it cut me deeply." He clung to her and kissed her hair.

"I'm glad you're here, Pa. Even though I'm not happy the accident happened, I'm glad it meant you're here."

"Silver linings, Darling."

"Yes, Pa."

"Well, are you ready, Little Girl?" He gave her his arm.

She nodded and tucked her arm under his.

Friends and family scurried to their seats as the harpist began to play. Callie's four younger sisters walked down the aisle in their beautiful yellow dresses. Katie sat in the front row with Rose and Lily. The harpist began to pluck out the bridal march. Everyone turned to look as Adam, in his red serge dress uniform, escorted the beautiful woman around the side of the house and stood at the end of the aisle.

The other man in red serge stood under the arch beneath the large oak tree. He gasped when he saw her and grinned widely. Marcus leaned over and patted him on the back. "Just breathe, Jon. You're a blessed man."

Jonny grinned and nodded. He and Callie locked eyes, and he shook his head. He couldn't believe this incredible woman was walking up the aisle to marry him. Adam's eyes brimmed with tears as they finally reached the front. He gave Daniel a nod.

The pastor gave his brother-in-law an encouraging smile. "Who gives this woman to be married to this man?"

Adam gulped back his emotions and choked out, "I do." He kissed her, and handed her over to Jonny. Adam caught the younger Mountie's eye and nodded. A message of great respect passed between the two, and from Jonny, a promise to always cherish her. Adam slipped in beside Katie and put his arm around her while they watched the ceremony.

*   *   *   *

At long last, the newlyweds opened the door to their new home. Jonny stood on the doorstep with his new bride. He reached for her and kissed her deeply. "Are you ready, Mrs Scott?"

"Ready for what?"

"To start our lives together?"

"Oh, yes, Jonny, I've never been more ready or more excited for anything in my whole life."

"Me either." He kissed her again, scooped her up in his arms, carried her inside and put her back on her feet. Reaching over to close the door, he kissed her again. They stood with arms wrapped around each other for some time. Jonny relished just holding his new bride in his arms. "I can't believe it, Callie. You're actually my wife."

"I'm so happy, Jonny." She looked up at him. "It was worth the wait."

Thirty
A Duty to Family.

Jonny walked inside with an armload of firewood. He dropped it in the basket beside the stove and eyed his wife up and down. "Mrs Scott, you look absolutely radiant this morning."

"Hardly, Husband. I'm just an old housewife bent over a stove." She laughed, and he came over to her and turned her around to look at him. She still had the oven cloth in her hand but put her arms around his neck, and he wrapped his around her waist.

He kissed her, his face shining in joy. "No way, Mrs Scott, you're no old housewife. You're my radiant bride. I can't believe we've already been married for three days. It's been the best three days of my life."

"You do exaggerate, Husband."

He grinned. "I like that word. Husband. I like to call you wife too." Then he became serious. "But, Callie, I'm not exaggerating; being married to you is like a dream come true. These last three mornings, I've woken up with you in my arms; I think that's about the best feeling ever."

Callie blushed and lowered her eyes. "Jonny."

"What, Darling? I'm just telling you how I feel about you. You've got me floating on a cloud. These have been wonderful days."

"But we've done nothing but ordinary things; cooking, eating, gardening and looking after our home?"

"Ordinary is wonderful when it's with you. In fact, when I'm with you, even the ordinary feels extraordinary. You're a wonderful wife, Callie. I appreciate the care you show towards me. The little things you do; bringing me coffee and my newspaper in the evening. Pressing my jacket for me. I just hope I can take as good care of you as you do of me."

"Oh, you do, Constable. I feel so safe, protected, and cared for here in your arms. It's my favourite place to be." She stepped up on her toes and kissed him and then laid her head against his red serge jacket.

"And it's my favourite place too, Callie. Having you in my arms is my greatest delight."

"I'm going to miss you when you're back at work."

"I'm not looking forward to it either, but Marcus told me a few weeks ago that there is one good thing about leaving each day; getting to come home to the one you love each evening, being greeted by her smile and embrace." He held her for a time in silence. He sighed contentedly. "Have I told you today that I love you?"

"Several times." She grinned. "But I can never hear it too often."

"I love you, Callie Scott." He kissed her again

"I love you too, Constable Scott."

"Well, are you ready to go? I'm anxious to show off my bride."

"Jonny! Yes, I'm ready to go."

"Would you like to call in on your ma on the way to town?"

Callie nodded. "I'll just get my shawl."

"Ma." Callie put her head in the door at her parent's place.

"Callie, Dear." Katie ran to greet her married daughter. She embraced Callie, then Jonny. "You both look so happy."

"We are, Ma."

"That's great news, Darling. Do you want coffee?"

"No, we're heading into town. Jonny has to start back at work today, and I need to do some shopping. I have my first guests for supper tonight," she grinned.

"And we can't wait, Sweetheart. Are the Murray's coming too?"

"Of course. Rose is going to bring an apple pie for dessert."

"Excellent, I'll look forward to it."

Jonny put his hand on Callie's back. "Sorry to run, Mrs Morgan, but we really have to get to town."

"Now, Jonny, please call me Ma."

"With pleasure, Ma." He gulped. "That's a rather special word to me. I never got to call anyone 'ma' before. I like it." He leaned down and kissed the woman on the forehead.

"I'm proud to have you as a son, Jon." Katie grinned and squeezed his arm.

They stowed Major and Maisy at the livery and walked arm-in-arm through town, wandering slowly along, just enjoying each other's company. Jonny carried Callie's basket as they walked and while Callie shopped. He paid for their groceries, and Callie gushed over the idea of having someone there to share these small everyday things with.

She retook Jonny's arm, and he smiled at her as they left the store and walked towards the RNWMP office. Jonny placed Callie's full basket on the desk and kissed her. "I love being able to show you off in town, Mrs Scott. "Having you on my arm makes me proud."

"Thanks, Jonny. I'm proud to be married to you too."

"Well, if it isn't Mr & Mrs Scott." Adam walked into the office to see them with arms around each other. Callie blushed and pulled away from Jonny, and he grinned back at Adam, his cheeks colouring too.

"Morning, Pa." Addressing her father as a married woman, she suddenly felt shy.

Adam walked up and embraced her. "Good morning, Mrs Scott." His voice trembled. "I miss you, Darling." He released her and grinned. "You look happy, Sweetheart. I hope your new husband is treating you well." He squinted at Jonny.

"Oh, he is, Pa. He's the most wonderful husband." She beamed at Jonny. Adam reached to shake his hand.

"Good to hear. You starting back today, Son?"

"Yes, Sir. I'm on duty, Sergeant."

"Well, good, I certainly need the help. It's been hard work without you the last few days. This town is really growing."

"I know. Rose told me there will be seven classrooms in the school next year," Callie said.

"Wow." Adam nodded. "I've noticed the settlement to the east of town is really growing. We'll be a city before we know it."

"Might be time to get more help, Serge."

"It's on my mind. But I'm worried if I get another Mountie here, I'll lose another daughter." He chuckled. "Not that I'm sorry. You two are perfect together."

"Well, I'll leave you men to it. Are you still coming for supper, Pa?"

"We wouldn't miss it for the world, Callie." Adam grinned and put his arm around her.

"You'll be our first visitors."

"We're honoured."

She grinned at Jonny. "I should go." She blushed and reached for a quick embrace.

"Callie, you're newlyweds. You don't have to hide your affection from me." Adam grinned. "You know full well your ma and I never do."

She blushed and stood on her toes to receive a kiss and a hug from Jonny.

"I love you, Mrs Scott. See you this evening."

"See you this evening,"

"That's more like it!" Adam grinned. "Never miss a moment to show each other your love. You never know when a moment will be your last."

Callie nodded, embraced her father, reached for her basket, and left.

Adam grinned as he watched Jonny follow her with his eyes and sigh. "So, how's married life, Jon?"

"Wonderful, Sir. That daughter of yours is quite a woman." He grinned.

"Yes. She's her mother's daughter. You got yourself a fine wife there. Of course, there's a chance I might be biased."

Jonny grinned. "A little, but I'm not disagreeing. I can't believe I ever managed to live without that woman by my side. Watching her walk away just now pierced my heart."

"I know exactly what you mean, but remember, Jon. She'll be there waiting for you when you get home!"

"Somehow, it makes me even more determined to do my duty, like I'll make her proud doing so."

"I understand. Treasure every moment of married life, Jon. A good wife is your greatest delight. And just wait until you hold your baby in your arms for the first time. There's just nothing like it." Adam's eyes sparkled.

Jonny blushed. "I'm looking forward to that."

"You want a large family?"

"Yes, if it were up to me, Serge. I don't have much family. One younger brother I haven't seen in ten years and my old uncle. So if we have a whole squadron of children, I'll be delighted."

"I hope you do. I'd be delighted to have a whole passel of grandchildren. What if you end up with all girls like me?"

"Didn't do you any harm, Sir." Jonny chuckled.

"Nope, they are the light of my life. Wouldn't trade a single one of them in for a boy."

"Do you regret not having a son?"

Adam grinned. "I get asked that a lot, as you can imagine. Not for a second. I would've loved whoever came along, but that army of girls I have is just fine by me. I never could work out why men feel disappointed when they don't have any sons. Having my daughters' arms around my neck and their precious kisses is the greatest pleasure of my life. Girls never grow out of that, even as adults, I think boys would've long ago."

"I can see that, Serge. I hope I get to have daughters too someday. Sure would like some sons too though."

"Some advice for what it's worth. Don't get your heart set on either. Just be prepared to love whoever God brings you."

"I will, Sir. I'd not begrudge an army of girls either." He grinned. They parted ways to head out on their rounds.

* * * *

"I sure am glad I built a large table." Jonny chuckled as the family squeezed around it. As it was, Hope and Sarah had to sit at a smaller table that Jon had set up for them. Callie fussed about refusing any help from her ma or sisters.

"No, I want to serve you for a change, Ma. Please take a seat."

Katie nodded and enjoyed the rare privilege of sitting in the living room with her family while someone else cooked.

Before he gave thanks for the food, Jonny got everyone's attention. "Family, my new bride and I, want to welcome you to our home and thank you for your help with building this place, putting on our wedding, and being there for Callie through her recovery. I can't believe we're finally here together in our own home. I'm so proud of you, Mrs Scott, for making this house into a wonderful home that I look forward to coming home to each evening. You're all welcome here anytime. Callie and I want to say we love you all very much."

He gave thanks for the meal, and they enjoyed their time together.

Adam put his fork down and looked around. He sighed loudly and ran his fingers through his hair.

"What is it, Pa?" asked Anna.

"I just can't believe I have two married daughters."

Lizzie rolled her eyes. "Oh, are you going to get sentimental on us again?"

Adam laughed and exhaled loudly in an effort to hold back tears that threatened to bubble over. "It's highly likely, Lizzie."

"What is it that touches you so, Pa?" Sarah asked.

Adam didn't speak for a moment. He looked at each face sitting before him. He thought about all the other people he called 'family.' He took a large slurp of water from his cup and wiped away a tear.

"I can't explain it." He finally began. "It's just when I get to thinking about you all, about my family, our many blessings, I get overwhelmed. It's a feeling of deep love, admiration, strength, pride, protectiveness, and crippling fear all at once." He chuckled at himself.

"Fear, Pa?" Hope foisted a large piece of potato in her mouth.

"Yeah, fear. There's something about having a family and being responsible for you all that is terrifying and yet so wonderful. Terrifying because I can't bear the thought of anything happening to any of you." He closed his eyes for a moment. "I'm so glad you're well, Callie, seeing you on that bed in the clinic, knowing all you'd suffered. It nearly tore my heart in two."

"But I'm fine now, Pa."

"Yes, and you're married and here in your own home, a grown woman, and still, I just want to wrap you in my arms and make sure you're safe. I want you all around me where I can watch over you. Whenever I'm apart from any of you, I ache for you all. I feel like a part of me is missing. Family is the most wonderful and yet heart-wrenching thing there is."

"If it's so hard, Pa, then why was it so easy for you to give us up?" Rose lifted a spoonful of mashed carrot to Lily's lips.

"Easy? You think it easy?" Adam's eyebrows raised.

"You practically told me court, Rose, Sir." Marcus laughed.

"And you asked me why I hadn't proposed yet." Jonny winked at Callie.

Adam leaned back in his chair and nodded. A rather crooked smile crossed his lips, and his eyes glistened. For a few seconds, only the sounds of eating could be heard. Adam sighed, and a single tear escaped down his cheek. "No, it wasn't easy. I gave up a piece of my soul when I gave away Rose and Callie. And I will each time I give up one of you."

"Then why'd you suggest I court Rose, Sir, and encourage Jon to propose? I don't understand." Marcus sipped his coffee.

Adam smiled and looked at Rose and Lily, with Marcus watching on. He looked deeply into Callie's face and watched Jonny's shining eyes. "Because look how happy you are...." He paused, his lips trembled, and his eyes flooded with tears. "That's all I've ever wanted for you."

He gripped Katie's hand tightly and smiled a grateful smile. "I'm a better man because of this amazing woman. I need her. She fills my soul, my mind, and my heart. She's who I draw my strength from." He closed his eyes. "I can't imagine my life without her, and I'm so glad your Uncle Daniel said yes to me marrying her. All of the hardships of life, all the difficulties, even my time in prison and losing a baby, have been made so much easier to manage with this woman by my side. How could I deprive my daughters of this kind of happiness?" His tears overflowed.

"My pain at letting you go, my darlings, is so worth it just to see you as fulfilled and happy as you are. And I will willingly take that pain four more times in the years to come, to see all of you as happy as I am. Besides, Callie and Rose, you're still my darlings, and I'll still watch over you, worry about you, and want to protect you and hold you in my arms until my dying day. It just means you aren't in my home anymore and..." He frowned. "I gotta share you with your husbands." He chuckled and swiped a sleeve across his eyes. "In all seriousness, my darlings, it's agony being a father, but such a blessed and wonderful joy! It's my duty as a father and a husband to see my children and my wife happy and fulfilled. It's my greatest duty." He finished with a raspy breath. "My greatest joy."

"Oh, Pa!" Rose and Callie said at the same time. No one spoke for a moment; everyone was alone with their thoughts.

At last, Hope said what everyone was thinking. "I think we all have that duty in some ways, Pa, a duty to each other."

"What are you saying, Child?" Adam grinned at her.

"A duty to family, to love each other the way you do. You have a duty to us, and you've shown us that all our lives. I think we have that same duty to watch out for each other forever."

All heads nodded.

Adam stroked her cheek and grinned. "You're absolutely right, Darling. It's not just me that has a duty to family. It's all of us. Thank you for reminding me of that. I know it to be true because you all take such wonderful care of me too, you've all saved my life over and over again. It's the duty we all have to each other. The duty to family, and it's the greatest duty of all."

About the Author

Jo Dawson grew up on a dairy farm in Wellsford, a small town in the North Island of New Zealand. She spent fifteen years as a teacher in New Zealand and abroad, before becoming a stay-at-home mum and completing her graduate degree in Theology.

She has lived in Australia and the USA for a time, and these experiences have added to her love of people and history. Blessed with a vivid imagination and the love of classical literature and historical fiction, Jo virtually grew up best friends with Anne Shirley, romping with Jo March and her sisters, sailing a raft down the Mississippi with Huckleberry Finn or living in the 'little house' with Laura Ingalls.

Born and raised in a strong Christian family, Jo's faith is at the centre of who she is, with a lifetime of being involved in churches and Christian camps. These two loves, literature and the Lord, have inevitably converged into writing compelling stories of strong Christian women, courageously facing the hardships of life on the frontier. It is her hope that women of all ages would find encouragement from her heroines' experiences that, while fiction, so often mirror even our modern lives.

Jo currently resides in the small North Island town of Waipu in New Zealand, where she lives with her husband, son, father-in-law and a very lazy cat.

Synopsis: Book Four
The Duty of a Father

"Never mind being a Mountie. Being a father to those six girls is the manliest thing I could ever do."

A heart-breaking choice to arrest someone he loves leaves one of Adam's girls lives altered forever. Another's life hangs in the balance and Adam must face the fear of losing one of his precious girls.

Falling through a second-storey window would lead to Lizzie finding her life's purpose, but her new calling brings with it the wrong kind of attention and Adam is called upon to save her from more than one man with vile intentions. With her father's love and guidance can Lizzie ever find someone who'll love her for her heart and not her station in life?

www.ingramcontent.com/pod-product-compliance
Lightning Source LLC
Chambersburg PA
CBHW051323250626
47155CB00007B/2429